LIFE
in the time of
HURRICANES

Previous Books by Rod Davis

Corina's Way
   –PEN Southwest Inaugural Book Awards, Fiction, 2000–2005

   –"In the tradition of Flannery O'Connor or John Kennedy Toole: a welcome romp, told with traditional Southern charm." Kirkus Reviews

American Voudou: Journey into a Hidden World
   –One of "The Exceptional Books of 1998." Bookman Book Review Syndicate

South, America
   –"A triumph of Southern noir . . . Rod Davis is the new mayor of the mean streets." Julie Smith, Edgar Award-winning author of New Orleans Mourning

East of Texas, West of Hell
   –"Rod Davis delivers not just a gripping story peopled with jump-off-the-page characters, but a heartfelt meditation on life, justice, and the murky areas in between." Sarah Bird, award-winning author of Daughter of a Daughter of a Queen

The Life of Kim and the Behavior of Men: Human Bondage in the After-market of War
   –"A moving and well-written war drama." Kirkus Reviews

   –Silver Award, Independent Publisher Book Awards (IPPY), 2025, for Military/Wartime Fiction

   –Honorable Mention, Foreword/INDIE 2024 Award Winners, War and Military Fiction; and previous Finalist in the general Awards Contest

   –Finalist, Military Fiction, 7th Annual American Fiction Awards, American Book Fest, 2024

   –Finalist, Author of the Year 2025, International Impact Book Awards, Contemporary Fiction, 2024

LIFE

in the time of

HURRICANES

A NOVEL

BY

ROD DAVIS

Fort Worth, Texas

Copyright © 2025 by Rod Davis

Library of Congress Cataloging-in-Publication Data

Names: Davis, Rod, 1946- author
Title: Life in the time of hurricanes : a novel / Rod Davis.
Description: Fort Worth, Texas : TCU Press, 2025. | Includes
  bibliographical references and index. | Summary: "Duane McGuane
  ex-journalist and owner of the Portia, an art house in Uptown New
  Orleans, has a vision while standing on the Mississippi River levee near
  the French Quarter that it is time to move on and produce his own film:
  The Southern Guide to Self-Improvement. The production of the film is
  accelerated by the arrival of Hurricane Katrina a few days later.
  Duane's efforts to survive Katrina and its aftermath bring him into
  alliance with his girlfriend Maybelle, his theater projectionist
  Moon-Ra, his Welsh lawyer Rhys, the hustler kid Boy Jack, a voudou
  preacher's son Paulus, and their extended families and friends
  throughout the city. After a terrifying night seeking shelter in the
  Convention Center, helped along by Scheherazade-like tales to ward off
  fear and intruders, the group-now called the Portia Family-decides to
  head to Texas, where Duane has been gifted a mysterious ranch in the Big
  Bend by his old friend Carlos, whom he hasn't seen since Duane's
  insurgent gun-smuggling days in Mexico. Duane tells the Portia family
  they can start a new life and help make his movie. They head out in a
  stolen church van, joining the thousands of evacuees from Katrina who
  can no longer stay in New Orleans as it struggles to recover. Their
  flight takes them from the city to nearby bayou towns, through Cajun
  country, into the racist fringes of western Louisiana and East Texas,
  and a pause in San Antonio to regroup. When they travel to the Rio
  Grande Valley, another surprise that will affect all their destinies
  awaits. Increasingly torn by their decisions and consequences, they
  press on to the mountains and deserts of the Trans Pecos to find Duane's
  new land. There, they encounter more surprises-spiritual, deadly, and
  transformative. Some who started the expedition never return to New
  Orleans. Others are pulled home by the city, as is its way, to pursue
  their own journeys through life in the time of hurricanes"-- Provided by
  publisher.
Identifiers: LCCN 2025029427 (print) | LCCN 2025029428 (ebook) | ISBN

  9780875659336 paperback | ISBN 9780875659428 ebook

Subjects: LCSH: Hurricane Katrina, 2005--Social aspects--Fiction | Disaster
  victims--Louisiana--New Orleans--Fiction | Environmental
  refugees--Texas--Fiction | LCGFT: Novels | Fiction
Classification: LCC PS3604.A975 L536 2025 (print) | LCC PS3604.A975
  (ebook)
LC record available at https://lccn.loc.gov/2025029427

LC ebook record available at https://lccn.loc.gov/2025029428

TCU Box 298300
Fort Worth, Texas 76129
www.tcupress.com

This book is dedicated to my daughter, Jennifer, and granddaughters, Moriah, Hailey, and Noelle. And to the people of New Orleans and those from other cities and states who responded unceasingly with hearts and help.

CONTENTS

Part IV The Howl

Part V Snow Leopards

ACKNOWLEDGMENTS

Special thanks for support, information, inspiration, shelter, and guidance to friends and colleagues, not limited to but including: Jessica Harris, Sarah Whistler, Pam Becker, Helen Thompson, Betty Moore, Randall Williams, the Reverend Lorita Honeycutt Mitchell Gamble and her family, the *San Antonio Express-News* and colleagues, Dan Williams and staff at the TCU Press, and the extraordinary residents of New Orleans, the most fascinating city in the US.

Flooding in neighborhood streets.
Photo by John Davenport/San Antonio Express-News/ZUMA Press.

KATRINA

And once the storm is over you won't remember how you made it through, how you managed to survive. You won't even be sure, in fact, whether the storm is really over. But one thing is certain. When you come out of the storm you won't be the same person who walked in. That's what this storm's all about."

—Haruki Murakami, *Kafka on the Shore*

CHAPTER 1

Tuesday, August 23

From the fresh gravel path on the Moon Walk atop the ancient city's levee, Duane McGuane watched the early-morning produce trucks clump around the French Market below. Drunks and derelicts that had survived another night mingled among the rigs like vampires. He wanted them all to go home. They never did. He turned to face the river. A grayish cast to the far horizon meant storm clouds were piling up out in the Gulf, and the Mississippi already had begun to moan. The crescent that gave the city its nickname was full of gambling barges and tankers, and it wouldn't be long until they were dispatched seaward or secured down on the docks of the river and the bayous. Early wind gusts churned the waters. Flashes of sun sparkled green, purple, and gold on choppy slicks of oil. In them, Duane saw Mardi Gras and king cakes and the tattoo on Maybelle's back. His focus refixed itself upon one of the ferries that ran back and forth day after day from Algiers Point to Canal Street. He watched it a long time. He felt very serene.

In that moment, that precise, discrete temporal demarcation, Duane saw what was to come—the great movement, the urge of migration he knew was the lot of his species and not just his personal burden. He heard the voice come from inside, and it was that of a great fierce dog atop a jagged boulder in the Himalayas howling of distant chaos. The howl was like a marvelous force inside his entire head and body and no one knew of it. But he did, and it had breached his world and he was going where it led.

A burst of wind blew bits of earth and litter across his cheek. Duane brushed his face and looked out to the southeast. So late in the season, this was likely a bad one, if it came this way. He turned his back to the river to face the city again; the place he loved, hated, exalted, and reviled. He pondered *otra vez* the aforementioned produce trucks and drunks, and now also from the corner of his vision a Vietnamese waitress in black pants and white shirt at Café du Monde shaking out a tablecloth on the sidewalk below. Also, in that exact second, he watched, from another angle still, his entire being as if viewed from the heavens, poised neatly on the Moon Walk, the impetuous idea of jumping into Old Man River just to see if he could survive the strong current having passed and morphing into something much finer.

Thus now did he see his new life, all at once and stretched out to infinity, and in that spectacle did Duane McGuane join the ranks of the prophets, and he had in mind a certain redoubt in Texas. From there they would begin it all, the fierce, stray, lost dogs of his acquaintance and yet of his fortune to come. They would howl from within that place where they would no longer have to deal with any of this shit.

Maybelle woke up from her nap later than usual, which meant she would be later than usual to work, a bent toward tardiness that disturbed her less than it might in others more inclined to guilt. You could include her boss in that latter conglomerate of sad and desperate clock-watchers. Also she could be cranky. Part of her wanted Arturo to just fire her and be done with it. But the part of her that didn't— that saw getting fired as the first stage in a domino progression that led to getting bounced from her duplex and sundry other privations of unemployment—made her bolt upright from bed, shake her head once to kick the gears into motion, and proceed with her ablutions.

When that was done and a rice cake and Community coffee in her stomach, she blew out the door and hurried to her old Toyota on the narrow street of small brick houses about a half step ahead of receivership. Most of the houses didn't have garages, so all the cars were crammed together on the curb, and it took her a good five minutes to wheedle herself free of the cramped space defined in front by an old Caddy and in back by a Dodge van with a bondo-packed fender. Except for the weather, it was looking like "just another day," as that Paul McCartney song went, for the best waitress at Arturo's, "the finest restaurant in the Irish Channel," as Arturo's ads went, no sense of irony at all in that man.

But she tried not to fault him any more than he deserved. Her own shortcomings were her long-term future, as her mother had put it. Maybelle herself had a sense of irony—but those were hard words nonetheless. *We didn't send you to Tulane to be a waitress or work in a department store or clerk for those communist lawyers in Baton Rouge* was the rest of her mother's verdict. The response—Then what did you send me to Tulane for?—was no longer answered, only sighed upon. But the department store wasn't bad, the argument usually went, because it was an entry point to becoming a buyer and then a ladder into management, which of course was what a degree from Tulane was for. That and marrying the right boy so she could settle in over by Audubon Park on Henry Clay or maybe even St. Charles. Which scenario her mother always duly denied, thus confirming it as truth. They never even talked about the storefront poverty law center work two years ago and all that had ensued from that. Sometimes Maybelle did think upon it herself, and every so often she drove up the River Road, the slow way, to William's grave and left some flowers, for him, for them. But that seemed long ago and a certain amount of regrouping was in order.

She went into the back of the restaurant and took off her summer smock and put on the black shift and low-heeled shoes of her station. She didn't really have a locker, just a hook on the wall on which to hang her stuff. A hooker, she frequently said to herself long after the joke had gone flat. Her purse went under the cash register out front, where she could keep an eye on it. As she disrobed, Benny, the other waiter for the night, unless it got busy, came in. He already had on his white shirt and dark pants, but they had changed in front of each other before and it didn't matter because he was gay, but in truth Maybelle wouldn't have cared anyway. Sexual interludes were far from her mind. And her, thirty-three years old!

It wasn't yet five, and a Tuesday, so nobody had come in, not even the early conventioneers. Benny went around fixing and fussing at the dozen tables in the dining room. Bertie, the creepy guy from New Zealand, cleaned off the marble counter in the long, dark bar and lined up the glasses hanging upside down overhead. He would get the first wave of customers, and he would lubricate them.

Maybelle waited for the onslaught in a high-backed, lacquered wooden chair against the wall, under a print from the South of France. She looked out the window toward the street, and at the parking lot on the other side next to the corner grocery. Two beige sedans with Avis stickers on the back slowed and pulled tentatively into the lot.

Four men got out of one car and four women out of the other, all dressed in suits or the equivalent, and rejoined each other, stiffly, then came across the street.

Seeing them, Bertie yelled to Lisa, the main bar waitress, to get some ice, and in came the people, their convention badges still hanging from cords around their necks. Maybelle had a theory about that, that people kept the name tags not because they had forgotten to remove them but because in an alien city it reminded them who they were. Maybelle knew how easily that could be forgotten. How easily anything could be forgotten if you put your mind to it.

Boy Jack pushed the crate as far as he could against the wall at the back of the storage room. The thing seemed to weigh a ton, which was about right, since it was full of brass and teakwood from Burma, a term Mr. Croydon always used and always added, "What we now call Myanmar." Croydon wasn't a bad boss, but sometimes Boy Jack felt out of place in a weird and prickly way. He had never been much troubled about other people's sex lives, but where he had been brought up, in Lafayette, "dainty" wasn't an adjective a man likely would take upon himself. None of Mr. Croydon's friends had ever given him a hard time about anything, but a couple of them had made passes at him, probably because they were all pushing fifty and he was barely in his twenties.

When he had caught his breath he picked up the stencil and paint gun and zapped "Fragile" all over the box and "Croydon's World Imports. New Orleans" in the corners and then the destination address, in Wichita, Kansas, on every side. He hoped to be finished by five so he could get it to the bulk container depot at the airport before they closed for the evening. He had plans for later, and if he worked the timing right, he wouldn't have to even go back to the store, which would be a bad drive through the traffic anyway.

The stenciling looked pretty good, although it filled the back of the room with fumes. He pushed open the loading door and wheeled the hand truck over to the crate. First, though, he cracked the door to the viewing room where all the art and antiques Mr. Croydon had gotten—in ways Boy Jack hoped to learn—filled the big space. There were bronze and ceramic statues of the Buddha, dark wooden carvings of strange Ivory Coast gods, big ruby-jeweled elephants and gold-flecked dancing Shivas, flat-head terra cotta figurines from Guatemala, lumpy piles of insanely heavy Turkish rugs, stacks of hand-painted Mexican hacienda pottery, cheap-looking brass Taiwanese decorations, thin-legged wooden Senegalese chairs, and slightly chipped 300-year-old church gargoyles from Peru like the one in the box heading for Wichita, for the office of an oil company executive whose wife had been "mad" for everything in the store.

Boy Jack saw Mr. Croydon talking to a husband and wife. Probably, they were just the tourist types who came in more often than the serious buyers. Still, you never knew just by looking at some of them, and Mr. Croydon said every fish was one that could be on your line if you weren't too lazy to bait up. That was what Boy Jack liked about the old guy—he was a real fanatic at the sales end. Just then Himself glanced back and Boy Jack made a thumbs-up sign to indicate he was ready to roll. Mr. Croydon nodded without saying anything, the light eyebrows on his reddish and very oblong face cranked slightly in the way they did when he thought he was going to land a couple of flounder and didn't want to be disturbed.

When the white van hit the exit ramp up to the freeway, Boy Jack was well ahead of schedule. He listened to the weather because it was August and some other damn storm seemed to be out there in the Bahamas or somewhere. It didn't sound like anything bad, but in the shipping business you had to always keep up with anything that could cause delays.

He smoked half a joint en route to drop off the packages because he figured he was finished for the day, and it relaxed him so that even the huge snaggle from the wreck near Metairie didn't bug him. In his head he practiced how he would handle the fish in his own store some-day. "Why, yes, ma'am, that's exactly right. You have a very good eye for the pre-Columbian. I wonder if you'd also be interested in some recent things we've gotten in from Burma—Myanmar now, of course, but when I used to sail there I learned it by the name the old hands called it."

Duane wanted change for everything. His friends. The whole city. But he couldn't get the city out of itself. Its very resilience, stolidity, stubborn stupid resistance to time ate at Duane, even though he knew that the only way to reconcile all his tensions was by getting the hell out.

But the Portia had its needs, too. The most pressing of which, apart from the possibility of having to board up the windows and tick-et booth, was summarized on the sheets of 8x14 paper he had tossed with altogether feigned indifference across the middle of the old desk perched in the arc of the bay window overlooking Milton Street.

He leaned back in the creaky chair that came with the desk that had probably been in the building, if not the theater itself, since the dawn of time, and put his boots up on top of the paper pile. The cup of coffee from JJ's Grocery, also on the paper pile, wobbled slightly, so that a trickle eased down the side and found its way to the documents. This was intended to show disdain for the words. But it was feigned disdain. From Duane McGuane!

He considered knocking the whole mess over. Too dramatic. Better for the cup to sit there, in uncertainty, full of potential mishap. Duane had learned the finer points of thespian pacing from the piles of cinema theory and movie production books he'd worked his way through in the last few years to jump-start himself in the business.

It was a pretty good old house, though, the Portia, and he'd gotten it for a price well within his resources, which were bolstered by a small settlement for wrongful firing from a newspaper in Houston over a story about the owner of a major car dealership, and, in a related incident—and a much bigger, six-figure payout—a lawsuit against the owner of said dealership taking a shot at him with a 9mm outside a Montrose bar. It was ugly and complicated and he rarely talked about it.

But the game-changer assets came from Uncle Walter, on his dad's side, who had lived a quiet, almost spartan life as a widower in Corpus Christi. His death from skin cancer revealed silent co-ownership of five coastal drilling rigs, the sale of which netted enough that "immediate surviving family," which probate said included Duane, put nearly $200,000 in his checking account. But two years later that nearly doubled because he'd reinvested the money into a high-risk account run by a genius stockbroker Uncle Walter had recommended in his will. The stock play was dicey, but the value bounced up to a post-recession high in oil, real estate, and foreign currency trading. When it hit $375,000, Duane pulled out of the market and put everything in the bank.

And then a lot of that went into the Portia. It was named after the wife of Mr. Thompson, the original owner, and was what they called an art house in the industry, with only two hundred seats and a three-row balcony, but also a real stage with thick crimson curtains that opened and shut for each feature. The downstairs lobby had been converted into a bar some years back, when the theater itself was bankrupt, but Duane hadn't wanted to put up the grease money for a liquor license, so he had a little coffee corner in the lobby that some of the locals liked to use whether they went to a movie or not. And popcorn. He had just about decided against getting the liquor license at all, even if Rhys could keep the bribe reasonable, because he figured it might change the tone somehow. But he hadn't ruled it out.

Some days he had a big crowd, usually students, but not necessarily, since he believed in mixing up his bookings. Foreign films and student perennials, but also there were the Chuck Norris Festival and Duke Saves America Week and so on, which were such big successes Duane had rethought his whole attitude about who sees movies in art houses, and that got into thoughts about art and what it was and who bought it, etc. Which in some ways accounted for his current plight.

When Duane was a kid in southeast Texas, the movies were at movie theaters, not malls. In Cartersville, before they moved, he'd gone to every Saturday matinee the Orion offered, or at least two a month. He loved all that—riding his Schwinn across town, past the community college to look at the girls, who were too old but not to look at, sinking deep into the furry red seats, coming out into the afternoon sun blinking with a head full of Alan Ladd and the Duke and Lana Turner and also of vampires and monsters stomping through Japan.

All of which no doubt had to do with the Greater Delta Day of Smut, because, at least according to Rhys, everything was everything, and also it was nothing, at some level. But Duane wasn't blaming his debacle on anybody else. He was the one who had booked *Barely Bambi*, *Romeo That Julie Ate*, and so on. Even now, though, and with all that had happened, Duane maintained that you'd think people would have had a sense of humor.

So now, what, smut wasn't part of the industry, too? The hand-lettered, neon-marker posters he'd put on the doors, "Abandon All Scruples, Ye Who Enter," weren't warning enough? The big XXX's on the marquee that day? "No one under 18 admitted" plaque on the ticket window? And this was New Orleans, for godsake. Sordidness and sleaze were not exactly strangers. You'd have thought. And you'd have thought Gretchen would have had the presence of mind to ask for IDs.

Duane sighted down his jeans legs to the coffee cup next to his boots again. He got up, carefully, and went to the window. The gray in the sky was definitely out there. He made a mental note to listen to the weather forecast, as if he could do anything about it. He sat on the sill a little longer and looked back into his office. The building must have been something back when Mr. Thompson owned it, and, thanks to freaks of financial benevolence, Duane might be destined to make it that way again. Maybe that was in the howl, too.

He got up and went over to the long oak table he'd converted to resting places for piles of posters and handbills, trade journals, and giveaways. He flipped through the PR scrapbook, saw the tiny *Picayune* article announcing the reopening of the Portia, with him standing out front so full of pride.

Eventually, he saw the subpoena again. And what was really on his mind. The letter from Carlos.

It was insanely hot, like being trapped in some cave at the center of the earth. Kind of a good description of his apartment in the Tremé, especially when the power had been out all day, which it had, again. But no matter. Moon-Ra knew his body reacted to the heat better than to any air conditioning chill; it funkified him even as it made him miserable, and his real fingers found the imaginary bass line right there in the imaginary groove in which it always lay if you knew how to feel for it, all third-eye. It was like the way you never looked at the frets; it was why he wore Ray-Bans. Not, like some of them said, to pose, but so he wouldn't have to look at anything. Also, Feliciana liked it.

The power jumped back on and so did the a/c and the Sansui and George Clinton. Moon-Ra picked up the beat without a hitch and within a couple of cuts he was animated and soaked in his own sweat because the a/c would take a while to catch up. Just like when they played in the clubs off Rampart. It brought to mind a recurring question: At exactly what level of risk is the electronic musician on a hot night on a band-stand without sufficient grounding? This was a much-overlooked work hazard and—

The power stopped. Moon-Ra opened his eyes and everything in his apartment was dark and silent. He felt like a damp rag. Wind toyed with the tree branches outside. He waited for the corroded circuits to find their own groove again. This was truly oppressive, especially at the end of such a long day. He could tell the landlord to fix the electric for the eight-thousandth time, but what could you really do? So he fingered the air bass of his mind, closed his eyes, and dealt. Moon-Ra, he smiled, is not dependent on the grid.

CHAPTER 2

Wednesday, August 24

Maybelle put her beer bottle label horse next to Bonnie's brontosaurus. "This is sad," Bonnie observed.

"It's more than sad."

"What's more than sad?"

"Tragic. That's worse."

"How?"

"Sad is your own fault. Tragedy is like the whole world is against you. It's fate. You can't avoid it."

Bonnie peeled another strip off one of the Dixie bottles on the Formica tabletop. She glanced across the coal bin light of Duke's. A couple of young guys hitting on girls with entirely too much eye make-up. A table of office workers who'd pushed two-martini lunch way past its limits. The music was too loud, too country.

"Plus," said Maybelle, "in a real tragedy it all could've worked out different for the character. Except you have a flaw in your character and you wind up trashing yourself."

"What's the flaw in mine? Bad origami?"

"You could make something other than a dinosaur sometime, I guess."

"It's a brontosaurus."

"There you go."

"What?"

Maybelle looked at their creations, and flicked them into a pile with the others. It was a graveyard of little beer-label animals, and that was what seemed sad. As opposed to tragic. "I want to get out of here."

"You want to go down to the Quarter?"

"No—I mean out of here."

"That again."

"It's tragic sitting in places like this. In the middle of the day no less—"

"Say, darlin', two good-lookin' women like you don't need to be sittin' over here all by yourselves." The man in khaki slacks and button-down checkered shirt leaned low over the table. "Damn, y'all artists or somethin'?"

Bonnie evaluated the man quickly, darted a glance at Maybelle, who shook her head, tragically, as if to elaborate the obvious.

"Maybe some other time," Bonnie said, unable by long indoctrination to avoid being polite, especially at inappropriate moments.

"No time like the present. Why don't y'all come over to our table"—pointing as he spoke to a not unpleasant looking suburban type over near the office worker party. "Or we could just come on over here."

Maybelle looked at the man and his friend. In truth, she considered the invitation. As Joe Blows go, they weren't that bad, and what was Duane to her anymore, anyway? That was a dumb thing to ask.

"Maybe some other time," she smiled, far too much tooth in it, like something Bonnie would have done. Maybe that stuff was catching.

The man looked at them, then backward toward his friend. For a moment it looked like he'd press the hustle a little further, but the smile on the woman looking at him wasn't really what it seemed to be, and he shrugged with the resignation of a forty-year-old and went away.

Bonnie rolled her eyes at Maybelle. "Where would you go to?"

Maybelle studied the little animals. Hers were definitely the best.

For a nurse, Bonnie had the finger skills of a bricklayer. Or was that the right analogy?

"I don't know. I have no idea. Somewhere else. Somewhere way away from here. I just feel like, you know, I gotta move. Or something."

"What about Duane?"

"I consider that a long shot. Anyway, this is something else."

Bonnie nodded. They both looked as the two men got up and left the bar.

"It isn't sad and it isn't tragic, either. Us," Bonnie said. "It's pitiful."

Maybelle laughed, although, from a strictly literary point of view, hers was the correct interpretation.

Duane gave thought to the potential effect of the potential storm on potential business and concluded that the results would be mixed. Some people would come, but more—maybe a lot more—would stay away because of the weather. But then again, the weather would draw others in who would appreciate the shelter and distraction. Duane hated when it got into those algorithms of what could be. He hated it even more now that he had a vision of what was to come. Anyway, Duane didn't want business right now. An empty house was the thing, because there was too much to do and Gretchen called in sick and he wouldn't have any time to put the thing in motion, the thing he had seen and the howl he had heard.

What would Carlos know about it anyway? Wherever he was.

Duane pushed the stack of return film cases out of the way and looked at the two big 35mm projectors in the small booth as though he knew what he was doing. Moon-Ra had shown him the basics and he'd bungled his way through threading it for a few nights, but mostly it freaked him in the way things did that seemed seductively catastrophic. Moon-Ra said he should get those new platter-loading projection machines because any damn fool could handle them.

Duane did not subscribe to that kind of optimism. New machine or old, things you could fuck up so fast and so bad invited an odd kind of obsession with the downside. Maybelle referred to this as a masochistic regression, to which he said, yeah, well, look who's working as a waitress.

Anyway, the sprockets and bulbs and gates looked good to him and if not, Moon-Ra would be in by four o'clock for the twilight Jim Jarmusch double-bill anyway. On the downside, Duane might have to take over again by the last feature, *Cannibal Women in the Avocado Jungle of Death*—you always went camp for the late show—because Moon-Ra's new band seemed to be getting a lot more gigs.

Duane peered down through the narrow slit for the projector lenses into the empty seats below. Dark, cool, very quiet. It was a good place to sit alone, and he often did. Other empty buildings weren't like that, but theaters were. People didn't actually have to be there for you to feel them; and the converse was true. You could be in the theater with the movie running and a full house and be the only one there. That was one of the reasons he had bought the Portia, shifted careers.

Journalism was a form of nonexistence, Duane had once told Wally, the wire service night editor back in Dallas in the '80s. Wally claimed he had no idea what Duane meant, but Duane was sure he did, because Wally died of cirrhosis, the disease of the nonexistent. And then Duane had left Dallas himself, got mixed up with Carlos. Alive, but definitely losing his sense of his essence.

All of this shit, begone!

Duane closed up the booth and picked his way down the balcony stairs to the lobby. It was already midafternoon, and the day was getting away. He took a bottle of water from the refrigerator behind the popcorn counter and on second thought also grabbed a couple of granola bars from the display case, reminding himself to reimburse the register later, bookkeeping being important to him after the last discussion with his tax accountant. He needed to call Rhys to find out what to do about the city and the lawsuit, but he didn't want to have that discussion, because he could guess where it would lead, and he was heading somewhere else.

He locked the lobby door behind him and walked out onto Milton. It was a steam bath, and the hot, thick breeze was almost wet as rain, so he decided to turn up Prytania and over to St. Charles, to sit on a bench and watch the trolley and the joggers.

Traffic was busy; sometimes it got that way during the season when the weather warnings went up. He had to sprint toward the median to get out of the way of a muffler-rattling Mustang with dark windows going at least fifty in a thirty zone. People said it was dangerous on the avenue anymore. But that wasn't the kind of shit Duane wanted to get away from. It was the other.

Not far from the park, he found a bench, newly painted, under a moss-draped tree and sat down. A Mexican woman in a maid's uniform came by pushing an expensive-looking baby stroller. Duane smiled and said hello. They both looked up at the sky in silent acknowledgment. He noticed a soggy Dixie cup on the ground a few feet away. It annoyed him more than it should have, and he picked it up and walked it over to a trash barrel. Then he settled in, tore the wrapper off one of the granola bars and ate it without pause.

He watched the street and old homes and cars and trees and people around him shift and swirl in a molecular alignment which could be seen only by people with certain kinds of vision, for example amateur movie projectionists and those who had heard the howl of the fierce dog from atop the levee.

He drank a big gulp of water, then realized he'd gotten the fizzy kind by mistake. It came streaming out his nose. When his eyes stopped misting over, he pulled from his back pocket the envelope with the Distrito Federal postmark he'd been carrying around the past two days. It had taken him this long to open it:

I guess you're sitting up there in the land of the free and home of the world's largest rapid deployment force. Congratufuckinglations. How you can stand it is way beyond me, but you know that, or at least think you do or at least ought to. You're probably putting money in your bank account every week and screwing people for the rights to see 120 minutes of total garbage in technicolor and Dolby and figuring it's the best you can do.

Yesterday I got back from a place I can't tell you about. Why you haven't heard from me. I won't be back to America, which is the point of this. I want you to take the ranch. Just take it, what's left of it. Probably not much. Do something with the land. Whatever you want. Just don't waste it. I don't want my sister to have it, or her spawn, who would otherwise if I don't show. You'll be getting a deed to it one of these days when I can get it done. I'm having the legal stuff taken care of in Dallas. I don't want to put where it is in this letter. You'll know. You remember Memo and that lawyer lady, I'm sure. One or the other has everything about the place. I don't want it. I don't want any of what's left up there. Couldn't do anything with it if I had it. Won't.

You figure it out, you let me know. What would you do, you could do anything?

He signed it "C." Like Duane wouldn't know. He read it again, not really seeing the words. But he'd read it many times and now the content was pretty much set in concrete. Moving, in concrete. The idea, solid. In his head.

Then it hit him. Just below his left eye. What was he today, a human target for the random parabolas of matter?

"Oh God, I'm sorry," the teenage boy said, running up, hesitating the closer he got.

Duane touched the sharp pain in his cheek and then picked up the purple and yellow frisbee that had fallen across his right foot. He pitched it back to the boy. "No problem."

The kid turned and quickly sailed it back to a girl standing across the median, just in front of the three o'clock trolley. It was full of tourists and office workers coming back from late lunch in the park. Nobody seemed concerned about anything.

Duane could feel a little blood in his mouth but nothing too bad. What you get for just sitting there.

He got back to the Portia just in time to catch Rhys walking away to his Jeep.

"I was going to call you later," Duane said, extending his hand. "Looking nasty out there, ain't it?"

"You can't fuck around, this stuff," Rhys said, adjusting his Orbison-style Ray-Bans, not about to get distracted with weather observations. He was young looking, although exactly Duane's age, forty-four, three months from forty-five. Not that Duane looked old. Just more troubled, say, a less handsome version of Jeff Bridges. Rhys Griffyn looked like a coal miner who'd done well in workmen's comp and union cases and liked to show it. "I got a meeting with Everett, that prick assistant DA, at 4:30. I maybe can talk him into dropping the charge. You might be interested, you know. That's why I asked you to call me."

Duane walked on toward the theater, pulling his keys from his jeans. Rhys followed, not happily. He looked off to the southeastern sky.

"Shit, what can I say?" Duane said when they got inside, pausing at the concession stand while he made a mental note to restock the candy. "This isn't even a shakedown this time. I got no chance. Why should I give those assholes the satisfaction?"

"They could as easily take you back in custody."

"We put up the fucking bond. Why'd they do that? Just more work for them? They don't like work, Rhys. That's why they steal people's property."

"That they will, boyo"—recently, Rhys had affected Welshisms, to everyone's mild embarrassment—"specially if you make it easy for them."

Duane walked up the first half flight of stairs.

"You listening to me?"

"Come on up. We got some new posters."

19

"Duane. I'm serious. This is serious."

Duane turned at the landing to the second half-flight and so to the upper story. He walked across the linoleum floor to his office. "Shit" came from below, along with tromping footfalls and something that sounded like grumbling.

Duane disappeared into the office, walked over to the bay window for a moment, then as if remembering why he'd come up, went over to one of the long utility tables and picked up a postal mailing cylinder from among a pile of unopened letters. He was prying off the top of the canister when Rhys finally came in, and the posters slipped completely out, uncurling as they did: *Jailhouse Rock, Blue Hawaii, Viva Las Vegas.* Ten of them.

"Damn," said Rhys.

"I told you."

"You've even got the Indian one."

"*Flaming Star.*"

"Damn."

"I was gonna use them for an Elvis Sighting Special, which never happened. But then I just made them prizes for different contests."

"These must be worth a fortune."

"Nah. Just reproductions. Take any of 'em. Take all of 'em if you like."

Rhys spread them out. "Look, but here's the thing. Don't distract me. The thing is why you ain't in jail right now. Why you might get out of this if you listen to the guy you pay for legal advice."

He looked over the array as only a serious fan would, but trying to keep in business mode. "Croaker checked the kids out. Your neighbor in that office building next door, Rouxbicharde, set it all up. Actually brought in that bunch from Church on the Lake that filed the complaint. They even got a donation for their Sunday school out of it. Shit, they could be in more trouble than you."

Duane could feel the beginnings of a smile on his lips. "It'll stand up?"

"Croaker got tape. You know the PIs around here. He put the fear in a couple of the kids, and their parents just shucked open with the 411 about how they got bribed."

"What'd it cost me?"

"Forget it. It's worth it. I'll make Everett eat that. They'll drop the case."

Duane was tapping the poster canister against the tabletop. Then he smacked it really hard. Smile gone. "So what? They want the building. They want the lot. If not this time, it'll be next time. That's what you ought to be telling me. Why'm I telling you?"

Rhys cocked his head. Like a dog thinking about some precipitate move. "I didn't think you'd fold, Duane. They fuck you, you fuck 'em back. Come on, what's the matter? This ain't shit to worry about."

Duane was leaning on the wall at the bay window.

"So tell me some stuff I can go to Everett with"—Rhys pulled back the shirtsleeve beneath his tan suit—"in an hour and a half, by the way."

Duane flashed a thumbs-up, but he was thinking about Elvis. His taste in music hadn't run in that direction as a kid. Only now, in later years, did he like him. He wondered why that was. Maybe it was because Elvis had become a fairly noxious piece of work, and there are times to be judgmental about such things and times to view the human condition as more of a long shot.

He didn't particularly want to see Maybelle. It had gotten to that weird place where every word was the subject of misinterpretation, every deed bungled and damp with malfeasance. Another good reason to move on. Clean slate and fresh start.

He decided to stop in Arturo's anyway on his dinner break, and before he had to go relieve Moon-Ra. It had a decent bar and sometimes a decent jazz quartet. Even Moon-Ra dropped in sometimes after a late-night showing. Duane didn't want to see Maybelle, but he was pretty sure he wanted to talk to her. What he saw now, had seen on the levee, the howl he heard, which was not the howl of the com-ing hurricane, although the moan of that much less cosmic howl was getting louder. And there he was on Camp, looking for a place to park.

Eventually, he found a spot near some construction sawhorses out-side an old house being refurbished, but he had to walk a couple blocks more than he'd figured. However, it gave him time to turn a quotidian dilemma into a Chinese jigsaw puzzle of a conundrum. In fact, he wasn't sure what he might want to say to Maybelle about his plan, if he had a plan. He didn't know if he was afraid she wouldn't like the plan or that she might. He just didn't want to see her.

Inside Arturo's, he spotted her right away, over at one of the tables in the dining room, and his little heart perked up. She had a funny way about her, and kind of a prominent nose, maybe, although he really liked everything on her face and really everywhere else, but the main thing was she had a light inside her that no shit illuminated him. He didn't think she had seen him, and so he pulled a stool from the bar to sit down, and just then, reaching for his wallet to buy a drink, realized he had left it on the floorboard of his car after taking it out at an ATM up near Napoleon on the way over. No way would he ask her to loan him money for drinks. Not wanting to see her and all.

He slipped back out and turned up Magazine, then ambled up lakeside toward his car. The wind seemed to have backed off a little, but that just made the heat and humidity more unbearable. Maybe the storm might blow down into Mexico instead of up this way. Thinking about that, and seeing/not seeing Maybelle, he had walked a block too far. He turned to fix the error, and realized two men had been gaining on him from behind. One was white and one black, both in dark ball caps and shades. As he passed them, he knew they were studying him. He looked away.

The thwack on the back of his head sent stars into his vision, which must have been his eyelids because he wasn't really seeing much else, basically just sidewalk concrete and some wax-leaved bushes. One of the men said, "Kenneth, what's the frequency?"

Duane crawled a couple of feet and turned on one side trying to sit up. He could sort of make them out but not really. The one with the question had a high voice. Duane thought it incongruous, considering. Then the other man kicked him in the neck.

"I said what's the fucking frequency, Kenneth?"

Duane rolled onto his back but nothing came into focus. He tried to tell if it was a black voice or a white one. "What are you doing?" he asked.

There was a blow across his stomach with some kind of stick or length of pipe. Then one man held his arms and the other turned him over halfway, feeling in his rear pocket. A couple seconds passed.

"Nothing there. What a dumb fuck."

The second one kicked again. That was all Duane knew.

Later, maybe not all that long because the sunset hadn't yet turned completely dark, Duane's eyes opened and he felt himself breathing. It took a moment, but he was able to get up on an elbow and then into a sitting position. He felt his face and everything was there, but it was wet and his fingers turned up bloody.

Two kids came along and stopped about ten yards short when they saw him sitting against a bush. Across the block, a couple headed for Magazine Street glanced his way and then looked elsewhere. Duane understood. They figured he was a drunk. Or a junkie. Or that they were going to get mugged. Well, Duane, thought, I've preempted that last possibility, at least on this block.

He managed to stand up. His head was throbbing and his left jaw was swelling and didn't want to be touched. He couldn't find his keys, and then it flashed that they had been waiting for him to steal his car, but that made no sense, not least because his car was a piece-of-crap Taurus that nobody would want to steal—the only way to own a car in New Orleans. He limped along to the end of the block and there it was. He kept a Hide-a-Key under the left bumper and let himself in. Next to his wallet on the floorboard were his regular keys. All told, Duane had been lucky.

At the emergency room at Touro Infirmary he got X-rays, and the ribs were slightly bruised but not broken. A young Vietnamese doctor stitched the place on his cheek torn by that last kick and bandaged another laceration on Duane's forehead. As he worked, the doctor talked to a medical student about how it really got bad on the weekends and then they started talking about a new Schwarzenegger movie.

Duane listened with a kind of professional pride, though his jaw hurt too much to offer the usual asterisk on the actor's politics. When they were done, Duane asked for some pain pills and the doctor said all he could write for him was Tylenol 3. He paid the infirmary with a credit card because his health insurance had lapsed some months earlier, an oversight he probably should have mentioned to Moon-Ra and Gretchen. Then picked up the pills at the pharmacy across the street. They gave him the refill, too, in case the weather got bad and everything was closed.

He drove back to his two-bedroom cottage-style house in the Marigny, which he'd bought really cheap because the previous owner had hanged himself from a telephone pole in the backyard. Rhys, who told him about the deal, said buying was actually cheaper than renting. And he would be an official resident of the city.

Duane liked that. It had taken some doing.

When his dad, Hank, who worked for a Big Ag corporation, got transferred to Atlanta, then back to Texas via Corpus Christi, life seemed in constant flux, so Duane pinned himself down by going to UT in Austin. That's where he met Carlos Robles, a bright and unusually serious kid from Juárez. They were both poly-sci majors and ended up sharing a cheap off-campus rent house.

They got involved with some of Carlos's even more serious friends and also in several protests against Reagan's policy in Central America, but then lost touch after graduation. Duane headed to LSU when he got a grad school scholarship and didn't really know what else to do. Baton Rouge helped continue the fascination with New Orleans that had started as a kid when Hank took him on various business trips to the Crescent City.

Later in the '80s, when Duane got into journalism as a kind of experimental career choice, Hank was murdered by the hot-tempered owner of a big farm up near Tyler. There was a contract dispute, but the proximate cause was Hank's objection to the farmer kicking one of his own dogs after a Mexican migrant worker had dared to pet it. Duane's mom, Sheila, never really got over the trauma and moved up to Seattle to live with Duane's older sister, Jane. Duane rarely talked to either of them.

His older brother, Shane (Mom thought it would be "fun" to rhyme everyone), was in Denver working at the airport. He and Duane talked even less. In fact, their last conversation one Thanksgiving was about their names, both connected to movies. Shane came directly from *Shane*, the movie with Alan Ladd, confirmed by Mom. But Duane predated the use of his name in *The Last Picture Show*, and it annoyed him because the Duane character, played by Jeff Bridges, also an ironic connection, was such a jerk.

Not sure what to do next, real-life Duane turned on WWOZ, sat down on the secondhand sofa in the living room, and kicked off his sneakers. But OZ was doing some kind of fund raiser. He turned that off and got a beer from the fridge. He thought of calling Maybelle. He thought of calling Moon-Ra to see if everything was okay at the theater. He settled back into the cushions and almost fell asleep, until he got stuck on thoughts about how a mugging might negatively affect his plans.

He wondered if it was just too much to be a coincidence? I mean, "Kenneth, what's the frequency?"! Wasn't that just unacceptably dated and trite? What kinds of muggers were out there roaming the streets these days? Fans of Assailants of Dan Rather? Was that some kind of underground retro cult?

Then his funk hit bottom and for no real reason bounced back up from the sofa like a hard rubber ball. He scrounged through his tapes in the old peach crates and found some jump jazz and actually danced around his front room. Then his head hurt and he had to sit down.

Something woke him in the night and he realized it was the throbbing in his face and ribs. He hadn't moved from the sofa, except to slump all the way down. It was pitch dark, inside and out. No noises, no sirens, no loud street arguments, no nothing. He lay still, feeling the pain, groggy from the pills that were supposed to stop the pain, pondering how he had ever survived two off-the-radar years of gun and medicine smuggling with Carlos after leaving the AP. Plus the other handful of runs a half-dozen years ago, because, as Carlos put it, knowing what you know, how can you not? Still an interesting question.

CHAPTER 3

Thursday, August 25

The city was filled with nothing. It had become hollow. Into the hollowness had seeped muggers in the Irish Channel and crooked politicians across the city and lying preachers and the entire fabric of mistrust and greed and dumbassness and violence that they engendered. In this had incubated a great wrongness.

In this, Duane admitted, do I dwell. Because I dwell, I cannot leave.

Duane knew that of such revelatory syllogisms much tragedy is born. It drove Socrates to the hemlock. It was Vietnam. It was Afghanistan. It was Central America. It was the tragic logic and the essence of New Orleans.

Thus had the vision for the film come to him: "The Southern Guide to Self-Improvement." Working title but it had legs. It would become the cultural icon for the rebirth of the city. It would deal with New Orleans on its own terms. It would embrace the flaws, the very exceptionally serious flaws and even the deeply original sins, and it would turn them into fuel to power up the good, the unrealized dreams, the greatness that everyone knew was there, if only there were a way to figure out what it was.

Duane McGuane would do just that. He would make the movie of all movies about the city of all cities. Assuming Rhys could help with the financing.

Stack on that the other great revelation he had recently experienced— the howl on the levee. Which it occurred to him might have also come from residual memory of *The Snow Leopard,* a book by Peter Matthiessen he had read many years ago and got him interested in Buddhism, or maybe from that poem by Allen Ginsberg. Or both. Or neither. Maybe it was just a howl that was only there on the levee at that day and that time and in that smidgeon of the cosmos and could only be heard by him. Provenance was not the issue. That was for academics and lawyers.

For Duane McGuane, the howl was the breath of newly forged resolve. In fact, he was already casting the film. Since it would be low budget, he naturally had to rely on people he knew and people they might know, but this would be fine. It would take care of itself. He was very confident. And he already had screenwriting software, so he didn't even need to order that.

Meanwhile, out in the Gulf, the storm became the hurricane and the hurricane took a name, and its name was Katrina, which coincidentally was the name of the girl Duane had been in love with in Austin and also the name of one of the Dutch stars featured in the Greater Delta Day of Smut festival, both of which had caused him great pain. It was dawn, and he finally went back to sleep.

By late afternoon Thursday the Tylenol-3 haze was clearing up, and he was back over at the Portia, hunkered at his desk and poring through ledger books and Excel spreadsheets looking at his basic financial situation, which with buying a theater and a house and running an operational budget usually in the red, had gotten tight. But Duane still could see a basis for launching a movie and attracting investors. If somehow the Portia could get free of the pending lawsuits, and somehow be unencumbered by any other liens, he could probably get seed money with a couple-hundred-thousand-dollar loan to go with what savings he had left. From an actual bank. If there were such a thing in New Orleans. Or even from a bank in Texas.

It was going to be a pretty decent fall season in the art house market, judging from the current line of industry gossip. Banks liked numbers for making loans, and even if the numbers went south, the good thing for the banks was that they could seize the asset. Who wouldn't want to repo a cool theater on a semi-prime, or at least sorta-prime, location? Even a default was money in the bank to a bank.

Thinking of that kind of outcome derailed Duane's train of thought. Which was still slightly fuzzy from the meds. He needed to give some real thought to losing everything. But he would not lose. He believed in his vision, and therefore was willing, if pushed, to embrace the ultimate fallback. In case his vision went dark.

He was willing to go to Rhys for bailout bucks. Which would, inevitably, mean going through at least some permutation of the mob. Duane had a very clear understanding of the relationship of art and commerce. But damned if he would lose his shot. He just wouldn't. That was also part of the art-commerce relationship. It depended on people who didn't believe they would lose. And sometimes didn't. It worked that way in the oil field wildcat business, too. Just saying.

The ranch from Carlos wasn't really a ranch. They just called it that. But it was at least twenty acres, maybe more, and mostly of nothing. But a good location, supposedly. Maybe worth something. Maybe a lot. Maybe nothing. Maybe something to sell, or use, to finance a movie. Maybe a place to retire. No way really to know. The mystery of the value of the ranch produced a thought Duane didn't like—exactly the kind of thought that could impede changing his mind about changing his mind about moving out there. Carlos never did anything without a reason. And the howl never howled in vain.

His head felt like it would explode. Besotted by great notions. Also by pain. He took a minute to just sit there. Maybe it was more than a minute. When he came to, he realized he had fallen asleep slumped across the top of the desk. A ballpoint pen was stuck to one cheek by either sweat or slobber from his mouth, and as he pulled it off and shook himself into focus, he looked around as if somebody might have been watching.

He knew he needed to tell all this to Maybelle. He felt there was zero chance that she would turn down a role in a movie and would probably even see it as a harbinger that Duane himself planned to become a better soul. Perhaps she could be right, but this movie wasn't about him. Or his soul. It was about the city. As such, it was about the South, and as such, about America, and as such, about the fate of the world itself and all souls in it. Duane felt very strongly that he could put all that in 118 minutes, the optimum running time according to recent articles in the trade magazines to which he subscribed or got for free.

Duane punched in Maybelle's number on his cell. He got her voice mail. He hung up.

He found a legal pad under one of the Elvis posters and started to flesh out the numbers. A half-mil for even a very low-budget film was foolish and fanciful, even in New Orleans. He couldn't get his head around the numbers and the scope of the possible production, and despite thinking he shouldn't, he called Rhys.

Whose reaction was less than supportive, much as had been his reaction to the mugging, which he thought was Duane's "own damn fault and kind of embarrassing." Rhys had strong feelings that people in the city who couldn't navigate the dangers should go live somewhere else. It probably followed that he would be against making a movie in said city. Especially based on a kind of revelation. Actually, his reaction to Duane's idea could be described less as strong disapproval and more as damnation and disdain. For Duane McGuane.

"You want to blow some money on this, or go into big-time debt, or whatever, why don't you sell that ranch you just inherited? I don't know where the hell it even is, but I'll bet unless some developer wants it, it ain't worth much. Probably just enough to get you started, though. Until you see how much a money hole a fucking movie can get you in. Especially one like you're talking about. So that would be a good fucking lesson before you blew your own money or got totally underwater on a big loan. You know?"

Duane let that settle in until he could hear Rhys breathing normally. He started by saying he had already thought on that, and also how he would be in good shape in a few months to talk to a bank. With Rhys's help, of course, and he would go into the "financial aspects" in more detail with him when he'd worked on them a bit.

But he said that wasn't really why he called, now that he actually had. He said he knew what he really wanted to talk about was the big idea. About the movie. Not the money. "I mean I do want to talk about the money, but not yet," he said, knowing he needed to emphasize. He could practically see the eye-rolling at the other end of the line.

Finally, some words. "Maybe we should get a beer, boyo. Or a dozen."

"Maybe."

"Duane?"

"Yeah."

"Never mind."

"It would work. I just wanted to—"

"Did you have a concussion?"

"I had a consensus."

"What?"

"Of ideas. I had a consensus of ideas."

"But your head is okay."

"Come on."

"Have you been watching the weather?"

"That and feeling it."

"It hit Florida. It might be coming this way. They think."

"They think. They never fucking know."

"This time I think they do. What will you do with the Portia?"

"We'll plywood it up. Put everything upstairs. Same-ol' same-ol'."

"You started?"

"No."

"As your attorney I'm advising you to get your shit together and take care of business and stop daydreaming about making movies that'll never get the time of fucking day. How much you actually got left in savings these days?"

"Two-hundred thou, maybe. Most of it went for the Portia, of course."

"Fuck, Duane. I thought you were breaking even."

Duane coughed, cleared his throat. "I am now, but in the early days, I couldn't get any loans. So I spent my own."

"But now. You're in the black."

"Mostly."

"We need to talk about this more."

"Come on, man. It's bootstrapping, this movie idea. I'm aware."

"That's being generous. But just to reiterate. You basically got about enough money to get yourself in deep debt when it all goes to hell."

"Okay, fine. I guess I could sell the ranch. Make you feel better?"

"You believe that letter is for real?"

"Carlos is a serious person. I thought you understood that."

"I understand you have a letter from a guy who may be dead by now saying he left you some property. And no deed and you've never even seen it or know fuck all about it. Letter's not even notarized. That cover it?"

"Anyway . . . I mean, I just found out about this. So why not spitball? I was thinking it might work for a base, you know. A working location. For a cheap studio. Some sets. For us to live on while we're planning and building. I mean, if it turns out it's not worth much money." He paused. "Plus New Orleans is way too expensive to shoot here. I mean, that would be crazy."

"I'll leave that for now. No idea at all where this is? The ranch?"

"Along the border, out in the Big Bend. If it's where I think. I have to wait for the deed to be sure. Carlos didn't say in the letter."

"Hhhn."

"I just need to call Memo, the lawyer up in Dallas. He'll have the 411."

"Well, boyo, it better be worth a shit ton. And you know, just to reiterate my earlier point, unless you sell it to bring in some money, I have to say, looking at it from the actual movie-making perspective, that I'm having trouble getting how a spread out in the Big Bend really stands in for New Orleans. You know?" Rhys choked down a laugh, or something that sounded like one. "Assuming for right now that this hurricane doesn't blow you and your incredibly profitable art house slash smut palace out into the swamps."

Another silence.

"Always with the negative attitude, Moriarty."

"*Kelly's Heroes*. Really?"

"Well. I mean, you know, as far as the landscape, you never heard of day for night in the movie business?"

"Yeah, dry mountains for bayous and swamps. Should work out great."

"You're supposed to be my go-to adviser. Not a nattering fucking nabob of negativism."

"Spiro Agnew? You're on fire with the references today."

"Look, I'm just thinking aloud here. I could use some insights. You know?"

"Well, my insight, and my professional advice as the attorney you love to ignore, is to let your brain work on all those angles but use your hands to fucking put the boards up."

"Jesus."

"Have you seen the weather forecast? The news? Seriously, are you okay? Are you taking too much medication? Like what, by the way?"

"I'm not. No."

"Bullshit, Duane. As your attorney."

"This is big. Too big even for bad weather. I have to say that I'm disappointed in your lack of imagination. Saddened."

"I have to say that I'm going now. I have to board up my own place. They're talking evacuation, for chrissake."

"Seriously?"

"Call me later, Marcello. Ciao."

"Fellini? Really? My favorite fucking movie? You slam me with it?"

"My turn for references. But you could use some *La Dolce* in your *Vita*. Bye."

"Bite me."

The dial tone came on and Duane hung up the phone. He paced around the office and then turned on the old TV in the corner and found CNN. He watched for a while and he called Maybelle again. Still no answer.

She always tried to make the most of her days off, but this one had gotten away. Her great-aunt Ouisa lived in a nursing home in Lakeview, and even though Maybelle had shown up at eight in the morning for the regular visit, by the time breakfast had been negotiated, and hospital administrators talked to, and arguments had about the proper cleaning of bandages on Ouisa's elbow, the one that had been broken, and surreal conversations in which Ouisa, who also suffered from Alzheimer's, ranged her memories in Homeric sweeps of time and distance and repetition, it was all but eleven. That left another two hours to stop at the storefront law office near Dillard to help the two young and hopelessly idealistic attorneys research and write up some briefs pertaining to the apparently endless exploitation of workers from Mexico and Guatemala.

It was work that Maybelle had sworn off doing since William's murder last year, but a few months at Arturo's had been eating at her façade of detachment, and of late she'd been putting in a half-dozen hours or so a week helping Eugenia and Lincoln. Who needed it. But they had known William, too, and they all had worked in Alabama and Mississippi and in the psychotic nightmare of northern Louisiana.

But they weren't the ones who found William's body beside the creek in Ruston. They were the ones still working cases out of the Gentilly storefront, though, and she wasn't. So it didn't matter what she had found. And what it looked like. Her colleagues in Ruston had understood when she left the team to go back to the city of her birth and dive deep into the cover of timelessness, and for a time, at least, never even cross the storefront doorway.

And now she was doing paralegal again. Part-time. Pro fucking bono. Go figure.

Lunch was a pit stop for a cup of jambalaya on Magazine Street, and then there were errands that in their own stupid repetitive banality bespoke a timelessness, too, and they could relax her even among the aisles of a grocery store, a discount pharmacy, a hardware store. And then it was three and time for coffee at No Quarter Books, which Duane's friend Gus Houston and his wife, Bonita, ran not too far from Arturo's. Everyone in the store was talking about that storm coming across the Gulf and speculating what, if anything, to do about it.

For the first time, Maybelle started thinking about it, too. It seemed unreal, and simply another of life's turbulences, and something she would just get through. Getting through was what she was all about these days, she had decided. And she had decided she was pretty sick of it.

She thought of Duane. She hadn't returned his calls because she didn't know quite what she wanted. They actually liked each other considerably, but since each was damaged in sundry ways, they seemed unable to do much about it. But it was nice having him out there. Question was whether she wanted him in there. Not inside her, which was fine, but in *there*.

She finished her coffee and went back to her duplex and plunged accidentally into a cleaning binge that took up the rest of the afternoon, and then the day was completely shot. And so she watched the news on TV. They were all talking about the storm and what to do, if anything. Being TV news, of course, they were very worked up about the ambiguity.

Boy Jack parked the van behind the loading dock and went inside to tell Mr. Croydon that the last shipment had been delivered. But there were five more to get out before Saturday, by which time it was pretty likely the freeway to the airport would be clogged even worse than usual. With any luck, Saturday would be a great day to lie back in his duplex and ride the bitch out.

Mr. Croydon was nowhere to be found, and Boy Jack figured he was probably out having a late lunch or early evening drinks with some of his crowd, what he called the Truman Capotes. Croydon told him not to use that term anymore, but Boy Jack knew he kind of liked it and so it had become a kind of inside joke between them. Even more inside than Mr. Croydon knew, since one of the TCs had become a kind of friend. Boy Jack actually liked Wallace okay, and the one hookup he'd allowed was decent enough considering Wallace was pushing sixty, but in truth they were exactly what they appeared. Wallace wanted a younger man, and Boy Jack got a Garden District patron who didn't mind helping with the rent and new brakes for Boy Jack's pickup truck. And nobody had to know, so it was definitely cool.

Boy Jack realized his days as a toy were limited, even in New Orleans, and even if he was what you might call bisexual, he wasn't all that interested in men in that way. But for now it was a way to get by while his larger goals—maybe an import business of his own or maybe just getting away to one of those Myanmar places where he'd be shipping the exports away instead of dealing with the imports and the people who bought them. Getting away, maybe real far away, had tremendous appeal for him. In fact, he knew his being accepted into city society, which was key to a business such as Croydon's, would be a joke in this town, even with his looks. He was another marginal kid from Baton Rouge who'd learned how to accommodate the interests of the rich. "Disposable" was the word Wallace had used once when he was very drunk and his advances had been rebuffed.

But Wallace was right. Boy Jack was better at it than most, but no one could escape their past—that was what his mother always said. She certainly didn't.

Disposable. Even his name was like having his fate stamped onto his forehead with a hot iron. It had cachet, but it also put him in a box he'd likely never get out of. John Caleb Pateau, from his birth certificate, was forgettable, and largely forgotten now except on his income tax and his bills, that kind of thing. Mostly he was Boy Jack.

After thirty what would he be?

He checked over some of the boxes in the storage room and pondered another trip out to the airport just to kill some time but quickly put that thought to rest. There were other ways to pass the hours. He waited for Croydon for another thirty minutes and then left a note saying he'd gone to run some errands and would be back tomorrow. The front door was locked so he was pretty sure Croydon had closed down for the day. It'd be nice to be able to do that, just stop for the day without having to clear it with anyone and without worrying if it would mean you couldn't pay the light bill later on.

He walked down the block to the parking garage where Croydon let him use a space for his F-150, checking out the sky. You could just feel in the air that something was coming, and he thought, the sooner the better. The Quarter was eating at him today, and he walked past the tourists without looking at them, because he didn't want to see what they were looking at. Along Chartres, not too far from the Monteleone Hotel, where the TCs liked to hang out, he half-tripped on an uneven bit of sidewalk, and as he was catching himself to keep from falling, he noticed a bright golden chain in the gutter. He walked another step and then went back and bent down to have a closer look.

In the Quarter, you never knew what you might find, so he picked it up, and as he did, the chain unraveled and a small cross slid to the end. He held it out and inspected it in the afternoon light. A man and a woman in business dress walked by and gave him a look like he was a bum. He started to say something but couldn't. He gazed upon the cross on the chain, not caring who else went past him. It was not an antique, and it wasn't real gold, and it wasn't something anyone else wanted. He put it in his pocket and walked along the loud and busy street.

Duane spent the evening at the theater, helping Moon-Ra and handling the concessions. Katrina's approach wasn't helping the Shannon Tweed turnout. The 9:45 showing only drew about forty patrons, and to make it worse, they weren't the camp crowd he tried to woo. A lot of them looked like porn store addicts.

While the last reel was playing, he got into a long conversation with Moon-Ra about film equipment. He didn't mention the movie idea, yet, but Duane knew Moon-Ra had the soul of a cinematographer and probably could also be one of the cast. Fellini would definitely cast him.

By midnight, when they were closing up, Duane considered taking an extra hour to board the place up, per Rhys, but all he wanted was to go home and sleep.

Moon-Ra took off for a late-night gig in the Quarter.

Duane drove back to his place, stifling an impulse to go to Maybelle's. He took a Tylenol-3 and turned on the stereo to OZ and fell asleep fully clothed on his bed in typical Big Easy mode, because tomorrow was always another day, and there was already sufficient evil unto the present one. He had absolutely no idea what he really wanted to do. He was perfect for the nothing city. Jesus.

The weight of time occasionally became a burden for Moon-Ra. For example, tonight, in the reassessment process of a sweltering city half-preparing itself for a half-acknowledged crisis, if that was the word. Which was why the gig got canceled. Which was more-or-less okay. Maybe for the best. Maybe he needed to devote some serious thought to this one. He had gotten out of that habit. And not just with him. It was a New Orleans thing. A tentative relationship with the real world. Not many of his friends actually believed the hurricane would hit New Orleans, and anyway, if it did, where would they go? The evacuation plans always pretty much assumed you had a car, and gas, and a place to stay once you got away.

When he called his cousin, Paulus, who worked in a music store on St. Claude over in the Seventh Ward, to see what he was going to do, the answer was basically to nail up some plywood over the windows and go home to his apartment and chill with his wife and kids. He said his mama, Corina, was putting up some pots and planning to offer up a chicken to Ogun, but she was still going to have church on Sunday and had ridden out every storm so far so wasn't going to change her mind.

She was a stubborn preacher woman everyone knew as the Reverend Youngblood, and also a voudou priestess, so Moon-Ra figured his aunt knew things. On the other hand, he believed in science, because music was like science. So he watched the weather forecasts.

Also, Moon-Ra and Paulus had been working on a plan to start their own band, sort of second-line funk kind of groove. They just needed to get a good horn player and a singer. But the singer didn't need to be Feliciana, who was again driving him crazy. She had it together extremely well with her looks, and her voice was throaty and sweet, but everybody knew you couldn't mix your personal life with your music or you'd wind up—who could count how many bands had gone off the rails because of that?

Really, no one knew how it was to be Moon-Ra. Never had. As far back as junior high in Birmingham, where he came up. College in Memphis didn't change anything. Nobody got what that was inside him—the spirit thing, the music thing, the love thing. That last made everyone think he was a softie. But to himself, he thought he was something like an alien. Not from Mexico or Puerto Rico or anything. From Mars or Venus or someplace like that. Maybe another solar system.

So he gave up the person no one could understand, baptized as Curtis Lincoln Boyard. He liked the music of Sun-Ra, and so the name just came to him one night looking up at the heavens while walking along Elysian Fields. He could see strands of the cosmos largely hidden from anyone else. He could see them right then and there. Thus he found Moon-Ra.

It took his family and friends a while to get the change of name, except for Aunt Corina, the preacher, who said it was his Oshun spirit breaking through. He argued with her, because Oshun was female, but the Reverend Youngblood said to shut up because it didn't matter, and that could happen, and anyway, it was the right one because he was pretty and you can't argue about those things, and shouldn't.

And you never argued with the reverend.

But Moon-Ra also had a side order of Chango, a tough guy for sure, which made him feel better. What did they say, "Everything is everything?" Confirmed.

The job at the Portia wasn't much more for him than a way to stay busy and also connect, even remotely, with the world of the arts. Also, he liked his boss. Duane seemed to get Moon-Ra, or at least enough that it felt like being with a kindred spirit. Being with like-minded spirits also was what New Orleans was all about. Each had come across the city in his own time, and now couldn't imagine being anywhere else. He and Duane had talked about that often. Even tonight, after the dumbass Shannon Tweed thing, which ended up with them both laughing and talking about whether the storm would hit.

The power was still jumping on and off so much that he couldn't work on some bass lines or for that matter even relax or think. Until it was fixed he needed somewhere else to be, and so, damn fool he was, he called Feliciana.

CHAPTER 4

Friday, August 26

Friday morning, Boy Jack remembered that he needed to go by and pick up the door prize for winning the drawing from the *Billy Jack* retrospective at the Portia last month. Yes, his nickname did have some connection to the movie. Word play of that sort ran in the family. There was Uncle Hondo, his older sister Scarlett, his dad, Big Jake, a dog named Rinny Tin Tin, the grandpa they all called Darth Vader, but not to his face . . . it was just ridiculous.

Hell, he didn't even like Billy Jack, self-righteous asshole. He really only went to the movie because he was bored and the mood just came over him and it was cheap. Maybe a little because it was *Billy Jack*. No matter. The first movie was the only one watchable and then they had the drawing and he had left after that. The cute girl at the ticket window and popcorn counter said he'd have to pick up the prize—a poster of either Elvis or Raquel Welch—later on since the office was locked and she couldn't get in. It was just so fucking New Orleans. Nothing ever worked.

He had some errands and one of them was to drop off an antique lamp for Mr. Croydon to some judge's wife at a house near Audubon Park, which was close to the Portia and he might as well get the poster before the damn storm showed up, which was looking more like it could.

It was nearly four when he got there, and a middle-aged man that looked like a less handsome version of Jeff Bridges was standing outside checking out the old theater building. Strangely. Probably the owner. Maybe he was thinking about the hurricane.

Boy Jack parked his F-150 and went over to introduce himself and get his posters. The guy seemed almost startled, like he was off in some other world, but was friendly and shook his hand. He had two small band-aids on his cheek and a stitch on his forehead. Boy Jack liked him right away.

Had a flock of circumstances no more meaningful than the flutter in a spider's heart not stuttered out of the cosmos, perhaps nothing of what eventually came to pass would have. However, this is not the way of said cosmos. In said cosmos, where all has happened anyway and those holding tickets in the currently running production are only relevant in the sense of being witnesses to the action, even if pressed into audience participation, there is no known ending. No script not subject to instantaneous revision.

It speaks the language of the howl. In its sonography, the sonography of all being and time, it is the only concept in which relevance even matters. These are things that are universal in nature and yet, for Duane, highly specific. Specific to the sidewalk where two freaks of some unknown cult kicked the shit out of him. To the emergency room doctor. To the empty seat he perched in last night just to look out in the half-empty theater to see exactly what kind of people would come to a Shannon Tweed festival, and the ugly and very un-hip answers that derived from that. And now, specific to the news that Katrina was moving across the Gulf after all, and had at least an odds-on chance it would hit Louisiana in the next couple of days.

He needed to board up.

42

These were the thoughts going through Duane's mind when Boy Jack had interrupted his reveries to introduce himself. Now came new mental meat. For example, casting his movie. Just looking at the casual James Dean-ishness of the kid, translated through an obvious Southern manifestation, suggested at least one new character—maybe even played by the very person who called himself Boy Jack.

Another of the great things about the city. You didn't have to spend much time making things up. They were always right there in front of you. Gus Houston, for that matter. Quite a story there, with his No Quarter Books store on Louisiana and unusual connection with Reverend Youngblood. Certainly a part for Gus, maybe for his beautiful fireball wife, Bonita, too.

For now, the main thing was that Boy Jack wanted the Elvis poster from *Jail House Rock*. Not the one Duane suggested as the prize—Raquel Welch in her *One Million B.C.* fake fur-skin bikini, a clothing option which many anthropologists seemed to have missed during their research. Duane said he had contemplated how the discovery of a beauty thus clad in the primordial ages might have affected subsequent debates about evolution, but it was purely fanciful and perhaps they really needed to focus hard on the reality of the day.

Boy Jack had no idea what Duane was talking about. "You get tired of looking at her tits, but you never really get tired of Elvis pretending to be a jail bird," he said. Neither of them believed that completely, but it was a good way to restore conversational focus and further impressed Duane in his secret consideration of Boy Jack for the movie.

Duane might have lured them into a conversation about cinema, which he was wont to do so often that Maybelle frequently called him out on it, but the "reality of the day," as he himself had put it, was too strong to avoid. Both complained how the coming storm was interrupting business and their daily lives.

Which happened also to be what people throughout the city were saying at that very moment. They were saying that hurricanes were nuisances. Nor were they inspired by or frightened into speculation of the larger impact. Despite ample evidence. They were what might be called dissociated from matters at hand. In that, they were but another indication that the city needed guidance, direction—something that actually mattered.

Yes, the people mattered. The city mattered. But the people in the city had become content to let the forces of nature, not to say commerce and capitalism, sweep through as though no kind of matter mattered. They believed in their arrhythmic and besotted hearts that whatever havoc the storms wrought, no evil nor nature nor human depravity could ever truly touch the soul of the pride of the Mississippi and really the whole fucking universe. And of course they were wrong. Not just wrong. Stubborn and foolhardy and deserving of utter annihilation for being fucking idiots. But it didn't do any good to say so, and thus another notch in Duane's dilemma. For that matter in Maybelle's and Moon-Ra's dilemmas, and so on. And in this kid, too.

Boy Jack stayed for nearly an hour, including a tour of the whole theater—far more camaraderie than either had anticipated. Boy Jack told Duane about Croydon's Imports, about which of course Duane knew, but not in such detail. They exchanged phone numbers. Boy Jack said if he needed help boarding up to let him know and if he wasn't doing stuff for Mr. Croydon, he'd come over and help out.

This made Duane feel good about the very things that usually made him feel sour on the city. So he hollered as Boy Jack walked back to his pickup with the Elvis poster that if he had another hour or so, maybe he could stick around and help right now.

Which is how they wound up driving to the lumber store in Metairie. The one on Tchoupitoulas had unexpectedly sold out of plywood sheets. There were more rumors, or at least what they heard at both lumber and hardware yards, that Katrina was a hurricane again after leaving Florida. Supposedly, the governor had called a state of emergency, or was going to. Those kinds of rumors were enough to begin the hints of a rush to buy batteries and water and ice, though not yet to purchase the more expensive things like generators.

Smart business owners, which arguably included Duane, were taking the most preliminary of precautions, which increased as the day went on. Duane bought the last eighteen plywood sheets the place had. About five more than he actually needed. In the cashier line he almost decided to cut back to just a dozen, but didn't. Who knew when such bulwarks against the chaos of the skies might come in handy in such a miserably chosen location for the soul of the American people, who at the time weren't even American, in the strictest, original sense. Duane felt himself reeling away in his mind again and he noticed Boy Jack looking at him funny, and then the cashier asking him to please move along in the line, and he noticed customers behind him with carts filled with the capricious cornucopia of survival. So he snapped to.

Riding back in the pickup, Duane and Boy Jack exchanged a few more sage remarks of surprise if not inklings of concern that people might not actually be taking this seriously, state of emergency or not. All the bars and hotels and restaurants and grocery stores and Wal-marts were open, and just then a pickup truck with a bunch of Little League kids in the bed drove past.

Audubon Park was full of runners and walkers and nannies pushing the prams of the entitled. It wasn't even windy or rainy, let alone threatening. Hot enough, though, and plenty humid, but it was August and that's the way it always was. The Saints were playing a night game against Baltimore at the Superdome for god's sake.

Back at the Portia they unloaded the plywood and a dozen 1x4s Duane also bought at the last minute to nail them up better. Duane gave Boy Jack thirty bucks for gas and beer, which he feigned to refuse, but then accepted, because otherwise it would have been awkward.

Gretchen called and wanted to know was the Portia going to be open for the second Shannon Tweed night. Moon-Ra called with the same question. Duane told Gretchen to stay home if she wanted, and she said she did. Moon-Ra said he could come in for the 6:25 reel, but wanted to leave after that, if it was okay. He said nobody would come, probably. Duane said probably that was right, but to come in for the 6:25 anyway.

He could tell Moon-Ra was hoping he'd just cancel the whole thing, but he'd already committed to showing up. So Duane held him to do it. It would be a good lesson to Moon-Ra about floating trial balloons. Then he sat in the back row of the empty theater and looked at the lightless screen for longer than he liked to admit, and then he called Maybelle.

She answered. Which busted a trial balloon of his own. He'd expected the voice message: "Hello. It's me. Say what you need to."

Instead, she said she was at work because they made her but she'd be off by eight and thought she might start planning to leave town. Her apartment by the Fairgrounds, really more a duplex except nobody lived on the other side because the owner used it for storage, was on a street of slightly gentrified shotgun shack houses. She said her mom and dad, who lived in Lakeview near Aunt Ouisa, were going up to Dallas to stay with the relatives they usually stayed with when they evacuated. They were going to pick up her younger sister and her family in Baton Rouge on the way.

"They're evacuating?"

"Not officially. But you know."

"I do?"

"Look around, Duane. Watch the news. Like that."

"Well you know, they never know where it will wind up."

"It's going to wind up here. Come on."

"Actually, that's why I called. Can you come over and help me at the Portia with some stuff? I mean, if you're not going with your mom tonight."

He knew that would piss her off, and it did, so it took a long silence for her to answer.

"What stuff?"

"I bought some plywood. I was going to board up tomorrow but maybe I should start tonight. You know, make it a party."

"A plywood party?"

"Just me and you and maybe Moon-Ra."

"So just you and me."

"Well, you just said it's coming. I feel like I'm doing the intelligent thing here."

"Jesus."

"So also I'd like to see you."

Another silence. Then, "I have to get back to work. This place is actually full. People are fucking stupid."

"So you'll come?"

"You bringing the plywood?"

"Maybe also grab some vino? *Por favor.*"

"You're a shit."

"I know. But I miss you. I got plenty of things to share."

"What, pizza?"

"I mean share. Like in discuss."

"That kind of share? You?"

"I'll tell you when you get here. You'll want to know."

"Huhhn."

"I will also have food. Not pizza."

"What girl can turn that down?"

She hung up but not in a bad way, and Duane's heart struggled with the good blood of pained elation.

He got up and swept the aisle floors and tidied up around the concession stand and wolfed down a bag of peanuts and generally waited for Moon-Ra to show up, because hurricane approaching or not, Duane had no real confidence in his own technical ability to make the damn machinery of the cinematic art do as it was told. He also called Eddie's for a pizza delivery but he figured Maybelle would understand or not care.

Moon-Ra got there in time for the setup and a little small talk, along the general line Duane'd had with Boy Jack, but different, about whether or not people in the city were acting weird thinking about hurricanes. They agreed that people were. Acting weird. But intentionally. By pretending nothing would happen. Like it was a proud tradition. Neither Duane nor Moon-Ra were interested in further speculation of what just seemed mass idiocy.

Moon-Ra asked about the stiches on Duane's face and Duane said he'd fallen down and it was a funny story but he'd tell him later, when it stopped hurting. He said he'd just taken the bandages off before Maybelle would be coming over and asked if there were scabs yet. Moon-Ra rolled his eyes and went upstairs to the projection booth.

At 5:30, Duane opened the doors and cranked down the air conditioning. The first customer, who looked like a bank clerk never allowed out of his cage, showed up at 6:04. At 6:25, Moon-Ra started the projector on the coming attractions, and counted nine people, all men, in the audience. Perve platoon. Too bad for them it was one of Shannon's soft porn nudie detective efforts, rather than the more purposely erotic groin-groan stuff. Moon-Ra dutifully sat with the projector for eighty-three minutes as the former Playmate bared large portions but not all of her body. He watched with great sympathy. The script no doubt hurt as much to perform as it did to watch. Probably. But the pervs were fine with the soft stuff, which was a win-win. Duane wasn't going to get any vice badges bothering him.

All the peckers and their owners were gone out the side exit doors as soon as the end credits rolled, but Moon-Ra let the reel play out as a matter of professional principle. Then he shut it down and put things away and went downstairs to say good-bye to the boss.

Which was when he saw Maybelle, perched on the counter of the concession stand in jeans, sandals, and a soft blue blouse. Duane was rummaging through a storage closet and emerged just at the right dramatic moment with a small chainsaw in one hand. Actually, a small electric saw for cutting wood Duane had picked up at a Sears.

"I thought you were gonna save that for tomorrow," Moon-Ra said, nodding to Maybelle at the same time.

"Might get started a little tonight after all. At least cut some of this stuff to fit the windows."

"It's his idea of a date," she said. "Plus, as you can see he's already cut himself, so odds are he won't ruin the evening with an emergency room run." Her brown eyes gazed toward the entry door as if it might offer an escape. "That would just be statistically unrealistic."

Duane touched the wounds of his mugging, frowned, and looked around the lobby. "Damn, I meant to get those sawhorses."

Maybelle looked directly at Moon-Ra. They didn't need to say anything.

"Well, it'll just have to do," Duane said, frowning even more at their indifference. "I can probably prop it up against the counter or something."

"They'll break on you if you do that," said Moon-Ra, walking to the concession stand.

"And then you'll amputate your hand or maybe your leg," Maybelle said.

"You got somewhere to go?" Duane said to Moon-Ra, who was pulling two hangers with a shirt and pants from a wall hook behind the counter.

"Or we could do all this cutting and nailing and injuring tomorrow," Maybelle said, sliding off the counter to pull a bottle of Cabernet from a plastic bag. "Wanna join us?" she asked Moon-Ra.

"Another time," he said, and headed to the now-vacant theater pit. "White shirt and black pants for this gig tonight."

"Where?" she asked.

"Over on Maple. Bar slash restaurant, something like that. Never been there but they want live music nine to midnight. Friend of mine plays with the Levee Rats and needed a bass. Feliciana coming by, too, for a set, maybe two."

"Well, good for you."

"I guess. Might be the last gig for a while if that storm keeps on coming our way."

"You never know."

"You never do."

Duane had disappeared down a small hallway that ran along one side of the theater pit but now came back, dragging a plywood sheet.

"Shit, I definitely bought too damn many of these."

"Never hurts to have too much plywood," Maybelle said. Moon-Ra closed the doors to the pit behind him, after one more quick glance to be sure all the pervs definitely were gone from all the seats.

"You know, that was exactly my thought," Duane said, and stopped, looked back down the hall where the rest of the lumber was stacked. Looked for longer than seemed necessary.

"Yeah. Well, how about that vino?" Maybelle was pouring one for each of them into the plastic cups normally used for soft drinks for people who didn't want to drink out of bottles or cans for whatever reason.

"To being prepared!" he toasted. Actual cups or glasses would have clinked. The cups sort of scrunched and crinkled and part of Maybelle's wine spilled onto her big toe. She looked at it like Duane had looked at the plywood, and drank half the cup.

"So this is what you're sharing? Boy Scout mottos?"

"Nope. I got lots more. You're gonna love it."

He glanced at the entry door, thinking he'd heard something, and saw a pizza box next to the ticket booth. He'd paid for the order by credit card but what the hell, why didn't the delivery guy at least knock instead of a dump and run? He would have to complain about that next time. For now, he brought it inside and put it on the concession counter.

"Right," she said, grabbing a slice. "Just like you promised."

He was right behind her.

"So I'm only eating because I'm starving. I didn't get to eat at Arturo's. But fuck you anyway for feeding me this way."

Duane's face showed due remorse. "But we like Eddie's. It's the best in Carrollton."

She chewed and shrugged at the same time, then drained and filled her wine cup again.

"See ya, keep in touch about tomorrow," Moon-Ra said, hurrying past.

"Looking fine," Maybelle said.

"Pretty sure we won't be open tomorrow night," Duane called out as Moon-Ra opened the door to the warm night air.

"Pretty sure I won't be here if you are," he laughed, and hurried to his blue Civic.

Duane watched him start the car and drive away, then got another slice and sat on the concession counter next to his girl. They let their legs swing like a couple of teenagers in the fifties. But they were in the new century, and glad to be together. And avoiding the contemplation, yet again, of what that meant or didn't.

He leaned over and kissed her on her red sauce-covered lips and she returned the pleasure and they sat on the counter a little longer because it was exactly where they knew they wanted to be. She put her free arm around his waist to bring him closer and when she touched his side, he pulled back and in the wince of pain on his sutured face she was getting an inkling that whatever he wanted to share was not going to be trivial.

Elsewhere, the city lay intact and its inhabitants held back their fears with the usual pretensions and diversions that made New Orleans the only place in the world for certain kinds of people to live. This would include Duane, Maybelle, Moon-Ra, and their various friends and families, sprinkled across the swamp that Bienville chose for his settlement like so many scooped-up, multicolored Carnival beads. It was easy to see how the bead that was Boy Jack could wind up with no place to go through no real fault of his own.

But he did have a duplex, and when he got back there was more than a little annoyed that he had to park a block away because of the fire trucks. The fire trucks were there because Walter, the moron drunk part-time security guard who lived on the other side, had done the classic of his ilk—fallen asleep on the couch while smoking. A fireman standing by the truck said they'd managed to get there in time to keep the flames from spreading, and the guy inside from dying. It didn't destroy the duplex, just charred the one side. Which wasn't the problem. The problem was that duplexes share way too much, and both sides reeked of smoke and burnt couches and probably Walter's cats.

The fireman had talked to the landlord, who lived in St. Francisville or somewhere, to see what to do. They decided Walter's side was no longer habitable, and that Boy Jack could stay in a motel for the next few days while they "evaluated the damage to the entire structure," if the insurance would pay for it, which the landlord didn't know for sure. Knowing the landlord's penchant for lying about almost everything, Boy Jack wanted to try to avoid a motel charge that he'd probably have to pay for himself. Either way he was about one step away from homeless. Just like that!

So he called Mr. Croydon, who was nice enough if a little crabby probably from the stress of the storm. He told Boy Jack maybe he could bunk for a few days in one of the warehouse spaces in Gentilly where they kept the antique back stock that couldn't fit in the store. It didn't seem all that inviting, or maybe even safe if the storm really came through, but it would do for the time being for at least stashing what was left of his stuff.

The fireman let Boy Jack get some of his things and open the windows to let the smoke and chemical stench ease out. But the clothes and other things he grabbed already bore the mark. He figured nothing in the apartment would be salvageable, and since he had no renter's insurance, he was looking at his own personal catastrophe dovetailing just perfectly into the one that was whipping itself into a frenzy out in the Gulf. Boy Jack was glad the ambulance took Walter to the hospital because he wanted more than anything to hit him with a baseball bat. Of course then he'd wind up in jail, but at least that would be a place to hole up until Katrina was come and gone.

Long way of saying that's how he wound up Friday night trying to figure a way to talk Mr. Croydon, or maybe Wallace or one of the other Truman Capotes, into a longer arrangement—temporary shelter but with an option for something permanent. Not a warehouse.

Which is how he learned that Croydon and Wallace—two of the

TCs—were evacuating Saturday, ahead of the fleeing traffic if possible. Now that Boy Jack had brought up a residence inquiry, Mr. Croydon wondered if he might be available to board up the windows at his house off St. Charles that morning. In turn he and Wallace would leave a key to the back door, which faced away from the probable hurricane direction, but to be used only as an emergency. Mr. Croydon cautioned, though, that it might be dangerous if Boy Jack stayed any longer than necessary and that he probably should get out of town, too. After the windows were boarded.

However, Mr. Croydon said, if Boy Jack did stay, he could use the guest cottage behind the house. Just for Friday night. But not during the storm, if it actually hit. Because the cottage wasn't sturdy and might be a possible insurance problem. Which is how Boy Jack realized yet again how he was viewed. As a possible insurance loss.

Nonetheless, he said yes, and spent Friday night in the cottage, as agreed, after nailing up most of the windows just for something to do. When he awoke on the cot at 3 a.m. in a sweat, he was still inside a dream in which he was on a floatie boat in a swimming pool that was inside a dark and tree-cluttered sea. He had a way of knowing things that would happen and dreams were often the informants. He may have gone back to sleep until dawn but he wasn't sure. But he was sure about the dream. He wasn't going to tell Mr. Croydon, but he damn sure planned on spending the next couple of days in the big house. He had no options.

They'd made it back to his house in the Marigny before it got too late and were in bed together within minutes. Now she was awake, next to him, and he was sleeping so quietly she could barely hear him breathe. She studied his face, and the cuts, and then turned onto her side and looked out the bedroom window, yet to be boarded up, but could see neither stars nor moon. Only clouds.

The first time she'd slept with Duane didn't actually involve sleep because it was, sort of like this night, after-hours at the Portia. But not in a bed—on the lip of the stage in front of the blank screen. It was good. It was fun. It was voyeuristic and unseemly. It was what she needed after the business with Will.

The seats were empty, and the front door was locked and no one could get in, but they were on a stage nonetheless in front of seats in which people often sat to watch things such as they were doing, but via the magic of chemistry and machinery capturing the images of life and dispensing them through thin air. His way of putting it was, "What good is owning a movie theater if you can't make your own movies?"

After coming together like the Beatles song, they lay together naked for a while and dozed off and woke up and did it again and turns out that was the beginning of a thing neither had anticipated when they met after she literally bumped into him on Magazine Street while walking, and it seemed comical enough that when he asked her to grab a coffee she said sure.

For more than a year it had progressed very little beyond that, although actually it had. At least enough that on this dark night she was with him, hurricane-prepping with pizza and wine, the sex smell still on them, and her thumb only a little discolored and sore from the impact of the hammer that she had fully intended to strike on the head of the nail to go into the plywood to keep the storm winds from blowing out the window of the ticket booth.

He had shared, all right. Just as promised. First off was the mugging, which he had to explain right away so that she wouldn't touch his right side ribs if at all possible. Which was asking a lot under the circumstances. Impossible, really. But he played through the pain pretty well and saved his groaning for when they were done.

Then the part about Carlos and the land in Texas. That was while he was resting his hand on the wetness between her thighs, curling his fingers in what might even be described as a joyful manner that surpassed mere coitus. He said he didn't know what to do about the bequest, and that he was plenty worried about his friend, and then he lay quietly, his fingers not wanting to leave her hair.

She asked occasional questions about the land, a couple of them legal-ish about the provability of the title transfer, a term that made his eyebrows arch even as he had to know it was a fair question, but mostly she just listened. Because it seemed the best thing to do because his sharing sounded so entirely dramatic and weird.

Then he sat up and told her about the movie. This was whole new territory.

She sat up, too, and looked into his eyes as he spoke, in that wild but exciting way he could get when ideas more vast than the capacity in his own head but not his soul overwhelmed him. It was basically what she liked about him. Seeing that in his eyes. Feeling it in his body. Ignoring all possible repercussions, like running a stop sign at ninety miles per hour on a narrow county road at midnight.

Actually, she really could see a guide to Southern living as a cinematic template of images and characters. The only thing was the plot. The not knowing the actual story, how it would play out, where it would go, where and when it would arrive. She realized he was talking about exactly what he *said* he was talking about—a way of looking at the whole country, the whole world, the whole thing. His soul truly was overwhelmed. He owned an art house theater because he *was* an art house theater.

When he was done with that she noticed he was hard again and she took him in her hand, and then her mouth, and then inside her hair and wetness and gripped his ribs and all until he moaned in real time in her arms and legs and there was no hiding one from the other. That was how she loved him, and when he had stopped and lay panting atop her, one hand over her breast and the other cradling her head, she knew that was how he loved her, too.

Or were they just making another movie, same as their first time together, and bound not only by love but by a concept, which anyone from New Orleans or from the South for that matter, understood? The true "force that through the green fuse drives the flower," and "that blasts the roots of trees is my destroyer," and so on. She was crazy about Duane, the concept of him, the reality of his green fuse blasting the roots of her trees. Where that all led. The creation of destruction. Of life. Of overwhelmed souls. Which is what he was sharing with her on a singularly strange and disturbing night in a city known for precisely that.

Duane awoke from sleep so deep it took a minute to realize where he was. Maybelle was curled on her side at the edge of the bed, one arm hanging almost to the floor. He didn't want to disturb her, so he eased away and for no particular reason roamed, naked, around the house looking at things that he owned. He owned things in the kitchen, in the living room, in the bathroom, on the back porch, in each of the bedrooms, although of course he did not own her. She was the woman he loved. They both knew it and finally had even said it to each other, but it seemed hasty at the time, and so they'd just let the actual profession of a feeling sit next to them like a ghostly spirit. The spirit was still with them.

He knew he'd gone on a little last night, with all that about the movie and what it could mean and how they could make it happen and change all their lives . . . and here he was elaborating again. To himself! He had started to notice that tendency more and more and felt that he needed to watch it. People would think he was odd. Which no doubt they already did and which Rhys in particular spared no opportunity to restate.

Maybe it all followed from getting his ass kicked by a couple of deviant thugs, exactly in the wake of hearing the howl on the levee and then the letter from Carlos. He couldn't sleep because he was having trouble putting it together. Plus Maybelle. Plus a debt-ridden movie house directly in the sights of his insurance office neighbor trying to get the city to close the place down and force a sale. Plus a hurricane.

Maybe. Probably. Maybe not. Possibly. The fuck knew?

It made him soul weary. He sat down in his old, badly cracked leather chair, which was cold as hell to his still-naked butt at first, and pulled a throw blanket on the armrest over him. He intended to go crawl back into bed with the love of his life, a description he always remembered said about the character Marge by the character Ray Hicks in Robert Stone's *Dog Soldiers* and the flawed adaptation *Who'll Stop the Rain* that followed, and he was thinking of how that all played out for Ray and Marge. Then he remembered Stone's *A Hall of Mirrors*, aka the Hollywood version *WUSA*, set in New Orleans and how that all played out for Rheinhardt. And then he remembered how it worked out for Marcello, because of Rhys's wisecrack. But he gradually slumped down in the chair and sleep took him and perhaps his dreams intertwined with those of his Maybelle—a possibility that true love and art, if not science, had to entertain.

The gig on Maple was inconsequential but paid well enough, and Moon-Ra felt it had been a good decision to take it, the necessity to play mostly cover tunes notwithstanding. Feliciana said it was a good gig and good money. They were surprised at how packed the place was, and the streets outside. She had hopped the trolley earlier in the evening and stopped at her friend Hannah's on the way. By the time Moon-Ra got there he'd had to park four blocks away and lug his bass and amp through the hot steamy night. Maybe the hurricane would come or maybe it would veer away—his friends seemed split right down the middle on the options. But he was starting to feel it coming, and instead of hanging around after the last set to drink or gossip about the music scene, he just wanted to go home. Feliciana said she was tired, too, and would just go back to Hannah's and crash. But when she kissed him good-bye she made sure he knew what he'd be missing.

When he got home, he put his bass and amps and speakers and assorted important things together in a corner of the front room and thought about where to stash them in case it actually did hit. The bathroom was always the best. As for everything else, it would just be a crap shoot. He wasn't going to board up because the house had wooden shutters and all he had to do was close them and drive in a couple of nails. Not his first rodeo for that kind of thing.

Still, worry had started to seep into his brain and it didn't help to think where his mom and his sister were. Mom in Nine Ward and Eluvia up in Gentilly. He needed to call them both first thing in the morning. His sense was that they had to leave. He knew their sense would be that they didn't. At least his mom's sense. Eluvia could be more reasonable. It occurred to him his Civic was on empty and he needed to tell them to gas up, too. The lines probably already were bad. People filled up even if they weren't going anywhere because that's what people did, like buy all the water they could cram in a shopping cart just because they could, no matter how many folks back of them in the check-out line would go thirsty.

He also needed to call Duane, and also Paulus and a couple of other friends. Feliciana most of all. He was not feeling good about the chances of avoiding the wind and rain, mostly the wind, but not letting himself feel bad just yet, either. So he took the bass out of its case and without plugging it in ran a free-form line off Fats's "Walkin' to New Orleans" until his head was chill enough for him to stretch out on the green couch. He wadded a Mexican blanket under his head for a pillow and listened for wind or rain or any other signs of what might be coming, but there was only silence. Thick, like the air. All he could feel was a sensation, maybe electrons readjusting. He felt all of them, jostling for position, pushing each other around for power. Felt them for real.

CHAPTER 5

Saturday, August 27

Saturday morning after making coffee and wheat toast, since he hadn't been to the grocery lately for actual food, and then taking Maybelle home over by the Fairgrounds, Duane headed to the Portia to finish up the boarding and planking and stowing that had been interrupted last night. She said he seemed wired and he said it was probably too much coffee. But it wasn't. Duane felt like every nerve in his body was sparking arcs. It was coming. You couldn't see it or smell it or touch it or feel it, unless you were Moon-Ra, but it was there. Even as it was not. Not in the sense of the "no there there" Gertrude Stein insult to LA, but in the sense of a there that was there, only it wasn't where it was going to be just yet.

Hurricanes are like that. All the dread is front-loaded, and then the storm shows up and the dread surges to simple God-fearing terror, and then it is replaced by the second dread, the hopelessness that all that could be taken has been taken and that you have to start again when you thought you'd been cleared from that particular responsibility.

Then comes the third dread, the worst. The third dread is that the dread will never end, but that you will. That time is not on your side. No one wants to admit that until they're drawing their last breath, but everyone knows it. Life in the time of hurricanes is very clear about mortality.

Mortality was what Duane had understood Tuesday, and also approximately one thousand years ago, while standing on the levee, then just the banks, of that river, though it would be unfair to criticize him for not comprehending the time linkage. But simply understanding mortality was not a bad trick in itself. Even when past, present, and future were so compartmentalized by human abilities.

The shock of understanding, of awakening, was divine no matter when it manifested, and where, and to whom. You'd think residents of the city would have a lot more of that kind of awakened shock, given all the opportunities on a quotidian basis. But in the Big Easy, intimations of immortality, or just plain mortality, which were the same thing, more often produced just the opposite of awakening: torpor.

Duane was not torporized. He was most definitely awake. So awake he was beginning to wonder if that was what was making people wonder about him. Maybelle listened well enough. Rhys barely at all. The kid who called himself Boy Jack did truly listen, and might be awake in his own way. Moon-Ra definitely was awake. He had been for way more than one thousand years. Duane took it for granted that Moon-Ra was not only an ancestral spirit or an avatar but also the incarnation of a future that Duane himself would never see, or maybe even comprehend.

Things were unblocking in Duane's mind, too fast and too chaotically, and shaping a vision. And he knew it was having an effect on Maybelle. "You are *so* wired this morning," she said for the third time, as he dropped her off and she air-kissed him walking up to her front door. He knew something in her had shifted, but he didn't know what, and he didn't even know how to speak of it to her, so he dismissed it in his head as just his own misinterpretation. Which, as time would eventually tell, it was not.

What he did know was that all this pouring out of him not only mystified her, it sent her retreating into her airtight, all-weather, magically translucent protective stainless-steel bubble around which people swirled with no chance of getting inside.

It was a trait he had noticed in Maybelle once or twice but never at this level. She might love him and no doubt did, but that didn't get him access when the bubble dropped down.

Was it his overly passionate summation of the theoretical movie? Of the ranch from Carlos? How could he tell? She was withdrawing so deftly—truly at the top of that form of her personal emotional art—that he was pretty sure she didn't even know she had left the building.

Duane had seen withdrawals all his life, in various people, including his mom and late father. He knew if Maybelle sensed there was something fundamentally off-center with him, way deep down, that she would disappear from his life forever.

These kinds of thoughts always brought Duane to a deep-lung exhale and a single word: fuuuuck. Still, he had an appointment with destiny. His dad had been in Big Ag. Duane was in Big Art. Or planned to be. Movies, esthetic visions, spiritual upheavals, masterpieces—the whole nine yards. Petty or grand, crazy or genius, tortured revelations of this sort had been eating at him all his life and intensified his resolve. Shaped his arc.

It went way past the rush of getting that first job out of grad school at the struggling TV station in Fort Worth, and then a step up to the wire service and postings around the country. Then joining and retreating from reckless adventures with Carlos and back into journalism, pretty much ending at the newspaper in Houston, except for occasional freelancing.

New Orleans was an easy pick to settle into some kind of stability, to work it out, find something that meant something. Those last, sporadic smuggling gigs with Carlos might have interfered with the Big Easy strategy if it hadn't been for Uncle Walter's bequest. Duane might still be way south of the border, dead or alive. But karma is what it is. So the lifelong movie buff found himself buying the Portia.

Actually "settling down." And finding Maybelle. Was it really such a stretch?

One of the constant updates on the radio from the hurricane watchers broke his reverie, which he realized had escalated to cosmic heights from reflections on the extreme mundanity of being mugged on an Irish Channel sidewalk. He shook his head like a dog getting back into the moment. That particular moment of pain—on the sidewalk—had been so bizarre and sadistic and decadent it barely registered as real. Compare it to Katrina. That was the definition of real. It was a freight train on water rails, and it would really lay waste to the city and all who tried to stay afloat inside it. Except Duane. Despite all vows to the contrary, he had decided to ride that bitch like a surfer on a great white.

Crossing Carrollton back over to the Portia, he touched the suture on his face and the bruises along his ribs like putting the final period on a complex sentence. By midafternoon he was finished with the hammer and nail jobs, and went up to his office to sort out paperwork and maps and posters and put everything loose into drawers or cabinets or the safe in the closet.

He carried his computer and important files and ledgers and anything valuable up to the projection room, which had no exposure to the outside, and put them into the incredibly heavy metal storage locker in the tiny closet. He remembered Rhys reminding him to turn off the gas and lights but leave the fridge and ice machine and concession stand coolers running. When all that was done he walked through the building one more time and padlocked the front door as he left.

He gave the building a last look. He felt it that it was completely secure and he'd performed admirably as custodian.

On the way home, he stopped at a deli in the Marigny that was still open and grabbed a few things and went back to his house to sit on the front porch to drink a beer and eat a sandwich and try to remember where he'd put the boards and plywood and nails he'd need to batten down the hatches at his own place before it got dark. He was glad to be focused. He was even glad to be where he was. Which might seem odd, if you didn't know what New Orleans could do to you.

Last night in Croydon's guest cottage behind the big house had been so uneventful that Boy Jack almost doubted the storm was still reaching so far west. Then he turned on the TV and saw how wrong he'd been. The keen sense of unintentional homelessness that had gripped him yesterday was back. He'd probably have to call Mr. Croydon before long to see what he might need to do that hadn't been done, or more likely, Croydon would call him.

He went out for a fast-food breakfast muffin and while he waited in the drive-thru lane he watched the thin, pale sky with one last fantasy of denial, but just the feel and smell of the air carried the true message. Sometime soon the wan effect of the day would begin the slow, undeniable shift to darkness and tempest, and before long the ride-it-out junkies, apparently now including him, would find out if their gamble would pay out.

He got his order and drove away one hand on the wheel, tearing at the egg and sausage and bread with his teeth like a trucker with a cheekful of tobacco and hating the adrenalin coming up from his gut. Whether he'd hoped to get out of town or not, fact was he was staying. Fact was, every junkie of whatever addiction needs a moment of truth from time to time to make all the pain worth it.

Moon-Ra didn't dislike going into the Lower Ninth, and he knew what it was all about and had spent a few years there himself, but he didn't really want to tread on his old tracks all that much and these days spent most of his time around the music and also, of necessity, around his job at the Portia. But he had to go now and try to talk his mother into getting the hell out of town for a few days. The biggest problem being that he had no idea how to do that. Actually, the second-biggest problem. The first was that it was miserably hot and humid, even for summer in the city. There were days when the Big Easy sauna could drain the life out of anything that moved, and this was one of them.

He'd called to tell her he was coming, but she didn't pick up and her old answering machine wasn't on, or probably even plugged in. When he got to the little two-bedroom a half-dozen blocks from the drawbridge at the canal, he parked along the nearly empty street and walked up. Nobody answered the door. He didn't have a key but knew where she kept the one for the back door, so he went around through the gate of the sagging chain link fence. Brownie, the mutt mix, barked at first, but he was as old in dog years as his mistress was in human, and didn't go to a lot of trouble.

At the back door Moon-Ra hollered out, but there was no answer. He went inside. He looked around, saw nothing to indicate any packing up or any particular concern about putting things out of the way. The aluminum shutters he'd helped put up a few years ago were closed, and that was about it. He ripped a paper towel off a roll on the kitchen counter and wrote a note that he'd been there and for her to call him right away. Before he left he called his sister. Eluvia said she was fine and that he didn't need to come up to Gentilly unless he wanted to and that Mom was probably over at some of her friends having a lunch. "You know how those can run into next week, practically," she said, and they laughed.

Moon-Ra went to the sagging storage shed in the backyard to get the pine boards and planks they kept for the windows just for this kind of occasion. He had nailed up a few when Feliciana called and asked him to come over and help her with the same thing. He finished the nailing, which took less than an hour. He didn't even look back driving away from his mom's place because that would have been bad luck.

On the way to Feliciana's he got caught up in traffic more than once and heard on WWL that everybody was recommending evacuating now, and it looked like some people already were. All he planned to do the rest of the day was stay with his girl and have a good dinner and maybe not even go anywhere Saturday night for a change. Duane had canceled the show for that night and shut down the Portia "until after the storm."

About nine, Moon-Ra called his mom again. This time she answered and said she was home and fine and her friends thought they'd just ride it out, and if it got too bad, she could go stay with Eluvia in Gentilly. "Curtis, I might be old, but you don't need to worry-wart me all the time," she said, before hanging up.

Maybelle spent most of the Saturday at the storefront helping Eugenia and Lincoln finish up legal paperwork and then putting the thick particle board planks over the two display windows—it was formerly a jewelry store—that faced the street in the small retail strip. On the list of things that could harm lawyers doing pro bono for the poor in the South, hurricanes barely made the top ten, although, as lawyers, they didn't discount any possibilities. So they assessed the structural viability of the office and made an action plan for evacuation.

The row of metal filing cabinets could stand up against damn near anything, and had so far, so anything on the desktops got shoved inside them. The computers were another problem, so they put backup copies of the files on disks and hoisted the machines and screens on top of the filing cabinets. They covered everything with blue paint tarps left over from remodeling when they had moved in, and then weighted all that down with broken bricks that for some reason had accumulated in the storage room. It was about all they could think of. If the winds got bad enough to break the boards over the windows, there wasn't much anyone could do.

The print shop on one side of the office and the used appliance store on the other side stayed open all day, but Lincoln said he'd talked to the people working there and they said the plan was to close down at five, and that they weren't sure about coming back on Monday. They heard Dillard might not have classes. It depended.

The hurricane prep was pretty much done by four, so Maybelle called Bonnie to see if she wanted to tempt fate at a happy hour at one of the seedy bars in the warehouse district, and of course she did, and so they met at Buddy's not too far from the Convention Center that lay along the river for blocks. They got clobbered on vodka shots, including one with green Jell-O, and somehow each made it home in heavy traffic and heavier air and fresh layers of foreboding. Maybelle called Duane to tell him she wanted to come over to his place but didn't want to get out again.

Meaning she shouldn't be driving. He said that was fine, that he was still tinkering with a few things at the house. Also drinking. He shouldn't be driving, either.

Tomorrow, they agreed, they'd ride it out together, either at her place or his, not quite knowing yet when or where it would hit. Sometime Sunday or Monday, was the latest. He said he'd picked up some beignets, in case the café closed down, and would save some for her. She reminded him she had stopped eating beignets. Because she had developed an addiction. That she wasn't kidding about it. He said he forgot, which was only partly true, and that next time he'd get some plain croissants. She said that was okay.

It was an entirely stupid digression. She said she was too tired, especially after the drinking, to figure anything out. She said she'd just call him in the morning. "I'll miss you," she said, before hanging up. She was under the illusion that she would get a good night's sleep.

CHAPTER 6

Sunday, August 28

Time travel as we perceive it is not possible through our level of analysis and technology, but there are those pesky intimations. In certain temporal moments, those who have the necessary chemical and cellular conduits and alignments in their bodies are known to "feel" things, intimations, that will happen. It might be hairs on the back of the neck, it might be a tightening in the gut, it might be a throbbing in the skull. To those in the African spirit world of New Orleans, this was often called second sight. It could also be attributed to voices from the spirits and ancestors and gods. For the storms of the sea, the messenger of the gods is Yemonja, mother of the oceans, or Oya, master of the winds, and maybe also of Elegba, merciless kibitzer of fate, a.k.a. the Divine Trickster, but whom Duane also saw as something of a sadist, on a cosmic scale where of course such human diagnoses were irrelevant.

Come from where they may, the intimations that had been gurgling all week in the necks or guts or skulls of the chosen mortals of the Crescent City approached ashore in force as Sunday delivered another rotation of the earth. The winds and water and sheets of unstoppable powers gathered on the eastern horizon of the Gulf, positioned to deal as they pleased with the so-called immovable forces of land and life where wild panthers and thick forests and then explorers and exploiters from around the world had gathered and built and bragged but now waited for payback. These same forces also were—had been—driving the fuse and howl inside Duane McGuane and becoming his visions and his own second sight and he knew it would be unshirted hell.

Duane was up early, made coffee, ran a load of clothes he might need through the washer and dryer in the utility closet, then unplugged both machines and killed time trying to get the TV to work while he waited for Maybelle's call. He tried Rhys, but got voicemail, and then remembered the boyo had hightailed it to Birmingham, leaving his not-quite-downtown office and his bizarrely decorated West Bank house in as best shape as he could. He left a message anyway.

Meanwhile, out in the labyrinth, the flow of traffic, which might have included Rhys, filled the interstates leading toward Baton Rouge, or Birmingham, or Shreveport, or Chicago, or Texas—places deemed sufficiently remote to be safe. Ha! For those too poor or stubborn or contemptuous of evacuation pussies to join the ritual exodus, hunkering down became the modus vivendi. Later, the percentage of non-fleeing leftovers who stuck it out, like him, would be put at about twenty percent of the city's half-million population.

Boy Jack spent Sunday morning dealing with an assortment of so-called emergency tasks at Croydon's World of Imports and then threaded the traffic nightmare back to Croydon's House of High-End Southern Decadence, which he decided to call it to lighten his mood. Which need-ed lightening, since the calls from Mr. Croydon never stopped. Always checking this, that, or the other thing that "we need to be sure is taken care of." In every case, it already had been.

But Boy Jack played it cool, and it wasn't like he had anything else to do. And he didn't mind making his employer, and now his temporary host, feel like he was in charge. Somehow. Of whatever Katrina might bring. Mr. Croydon affected to sound relatively calm, but the tinge of fear in his voice with each call did increase considerably as the day wore on. Nonstop calling was just his way of coping. Boy Jack was rightfully proud of himself for having the maturity to know that.

By nightfall, when the rains from the outer bands of what was said to be a Cat 5 began to announce its might, which was like over 130 or was it

160 miles per hour and much faster than his pickup could race on a wide-open freeway, Boy Jack had to tell Mr. Croydon as firmly as possible that everything was bolted down and it was dangerous to keep going outside. Mr. Croydon didn't answer right away but then, in a nicer voice, said that was fine. And thanks for everything. Boy Jack smiled because no one else could see it and said thanks back. He said he would probably have to stay the night in the upstairs bedroom if that was okay. It was.

After that, Boy Jack didn't answer the phone the rest of the night. Not that he could have, since the cell towers were going down like broken fingers all across the coast. So, thinking he had isolated himself of his own accord, he got stoned, and retreated upstairs with a pile of Croydon's videos to watch on the TV screen. It wasn't long before the power went off and on so much as to be insufferable, and he gave up the box completely. He wasn't getting any phone calls, but he was too zonked to make the connection of disruption to phone service, so kept his cell by his side just in case. Eventually, he just sat on the top of the bed, never turning down the covers, and listened to the world around him. By morning, he wouldn't have words to describe what he had heard.

Maybelle had been up since 3 a.m., when she remembered she'd done almost nothing to secure her own apartment. But after some tossing and turning she fell back asleep for a few hours. When she got up, she made a hasty but efficient round of closing windows and turning off lights and water faucets and putting things away that could be easily damaged. The landlord had installed weather shutters outside, so all she had to do was close them up and secure the latches. She figured Mr. Manglamere might come and check on his property anyway, so she decided not to stress too much. She was done by nine, called Duane, made a final check that everything was shut tight, and waited for Texas Fellini to pick her up. They'd decided to shelter at his house.

He'd already made coffee, but when he got back with her he made another pot and broke out his sack of goods from the deli and spread them on the kitchen table. Pointedly, she grabbed the blueberry muffin over his beignets, just the kind of show of independence and fuck-you-ness that eventually dooms even the best of affairs and marriages.

They talked over how to spend the day, but as the news and the winds worsened, they reasoned that Duane's small house might be too close to where the storm would probably hit. Really just a guess. They similarly guessed that while Maybelle's apartment was farther enough into the city to probably be safer, the best haven of all would be at the Portia, upstairs in the interior projection room. The building was brick, while both his place and Maybelle's were of wood construction, and everyone knew how that went for the three little pigs.

TV was mostly static, so they monitored the news on Duane's portable radio, which fortunately had fresh batteries. They heard that the Superdome was open for anyone who wanted to come. They talked about whether that would be an option. Dismissing the idea took less than a minute.

A little after noon, they packed some things in Duane's Taurus and pushed on to Uptown. The rain was coming in, and the streets were full of cars. They barely talked, instead looking constantly for puddles, sink-holes, incompetent drivers, or anything on any building that might be on the verge of falling on top of them. They made it, sticking to Magazine Street rather than Tchoupitoulas, a choice based only on Magazine being slightly more distant from the river.

Duane parked on the lot to the side of the Portia mostly away from the storm winds direction and the river. He didn't lock the car because he figured anyone who would steal that fucking Taurus deserved to crash and die. They carried in the food, water, wine, and clothes that each had brought.

The waning afternoon passed quickly enough given the ambient terror. They went outside a couple of times, because the a/c was off and it was hot and stuffy. By evening, as the weather worsened, they milled around inside, listening and looking outside where they could, constant-ly tuned to the radio.

Maybelle said the Portia seemed bigger when it was empty, which led to a conversation about things half full or half empty or just fucking empty altogether. Talking reduced the anxiety. The lights flickered and then went off for good, but Duane had a stock of candles and flashlights with boxes of spare batteries. Always a must for the responsible theater owner. What he didn't have was a generator—he insisted he had been "about to" get one—so losing the a/c slowed them down considerably in what was still insufferable heat.

They tried going outside once more for fresh air, but the worsening rain felt like BBs in the face and the wind was loud. So they retreated into the lobby, still insufferably hot. Maybelle held open one of the entry doors enough for a little air but not the rain, which wasn't easy. Duane found a full case of Coke cans behind the concession stand to prop the door open so Maybelle wouldn't have to keep standing there. Both lobby entry doors were especially heavy with plywood nailed and taped over the glass. But the wind got stronger, and the open door almost blew off its hinges before Duane managed to push it shut and lock it, with Maybelle's help. It sucked to close the doors, but being hot was better than being dead.

They listened for any news. Everything that had sounded bad an hour ago now sounded worse. A little before midnight they went up to the projection room. It was hot and stifling, but quieter, although the roof sounded like a wind tunnel. They discussed whether it might blow off and if they should move down into the amphitheater, maybe on the stage. So they did.

Carried everything down the stairs again, and closed the projection booth door behind them, as if somehow that would help if the roof did fly away. They considered the office, but it had too many windows. The balcony felt too exposed, and also might fall down. They laid out their things stage right in front of the screen, and then Duane went around to check all the downstairs exit doors. Which is when they wondered if maybe those doors might blow off just as easily as the lobby doors and thwart the entire effort of moving.

So they carried everything back upstairs. In this, they had been drinking wine so all the up-and-down in the face of the arrival of a hurricane seemed less foolish than it otherwise might have been.

Back in the projection room, which was still hot, even with the door left open, they took off their clothes and stretched out on a quilt on the floor next to the stack of movie reels that Moon-Ra or Gretchen really needed to get back to the distributors. Duane remembered there was a small floor fan behind some cabinets and brought it out but of course it didn't work because there was no power. They used old industry magazines as hand fans but they did little good. Thinking of how the reels might never get back to the distributors and whether his cheap insurance would cover such an eventuality caused Duane to become morose for a short time, until Maybelle bullied him into not being such a wuss.

So they put on brave faces and even kissed and held each other, and because they were naked, things happened. But in truth, making love in such circumstances might have worked well in a number of films, and not just those starring Shannon Tweed, but it was like talking about half-empty glasses—an exercise in distraction. When finished, they lay on their backs, sweaty and unaccountably shivering, and listened to each other breathe. She took his hand in hers.

He gripped it tight. His intention was to sleep through landfall, which would probably be close, because he just wanted it to be over and gone so he could get back to his plans. "You know what they say about plans, and God," Maybelle whispered into his ear just before they fell asleep.

But he awoke in the wild darkness. He heard again the howl that he had heard on the levee. He knew that if he could hear it, it now penetrated the city, capturing it, confirming with absolute clarity what it had intimated: That all before it would be torn asunder never to be the same again.

Moon-Ra called Eluvia shortly before 8 p.m. to say he was going to get their mom whether she agreed to come or not, and he was going to bring her to Eluvia's place because it had more room and was more solid than his. She said she would go with him but he said he wanted to make the trip as short as possible because the wind and rain had gotten bad. So he'd just drive over to get her out. Which he did, even though once again she wouldn't answer his calls, but the phone lines were down already in the Ninth.

Almost everywhere he passed was dark, or flickering. Crossing the draw bridge on St. Claude was unnerving, even though hardly any cars were on it. When he pulled up to his mother's house he had to hold his arms against the wind and stinging rain as he ran to the door, fortunately unlocked. She wasn't there. He called out. He looked in every room, even in the backyard. No mom. Nowhere.

He tried to call Eluvia again but the window on his phone said "no service." He looked down the street, but he could only see a few places where lanterns or maybe candles were burning. Maybe candles to the spirits, or Jesus, or to the night itself.

He got in his car, drenched just from the short steps from the house, and drove down the street,. He stopped at two places where she might be, but wasn't. Mrs. Landon, the eighty-year-old in the first house, seemed stunned beyond fear and just looked at him through the rain and said she ain't see Miz Claudia and did he want to come in. Which he didn't.

At the other house, where the Gulauts lived, Mr. Gulaut said Moon-Ra should get on back home right away but maybe his mom went over to her friend Malia's on Elysian Fields? Or maybe there was some people went to the Superdome and she could've maybe gone there. He said that was the best guess, but he didn't know because none of the phones worked right. Then he said again for Moon-Ra, now dripping wet, to go home, get out of the weather. He said Miz Claudia knew how to take care of herself and added that Moon-Ra should just take care of himself, too, and figure out where she was tomorrow. He said there was nothing else could be done.

Moon-Ra had no intention of going home. He drove toward Eluvia's in Gentilly, shivering and constantly wiping his eyes dry. He tried his phone again to call his cousin Paulus in the Seventh Ward but couldn't get a signal. He considered taking a detour to see if maybe his mom had gone there, or to her sister's, Aunt Corina's, or maybe to Corina's church. But it seemed too much a long shot and the rain was too hard to mess with in the pitch-black night. Eluvia's made more sense.

When he arrived and got inside, she hugged him more than he could ever remember, even though he was dripping wet, and told him to stay on the mat until she got some towels.

She had her two small boys, Edwin and Samuel, five and seven, in one of the bedrooms. Timothy, her estranged husband, or her "strange husband" as she usually put it, had gotten stuck at an airport in Atlanta where he was working for the power company and couldn't get back. She'd called a dozen times and couldn't get his cell. And he worked for the fucking power company. She said maybe their mom did go to the Superdome because that's where people were going, they said on the radio, but neither of them knew for sure and they were almost unable to talk about it.

He decided, over his sister's objections, to drive downtown to see for himself, despite the dangerous streets. She was still yelling at him as he backed out of her driveway. But he made it downtown and tried to get as close to the Superdome as he could. There was nowhere to park, and too many streets or alleys blocked or congested. The only glimpse he got of the Superdome entry was blurred by rain and bulging lines of hundreds of desperate people trying to find shelter. He knew he had no chance of making it inside.

He turned around and drove back through the flooding streets to Eluvia's. It took nearly two hours coming and going. She scolded him plenty and he had to admit he felt it was a miracle he had made it. He toweled off again, and this time she gave him one of Timothy's sweatpants and a shirt to sleep in while his clothes dried out. They agreed to wait until morning to do whatever else they decided. Eluvia rarely took hurricane warnings seriously, but she was scared out of her head.

He also wanted to find Feliciana, but knew it was too late and dangerous to go anywhere. He reasoned that she would be okay up near Tulane, that she was strong enough, and she lived far enough from the river that storm waves couldn't come up to get her. He tried to call, and after maybe two dozen attempts he got a short, static-filled answer. He heard her voice and she heard his and she said she was safe and he said the same and that he'd get over to her place as soon as the sun came up. But his sentence got cut off as the line went dead. He sat on the La-Z-Boy in the front room, exhausted, phone in hand, and fell asleep.

And then it was dawn and Katrina hadn't veered away or stalled out or calmed down or succumbed to any kinds of prayers or given succor to any of the ride-it-out crowd. He could hear the youngest boy, Edwin, screaming at the sound of the wind and the cracking of trees and powerlines. He could hear Eluvia trying to comfort him. She could not.

CHAPTER 7

Monday, August 29

Just before 9 a.m., when Boy Jack awoke, or more accurately came to, things were about the same as when he had finally fallen asleep: "The winds they were howling and the snow was outrageous." Except rain for snow. He was always surprised when he told people he was a Dylan fan and they looked at him like he was lying. Now all he could think about was whether the howling would ever stop.

With daylight he could see what was going on. None of it was good. He didn't know how strong the winds were, because he didn't have electricity, and his phone didn't work, and it was just a wild guess but he figured around seventy or eighty miles per hour, if they had been right about it being a Category 3 or maybe Cat 4, but he really wasn't up to date on all the rating criteria of the National Hurricane Center. Not that the categories mattered in any way if you were in the center of them. Which he was sure he was.

He went downstairs. Two of the living room windows had imploded, and more than a few of the plywood boards he'd nailed up had sailed away or were pushed through other windows into the house. A ridiculous time for "waste of money" to come in his head, but really it was open season on any kind of thought at all. Because if you were thinking, you must be alive. He thought of himself as clever for coming up with that but vaguely thought he might have heard something like it back in school. Meanwhile, he watched where he stepped. The living room was filled with puddles and odd bits of trash like paper cups and broken glass and a hubcap.

There was nothing to be done until the winds stopped and the power came back, so he checked out the rest of the house. Three more busted-in windows, two in the kitchen and another in the foyer. You'd think the upstairs would have had the most damage, but really only one more window was out. So maybe it hadn't been that bad.

Then he heard something flapping on the roof. The ceiling was still dry, so it might not have been more than a few loose shingles. His eyes wandered to the backyard and noticed the trunk of the old pecan tree bisecting the top of the guest cottage, and the roof on the garage half torn off and rising and falling with each new gust. It made him revise his estimate of what might be flapping on the roof just above his head.

He wanted to call Mr. Croydon and also didn't want to, but the issue was moot without phone service. He didn't even have a camera to take pictures of the damage. If Croydon ever got through, maybe he could say if there was one in the house. Boy Jack made a mental note to check for photographic equipment later. When the wind left. And the rain. And the incessant howling. And it was like a fucking sauna.

There was a little slackening of the storm, maybe, after about a couple of hours, but he wasn't sure if that meant the eye was yet to come or if it had passed and he was on the backside, which was the worst. He ventured outside to the sidewalk to look back at the place, even though he was drenched almost at once. Slack or not, it was still a ton of water. The limb of a big live oak was dangling over the left side of the house, just above one of the bedrooms, and it was anybody's guess when it would fall. And yeah, that flapping sound he'd heard came from a whole section of roof bare down to the tar paper. What was left of the tar paper.

The gusts picked up again, and so did the rain, but Boy Jack didn't want to go back inside yet. He looked down the street, just a couple blocks lakeside of St. Charles, and every place looked about the same. Like it had been run through by a herd of rabid flying elephants. But at least everything was mostly standing. He figured, yet again, in that New Orleans way, that maybe it could've been worse.

The rain was refreshing, if pelting, and a true energizer of both his body and his mind. Maybe his soul, but not a good moment to focus on that. And he'd had enough of being outside.

He went back inside and turned on the gas stove to try to make coffee and was delighted to see the flames come on, so he boiled water. He started to shiver, so he took off his shirt, wrung it out in the sink, and set it on a chair. He used some paper towels from the cupboard to dry off as best he could. The refrigerator was off, but the half and half cream was still reasonably cool and so was the OJ so he at least had sustenance, that and a swath of peanut butter on a slice of artisan whole wheat that Mr. Croydon kept in one of those special pastry containers.

After that he finished off last night's roach and slumped on the one dry cushion on the big blue couch in the living room, facing the broken windows. He leaned over to pick up the remote for the TV off the coffee table but no matter how many times he pressed the button, nothing came on. He tried his cell again but nothing. He wondered if Mr. Croydon was the type to keep emergency supplies in the house and he pondered on that off and on for the next half hour or so, deciding he didn't know, but very alert to the same sounds that had rendered him speechless last night. Truth is, he had no idea what to do or who to call or where to go.

Maybelle slept so fitfully she wasn't sure just how long she'd actually been out. Each time she woke, Duane was either lightly snoring or so lost in his dream world that even when she tried pushing against his side, the one that was supposedly healing from that seriously strange mugging, he just grunted and turned away. So she heard everything and he heard nothing through the screaming murderous maniac of a night.

Then came morning light, floating in through the open projection room door and gray with dust. Which meant there also was finally light outside, light of the sun. It might be getting into the Portia from cracks in the building and worse, and what it illuminated would certainly be filled with water and chaos, but the night was over.

She closed her eyes and almost drifted into sleep again, sleep as in numbness, but then Duane began to stir. He sat up, rubbed his own eyes hard enough to gouge them out, yawned, and nudged her with his left hand.

"You're awake?" he asked. They looked at each other like animals realizing the cage doors were open.

Moon-Ra was up before the sun, about the same time Katrina destroyed Plaquemines Parish and all that was nearby, and sliced east into Mississippi to level an entire coast and most of a state. But the outer bands of winds had hit New Orleans hard, and not just by tearing things apart like the roof of the Superdome. They also pushed water up through the channels and canals that were supposed to make ships easier to navigate and ensure that flooding in the city would drain like clockwork into Pontchartrain and that would prevent even big Gulf-bred hurricanes from destroying the city.

The battery radio worked for the sunrise news, and then with a static-filled, ten-second call from Feliciana that managed to get through, Moon-Ra knew that nothing was going to be the way they had said. She was holed up in her duplex, and scared. "Streets are flooding and the houses, too. You might have to leave right away." Her voice had never sounded like that before. Then the connection fizzled.

With a quick glance at the brown liquid mush coming in under the front door, he could already see that Eluvia's house was in trouble. Not from riverside, pushed in by the storm, but opposite, pushed back down from Pontchartrain. It would be awhile before he knew that it was really coming from the broken levees on the 17th Street canal, or maybe the London canal, but definitely from what seemed the wrong direction.

He called out to Eluvia, who hadn't slept at all, to get the boys and pack a bag because they had to leave. He said the best place would be the Superdome, even if they had to wait, because it would never flood and in a couple of days they could go home. So they piled into his car and that's where they headed.

The water on the streets was still deep, if not deeper, and it was hard to figure out anything with the wind blowing so hard it pitched a tree branch into the windshield and ripped off a wiper on the passenger side. The boys laughed for a moment and then went quiet again, holding tight to each other in the back seat.

Moon-Ra wasn't sure he could even make it into downtown, but he finally found a place along a curb several blocks away in the warehouse district. He squeezed in between an SUV and a minivan. A handicap spot. But he figured everyone in New Orleans was. Handicapped. Not like in a horse race. Like in mortal danger.

It would be quite a hike to the Superdome but they trudged over to Poydras through the flooding, Eluvia carrying Edwin and Moon-Ra clutching the hand of Sam. Moon-Ra looked back at the Civic a couple of times as if that would keep it safe, but he knew he might never see it again. At least in running condition.

Ahead, he could see a line on the pedestrian bridge leading from a hotel into the Superdome and eventually they found a way to get to it. They waited, barely talking, for a long time. and then they were past the entry doors and inside. He couldn't believe they'd made it, but Eluvia looked at him like he had just second-lined them into their own coffins.

It was a human horror of cots and meandering people and all manner of crying and yelling and mumbling, and they had no idea where to even go. The heat and humidity alone were punishing. Above, rain came in from where the roof had been ripped to flap up and down. They pushed their way to the stands around the playing field and found a few seats together. They seized them like spaces on a rescue raft, holding their small bags like treasure. The boys' eyes were wide with excitement and fear. Eluvia's face was like someone looking into a firing squad for the final seconds of her life.

Moon-Ra tried to strike a strong pose, but his mind raced with finding ways out as soon as possible. His own eyes scoured the seats and the human misery on the water-soaked artificial turf below for any sign of his mother. As far as he could tell, she wasn't there. A middle-aged man in nothing but a Saints T-shirt and wet purple shorts a few seats over offered that he heard that they might open up the Convention Center to get people out of the Superdome since it was easier to get into and wasn't leaking any water, but maybe not until later. But maybe it was just rumor, like everything else.

By late afternoon, soaked in the stench of urine and shit and sweat, when the crush of the weight of death had settled around them and they were fully able to see what lay in their future, Moon-Ra told Eluvia they had to get out before nightfall. Even though they'd just spent so much time and energy getting in. More talk was going around about the Convention Center and someone said it was on the radio. Eluvia said they should try. Anything was better than staying where both were certain they would die.

They gathered their things and descended the crowded and filthy stairs back down onto the field, pushing past bodies moving around like zombies, and on to the entry doors they'd worked so hard to get through earlier. Some kinds of constables or cops told them they couldn't leave once they'd been admitted, but Moon-Ra said they had a message from his mom to please come get her right away, and after some talking and crying from the boys, the guard told him to get the hell out if that's what he wanted but never try to come back.

They said thank you and pushed out the doors and into the crowd of terrified and destitute innocents trying to get into what they imagined was safety. It was push-and-pull until they could get back downstairs and into the streets that had become streams and ponds and were already thick with garbage and dead animals and one woman in a floral dress facedown with her head jammed against a parking meter.

On the exhausting slog to the Convention Center, they came within a block of his Civic, water already midway up the doors. Nobody saw it but Moon-Ra, and he didn't tell Eluvia, whose full concentration was on watching her children. The fate of a car was nothing. It was enough not to drown for, or run into downtown gangs or get separated for. It was enough not to die for.

Hurricanes came with the earth, with the necessary balances of land, water and atmosphere. The compositions were as unique as snow-flakes with different pressures, content, physics, trajectories, lifes-pans. In the Pacific they became known as typhoons, but in the space between Africa and the Americas, hurricanes, after the Spanish *huri-can*, became the impossibly insufficient attempt by language to define the limitless power of nature and the fragility of all who found them-selves in its path. The hurricanes became as regular as the seasons, and could neither be stopped nor predicted. Endured is really the only term that can approximate what separated their arrival from their departure and the efforts at rebuilding civilization by those who survived them in some way. Among those who didn't survive, there is no word, because words no longer exist for the dead. Only for the living who attempt to find a meaning in an attempt to carry on.

No efforts at meaning came before the humans arrived, with their languages and attempts to convey thoughts and harness actions. The animals and trees and plants simply confronted and endured or died. In time the first tales of the power of these great storms filtered back from the Caribbean and Gulf. Soon there were stories year in and out of ships gone down, people drowned, settlements and cities destroyed. Gold from Spanish galleons was said to lie in wait at the bottom of the waters, and many died pursuing the treasures that they never found.

Some of these stories made their way centuries later into the early swashbuckler movies that on at least two occasions had turned up at special weekend showings at the Portia. Duane had seen many more of them in the matinees of his childhood. Hurricanes always dashed fortunes and wreaked havoc.

He knew a little of that himself. He had been through near misses in New Orleans and had heard of the direct hits from Betsy and also, nearby, the big ones like Carla in Texas. He had learned of the storm,

Isaac, that had flooded Galveston in 1900 without warning and killed almost everyone who had been stranded because it struck in the night and without mercy.

He knew about the Mississippi flood of 1927 that wasn't really a hurricane but revealed the same soft underbelly of the city that would never toughen up and that with Katrina damn near would kill it. Everyone thought they were smarter now with computers and advanced predictions that could show what was coming and more or less when but were powerless to force humans to do anything sensible about it. And not just during the storms, but before, when it might really make a difference.

By the time Katrina came, oil rigs like zits on a wretched child dotted the Gulf. Canals to service said rigs cut and dissected the natural marshlands and outer islands so that although the floods come from one direction and hit the levees, nature could reverse the danger, surging into and backwashing the very drainage systems designed to alleviate the flooding. Katrina was the first to make that perfectly clear, and to bring the city to its knees in a way that had never before been possible, and that would now forever be inescapable.

This was the world in which Duane McGuane found himself on the morning of September 29, 2005, and in which those around him would suffer and die and escape for years to come. He was not able to fully understand, nor was anyone else on that morning, the extent of what was around him, that eighty percent of the city was under water. But they would learn, and it would all but ignite an anger which, unlike Katrina, would never leave. And that was in the future that could not be seen other than by those with second sight who had not perished in the waters that were not holy but had inundated their holy land.

In Duane it had precipitated the howl, the howl beyond the weather, the call to movement, the force that drives the reluctant pilgrim. He knew it before he knew he knew it. But he knew it.

Bonnie didn't make it. At the last minute she went to her brother Charley's place in Chalmette in St. Bernard parish, at the far eastern edge of the city. He was a single dad and wouldn't get home until late, if at all, working as a supervisor on power line systems. His place was a nice three-bedroom, but very close to the Mississippi River–Gulf Outlet, which everyone called Mr. Go. It led up from the Gulf into the Industrial Canal. The idea was to facilitate big ships and tankers, but Katrina proved it had another function—a high-capacity reverse funnel, pushing water from Lake Bourne and the Gulf right into the parish.

Charley did make it home just after midnight. Just enough time to join his children and Bonnie, in deep sleep from exhaustion, when the early-morning waves hit his house like a nuclear plow. In ten or fifteen minutes the water was over six feet and rising and then the force broke the house itself into pieces like it was made of toothpicks. The roof and rafters and walls fell atop them and trapped them so that they drowned, holding hands before they were even fully awake.

In death, the hands separated, and although Charley and his girls were identified quickly, Bonnie's body got separated and floated away for hundreds of yards and was trapped under brush and debris for more than a week. It was so desiccated by nature that the morgue in Baton Rouge took almost two weeks to identify her by matching a missing person report to three scars still visible in her abdomen, inflicted by stabbings with a broken bottle that she had endured when she was nineteen and walking home in the tough part of Uptown, where she ran into two drunk Cajuns from Alexandria who weren't done having fun that night. She also had two titanium implants in her upper right jaw from the same frivolity.

The forensics team, for whom one could have nothing but ever-lasting empathy, tagged and identified more than a thousand bodies. They said the one named Bonnie had been verified based on the scars and then the implants. The Baton Rouge office was able to trace backward to locate Bonnie's twice-divorced mom. She came in from Jackson to claim the body but refused to look, and complained about all the trouble.

Bonnie was cremated because that was cheaper. Her ashes were spread in the Mississippi in early November when her mom went to the casino in Tupelo and ended up going to Memphis for three weeks with a FEMA cleanup contractor. She eventually shot him in the face in a drunken argument over money and disappeared into the void, as far as anyone who might have cared about her was concerned.

CHAPTER 8

Monday, August 29, *continued*

The morning passed in thousands of terrors as the flooding surpassed the hurricane itself in lethality. The city that French opportunists thought would sit just terrifically in the forests and swamps of 1718 seemed to have returned to its primeval stature. Almost no one understood the residue of danger as Katrina pushed on to wreck Mississippi, parts of Alabama, and lesser states to the north and east. All anyone knew was that things were not as they were supposed to be. The hurricane had come, gone, done its thing, and now people could get out of their hunkering spots and start clearing out the debris and nailing back things that needed nailing.

But on WWL, the only station most people could pick up and the only one with any real information, Garland Robinette was telling another story. Anyone with a radio could hear it and anyone who was in the story who was not dead could feel it and wade in it and smell it. Duane and Maybelle turned the transistor up loud enough to hear throughout the Portia and it was more than background—it was fuel to their other plans.

They stayed inside until noon, giving a quick inspection to the office, which had broken windows but was otherwise spared destruction, and the amphitheater and balcony, also okay because the roof had held. The lobby was a complete mess because the doors had been blown open and the plywood ripped away. But it could have been worse. Much worse. Which allowed them to think about their own places.

The Taurus was covered with wind-blown branches and leaves and a soggy red blanket from somewhere, but it started up. They thought to try to get over to Maybelle's first, and then on to Duane's, and hole up in whichever had the least damage and start cleaning up the mess.

The streets into and around Maybelle's Fairgrounds neighborhood were impassable. Duane found a debris-tinged route to his place in the Marigny, but it took two hours and a quarter-tank of gas. And gas was hard to find. The solution to getting there had been counterintuitive, as was just about everything in the city as the day wore on. To cross the city, Duane realized he had to get closer to the river, not farther from it.

The streets where Duane lived were puddled up and full of trash and branches but not flooded. When they finally got to his house the reward was seeing the broken-off utility pole in the back having not quite hit the roof, and parts of a neighbor's tree pushed up against his front porch but not breaking anything. The windows were not so lucky, four of them broken, inward, from the wind. The pieces of plywood to protect them were strewn around the yard.

They parked against the curb and went inside. It was a freaking miracle. Except for wet spots where the rain had blown in from the broken windows, and a wicker night stand in one bedroom blown over, breaking a lamp, there was no real damage. Definitely none of the flooding. Duane picked up the plywood flats, and they wedged them back in the window frames as best they could, since he couldn't find any nails. He could follow up later. Maybelle helped, but he could tell from her face, though she tried to hide it, that she knew it would be a different story at her place.

They decided to go back to the Portia. It had real damage and also really needed immediate attention, not least to deter looting. No telling when they could get to Maybelle's, and staying at Duane's wouldn't really accomplish much, other than boarding up the broken windows, which would be fairly easy.

Neither of them wanted to just sit around. They could make

the Portia more comfortable, maybe sleep in Duane's office, where the upstairs windows that remained could stay open at night without worries about security or vicious winds.

They picked what food they thought they might need for a week from the pantry and took everything from the fridge. Then Duane wiped the empty fridge shelves, pulled the wall plug, and propped open the top and bottom doors to avoid mold, something he'd heard about on the radio, or maybe it was from Eluvia.

Since he kept all his business things at the Portia, nothing else on the bookshelves or the desk in the study in his house was worth taking. The only other things Duane thought he needed were some clothes for the week, a shaving kit, and the Tylenol-3 from the mugging. His ribs were still a little sore but the meds also helped with sleep. Maybelle took a few of Duane's shirts, boxer shorts. She also found a pair of jeans and a few other mismatched wardrobe survivors and hairbrushes she'd left over there a while back. She said they'd have to do until she could get into her apartment or stop at any place that sold clothes that was open. Except tourist shops. She said she'd rather be stinky or go naked than give them her business.

On the return drive to the Portia, basically up Tchoupitoulas this time with a few zigzags, they just stared out the car windows at what Katrina had done. Every house was dark, all the traffic lights were out, bits of roof and siding settled onto the road or parking lots or just flapped as the wind slackened off. At Jefferson Avenue, Duane was tempted to turn north to see if there was another way to get around the water and hazards, but he saw fire trucks and police cars in the distant intersections and kept going along the river. Maybelle said it looked like you couldn't get anywhere without a boat. On the radio, Garland was saying that flooding was getting worse by the hour.

Once back at the Portia they carried things inside and took a break to open some Ritz crackers and peanut butter from Duane's kitchen stock. They put the frozen meat and veggies and perishables inside the small cooler behind the concession stand but they knew they'd have to throw it all away probably tomorrow and never should have lugged it over in the first place.

The concession counter still had soft drinks and bottled water, of which they partook, and then, because it was late afternoon and they had barely slept, they fell asleep on a dry patch on the lobby floor. They couldn't lock the doors shut because wind bursts had blown them open despite the plywood sheets. But that was okay, because air circulation felt good. As with everything else for hundreds of miles around, it was like a fucking steam bath. It was the first time Duane could remember that he had gone to sleep not knowing, or caring, if he would wake up.

By evening, people were gathered for blocks outside the Convention Center like washed-up wreckage on a Gulf beach. It was a huge warehouse of a building, designed to house the kinds of trade shows and conferences that otherwise might be drawn to Vegas or Atlanta or Houston.

Moon-Ra and his sister and the boys had been wading and walking for at least a half hour and finally came up near Harrah's, almost at the end of Poydras. They could see a crowd around the Center, and as they got closer, a small strip along a boulevard where the crowd parted slightly. They headed for it. The boulevard and sidewalk out front of the building was jammed. No cops were around, and no one seemed to be in charge of anything.

Nothing about what Moon-Ra beheld looked remotely inviting. Except that the massive building looked dry. Not even damaged. Otherwise, why would so many people be packed on the sidewalks and trickling through the doors inches at a time?

Maybe it was at least a refuge, at least for the night. He glanced at Eluvia, whose expression in the crush of the crowd confirmed that neither of them thought the rumor about the Convention Center being officially open as a rescue shelter was true. It was open all right. To whoever could get there. Neither rescue nor shelter would be the way to describe it.

"We have to check it out anyways. We can't last out there," she said, hoping he could hear her over the noise and voices.

"I guess."

"I'm not guessing. We're already here and I can't go back in that water and I can't carry Edwin anymore."

Eluvia wasn't a complainer. If she said she was done, she was. Eluvia said "sorry" to a wild-eyed teenage girl with a baby in her arms that she just bumped into. The girl shrugged it off. Then Eluvia asked if the building was okay to go in. The girl said you could do whatever you want. She said she was going in as soon as her boyfriend came back out and found her. But now she couldn't get back to the boulevard because there were so many people they were pushing her in. She looked at Eluvia like people do when they have lost hope. In the next few minutes the crowd had separated them and Eluvia never saw her again.

In another fifteen minutes they were swept inside. Moon-Ra stayed in front, Eluvia behind, clutching her boys with an iron grip. Their eyes had to make a quick adjustment. Outside it was blindingly bright. Inside it was night. They appeared to be in a very long hall. The only illumination came through giant windows along the outer front walls. They regrouped as best they could.

Moon-Ra could see enough to see nothing, except more people moving past them and other people milling around on what seemed acres of red carpet. It reminded him of shots he had seen in movies of giant airplane hangars or sci-fi flicks with massive caves full of weird semi-humans and forgotten civilizations deep under the crust of the earth or millions of years in the past or in the future. *Planet of the Apes* indeed. It made him catch his breath.

He could see Eluvia was wilting so he took the hands of the boys and they made their way farther into the worst place they had ever stepped into.

It took another half hour to find a spot that might be safe

against a wall along the endless corridor. They were so tired they sat against the wall in a half-circle for hours just watching the incomprehensible. Then the boys had to go pee and that was a trip to restrooms of indescribable filth. Moon-Ra decided they'd never go back in there. Eluvia had the same report from the women's.

They reassembled and realized they had no food and only two water bottles Eluvia had carried in her shoulder bag. The boys were hungry and restless but then suddenly fell asleep on the carpet. Moon-Ra and Eluvia tried to stay awake, but eventually fell asleep on each side of the children. But not for long. Awake, they planned to leave quickly. If not, they would die of dehydration, if not something else.

But they were wrong. It would be their home for most of the next three days. And stay in their minds and souls until they grew old, died, and were buried decades later outside Baton Rouge in a crowded cemetery near a dozen other deceased members of their family, all of whom had known and lived in the time of hurricanes.

There was still an hour of daylight left so Duane and Maybelle did what they could inside the Portia, which was lucky enough that its main equipment stayed dry. Probably would work fine, although without electricity it was just a guess. Duane gave up on his brief idea of holding a free screening for the neighborhood of whatever films he had not returned to the distributors. It was a very good and community-building idea, given all the destruction and scattering of humanity, plus the pets, but without juice in the electrical sockets it had no purchase in reality.

Often enough, reality was not an obstacle for Duane, according to Rhys, but in this case it was just raw physics.

Duane thought a moment about Rhys in Birmingham, if he'd actually left town, but the phones were still worthless. But he was not worried. Rhys was a man of great practicality, in a grandiose sort of way, and Duane felt confident he had not only weathered the storm, wherever he was, but was already figuring ways to file damage lawsuits for his clients. Which, Duane realized, would have to include himself.

These digressive thoughts were beaten down in short order by the immediacy of the encompassing horror. Maybelle said she wanted to get out and explore as much as they could before dark, and make a plan for the week.

For the exploration, they made sure to take the lanterns and batteries out of the spare parts closet upstairs, and also assembled a sufficient supply of nutrition in the way of snacks, soft drinks, and water bottles in case they might get stranded.

They headed vaguely through Uptown in the Taurus, which worked but made funny noises that Duane had never heard before when starting. It was slow going.

Streets were flooded or not flooded in no apparent pattern, other than, as Maybelle suggested, their elevation above sea level, often a variance of only a few feet. St. Charles was clear in spots but not enough to drive, so they zig-zagged constantly.

The closer they got to downtown, the deeper the water. The projects close to I-10 and the neighborhoods around it were virtually submerged. The interstate and the bridges and overpasses were crowded with people on foot, many of them waving signs and articles of clothing. Helicopters were flying overhead.

It started getting dark sooner than they had expected, and Maybelle said they had to go back. Now. She had guts of steel but also excellent instincts, and Duane did not second-guess. They retreated.

Two blocks away from the Portia, Duane swerved to miss a dead dog in the street and ran over a clump of wooden planks. Which had nails. By the time he got to the parking spaces in front of the theater, both front tires were hissing and presently completely flat. The back ones might also have picked up nails, but it was too dark to see. He decided the flats were too little to worry about, given that cars were essentially useless and nobody knew anything about anything at the moment, other than on the radio, where the news was that levee after levee was breaking. New Orleans was sinking.

Inside the Portia again, they made sandwiches from the ham and bread sure to go bad in a day or so. They drank more water, then went outside to listen and watch. Even with night, the heat was still in the nineties and the humidity at least that, and the winds, now that they were really needed, had blown themselves out. No one other than the occasional wanderer on foot or in a slow-moving car ever went past. What was left of the trees overhead seemed to enclose the sum of the day's events and hold it fast like a secret that could never again be whispered without fear of repetition. Also, the mosquitoes were back.

Duane and Maybelle picked up a little of the scattered trash and debris in the lobby, until mosquitoes became so thick that they went upstairs to Duane's office, hoping to get some relief. He was amazed again that except for the blown-in windows, including just one pane in the bay, and minor rain damage, it had fared pretty well. Mr. Thompson had chosen a good brick building.

But it had no effect on mosquitoes. Duane remembered the can of mosquito repellent, but not where it was. Searching while swatting, he finally found it behind a file cabinet next to the safe. The can was full, and the spray a baptism of protection. A few of the blood-suckers got through the aromatic wall of chemical death, but they could easily be swatted. A breeze helped, too. Duane and Maybelle could have gone into the projection room and shut the doors against the bugs, but didn't want to take that shut-in heat again. Somewhat relieved by the repellant, they sat in the office and talked, never really arriving at a plan, until they fell asleep on the floor.

Boy Jack knew he had to spend at least one last night at Mr. Croydon's, as ad hoc caretaker, but he knew the old guy and his friends would be home from evacuation and converging at any time and without warning. Not just to check on the house, but to stay there, since there wasn't anywhere else to go once they got back into the city. Which was Boy Jack's concern before falling asleep as the day of the hurricane wound down. He didn't want to be in the house when Croydon or the Truman Capotes came and saw what had happened. It was irrational, but he felt that he would be blamed, somehow. Perhaps not boarding up enough, or not closing a window, or not doing this or that.

Fairness or innocence would have nothing to do with it. Boy Jack knew Mr. Croydon would be mad as hell after the shock passed, and would be fed by those damn queens who would support him in his anger so as to ingratiate themselves for his money and social connections in the days to come.

Boy Jack did not consider himself a cynic in any way and in fact he liked Mr. Croydon and knew that the feeling was mutual, but Katrina had come between them, and he had plenty of experience at people getting pissed off at him for things he'd had nothing to do with and he wasn't going to go there again.

He couldn't set the alarm on his cell because he needed to turn it off to save batteries until the power came back on, which could be forever considering the sense of urgency that had never burdened the city of New Orleans, and probably the phone companies that did business there. Anyway, he couldn't leave the phone on.

He fixed up a spot so he could sleep away this last night with his face toward the broken windows. The sun would wake him Tuesday at dawn, per his plan, if nothing else did, and Mr. Croydon was not exactly a morning person anyway.

Boy Jack figured he could be out of there at 8:00 a.m. at worst. What he couldn't figure was where he would go. He was familiar with life on the streets, way too familiar, and knew he'd find a way or find someone who had found a way and follow them. Fact is, he didn't really know, but he was exhausted, and groggy from the joint wearing off. So he slathered himself with Raid insect fogger since there was no actual repellant to be found.

Almost at once he fell asleep—as, around the wreckage, sleep had found Duane and Maybelle, or Moon-Ra and Eluvia and the boys, or Feliciana, or Gretchen, or Paulus, and even his mother in her dreams to the spirit world. None able to reach the others, hived though they were as one mournful soul in the half-submerged city, strangers in disaster but brothers and sisters in blank, numb terror and unimaginable ignorance.

CHAPTER 9

Tuesday, August 30

Moon-Ra didn't want to leave Eluvia and the kids behind, but something had to be done, and he was the only one who could do it. He hadn't been able to sleep except in fits and starts. Just before dawn, he told his sister he was leaving and to try to stay where she was so he could find her when he got back. Hopefully midafternoon. She agreed because they were desperate and had nowhere to go. He made his way through the bodies awake and asleep on the dirty carpet in the Convention Center's front corridor.

Outside, the air was thick with humidity, but it was better than what they'd been breathing inside. On the sidewalks, the split between the sleeping and the awake was about the same as it had been inside. He stepped carefully, only accidentally tripping over one leg, a grumpy teenager's, and apologizing despite being cursed. Then he passed an old man on the boulevard median who was definitely not asleep. Sleeping people didn't bloat like that, stomachs pushing up through their shirts like beach balls and faces swollen like they were stuffed with wet cotton. He thought about trying to cover the body with something, but nothing was at hand and that wasn't his mission.

He turned up the boulevard and made his way to the big overpass, where people above were huddled and trying to get across to Gretna or Algiers, and eventually found his way to Tchoupitoulas, which was strewn with debris but dry. He thought that, unless it was flooded down the way, it would take him to the Portia. That would be about five or six miles upriver, curving along the docks and levee to Audubon Park. He had no radio, and no contact with Duane or anyone else, and understood the hazards of guessing after a hurricane. But Eluvia had reminded him on their long walk from the Superdome that the city was like a bowl. The middle always took more water than the rim. That's what her family had always said, too.

He hoped his sister was right but even if not, he had to try. And he knew if he could get to the Portia, he'd find plenty of food and water. Assuming it hadn't all been torn down by the wind or flooded itself. So he concentrated on his steps past the stinking pools and sharp debris and as much of the route as he could see ahead. Assumptions would prove out or not. Family wisdom the same.

His mission was to hunter-gather the hell out of anything edible or drinkable and put it in trash bags and carry them back to his family. With any luck he'd come across an abandoned grocery cart or bicycle to help with the weight. He didn't know if they would be able to get out of the Convention Center, though, or the city, or where they would go if they did. He didn't even know for sure he'd even make it to the Portia.

The skies were still gray and dark in the predawn, and weird noises and howls were everywhere. He knew if he ran into any gangbangers, they'd take anything he had and maybe kill him just for sport. Himself, he was more than prepared to break into a house if thugs stole his Portia haul and left him alive. He would take whatever sustenance was needed for his family. Because that is what things had become since yesterday.

Boy Jack's plan to break free of Mr. Croydon had one flaw. The detached garage where he'd parked his truck was just low enough at the end of the inclined driveway that an impressive mound of tree branches and mud had floated in and settled against the doors.

They were old-style and had to be pulled open from the bottom to rise up in an arc and slide into the overhead rails. So they wouldn't budge. He could get into the side door and was glad to see his truck hadn't been damaged. He could have spent the better part of the morning clearing away the mess, if it was even possible by hand, but there also was a half-uprooted maple or oak that seemed ready to fall across the driveway at any minute. The entire idea was to be gone, not salvage the wreckage, so he took off on foot.

On St. Charles he passed a dozen or so people, black and white, all women and children except one grandfather type. They looked like scared, half-drowned ducks like you'd see in the bayous scooting and flapping away from turtles or gators. He called out to ask if they knew anything about shelters or somewhere to get food. The old man turned his head slightly and said they were going to the Convention Center because they had heard that was better than the Superdome, which everyone knew was awful.

Boy Jack said it was quite a hike but nobody answered, just kept walking. He watched them for a half-block or so, and then fell in behind. He figured he could at least scrounge something to eat along the way or once he got to the Center, and then rethink his options. After Mr. Croydon had time to cool off from watching the damage reports on TV, he could try giving him a call. Maybe go back for his truck.

Picking his way amid the trash and dark pools of water, he started to get a sense of how bad Katrina had been, and how fickle. Some streets and houses were okay. Some had been smashed up. Some streets had water. Others didn't. He followed the family of ducks as they picked and sorted their way. One of the young girls turned to him and waved for him to hurry up and join them. He waved back and tried to smile but he could not make himself quicken his steps. In truth, each one became harder and more leaden because each one seemed to be leading into a cold dark forest on a moonless night. Except that in New Orleans the sun was out and bright and already boiling up the thick moist air in a dirty soup of misery. There was no way to see where you were going and what might be there if you arrived.

At dawn, with only a few hours' rest, Duane and Maybelle got dressed in the same clothes from last night and went downstairs to get water from the concession stand, wishing it were coffee, and then outside, where it was slightly cooler but just as waterlogged. Also more mosquitoes. Duane went back for the spray and they spritzed themselves.

Maybelle said she wanted to try reaching Bonnie, and maybe her mom. Duane nodded and said he wanted to check in on Gretchen. She lived alone, and he hoped she had gone to stay with friends, but she was an independent sort, especially fond of sur- vivalist loner movies whenever they showed up on the bill. Good worker, though. Never late. Never complained unless there was a good reason, which was fairly often. The Portia was not the tightest ship in the harbor. It made him smile to think of her. And then lose the smile for the same reason. No answer. So he punched in her number again. Time of day didn't matter anymore. No one would be asleep. No one would be okay.

Maybelle spotted Moon-Ra first.

She elbowed Duane, who was still looking at his cell. He gasped, possibly from the pain in his ribs from Maybelle's jab, but just as likely from seeing his friend walking toward them, alive.

He was at the corner of Martin Street, pausing for a moment to look in the early light toward the Portia, at the fallen trees, broken windows, and what was left of the marquee, now a kind of stub of broken metal, plastic, and wires.

Then he saw them, too, and did not gasp but exhaled so heavily it might have been a gust of wind from the storm. Duane shout- ed out, Moon-Ra shouted out, and they all rushed together. They embraced because at first no one knew what to say. All that was real was what they could see. They could see each other.

"You're okay!" Maybelle exclaimed, because it was obvious and because nothing else had any meaning.

"You're soaked." Duane looked him over for injuries.

"Well, y'all are sights yourself."

"Were you out all night?"

"Convention Center."

"What?" Maybelle said.

"It's where everyone went."

Maybelle looked at Duane, then back at Moon-Ra. "How did you get here?"

He looked down at his wet, muddy sneakers.

"That's a hell of a walk," Duane said.

"Yeah."

"It wasn't flooded? Getting here?" Maybelle said.

"Parts. I went around it. It's weird."

"Definitely that. But shit, man, you're okay?" Duane said.

"Not really."

"No?"

"You?"

"You know."

"I definitely know."

They laughed after a fashion.

"So man, I came up here for food and water. I figured it was in the Portia." He looked them over. "I didn't figure you'd be here. I mean, you know."

"We got stuck," Maybelle said, and made a flourish pose as if at a fashion show.

Duane scowled.

"Me, too," Moon-Ra said. "But . . . I also got my family."

"What?" Duane said. "Who?"

"Eluvia, the kids. Back in the Center. I think my mom might be there, too."

"You don't know?"

"I haven't seen her. I can't find her. It's just what one of her friends said."

"Sorry."

"I mean, unless she got up to Baton Rouge or Lafayette or somewhere, I don't know where else she'd go. The Lower Nine is fucking flooded, man."

"They said on the radio," Maybelle said.

"It's all fucking flooded." He looked around what was left of the parking lot. "Look, can you help?"

"Tell us what you need," Maybelle said. Duane nodded and touched Moon-Ra on the shoulder to show support, but he flinched. Moon-Ra quickly returned a look that he was sorry, it was just a reaction, and patted Duane's shoulder. Then he told them what he needed.

They loaded everything they could from the concession stand into a half dozen black trash bags. Although Moon-Ra hadn't come across a grocery cart on his trip to the Portia, there was one in the supply room that Gretchen had pushed in two weeks ago after a homeless guy left it outside the ticket window. It was from the new health food store. Gretchen had decided to keep it since the yups could probably live without a cart and she had plenty of things she could do with it to keep the Portia from clogging up with crap.

They managed to cram in all the bags and Moon-Ra told them a little about life in the Convention Center. Then they grabbed warm Cokes and breakfast bars Duane had brought from his house and sat down in the lobby near the open door. Moon-Ra said it felt good to eat something. Duane asked Maybelle to come upstairs and help him with some things they'd left in the projection booth while Moon-Ra rested. She did.

"I think we should go with him," Duane said, softly, when they were in the booth and out of earshot. "I mean, I don't know if he can make it back with all that. And then there's Eluvia and the kids. Maybe his mom."

"You mean stay in that place?"

"I don't know. It sounds crowded but maybe just for a day. Or maybe we can get them back here. Find Miz Claudia. Not that there's anything here except maybe a little more space."

She looked at him closely. Like there could be any other answer. Like they even needed to say anything to each other. Like this was the bond between them. Like this was their new life. And it started now. It started with their friend. It started with who they had been, but mostly who they would be.

"Don't forget toilet paper," she whispered, kissed him, and then grabbed the bag she'd previously brought from her apartment and bounced down the stairs. "Hey, Moon, you got company!"

Duane locked the doors to the booth and his office. Going downstairs, he remembered the safe in the closet in his office and went back up to open it. The safe was an idea from Maybelle, who praised the one at the law office as safe from thieves and also "forces of nature," as the insurance certificate had said. So he bought one. His was not as big and probably could be stolen, until in a fit of DIY maintenance a year ago, Duane and Rhys bought some steel holding bars and various nuts and bolts and electric drills and fastened the thick metal contraption into a corner that at the least would take more work to free up than the average thief had time for. Even if they could break the combination.

He opened it, double-checked the $2,500 in operating cash he'd been saving inside, and went back to the projection room for his laptop, and put it in the safe, too.

When Duane got to the lobby, Maybelle and Moon-Ra were adjusting the bags in the shopping cart again to survive potholes and bumps. Moon-Ra looked at Duane and said nothing and in a very unusual move came up to him, gave him a short but strong hug.

"You didn't have to, and thanks."

"Well, hell, I gotta see this place," Duane said.

They headed down Milton to Magazine Street and Moon-Ra guided them over to Tchoupitoulas. They avoided all but a few street-lakes but were masses of sweat within fifteen minutes. Maybelle said at least it felt like they were doing something. Duane wasn't sure, but he kept it to himself.

Moon-Ra walked ahead, since he knew the way. Duane had to ask him to wait up several times as the cart wouldn't go fast and already had nearly tipped over twice. Moon-Ra didn't slow down, but he did wait when he got so far ahead that he was afraid of losing them.

He got quieter as they got closer. The only person he wanted to talk to, his mom, was missing and the only place he knew to look for her was in a warehouse of snakes and scorpions and flying bloodsuckers. It took the rest of the morning to get to the Convention Center, and when they arrived, it felt like they had trekked across the coals of hell only to fall into the furnace.

The withering heat that Katrina left behind along with the destruction hadn't relented, and inside the Center it was as bad or worse. Eluvia and the boys thought they might go mad, and it didn't help that they couldn't reach anyone by phone. The immediate concern was Moon-Ra's mom, but Eluvia couldn't reach her own family outside of New Orleans either, to let them know she and the boys were alive.

So although she'd agreed to stay where Moon-Ra could find them, Eluvia led the boys outside. There were rumors that people were being forced to stay put but no one said anything as they left. They crossed the median boulevard to a parking lot across the street where some TV news trucks had parked. She thought they must have phone service or they would have set up somewhere else.

She was part right. She got a weak signal and managed to reach her almost-ex, who turned out to still be at the Atlanta airport. The line was crackly, but Timothy said he and his crew had decided to just drive back if none of the flights for the day came through.

She told him where she and the boys were and that they needed help. She hated him over the affair he denied, but that didn't need going into at the moment. He said that even if they drove, he could be there by maybe noon Wednesday or earlier, depending on the roads. Problem was they couldn't come in through Mississippi because it was as bad or worse than New Orleans and anyway if they did come that way, the I-10 bridge was down.

He said maybe the phones would be better by tomorrow, but if not, he'd just get to the Convention Center and find them. Noon Wednesday at the latest, he said again, which they both knew was nothing more than a wild guess. But it was something. He actually told her to hang on and try to stay calm and safe and was glad Curtis was with them. He hated calling him Moon-Ra. She was going to let him know her feelings about staying calm and hanging on but the connection went out.

After fifteen minutes she still couldn't get it back and her phone batteries were under fifty percent so she decided to go back inside. They could probably get close to where they had been, or close enough for Moon to find them, and she could set up the same kind of perimeter. They had one bottle of water left but it would have to do, unless they could find more somewhere inside.

But if he wasn't back by night, she felt like they should leave and try going into the Quarter and maybe at least get some food and sleep on one of those sidewalks where the homeless people usually did. She told the boys it wouldn't be that much longer in the big building, but the truth was they were so ramped up by the chaos that the whole thing seemed like more an adventure to them than a burden. Kids. Who knew?

As they crossed the boulevard from the parking lot back to the Center, they picked up the attention of two young hoods, probably from the projects, who decided to throw a wolf whistle and half-ass follow, even though she had children in tow. She led the boys to the sidewalk fast and they blended into anonymity among the thousands trying to camp or just survive. She looked back, and the hoods were gone from view. Either looking for whatever they were looking for somewhere else, or running into somebody tougher and stronger with the same thoughts in mind, or maybe just worn out and tired of pretending to be thugs and ready just to collapse and moan inside their own heads until their time was up. And maybe already was.

CHAPTER 10

Tuesday, August 30, continued

They found Eluvia near where Moon-Ra had expected, and immediately gave her and the boys waters and the last of the granola bars from Duane's house. But, seeing the attention they had drawn with the shopping cart, Moon-Ra said to wait to eat until they got back to their old spot down the endless hallway or one they liked better, and less exposed. But they could drink the water as they walked.

They found a relatively uncrowded spot after a short search. The four adults worked quickly to assemble against the hallway wall a small, three-sided barricade of sorts, actually a pitiful joke of a barrier, with their backpacks and the cart and two cardboard boxes someone had abandoned. A campfire and marshmallows would have been ideal, had they been in a Boy Scout campground. Here, a campfire would become a real fire that no one could put out and they'd all die in post-hurricane flames, instead of drowning in filthy, frothing currents of Big Easy flood water. Which began to seem increasingly more apropos, given the heat.

Duane had been ruminating on just that—which would be worse, the old fire or flood dilemma—when fatigue called his bluff. He couldn't stay awake any longer. In truth, he had not slept more than a couple of hours since sometime Sunday, and had lied to Maybelle saying he had. He told her not to worry about it. Also a lie. After they had settled, and Eluvia and the children could eat and drink as much as they wanted, he fell asleep, back against the wall, almost in mid-sentence.

In comparable truth, Maybelle hadn't slept either, but she was far too wired to be anywhere involving sleep now. She sat near Duane's prone hulk and watched as Eluvia and the boys also dropped into sleep, snuggled together on the carpet like animals in the wilderness. But after maybe an hour, despite her resolve, Maybelle dropped off herself. Like she'd done dozens of times on a break at Arturo's. Which made her think of the restaurant and whether it might have survived.

Moon-Ra, who was obsessively trying to make calls on his cell phone, watched the sleepers, and studied what was around them. It was not good. "Not" being an absolute. It was absolutely not good. More people were coming in all the time, pushing and shoving, raising their voices when transgressed, scavenging for anything at all that was loose, finally staking out their own parts of the carpet. The air morphed from merely stale to hot and stale to hot and stale and foul with the odors of human digestion and excretion. Like the Superdome, only more so.

After a few hours, the boys woke up and then so did everyone else. Samuel and Edwin both needed to pee. Eluvia sighed and looked up at the ceiling, shaking her head. Biological functions had escalated from a nuisance to an unpleasantness to a dangerous problem to health and personal safety. Already, everyone inside the Center had learned not to use the restrooms up and down the hall because the toilets had stopped up in all of them. If you tried anyway, you encountered floors wet with pools of piss and sloppy with shit and clogs of toilet paper.

Moon-Ra and Duane took the boys on a long walk, almost a city block, to a distant and upriver part of the Center, stopping at a wall where no one was closer than fifty feet. They could pee there. It was worse for Eluvia and Maybelle, because even when they found a place, and squatted close to a wall or corner, men and women, but mostly men, could see their butts and their pee streaming and it was like eye-rape every time and put Eluvia into a funk.

Maybelle had more of a capacity to close things off, and did, but it was still the same.

When they got back from nature's calls and sat in their circle trying to figure what to do, Moon-Ra told Duane and Maybelle that as bad as things were in the day, the night would be "orders of magnitude worse." He shot a quick look at Eluvia, and then both of them looked at the boys, and decided not to elaborate. Nor would it get any cooler, he said. It would just get dark, and the pervs and thugs and killers would be concealed by the darkness and their sounds muffled by the crying and screaming and wailing that came from the mouths of babes and of their grandmothers and brothers and sisters and mothers and fathers and uncles and aunts.

It was a ceaseless thing, Moon-Ra said, which was why he had left that morning as soon as the first tinge of dawn gave him enough light to make his way outside and into the streets toward the Portia for supplies, not even knowing Duane and Maybelle would be there. Knowing he had left Eluvia and his nephews behind. She had a kitchen knife she had put in her handbag before they evacuated her house, but it was more a symbol than a weapon. He had left them to save them, huddled in their spot in the hall throughout the dawn and the morning like the first humans clinging to each other in their caves against the coming of the panthers and killer apes. Having returned, he wondered if he had succeeded or put off the inevitable.

Afternoon became evening. Nothing to do. Nothing to say. Moon-Ra couldn't get his mind off his missing mom, and said he was going to walk up to the far end of the Center, past the pissing spot, before nightfall and complete darkness. They had settled at the downriver end of the building, bordering on the big parking lot and Harrah's, so it was quite a hike up and back. Duane said he'd go with him, but after some discussion it seemed better that he stayed. It didn't matter that Eluvia had the knife, and that Maybelle had once taken self-defense training. They would look to predators like two women with two small children as not much defense at all. Either Duane or Moon-Ra needed to be there at all times, until they found a way out. Which at the moment they could not.

Moon-Ra was unwilling to leave until he found his mom or knew for sure she wasn't there. With the phones worthless, the only way to search was the oldest. By foot. He took off to find her, not fast but deliberately, trying to get a good look at every person or huddled group that he passed.

He wouldn't miss checking out anything except the outside sidewalks. That stretch of human misery would have to wait for daylight if he didn't find her inside. He hoped that's where she was, that if Miz Claudia was with anyone, that they would have had the sense to get inside. On the other hand, it was so bad inside that maybe the sidewalk wouldn't have been any worse.

Neither place had any kind of police protection except for a few cops on foot who sort of passed through the assembled mob like they couldn't wait to get back out. Moon-Ra kept walking and tried not to overthink that they were in hell. But the metaphor popped up like an annoying song with his every step. Like those paintings that showed medieval people being tortured in the caverns of misery for eternity.

He wanted to hurry, anxious and fearful in his search, but kept to his slow, deliberate pace and scanning every face he could. They were getting harder to take in. Especially the ones that said everything with their expressions, their eyes. Cold eyes. Dead eyes. Terrified eyes. Godforsaken eyes.

He'd actually been in the Center once before, doing a gig for some kind of sales convention for engineers, and he knew it was monstrous big. But not until his mother was swallowed by a hurricane had he ventured this far into its guts. The daylight was fading fast and he had far to go. He knew he had to move faster. He began bumping into people and being bumped. Curses for doing so. But he never lost his focus. Which of them could lead him to his mother? It was impossible. If there had been a couple thousand people in the place yesterday, there were ten times that many now. Not a breath could be taken that wasn't wet with the exhalations of twenty thousand lost souls.

It challenged his concentration. His brain sorted the images in milliseconds, throwing out any that did not approximate or match Miz Claudia. He did not fear being harmed. But it was certainly hell. He had seen plenty of homeless people, plenty of poor people, plenty of sick people, plenty of people at loose ends, plenty of desperadoes, but never such a forlorn herd.

The old ones were the toughest to behold. They seemed to have all but given up, sitting and slouching and half-falling in metal folding chairs liberated from the equipment closets whose broken and half-hanging doors were but another sign of surrender.

The old folks in particular had the thousand-yard stare that Moon-Ra had heard his Uncle Terence talk about from time in Vietnam. Uncle T wasn't around for Katrina. He put a bullet into his head a decade ago when the wait for his VA appointments got months long, while his despair and hard drinking arrived on schedule each day. "Nothin' ain't nothin'" was his favorite saying, almost a mantra. Only recently had Moon-Ra started to see what it meant. From a thousand yards.

He didn't find her.

Back at the makeshift fortress, the boys were finishing up crackers and candy from the Portia concession stand. Eluvia saw the look in Moon-Ra's face as soon as he returned, and her own dropped into sadness and desperation.

Duane saw them both, didn't want to barge into their pain. He knelt inside the barricade so everyone could hear him without shouting. "I just wanted to say it's going to be a long night and we need to stay tight here as long as we can. There's people walking around that'd scare a con from Angola. And then there's the ones just so damned pathetic you can't stand to look at them and think what shape they really might be in."

Moon-Ra stood at the opposite end of the barricade. "Tell me about it, goddam it."

"I didn't mean it that way," Duane said.

"Fuck, I just got back from walking through all that."

"I know."

"You don't, really. If you ain't seen it."

"It's okay, man."

"Nobody's gonna get much sleep tonight," Maybelle said, watching the flash of frustration between two men she was crazy about in different ways.

"Oh, it'll be okay. We just camping out here for a while," Eluvia added, shooting a quick glance at the boys and then back at the adults.

Moon-Ra and Duane got what she meant and nodded at each other. The boys swarmed their uncle, and it comforted him.

Duane and Maybelle busied themselves pulling the ersatz barricade blockade a little closer so their circle got smaller. They'd just finished when a voice down the darkened hall cried out, "Curtis, yo! Moon-Ra! Been trying to catch up with you, cuz."

Everyone looked.

"It's me. Paulus. Damn, thought I lost you."

"Paulus?" As soon as the figure came closer, Moon-Ra could see it was his cousin. It was unbelievable and unexpected, and both of them just stared at each other a few seconds, then smiled, hugged, did a handshake, and hugged again.

They exchanged quick explanations, loud enough for everyone in the barricade to hear, of how they got to the Convention Center. Paulus told him he and his family were out of water since about four o'clock and almost out of the bananas and oranges his wife, Nadia, had grabbed rushing from their house with the water coming in. He said Nadia and the two kids, Elena and Rael, the girl maybe six or seven, the boy about half that, weren't so much scared as half-dead with dehydration and exhaustion.

Moon-Ra told Paulus they needed to go retrieve his family right away and they took off. Duane and Maybelle stayed with Eluvia and the kids to guard their spot on the floor and protect the supplies.

Moon-Ra was leading Paulus and his family back in thirty minutes, about twice as long as it would have taken under normal Convention Center circumstances. Which no longer existed. Introductions were exchanged, the circle was made, and it would not be broken, even if everything that formed it already was.

It turned out that seeing Paulus again made Moon-Ra anxious again about his mother. He told Duane that he was going out into the nightmare one more time to search. He didn't wait for Duane's answer, or anyone else's opinion. He pushed once more into the long, teeming lobby, but even faster this time because mostly he was seeing the same thing, but with almost no light.

Moon-Ra was a devoted son and good man. But it didn't matter. He didn't find his mom. Nor would he. He didn't know it yet, any more than Maybelle knew about Bonnie, or the families of more than a thousand lost souls knew of their friends and relatives. The darkness that came on the first night after Katrina left the building would not lift for a thousand days, each day with ten thousand thousand-yard stares.

But no one knew.

Only they knew never again to joke "come hell or high water" and that continuing to breathe was a task sufficient unto itself. The darkness rendered the inhabitants dumbstruck with anger and despair. It had fastened to the throat of the city they loved and thrashed it like a drowned child's pillow and left them to find some kind of light.

Of this horror and destruction would come Duane's hejira to Texas. He didn't know that yet, either.

CHAPTER 11

Tuesday, August 30, night

"We thought we'd be okay that far from the river, but it was the canal, and we got water so fast we barely got out of the house. Brownie and the two cats never made it. We think they were outside when it all came and got trapped or something." Paulus laid out his family's story as everyone tried to settle in for the evening. It was easy to lose track of time, and quite a surprise when Nadia reminded them that it was going on nine o'clock.

Rael started to tear up at the mention of the lost pets, but Nadia wiped his cheek and whispered something into his ear and he sniffled and stopped. They all tucked the sadness away because in just a day of hurricane life they had learned to do that if they were going to make it to the other side.

Duane and Maybelle had moved the boxes and bags and cart and broken chairs into yet another configuration to make more room to sit or sleep. It was pushing the outer rim a little closer to the human traffic, but it still felt like a bulwark against the creatures of the night.

They were using the four lantern flashlights, with extra batteries, that they'd brought from the Portia for intervals of ten or fifteen minutes until their eyes got used to seeing in the deepening dark. Just enough illumination, added to intermittent light from the street, that they could recognize each other. And anyone who came within a dozen feet. The people silhouetted against the windows looked like puppets sagging against their strings.

"I don't know about my mom, or my other brothers and sisters,"

Paulus said. "Man, we don't know anything."

"It's like we was cut off from the world," said Nadia, holding her kids against her side. Moon-Ra, back from his search, passed them more snacks and soft drinks.

"I think my mom might be in Ruston or either Houston," Paulus said after a silence.

"I don't know about mine at all," Moon-Ra said. "Just what some people told me. And I can't get any signal on this phone."

"We can't get the cell, either," said Nadia. "All we know is from this little radio." She pulled a small black transistor from a bag. "I keep it turned off mostly because the batteries." She looked at Duane. "Any double-A's in there, maybe?"

"Just those big ones for the lanterns, but I'll go through the boxes again."

"What y'all need, for the kids?" Moon-Ra said. "I got a few band-aids and some aspirins. About all, though."

"They're working on what you already gave them," Nadia said. "They ain't cut or hurt, praise the Lord."

"I hope to hell we're out of here soon as morning comes," said Eluvia.

"Where to, though, that's the thing," Duane said, digging through cords and light bulbs and batteries. "Any of us got a car somewhere that'll still run?"

"Mine, maybe, that we left when we went into the Superdome. But I'm pretty sure it's under water," Moon-Ra said.

"You know that," Eluvia said.

"Mine might work," Maybelle said. "But I don't even know how we'd get to it."

"Pretty sure Fairgrounds and all around there is flooded out, too," Moon-Ra said. "So probably not worth the trouble."

Maybelle looked at him. "I was hoping otherwise."

"Pretty sure I heard everywhere around there took water."

"Ours is drowned for sure," said Paulus. "Seventh Ward's a lake."

"Mine might start but now there's two flat tires. Maybe three," said Duane. "Not too optimistic about finding guys to fix them."

"Nah. And we'd never get spares or patches," said Moon-Ra.

"Damn, this is fucked," said Duane.

"I'll add a damn," said Maybelle, slumping back on the carpet on her elbows. "Also a fucked."

"Hey, found some," Duane said. "Two double-As, actually. How many you need?"

"Two is good," said Nadia, reaching over to get them.

"Okay, then, we can listen in to Garland off and on," Duane said.

"Nobody else really has a clue what's going on," said Paulus.

"What have you heard?" Moon-Ra asked.

"It's like three or four of the levees broke somewhere. I know the Industrial Canal got us, and Nine Ward. And nobody to help do anything. What my cousin said about the Fairgrounds, he's right. It's like the opposite what you'd think. All the water in the middle, not around the edges."

"The old-timers always said that," Eluvia said.

"They did," said Paulus.

"Assholes," Maybelle said to no one in particular. "I mean the city, the state, all those types."

"They leaving us to die," said Eluvia. "Real bad in Gentilly when we left."

Maybelle stood up to stretch, and then everyone else did, too. None of the children had to pee, at least at the moment. They had nothing to say. All they could do was look at what was around them with eyes big as cable satellite dishes.

"Is this our new family?" Samuel asked Eluvia.

"I guess. Mr. Duane from the Portia, where your uncle works, and his lady friend, name Maybelle, and those are your cousins, you know. But I guess, yeah."

"So we're the Portia family," he said.

Duane looked at Samuel, smiled, gave a thumbs-up. It was maybe the best thing he'd heard all day. But best was not a high bar.

Once they had settled, the combination of boredom and terror reasserted itself. Nothing to do but gaze upon the spectacle, listen to the passing conversations. If there were twenty thousand people, which was the rumor, there were forty thousand arms and hands at rest or waving or tight against chests or wiping sweat from forty thousand eyes, forty thousand legs and forty thousand feet, some in wheel chairs or on crutches or some long since amputated. All barely in sync, trying to find a place to rest without being hurt any more.

The math also produced twenty thousand mouths trying to find something to say and eat, twenty thousand noses struggling to breathe and filter horrendous odors, twenty thousand brains trying to make some sense of hell, twenty thousand souls on twenty thousand quests for even a single soupçon of meaning.

Of all that, what floated across the perimeter of the Portia family were the audio fragments, the disconnected sound bites of frustration and anger and despair that became a sort of mash-up group conversation, a poetry slam. Like this:

Outta my way motherfucker. Fuck you doing? Mama? Somebody go get Uncle Bill, he don't know where he is. I'm so hungry. Where Tommy? I'm nothing but sweat and no damn water anywhere. Anybody find a toilet ain't backed up? Mama? Hey, man, can I have some of that? Girl, I got my eye on you. Stay the fuck away asshole. Anybody see a cop? I heard they's bodies all over the place. Is that a ambulance? Where's the water? Hey, leave that girl alone you fucking perv. God, it is so hot. I got to get outside, me. It's dangerous out there. Fuck, man, somebody shit right on the damn rug. Fuck. I just wanna go home. Anybody from Nine Ward? What's going on over there. Goddam, lady, don't let that boy pee on the window. It's all fuckin flooded, man. We just gotta get through the night. Tomorrow we go home. Did you hear that? Keep walking, I don't wanna go to sleep. Get that baby something to shut up. Fuck . . .

Listening to the voices—all ranges, all accents, all accents and colors—put a kind of rhythm in Duane's mind, like watching the river from the levee in the Quarter and hearing the howl, not the Katrina howl, but the one that had found purchase in his soul. That it was speaking to him again, and to those around him, and he felt love for them all as they leaned in to the center of the perimeter and looked across at each other's eyes, which were having conversations all their own. It gave him an idea.

"Let's tell stories," he said.

Maybelle gave him a glance of uncertain meaning, and then he saw Nadia look up from her children, her mouth purse like giving it some thought. Paulus stared without any sense of what he was thinking. Eluvia exchanged glances with Moon-Ra, who was rocking softly to some kind of beat that only he knew. But Duane knew that Moon-Ra got it. Was probably way beyond it.

"You know, to get us through this night."

"Go for it, big boy," Maybelle said. She lay back down on the grimy carpet and laughed. "It's your fucking all-night show, Mr. Movie Man." She laughed again. "Too bad about the popcorn."

"Popcorn?" Rael said to his mom.

"She was just making a joke," Nadia said. Then, to Duane, an upbeat lilt in her voice, "Okay, yeah, let's hear some stories. You know, for the Portia family."

Maybelle didn't move but Duane could detect her Mona Lisa smile.

Inside Convention Center.

Photo by Lisa Krantz/San Antonio Express-News/ZUMA Press.

PART II

SHELTER

"

And so what we could do had everything to do with being able to understand where we came from, what happened to our people, and how to honor them by living right, by telling our stories. She told me the world was made of stories, nothing else, just stories, and stories about stories."

—Tommy Orange, *There, There*

CHAPTER 12

Tuesday, August 30, night

Duane stood, then crouched back down on one knee so as not to draw too much attention from passers-by, some of whom had looked at him, standing up, in a way he didn't find comforting. "I was thinking, maybe one of the kids could get us started off. You know, if one of them wants to. I guess I'd like to know a story they might be thinking about right now." He felt like a camp counselor trying to liven up a room of sullen teenagers.

Samuel raised his hand. So did his brother, Edwin, but Eluvia said Samuel could go first.

He stood. Then Eluvia told him to sit down. "This one just for us," she told him. Then, to the others, "Kids don't need no special attention in this place."

Samuel scooted slightly into the circle, but couldn't help looking out beyond the perimeter. That must have been what derailed him. He got a few sentences out about these two surfing dogs who rode some big waves in from the ocean all the way to Pontchartrain, and it would have been interesting to see where he took it but one more glance out to the people moving outside in the darkness and he began choking and shaking, then rocking back and forth.

Eluvia zoomed across the carpet. She held his mouth open to see if anything was choking him, but it wasn't. "My God, his eyes is like big saucers, and he ain't even looking at us," she said. Moon-Ra was beside her in a flash and helped keep Samuel's arms from flailing as Eluvia tried to hold him.

A few people passing by holding paper sacks and bulging pillow-cases paused to watch. "The boy okay?" asked one older man. Moon-Ra held up his palm to indicate he was. "It's just got to him is all."

"It's sure got to us all," the old man said. He watched for another minute as Samuel's body started to relax, and then moved along, like someone who cared but had no way to show it.

Duane sat quietly, letting Eluvia handle it. Like the old man, he knew there was nothing to be done because of what already had been done. To the whole city. Samuel was in no danger. In fact, he might have moved past it.

"Amazing," Maybelle said softly. She and Paulus shared a glance, and then both caught Moon-Ra's gaze.

"He needs some water," Eluvia said. "He'll be okay. He'll be okay." Edwin was next to her, taking it all in.

Moon-Ra touched Samuel's forehead, looked him over as closely as he could.

"Boy's warm. And he needs some sleep."

"Here, take this," Nadia said, passing Eluvia one of the water bottles from the Portia.

Eluvia managed to get Samuel to drink. First just a sip. Then he drank it all.

Moon-Ra had gone around to pull some clothes from a bag to make a pillow and Eluvia helped her son lie back. He looked up at her and said nothing, but she was comforted to see that the pupils in his eyes had returned to normal size and the shaking was gone. Samuel grabbed her hand and squeezed it harder than she could ever recall. She cuddled Edwin, looked at Moon-Ra, and at Nadia, told them she thought he was better. When she looked at Samuel again he was asleep.

The adults kept close watch on the continuing swirl in the hall.

Paulus helped everyone resettle. Seeing them all like that, in that place, allowed it all to sink in, and suddenly he was transported somewhere else. It was a street in the Quarter, back when he was a teenager, and those Cuban men had beat him up for no reason that he knew at the time. Later, he found out they were trying to scare his mama, who everyone called Reverend Youngblood, from trying to stop what was being called a Superbotanica, big as one of those discount stores, from getting built near her church. In some ways, not knowing, at least at first, why he had been attacked left a lingering pain longer than the wounds.

Everyone sat quietly, only speaking to ask for water or when Nadia said she knew Elena needed to pee and that she was scared to take her. Eluvia told her where they could be safe and said she'd go with her, and Maybelle said she'd go, too.

By the time they got back, the worry over Samuel had decreased, and the reality of the rest of the night to be spent in the Convention Center reasserted its dominance. Duane stood, stretched. "Sun won't be up for six or seven hours yet. I can't sleep. Who wants to try another story?"

"Jesus, Duane," said Maybelle. "We're exhausted with this. You can't see that?"

"I absolutely can. But I know you can't sleep either. Any of the rest of you?"

Eluvia had already slumped down and fallen asleep with her boys. Everyone else mumbled something like "probably not."

"Come on, Maybelle," said Duane. "You got some stories. Tell us just one. It might even relax you enough to get a nap."

The look she gave him was not friendly. She regretted it immediately, because where they were huddled was very probably not sustainable or survivable for very long and it was no place to sleep, especially with children. The part of her that was familiar with how sudden violence could explode out of nowhere, as it had with William, slapped her inside her brain to wake up and smell the urine.

"Okay, bubba." She looked around the circle. "Want to pull an all-nighter?" She leaned back and did a little stretching, careful not to kick over anything. "Hey, Moon-Ra, pass me one of those Cokes."

"They're warm," he said, reaching into a box.

"Perfect," she said, and sat back up, then stood slowly, like a battered athlete, as if every muscle and bone in her body carried the pains of centuries. She faced the passing legions of the damned.

CHAPTER 13

Tuesday, August 30, *around midnight*

"I'm not a good storyteller, so I'm just going to tell you something that happened, although it's definitely a story." Turning her head to Duane. "That meet your criteria, Professor McGuane?" Back to those passing by who were slowing to see what this was about. "And not just for us—for this whole audience that wants to take in the late-night matinee. I got that right?"

Maybelle tried for a smile, and made a quick visual recon of what was around her. "Okay then, we'll settle in," she said, raising her voice a few notches to cut through the ambient noise. "And yeah, all y'all out there walking by, you wanna eavesdrop and get a little free entertainment, you're in the right place."

About a half-dozen had slowed or stopped and now maybe a few more, although it was a good bet they weren't looking at the strange woman but more at the clump of cardboard boxes of food surrounding an odd clump of people.

Noticing the stares, Duane stood up, on Maybelle's right. As did Paulus and Moon-Ra, on her left. They assessed her surroundings, and the gawkers, about half black, half white, mostly middle-aged or older. At various places down the hall, flashlights or battery-powered lanterns flashed and off, not exactly in sync but enough to provide a semblance of campfire-like visibility beyond what light from the streets came in through the hall windows. It would stay that way until the predawn. Enough illumination to see the fear and enough shadowy dark to see the same.

Maybelle gave Duane an okay hand sign. She could see the drop-ins weren't gangbangers, just lost souls, and nobody wanted a fight. Although a woman in an out-of-place yellow lounge suit and the man with her in burgundy and dirty white golf clothes shook their heads in disgust at being scanned by the men in the circle and walked away. "Ain't nothin'," another man, older, said as the pair shuffled away.

"Didn't mean nothin'," a woman's deep voice called out from the other side.

Beyond them, the larger tide of exhausted bodies kept moving. It really was looking like a river of people, filled with bends and curves and rapids and rocks and shallows, and deep, cold currents where nothing lived but through which much passed. Or like looking at the thick flow of oil from a wrecked tanker. Metaphors were one of the few things not in short supply after a hurricane.

"I hate this shit," Paulus told Duane. "Nobody knows what to do and nobody from the city even in here to help."

"It's like this everywhere," Moon-Ra said.

"I can handle them," Maybelle said to her three bodyguards. "I mean, that's the whole fucking point, isn't it? Tell stories. Keep them from killing you?" She made a shooing motion with her arm and Duane nodded and he and Moon-Ra and Paulus moved back to the family circle. "I'm good."

With that, her exhaustion vanished. She gathered up tall and straight, as if behind a mike stand, but also floating in the dark. Something was going on in her head, and you could practically see the corona of energy it produced. Like actors falling into character, Duane thought, but did not say.

She knew exactly where she was, and why, and she needed to watch what she said. She also knew she had every right—everyone in the building had every right—to be angry and on the edge of the edge. Anger had brought them all there and remained, at least in potential. But it was real potential and it required but a spark, a quirk, a flaw of fate to manifest.

In exactly that moment she changed her mind, or, as she might have said later, her mind changed her, about what story she would offer. In mitigation, in respect, in a truth they could only begin to comprehend.

She took another moment to survey the movement of the displaced. Then, staring down the void, the putative love of Duane's life began talking in a voice he had never heard.

MAYBELLE'S STORY

"My old and true name is Xóchitl, which is from the Aztec language, or one called Nahautl. It's pronounced like I just did, SO-Chee, or some say SO-Cheel, but if you saw the word you'd think it's spelled kind of funny, like with an X instead of an S and like that. Anyway, somewhere long ago a Spanish last name got added, Miramundo, maybe because there were so many Xóchitls. I don't know why any of that. The names just come to me.

"I was born, or became a life form, before anyone can remember, and I lived more lives in more bodies and had more names to go with them than anyone can remember, even me. I came and went all around the world, I'm pretty sure, but mostly on this part of where the planet curves with its land and its water. So my names have something to do with geography."

A few of the passers-by were pausing. Others kept going but turning their heads to listen on the way.

"Three or four hundred years ago, the body that I got into was on the islands down in the Caribbean, they called it, and I lived three times there. First time, I got sick from the mosquitoes and died when I was a teenager. I think it was on what they call Guadeloupe. Second time is when I was hiding out with the maroons up in the mountains in Jamaica and I had a good life and was in love so much with a young man who thought all the slaves could be free again. So they killed him, cut off his head and everything between his legs and put him on a big wood pole outside the city until the animals

127

ate him all up.

"And then it wasn't long after that they caught up with me and my friends and my little family and they caught us in a valley between the mountains and they couldn't get us out so they blocked it up with rocks where we had gone in and then started a big fire. So we all got roasted alive, except a couple who also got shot or run through with those big swords the soldiers had."

When she paused, it was fair to say that everyone in the circle either took a deep breath or simply looked on with open-mouthed astonishment. Absorbing the words as best they could but more like dumbfounded that this woman among them had gone insane and was finally admitting it. But also realizing she was telling a story and that it would be a good one. Mesmerized would be a fair description.

Duane looked at her with an expression that he hoped was not alarmist. He was truly interested in what would come next. Also wondering from exactly where this particular story emanated.

Moon-Ra was staring at Maybelle like he'd just seen evidence of interplanetary life-form and knew all along that they were coming. Maybe already here. Maybe in human disguise. She caught his look, just enough so that he knew she had.

"So that was two of the lives. The third life is what's relevant here."

She stopped, looking at a new clump of the hall-walkers pressing in. Duane began to stand but she waved him to let it be. "Greetings to all you people of earth joining us tonight," she called out. A few of them left right away. Others stayed put. A few more paused as they passed by.

Moon-Ra adjusted his body a little and felt the spirits in his soul begin to twitch. He looked at Paulus. Maybe his cousin had moved past what the preacher and priestess who was his mom and Moon-Ra's aunt, had poured into him, but he was still a vessel of the spirits. He and Moon-Ra would be receiving whatever message that whatever was inside Maybelle was transmitting. He could see that Paulus understood, exactly.

"The third time," Maybelle called out, her voice loud enough to bring the circle and the onlookers back into her realm, "I was a little French girl and the island was Haiti, I think. My dad was some kind of banker and handled money from the ships and the soldiers and the plantation owners and also had a side thing handling money for the poor whites and some of the Africans who weren't slaves anymore or mostly weren't. It was a good life for me, I guess, and I made it in comfort until I was a young woman, about to be married to a nice young officer who wanted us to elope and get across the sea to the big country of America, maybe either Florida or Louisiana.

"Which we might have done that until the hurricane. In those days you didn't get a warning, except right at the end when the skies and the winds told you what was coming. But it was always too late. And on an island, no place to run to anyway. Not like around here where you can get in a car and drive way the hell into Texas or Arkansas or wherever until the storm is gone. Not like that at all."

She closed her eyes to follow a thought. "Well, maybe it is like that around here, too. I mean, *look where we are.*"

The children flinched because Maybelle had raised her voice to almost a shout. The audience, now maybe a couple dozen, had gathered the way a crowd gradually increases in size around a car wreck or a fight or some mad street preacher in the Quarter calling out salvation to people just looking for a show.

She resumed, voice back to normal. "So it hit us almost by surprise and the wind was so strong it crashed down the roof of my family's house, which was down near the shore. We didn't drown. I mean some of us did but more as an after-effect. The main punch was we were crushed and trapped by the big logs and pieces of window iron that pushed into everywhere. Then we were all covered with water and the ones still breathing drowned that way.

"That was how I went. I had a broken back and legs and I couldn't move and the water went over me and I couldn't even raise

129

up my head. Nobody found us for a week or two and then they had a hard time telling one from another, with all the animals eating on us all that long, and the flies and insects and birds.

"But I was long gone from my body by then and from the islands. Like I said, I had a lot of lives. By then I was up in a farm in Ohio, but that didn't last. Some kind of fever took me when I was only ten—people were always dying of little things then that today we can fix with a pill from the drugstore. Anyway, none of my lives lasted too long up that way."

Everyone was really listening now, not questioning—like they'd chanced upon some hair-raising revival sermon.

"Next time that really mattered I was jumped into a new life about the time of the Civil War. The body I was in was in the Carolinas up in the mountains with some kind of family that probably was smugglers or something like that, but before I got a handle on it, I got shot. Turned out there was a boy down the road a ways who was hunting for deer and but he missed and the bullet traveled on farther than he'd expected and caught me out in the field behind our house. It hit me in my side and went all the way through and exploded my stomach. It was kind of funny because he didn't know he'd killed me until the next day.

"My mom was crazy scared because I hadn't come home and I was only fifteen, and some of the men around there came out to look for me. They found my body hidden by an old tree log. The war had started and even though there were armies and uniforms we all knew that anybody could be killed for any reason at any time and probably nothing would ever come of it. But fact is I was killed because that boy, name of Harold, only fourteen, didn't hit the deer he was aiming at. Weird, huh?"

Rael and Samuel, no longer asleep, nodded their heads as if they understood the show. The adults exchanged looks, raised eyebrows, mild head-shakes, but absolutely no words.

Maybelle bent down, picked up her Coke bottle, and took a long drink. "So anyway, by this time the people knew that boy

Harold had done it and knew it was an accident because even if I was only fifteen, I was a woman already and Harold's older brother Ervin had in mind marrying me when he got back from fighting over in Virginia or Tennessee. Which he probably never did. But I was long gone once again and so I never found out if he got killed, too. I think my name was Annie.

"So you know, I'm glad this body isn't really mine, though. I can just fit into one body after another like changing clothes because otherwise all that would be extremely painful and horrid. I mean, having the same body doing all that? It would be quite a wreck and people would turn away whenever I got within their eyesight."

Maybelle looked down the length of her body like it was something she barely recognized. "I need to take a minute." Then she sat, legs crossed, inhaling loudly a few times.

No one left. It felt like an intermission. Maybelle finished off her Coke. Duane offered her a water bottle, but she waved it off. Maybe him, too. She never even met his eyes. Eluvia stretched where she sat, and the others in the family did the same, and sipped at their own bottles of whatever they had found or brought.

Duane and Moon-Ra realized at roughly the same time that looks from the hall were coming their way again. "Put our bottles down," Moon-Ra said, in a whisper.

"And cover up the other stuff," Duane mouthed to Moon-Ra and Paulus. They did, as subtly as possible. They also sat up a little straighter and measured the crowd. There were at least five pairs of eyes out there that seemed more than capable of assault and theft. Duane stood, as did Moon-Ra and Paulus.

It seemed to have the same protective effect as when they had stood up together earlier in the evening. Except now more a sense of impatience out there than aggression.

"So what happened?" came a voice from a young woman. "Yeah," said another. "Get back up here. Tell us. Ain't like we got no place else to go or somethin' to do." The ripple of laughter was out of place under the circumstances but also exactly in place, and it seemed to relieve the tension.

It brought Maybelle back from wherever she was in her time out. She stood, breathed in and out deeply, stretched, then raised her hands and clapped. She stared out beyond the family circle, into the crowd, and clapped again. Harder.

"So that's how I got to Louisiana."

She used her pay-attention voice, and it worked.

"Now thank you for being so good and wanting to hear more." Someone yelled out a "Whoop!" Then came a smatter of applause.

"And I'm gonna do just that," Maybelle said, her voice big and commanding. "Tell you more. I just needed, you know, a little breather. I mean, it's a lot has to come out, so I hope you're really ready."

The crowd tightened as people moved forward. Others began to join them from the flow in the hall. The next story was even more blood-soaked and dark, and even further beyond anything Duane would have expected before this scene in the hurricane.

She went from reiterations of herself as a sharecropper in Alabama, raped and killed by Confederate bounty hunters, an actually good life working in a restaurant in Memphis, a street-walker in Chicago during the Depression whose only way out was suicide. She glanced at the children who were still awake a few times to see that they weren't too scared. But they needed stories as much as anyone.

After that, she had reincarnated as a teacher in Miami, things going well until a hurricane came through and knocked down a powerline that fell in a puddle she walked through and fried her. She remembered her name from that one, Sally, because that's who Raul, her boyfriend, had called out as she fell into a spasm.

"You making all this up, lady?"

She shook her head.

"Leave her alone" shouts erupted from the crowd.

"Anyway, I guess it was a good thing, all those ways of being a human woman, especially the last one, which ended up putting me over towards Baton Rouge, where I grew up sort of normal, and when that was over, I finally wound up here, child of New Orleans. Just in time to meet Katrina and all y'all."

She looked around. "And that's how I got to this story that was all stuck inside me for all this long time. And I have another story, one from right here in this time of my time. And I want to tell you." She paused and her voice dropped to barely audible, and turning hoarse. "But thing is I got to rest this human throat, and maybe this whole body."

"No!" came several cries.

"Just give me a little time. And now we're close to the sun show-ing up, and that's what I was trying to help with. To keep us all safe while we're all in here this night, all cooped up and scared and it's even more damn dangerous to go out in those dark streets."

"Stories!" someone yelled.

"Let her rest up. She all our friends," said another.

Maybelle waved, and was surprised how many waved back. "So if you need to go pee or anything, this would be the time. Or if you got somewhere else to be, I'm glad I was able to talk to you. I mean, I never do anything like this. And I'll never forget you."

She stepped back toward the barricade and met Moon-Ra, who gave her another water bottle. A quick burst of applause rang out from the crowd and faded.

Moon-Ra could hear the scratch in her voice as she thanked him before downing the water. Then she dropped the bottle and stretched to the limits of her muscles and joints, which felt really good. But abruptly stopped when she realized some of the men in the crowd, even in the dim light, were watching her breasts rise and fall beneath her T-shirt.

It didn't creep her out so much as remind her of what she and Bonnie had often described as the constant, unstoppable, offending presence of men in the world of women. That should be the world of women. But wasn't.

Except for Katrina. Now that was a woman had something to

say. To the men of the Big Easy and the Mississippi coast and any other XY chromosomes in her merciless howling path as she continued on what Maybelle was starting to feel was a fuck-you mission against the male world at the heart of every hurricane that men themselves in their remarkable arrogance had named and thus blamed on women.

But fuck them. Katrina made it pretty clear the story would be the way she wanted it told. Period.

Maybelle took a few more deep breaths, fuck anyone looking at her tits. She sat down close to the barricade. Duane came over. Hugged her. Sat next to her. It felt like she was on a cloud. From somewhere else.

CHAPTER 14

Wednesday, August 31, *wee hours*

The crowd had thinned considerably, but at least a hundred or more were still there. Because where else could they be? Cries of "Tell us more, sister," and so on, cropped up again.

Maybelle ignored them except for another hand wave and a slight dip of her head. Duane and Moon-Ra exchanged glances. They were still far from relaxed about supplies and safety and the family. Now even more so. Without stories, there wasn't anything to mollify or distract the drifters. The perimeter of boxes and backpacks wouldn't withstand anything, and the dark hours would soon surrender to the warnings of a new day.

Moon-Ra stood where Maybelle had been. "We're gonna make it," he said, loud like the closer in a nightclub or rowdy bar trying to be heard over the drunks.

Which maybe there were. Drunks: "More stories!" "More hottie girl!" "Give us our money back!"

Moon-Ra held up his arms to quiet them. "You want some more stories?"

Scattered half-shouts of "yeah" and "keep it goin'." Smatters of applause.

Moon-Ra looked at Duane, extended one arm in invitation. He didn't have to say why. Duane knew. He'd got the whole thing started. He signaled okay with a less than enthusiastic thumbs-up. Moon-Ra laughed without meaning to and held his arms up again for the crowd.

"So the next storyteller on tonight's star-studded triple feature is my old friend Duane here."

Duane bowed slightly. Moon-Ra responded in kind.

"Y'all might know him if you ever saw a movie at the Portia theater." Nobody said anything. "You know, Uptown, kind of near the zoo." Nothing. "Anyway I work over there, too. I mean I did. It ain't never gonna be open again, though, probably."

Duane nodded with forced enthusiasm and raised his right hand with another thumbs-up sign. Paulus grinned at them both, but also keeping an eye on the crowd.

Maybelle sat very still, her arms tight around her knees, which were drawn up under her chin.

"Damn, that was something. I don't even know where to start." It was the first chance he'd had to talk to her after her story. But in his eyes were mystery and even worship. At least that's what it looked like to her, from her cloud.

"Ol' Duane here has seen a lot of movies and he's a man can tell a story," Moon-Ra called out.

A woman's voice responded. "Anything better that just hanging round without no TV or nothing." Then a teenage boy, or girl. "Bring it on!"

Moon-Ra raised a fist.

Off in the distance down the hall, a small group of bandana-wearing thugs were pounding the body of a middle-aged man sagging to his knees and then crumpling and adding his blood type to the stained carpet. Then came some kicking. Some screams.

Paulus tilted his head in the direction of the mayhem so that Moon-Ra would know, and also toward Duane, but then the screaming and yelling stopped. Duane looked out at the newly gathering crowd. Moon-Ra and Paulus moved to each side of the circle, but not in a way to alarm anyone. Maybelle still not moving.

It was late. Actually, very early hours in the new day. No one had slept, and anyone still awake was beyond miserable. But it seemed better to keep a crowd amused than to be left alone with no more protection than a perimeter of a shopping cart, a few boxes, and trash bags of snacks and clothes.

Duane took a deep breath, stretched his arms, and tried to make eye contact with anyone who would let him. Then he took another breath, and then a third, and finally got his mind back in the game. Of storytelling away the long night. Of keeping the peace with words. Of making it up as you go. The whole scene could be looked at in different ways, not all possible, but for him it was a triumph of communication. It was, put another way, a focus group.

If he could try out the sales pitch of his cinematic vision to people in as dire straits as conceivable this side of hell, he might have just the kind of gut-punch mindless spiritual appeal that explained the success of films as god-awful and manipulative as *E.T.* and as brilliant but deeply flawed as *The Searchers*. Films that everyone had to see because they had to and they didn't even know why.

"Duane, man, say something." Moon-Ra moved up next to him. "They're going to walk off if you just stand there with your mouth shut."

Lacking a mirror, Duane could not see his own face at that moment, but if he had been able to, it would have resembled Maybelle's when she was traveling through time and lives never before revealed. But without glow, without fascination, without mystery. He was a hustler. She was a force.

"Damn, sorry," he said to Moon-Ra and waved his arms to the crowd, which was on the verge of breaking up and maybe turning to mayhem. Which Duane felt was unfair. At the most, his inner assessment thoughts on the value of this opportunity couldn't have taken more than a minute. "Hello, friends. Welcome to the show!"

Very loud. Like a circus barker. A tent preacher. It was perfect. Moon-Ra tried to start some applause. Got a little.

DUANE'S STORY

"The thing about being from the South is, you get this," he shouted out, hoping to get attention right away. "What we're going through right this very minute. You get it. I mean we all get it. Because we're all in it. We *are* it."

Slight pause as he waited for the yawning and muttering to settle.

Eluvia sat up suddenly, as if startled, then yawned, lay back down. Paulus looked at Nadia, who was snoring lightly. The children were solid asleep. Maybelle, exhausted, had slumped down and was now fully prone on the carpet, no matter its germ count and the possibility of someone stepping on her face.

No one left. He considered it a victory.

"So the South, what I'm saying, is a place that is and isn't at any given moment, you know, because of what it was and what it will be. Whatever it is at the present is never, you know, real. What Faulkner was always getting at. Just look around. By the *South*, what I mean mostly is this city. New Orleans. You know all about New Orleans."

Those that had no idea what he was talking about were roughly evenly matched by those who did, but didn't care. He would bring them all into the tent. If this was a test run for his big production, it was going to be one to remember.

"What you are seeing and smelling and stepping in and getting pushed around by in the belly of this whale—and I'm not going Biblical or anything but damn it seems like that sometimes—anyway it won't be like this tomorrow. Or a week from now. It will be gone. Like every day. Once it's gone, it's history. This—here, now—will be only what you remember of it. Like a second line parade."

He mulled the analogy as soon as he said it, nodded to himself that he was right, got back on topic. "So it is with our idea of New Orleans, where we live."

A dozen or so more people showed up at the back of the crowd. Or maybe just thought they had to stop for a traffic jam.

"And that's why I'm going to make a movie. That's what I want to talk to you about. What I'm trying real hard to tell you about here in the middle of the very essence of the South—good and bad. I want to make a movie about how that works, and doesn't. So I'm calling it, at least the working title, The Southern Guide to Self-Improvement.

Right here in New Orleans!"

He paused to see if there might be even one hand clapping. Not even. He wasn't sure if anyone had really listened. And, you know, Maybelle was a hell of an act to follow.

"It's that title because it's about people in the South, in particular in this city that is the South writ large. Like, you know, like some kind of half-discovered island lost in the ocean mists to everyone but itself."

Blank faces. Those were the most friendly.

"Although it is definitely a part of where it lies, our city is what it is. That reminds me, ever see *Play It as It Lays*? No? Nothing? Never mind. But look, New Orleans lies at the bottom of both the state and the river. But it's the whole South, too. It's what the college professors call a synecdoche. A little thing stands for the whole thing. Like roux in a gumbo. New Orleans for everything we know." He paused to catch his breath from having to talk so loud. Also hoping for a little response. In vain.

He cleared his throat and plunged back in. "So it's about coping with whatever the hell comes our way, is my point. Even now. I mean especially now. Us. Right here. In this place now and before and after. But through a weird kind of lens. You see? It's where we learn how to improve. However we want. You know? I mean like that."

He realized he was communicating in the extremely tall weeds of very deep shit. What expressions he could see in the grayish light could charitably be described as impatient or bored. Or pitying.

Moon-Ra's was the only face with any kind of emotion at all, and Duane was pretty sure it was from being miffed. Duane could almost see the thought bubble above his head: "Movie? You're planning a fucking movie and you never tell me about it until we're here in the middle of the fucking sewer?"

Duane did not let the reactions of his closest comrades deter him. Much was to be discussed later. The problem was the restless audience. He had to do better. It was very important to keep the zombies at bay and thinking of things other than stealing all the Portia family's supplies.

As for Moon-Ra, though, Duane was pretty sure he had mentioned making a movie. Maybe not this specific one. Wasn't it that time after they'd watched *La Dolce Vita* and got into a dispute about Marcello's character and values when they went for a drink? Anyway, who's to say this wasn't the best time to present an artistic revelation that had itself arisen in chaos, between a mugging and a hurricane?

Surely this was something Fellini would capture and shoot.

As his attention wallowed in these thoughts, which he realized were in his head again and not coming out of his mouth, Duane was brought back into the moment by loud angry yells and cries of pain and what probably was a gunshot.

All heads turned to the direction of the noise—far down the hall, maybe that big lobby area. Then, once again, all seemed to go quiet.

"Fuck your movie, man," someone yelled. "Somethin's goin' on."

Duane held up both hands in a kind of wave of acknowledgement. "What I'm saying is, in a nutshell, I'm going to make this movie and it's about New Orleans. And the South around us. And about you and me and the shit we go through and how we cope with it. You know? America itself. And you're all going to be in it. Somehow—"

"Run," someone shouted. "They got guns and hatchets."

CHAPTER 15

Wednesday, August 31, wee hours, continued

The audience instantly fragmented into individual parts in a pretty good version of a stampede. Duane felt like a vaudeville performer who just got the hook.

Moon-Ra and Paulus tried to get everyone awake and back against the wall.

"Shouldn't we get out of here?" Eluvia said.

"No," Moon-Ra said, "we just draw in tighter. Safer until they go by, whatever it is. Move that cart and the bags and boxes in tighter. Keep the kids all together," Paulus shouted. Eluvia and Nadia posted on each side of their own like knights on a chessboard.

Duane hurried over to Maybelle, snoring, as she did sometimes when exhausted, and had to shake her shoulders hard to wake her. She took a half-swing at him, but he stood back until she could get her bearings. She sat up, slapped her cheeks. She looked around, still groggy. "What the hell is going on?"

"We don't know. They just started running from something up that way." Duane pointed and passed her a lantern. Not for the light. For swinging at any attackers.

The noise and crush of the panic increased.

Whatever was pushing in was now maybe only a half-block length away. Duane told Maybelle it was like being in the bowels of a cosmic whale, or more aptly inside a boa constrictor. She looked at him with what might have been an eye-roll if he could have seen it. But he couldn't stop. He said the thing about some poor prey being inside a boa, if it was still alive, was that it only dimly knew what was going on and would presently succumb to digestion unless it could get the fuck out of there.

He said, "That's what we have to do. We have to get the fuck out of here."

She looked at him, the eye-roll now just wide, unblinking eyes, and then back at Moon-Ra, to see if he was listening, which he wasn't. Then she hoisted up a lantern by its handle to make sure she could swing it to crack someone's face.

"I mean it," Duane said, widening his stance in a more aggressive mode as some of the people came too close on their flight path.

"For god's sake, Duane," she said, "for once just pay attention to what's really happening, can you?"

Before he could respond, which probably would have been a mistake, it became impossible to hear anything over the crescendo of trampling feet and screams. Much of it in variations of "get the fuck out of the way."

Maybelle and Duane stood firm, with their lanterns, and Moon-Ra joined them. Warrior Trio of the Convention Center.

"This might not be all that intimidating if they're a bunch of thugs," Maybelle said. "If they want our stuff, we should just give it to them."

"Then we have no water or anything at all," Duane said.

"So what? We're getting the fuck out of here, *correcto*?"

Duane gave her a side glance.

"She's right," Moon-Ra said. "It's not worth a fight if it comes to that."

"I mean, that's really our only goal. Getting out of here," she said. "Right?"

"Fucking A."

They looked down the hall but couldn't see much beyond the inmates. Then, suddenly, a half-dozen or more young men, black and white, all looking like dead-end drug enforcers, pushed through the human clog and sure enough one of them took a hard look at the Portia circle. He pointed and said something to one of his comrades. The gang began to veer over.

Duane set his body hard and ready to clobber somebody, but when he looked at Maybelle, she shook her head. But damn, did she look full-on Amazon warrior.

"I'll talk to them, when they come up, to stall them," Duane told Maybelle. "But you guys fall back and help get Paulus and the kids out of the way. I mean, just leave everything."

"Done."

"Wait. Let me talk to them," Moon-Ra said. "Mostly I see a bunch of brothers." "They won't give a shit what you say."

"He's right," Maybelle said.

Suddenly, they heard Paulus yell out from behind them. "Cray-Cross! That you?" He was looking toward the opposite end of the hallway from which the gang had emerged. He began waving both arms in the air.

The reply came within seconds. "Paulus?"

Duane looked at Moon-Ra, who looked at Maybelle.

"It's me," Paulus yelled.

"We comin' over now. Don't be afraid," came the yell back.

"Hell, no. Come on."

Paulus motioned to Nadia and Eluvia to stay down and rushed over to Duane and Maybelle and Moon-Ra. "It's my half-cousin Craylon, we call him Cray-Cross. With the Sanctified Knights."

A small group of young black men began to separate itself from the crowd.

"They're friendlies, right?" Duane said.

"Mos' def."

"I heard of them," Moon-Ra said. "They work the streets out of his momma's church. Like a gang but mostly good."

"I heard of them, too," Maybelle said. "I think we had one as a client."

"Hurry," Paulus yelled out again. "See those boys coming on from down there the other way?"

"We seen 'em before. Stay put," Cray-Cross answered.

Within seconds he and the Sanctified Knights were at the circle. They all wore black, with white crosses on their shirts and black bandanas with crosses on their heads.

"These my friends. We're holed up like a fort here until morning," Paulus explained to Cray-Cross as he approached. He swept his arm to indicate who he was talking about. "We been fine, mostly," he said, "but those guys coming—"

The thugs stopped short a few yards away, as if they'd hit an invisible wall, or maybe a turf boundary. Three or four of the gang leaned in to talk like they were doing a quick huddle, all of them eyeing the Sanctified Knights, who had quickly formed what looked like an assault line.

Cray-Cross said something to his crew, who bunched up even tighter, Roman Legion formation. They played eye games with the gang but said nothing. After a minute or so of tension, the gang boss uttered, "Fuck this bullshit," and strode back into the hall. The others followed and they disappeared in the flow.

The Knights held formation until Cray-Cross raised a fist. They relaxed and cracked wise with each other for "beating those punks down with our mind-control," as one of them said to an array of fist-pumping.

"They just terrorizing everybody because they can," Cray-Cross said to Paulus, looking in the direction where the gang had gone. "We seen lots of this the last two days. That's why we stayed inside this place. We figured the Lord be glad for us to watch over all these poor people in here. At least the ones we can get to. They's so many. So many."

"Amen," from the Knights behind him.

"You been here that long?" Paulus said.

"Yeah. We couldn't get into the Superdome without giving up what we need"—he lifted his shirt to display the handle of a pistol. "So we heard we could at least get our bearings down at the Convention Center so we come here. Nobody checks nothing.

Then, you know, we had to stay."

"I wish I'd seen you before," Paulus said.

"Well, you know, it's hard to find anybody in this mess, except the troublemakers."

"True."

Duane held out a hand to Cray-Cross. "Not sure we'd have made it. I mean, I'm sure. We wouldn't have."

Cray-Cross seemed to consider shaking it, then did. "You planning on leaving soon?"

"Come morning, absolutely."

"Good idea."

"Look, we've got water and enough food to share. Come sit with us a little and rest up, eat."

Cray-Cross looked toward his crew. "I could use something to drink," one of them said. "And eat," said another.

"Stay," said Paulus. "We can catch up. Maybe you can leave with us in the morning."

"I don't think the Lord's ready for that yet. We have to see," Cray-Cross said, looking around. "But sure, we could take a little rest here. We been on our feet since this afternoon."

With that, Duane and Maybelle and Moon-Ra opened the circle and dug out water bottles and boxes of concession snacks from the Portia. Cray-Cross and the Knights inhaled the food and sat or stretched out on the floor. They were clearly needing a break. Cray-Cross told them it was okay to grab some sleep, because they'd be headed back down to the lobby at the end of the hall soon to see if they could do anything about the entrance and exit. He said that he or Paulus would take the watch because they couldn't sleep.

The two shared snippets of family gossip that neither particularly cared about, but some small talk seemed useful after not seeing each other for many months. In a strictly structural way, it almost seemed like a picnic.

Except it was coming up dawn pretty soon, they were refugees from a Cat 4 or Cat 3 or however many Cats, their chosen place of shelter was a swarm of terrified pseudo-zombies, and there was as much danger inside as there was outside on the flooded streets of the city that would never again be the Big Easy.

CHAPTER 16

Wednesday, August 31, O dark thirty

Once the immediate distraction of being stalked by thugs had subsided, and the boredom of collateral captivity had returned to the hall, and the sun yet to shine, Duane said they should resume the storytelling. If nothing else, it had smoothed out some of the night, and protected their highly vulnerable haven. As the recent rush of danger had shown, the Portia circle couldn't withstand armed attackers. And wouldn't have without the arrival of the Sanctified Knights.

He got a yes vote from the family, mostly awake again, since sleep was no longer an option for anyone but children. Cray-Cross and his Knights hadn't been in on the earlier shows and also gave it a thumbs-up, but really most of them wanted to catch some zzz's and were stretching out on the carpet.

But Duane didn't want to do it again. Maybelle thought about it but felt too spun out. Which basically left Moon-Ra.

Duane set it up again, using his carny barker bellow to lure the current strain of passing *misérables.*

"Okay, everybody . . . Here we go . . . Story Time Number Three. Triple Feature. Take a minute to join us. That's right, just come on over. It's a free show for everyone trapped in this miserable, smelly hell's ark. And this time the storyteller we are graced with is the great blues and jazz musician and master of movie theaters and son of one of our city's great preachers—our own Moon-Ra!"

A handful of people paused, curious. So Duane repeated more

or less the same pitch, several times. Each time luring a few more who, as before, really had nothing else to do. He was surprised, in a good way.

When maybe fifty or more, with more stopping, had gathered, Duane raised a fist as a sign of solidarity, beckoned Moon-Ra to come stand with him. Which Moon-Ra did, after Maybelle embraced him and kissed him, which drew unseemly whistles from the crowd, but definitely put Moon-Ra in a more relaxed mood. At least relaxed enough to take the plunge into early twenty-first-century ersatz crowd control.

"So let me tell you a story of my own," he began, modulating his voice and straightening up as Maybelle had done so he could look the part. He'd done that a lot playing bass in the clubs, so it came fairly naturally. He had a presence.

"It's from the beginning of time in the endlessness of the sky above." He spread his arms as if enveloping the universe. "Not that we can see the sky right now, but we will before long. Meanwhile it can see us, and so what I want to do is take us all up there now, in a time of our blindness, to see that light that I know is up there. Is out there. Is in all of us.

"My name is Moon-Ra and I grew up in this city but I come from up there." He pointed to the sky, or at least the ceiling.

"That sounds more like it," a voice yelled.

"We got us a preacher man now," said another.

Moon-Ra waited for the audience to settle into the groove, and then took it much deeper.

MOON-RA'S STORY

"I wasn't brought up by my name, Moon-Ra," he began, "because it wasn't until I was nearly twenty years old it came to me who I really was, and why. Before that I was just Curtis, just another kid in Lower Ninth and then Seventh Ward in this city doing his best to get through school and not get killed or pulled into a gang or all the other things that happen around us every day. And which"—he gestured to Cray-Cross and the Knights—" fine young men like my second cousin over here and the Sanctified Knights do what they do every day and night to keep the evil from running over all the young men and ladies of the ward and anywhere else."

He clapped for them and somewhat to his surprise most of the new, and expanding, crowd did the same. Cray-Cross stood, bowed, and raised a solidarity fist. Duane did the same. Maybelle smiled and let out a big breath.

The clapping and shouts of approval subsided. All eyes seriously on Moon-Ra. It felt like playing a great gig in a noisy club. He set about it.

"Like most of you, I guess, I always thought we got here the way the Bible said, when the Lord made the world and Adam and Eve got it all started. And that was fine, and I got nothing against that at all. But I often went to my Aunt Corina's church, mother of Paulus over here"—he pointed him out—" you probably know her as Reverend Youngblood if you're from that part of the city. And over the years I listened. I listened to the way she talked about the stories in the Bible that were also about more things that came out of Africa. It kind of put the Garden of Eden in more perspective. But being a little kid and then a teenager who normally didn't listen to no one, I never really contemplated it like I might have.

"And then one day I was over helping my aunt dig up a broken water pipe in her yard so it could be fixed and after that I sat with her on her back screen porch and drank some cold tea and she told me this amazing story. It took her almost three hours." He put up his hands like making a stop-right-there signal. "You don't need those looks. I'm not gonna take near that long. Just the basic 411, you know? So you'll know how all this came to be. Even what we doing being right here, right now. How this came to be."

Some laughter.

"We got all night, or what's left of it," one old man's voice yelled out, and more ripples of laughter. Moon-Ra knew he had them, smiled and gave the old man a thumbs-up.

"So just stay with me, brother. Now, what I was saying—you look at things that way, you know, like my auntie the preacher told me, about how all this came to be. Even if it's bad, you can see how it fits in. You can see maybe how even the worst suffering, which we have to be pretty much in tonight from here all the way over to Mississippi and even Florida"—spontaneous groans from the listeners— "even that kind of suffering fits into something bigger. You can't really call it 'beautiful,' like a lot of people say sometimes about the way the world fits together. Because nothing about this hurricane is beautiful. But our suffering does fit into some other word that only God and the holy spirits might know but that covers us anyway."

The faces out there, now regularly popping out "amens," reminded him of what he had seen in the St. Claude House of Spirit Glory where Aunt Corina preached. Where Moon-Ra had sat many a Sunday alongside Paulus and his older brother, Jean-Pierre, the brother that got shot at Jazzfest that time. Something like hope and despair all scrunched together in a single word. Or maybe he was just being vain.

"So even though this world was created by God, it was always part of something more. Way more. And that's what auntie wanted us to see. Or learn how to see. So join me here now and just give that a moment." He closed his eyes. Maybe some in the hall did, too. "So think that everything we know, that we see, all around us, from the darkest swamp to the brightest spot on the sun, is just a small little flea of a thing on the back of some giant beast you can't even see but parts of it at a time galloping through space."

"Fuck is he sayin'?"

"He blasphemin'."

"You people, can you just be quiet so we can hear the Moon-Man?"

"Yeah, shut up. You got something better to do, go someplace else."

150

Moon-Ra paused. He'd heard all that kind of thing before, people talking about his aunt and what she said about voudou and the spirits and Jesus and God all rolled into one.

"Look, take it easy. This just a story, okay? Pretend you walked into a movie. You want to see what it's all about? You don't believe there's really a Godzilla or Darth Vader or King Kong or any that, right? So hear me out. Or don't. But I'm testifying anyway. This is what the Reverend Youngblood, my Aunt Corina, said was really behind what we're all about." He nodded to himself. "Yessir. All about."

"Man wants to enlighten you. Do yourself a favor and let it happen." It was Cray-Cross, stepping forward, arms folded across his chest. The catcalls and wisecracks stopped.

Moon-Ra nodded to his cousin, then took a step or two forward toward what he had just noticed was an upturned wooden produce crate, abandoned by someone. He moved it back to his spot near the perimeter and pushed down one leg and then the other just to test it for strength. He stood atop it.

"This world isn't the beginning of anything or the end," he said. "It's just a place on the way. That's what she explained to me, and said the truth of it all came from where it all started. Africa. Only not from there. It came from the spirit connection that Africa had with the serpent that surrounds and protects all life, and his name, African name, is called Damballah-Wedo. That's what she told me.

"She said maybe other countries or other universes call it something else, but that's how she knew it when she was coming up because that's what her own great-grandmother, who was a slave who came over from around Nigeria, that part of Africa, told her.

"Her great-grandma was just a little girl when she was packed on one of those slave ships. She didn't know hardly any English words all her life, and at the end, her throat had the cancer, so she couldn't talk much, but Aunt Corina said she understood her great-grandma anyway, they called her Mama Leona from the name the owners gave her.

"Auntie said her own soul felt the parts that didn't have words from Mama Leona, and that's how she got into the saving souls and second-sight business herself once she grew up over in Algiers and the Lower Ninth."

"Where I live," someone said. "Us, too," said another.

Moon-Ra put his palms together as if offering a prayer to the Ninth, then went on. "So back to the big snake. So it had more worlds than we can count in his belly, like we were all babies being protected and coming to life and none of us knew about the others, or maybe just a few did but nobody would believe them. And it went on like that for more millions of years than you have hairs on your head and there weren't any wars or fighting because there wasn't anything to war or fight about. I can't really tell you more than that because it was too far back and even Aunt Corina didn't know, so I don't. But I know what happened next."

"They put you in the insane asylum?"

"You stopped smokin' weed and sobered up?"

Cray-Cross stepped forward toward the wisecrackers. So did two of the other Knights who had nodded off at the circle but now were engrossed in Moon-Ra's story. The comments stopped.

"It's okay, it's okay," Moon-Ra said. "I know this all sounds made up and weird and stuff. But let me tell it out."

"Tell it."

"It's blasphemin'."

"Finish the story, man."

Moon-Ra paused, held up one hand to signal Cray-Cross to let it go.

"So before time was even time, and Damballah-Wedo went across the skies that nobody could even see or imagine, he was just minding his own business, or her business—Auntie says the serpent had to be female, logically—and out of nowhere, literally, something like a hurricane wind, times a gazillion gazillion, and blinding white-hot, smashed into her belly.

"There's no kind of force we know to relate to how powerful it was. But it was powerful enough to knock that huge snake-mother-incubator into another dimension and to force her to cough up the worlds inside her and spew them out into the new darkness of an entirely new and strange part of existence. It's what we call our universe, and there wasn't anything in it at the time. But when Damballah-Wedo was pushed through, and the worlds came out, so did billions of other things we would call stars and planets and asteroids and all the things that we live in now.

"And most of those worlds died out or got lost, but in one of them a few people were saved, and some animals. They didn't look nothing like they do today but they were alive, and eventually they figured out who they were and what they were supposed to do."

Moon-Ra began to cough with the thickness of the motionless humid air. No catcalls this time. One of the Sanctified Knights handed him a bottle of water. He drank half of it and the cough cleared. He looked out into the dimness of the hall to see that the crowd around him had increased. And dawn was definitely coming.

People would be antsy.

"Mother Damballah didn't have emotions like we do, but she knew she had been disrupted by a force she could not name or fathom. She knew everything was different now, and all that she had been guarding had been hammered out of her belly. And now wherever she was had not even existed but it was a part of her down to every last and tiniest element. As soon as she knew that she knew her new place. She did. She surely did.

"She unstretched her body beyond what could be seen or even imagined and with a whip of her tail pulled herself into a coil that marked the farthest reaches of the new universe and allowed her to feel the tingle of other things behind that. But inside, it was the life and worlds she had created, and pushed out from the power that struck her. And she would guard that now and forever, and within her coil of protection would be worlds beyond worlds, creations within creations, life within life, cold nothingness and fiery entrails of light and heat.

"She was above time and creation and any measurements of any kind and she would never again be struck by the unknown winds and lights. And she settled."

Moon-Ra caught a breath. "When we get out of here, whenever the clouds are gone and you can see the sky again, look up, and even if you can't see her, she is out there."

"Jesus save us."

"Load of crap."

"Let the man talk, dammit. Why you people can't just listen?"

"He goin' to hell for sayin' all this."

"I heard of that snake. I got a grandma, too. Over in Mississippi."

"That it?"

Moon-Ra let it simmer down again. The Knights did the same.

"Well I know it ain't what we learned in the Bible, and you don't need to worry if you don't want to think about it. What Aunt Corina said was even if we are protected by Damballah-Wedo, and we can't even see her or really imagine it, doesn't mean that our own God and Jesus couldn't come up over the years for us. And doesn't mean that where the first people still had some kind of way of sensing Damballah-Wedo, and then the spirits that came up around her in Africa, that those African ways people call voudou or like that can't be part of the Jesus we also got in church.

"Really, Aunt Corina's whole life is based on trying to explain that to everyone. I guess a little like I'm doing now, so that you can have something else to think about besides where you're actually standing right now and what you're going through right this minute in this horrible place."

"You believe in all that?"

"I do."

"That why they call you Moon-Ra?"

"Well I was starting to say that before. Maybe a little. I didn't feel like the name I got when I was born really suited me. I was a guy named Curtis and I looked up at the stars at night all the time and I daydreamed a lot. I even went into sort of trances sometimes when I was really into a strong bass line, like in jazz or reggae especially. 'Rivers of Babylon,' you know, man, that pretty much says it.

"You all heard of Sun-Ra, I'm guessing or hoping. I always liked that name and his whole thing, but it didn't seem me and anyway it was already taken." He looked at Cray-Cross, who, like Moon-Ra's relatives and close friends, knew about the name change already. "But I was most definitely Moon-Ra. So that's what I asked everyone to call me from then on."

He laughed, and then everyone did, as people laugh when they've just come from a very strange place.

Then Duane walked up and said something to him no one else could hear.

"So my former boss-man Duane here says it will be breaking light in maybe a half hour. I know all of you can't split right now because you got nowhere to stay and no house left to stay in. And I hate to leave you. But just stay safe a little longer."

Whoops and random catcalls.

"I love you and I thank you for sticking with me and all of us and we were just trying to make the night a little shorter by all our blabbing and storifying. So good-bye and good luck."

The audience held together briefly, multiple conversations and muddled shouts, then broke apart as if a rubber band around it had popped.

Paulus and Cray-Cross came up to shake hands, as did Maybelle and Duane. Cray-Cross and Duane promised to get in touch after all this was over and the Knights told everyone good-bye and pushed into the hall.

Paulus and Moon-Ra took charge of repacking anything that was left from the Portia's store of water and snacks, which wasn't much after the giveaways.

Nadia and Eluvia gathered the few small bags of clothing and essentials they had brought in. The four kids watched all the

155

adults and then Rael and Edwin needed the bathroom. Paulus volunteered. Their old spot to pee had been taken but they found a new one a half-block down. Then everyone sat, quietly, as the light came.

CHAPTER 17

Wednesday, August 31, first light

Boy Jack had a bad feeling the hotel security would find him before long, even though he'd been cagey as hell getting inside and up the stairs to the fourteenth floor and then into a room where he didn't have to bust open the door, which would have been a sure sign to the dicks. The water was running, which was a good surprise since he only had a few plastic bottles. It was the only surprise. No lights and no air conditioning and nothing at all from the grid. But he had a good view of the river and also the lower half of the Convention Center, increasingly decorated with sidewalks swollen with people in far worse condition than he was.

He did appreciate his fortune. The family he'd followed up to the boulevard in front of the Convention Center two days ago had gone inside, he was pretty sure. But one look and he'd known it wasn't for him. That's how he decided to hike down the street toward Poydras Avenue, maybe he'd find something over in the Quarter.

En route was when he thought to check out a big hotel more or less across the street from the casino. He'd made a few deliveries there for Mr. Croydon. Mostly small vases and statues for well-off clients who couldn't be bothered to come to the store and pick up their purchases. Boy Jack liked those kinds of clients, though. In addition to the delivery fee, half of which he got to keep, there was also a fat tip every time, and he got to keep all of that. Also, they were frequently drinking or otherwise high and that increased their generosity.

As he got closer he could see that the hotel's front door was shattered and blown off its hinges. He walked through the empty but litter-strewn check-in island and taxi loop to take a quick look into the lobby. His main concern was po-po, but no badges and no squad cars. And nobody else there except some bewildered-looking tourists and a few homeless who probably would be headed for the Convention Center since nobody was around to give them any money.

He waited until the loop had cleared completely, and slipped inside. He spotted a door to a staircase just past the registration desk, and went to it, watching and listening all the way. But it was just him, at least for the time being. The staircase door was unlocked, which was the law. He went into the stairwell and started climbing. At the fourteenth floor landing he had a gut feeling it would be safe to look around, and did.

Turned out his intuition was solid. As soon as he stepped into the beige-carpeted hall, he could tell the fourteenth was both innocuous enough and in decent enough shape. For sure, doors had been blown off some of the rooms and lay in the hall or hung loosely from hinges. He peeped inside a couple, and it was mostly shattered windows and broken glass and everything soaked. A few with standing water. But he found many of the rooms still intact. One was especially clean and dry, like it had been vacant when the storm hit. He took it. Pretty decent foraging, he said to himself. Still had the touch.

He felt like a king that first night, albeit without power and only trickles of water. Up where he was, he could push open the sliding glass door to the narrow balcony to let in fresh air, and a bit of ambient light, although the city was mostly dark itself. The open door also meant he could hear the yelling and the crying and the cursing and the sirens, sirens, sirens. Even a helicopter. That was fine. He was inside, dry, and with enough snacks and bottled water from Mr. Croydon's house for maybe two days, after which he figured he'd either move on or the dicks would be throwing him out if they found him.

If he'd gone inside the Convention Center, though, his life expectancy already would have expired. He knew he'd be no match for whatever was in there. Poor Mr. Croydon would have gotten his body, because the police no doubt would have found one of the Croydon Imports business cards inside a wallet, or, if that were stolen, a pocket. Boy Jack mused on the permutations of his soul had he played the last few days differently. But he couldn't keep the thread and anyway croaking was probably not the sort of thing he should be thinking about. He should be thinking about how he was going to live.

It had been two days and two nights. Maybe he could hold out longer, but his gut said time to vamoose. Also, he was getting tired of no electricity, and just the feeling of being trapped. He'd slept later than he intended but had time for a rinse-off in the shower, which still had a little water in the pipes. He started packing up what few things he had acquired and to his surprise in the pocket of a spare shirt he came across the butt of a joint he must have smoked before Katrina dropped by. He could think of no solid reason not to enrich the situation with herb and also calm his nerves. He took a Bic lighter from the plastic sandwich bag serving to hold his toothbrush, razor, and other basic needs, and got appropriately buzzed.

Out on the balcony he leaned against the guard rail and beheld in the soft morning light a swath of what was left of the city. Across the casino lot toward the river and then on to Algiers and, although he couldn't see that far, the marshes leading into the great Gulf from which the hellion had come and made short shrift of the vanity of humanity and its habitations. The view was majestic, in its own way. And terrible. Boy Jack was so fucked up by the doob that he knew being fucked up to analyze and reflect on his circumstances was completely and totally right fucking on.

Elsewhere, dawn brought its own terrors. As the sun's heat gives new fuel to hurricanes, so does it ignite fits of aggression and its sister, purpose, to animals. Humans, specifically. Now red-orange rays slid over the deep blue-black of vanishing night until the daily burn filled the endless scarlet corridor of the Center with ugliness and clarity. Duane watched the movements of the trapped people, now fully illuminated, as they hurried around as if they would actually accomplish anything. They seemed oblivious that their efforts looked even more pathetic than in the night.

They remained utterly destitute. Still no food, little if any water, no changes of clothes. If they brought in their babies, they also had diapers and baby clothes full of baby shit that had nowhere to be discarded, except on the floors. Which accounted for as much of the choking odor as any kind of adult urine puddles or piles of excrement. The restrooms grew more vile by the hour. Only junkies could stand them. Odiferous hiding places where they could shoot up or snort or maybe ambush some clueless refugee who unknowingly wandered in.

As lawless chaos and complete breakdown of the social order, the Center was in a league of its own. Duane granted this rarity a certain respect, although he still had enough sense despite sleep deprivation to know not to convey such morbid cynicism aloud. He had already told the Portia family what was important, beyond the mess, the suffering, the nightmare: "We have to get the fuck out of here."

Paulus and Eluvia, the only others already awake, joined him in gently nudging the dormant family to rise and saddle up. It wasn't easy. They'd only had a couple hours' sleep. Although the kids might normally have been the biggest balkers at such an early alarm, Edwin, Sam, Elena, and Rael sat up right away, trying to take in what they could now see around them. The adults stretched and groaned. Then they moved quickly. The Sanctified Knights had already gone.

Within fifteen minutes the bags and supplies were ready. Exactly when screams broke out at the upriver end of the hall, the opposite direction from where the Knights had gone. Then a fast burst of gunfire. Another human wave of terrified innocents surged past. Then a half-dozen more shots.

In the light, Duane could now see uncountable wheelchairs, mostly overturned, and one metal cart on wheels that looked somehow imported from a hospital. Here, it was being used to carry a very thin and sick-looking young man in a hospital gown and sweatpants. As the cart veered out of the main rush of people, Duane could see the man's eyes, locked and glassy, the kind of stare that comes shortly before nothingness.

"Back, get against the wall tight as we can," Paulus yelled. They did, the children protected by the adults. It took nearly ten minutes for this latest push of the terrified to pass. Each minute a possibility that someone would lose their shit entirely.

"They don't even know where they're going," Maybelle said. "When they get to the end they'll just have to turn back. Or try to get outside."

"Cray-Cross told me the cops out there are trying not to let anyone out. At least last night," Paulus said.

"I feel sorry for them. My God, do we look that bad?" Eluvia said.

"At least," Maybelle said.

A middle-aged white man wearing only boxer shorts veered against the Portia line, glancing off Maybelle and knocking Nadia and Rael, just behind her, off-balance. Moon-Ra immediately caught the man by his arm and hurled him back into the wave. The man stumbled into another person, who also pushed him, and the man fell to the floor. He got up quickly, wobbling slightly, and looked back at the Portia circle. He never said anything. His bloodshot eyes implied he had no idea what he was doing or where he was.

Moon-Ra shook his head. He wasn't angry. But no one was going to touch anyone in the family. The thought occurred that he would have killed the man without pause and never regretted it, had it been necessary.

The panic and chaos were weakening, but the adults still stood tightly together in front of the kids. No way of knowing if a secondary flow of gunshot refugees would erupt.

"Did you hear that woman say somebody was dead up there?" Maybelle said. "That one in the orange gym pants and the red hair?" Apparently no one did.

"There's rumors of dead people all up and down the building," Paulus said. "Or put in the freezers up there in the kitchen. Cray said he was pretty sure he'd seen a body or two out on the boulevard in front."

The adults shared looks of alarm, but let it go when they realized the children were paying close attention.

"Okay, I'm gonna check one of those doors near where we came in, up by where Cray-Cross was going. I think we can get out through it,"

Moon-Ra said, breaking away. "I'll be right back." He was gone before anyone could answer, moving through the zombie bodies with a surprising deftness. In his mind he thought it was like a bass line through a complicated riff, and he had no idea how that thought had even emerged.

"Form up behind me while we're waiting, along the wall," Duane said, turning to the rest of the family. "We'll be ready to step off as soon as he's back. Paulus, you and Maybelle take up the rear. Everybody else in between. When we leave, don't let anybody follow us. When Moon gets back, we'll plow through that field of people. We'll just go straight for the door he found and get outside and keep going. There's a bunch of people on the sidewalks, though. So when we're out, just follow me." He paused, looked at each of them. "Good with y'all?"

"Good," said Paulus.

"We're going back to the Portia?" Maybelle said.

"Maybe. If we can all make it that far. Anyone?"

"We're in. At least that far," Paulus said.

"I don't even know if we got a house to go back to. Or any place," Nadia said.

"Nobody does," said Eluvia. "I say go to the Portia and get our bearings."

"That's the plan, then," Duane said. "We can stay there as long as we want, as long as we need to come up with the next plan."

"Like that movie you was talking about doing?" Eluvia said. Her mouth twisting into a weird smile, her eyes unable not to roll. "That plan?"

Duane shrugged. "I guess it does seem kind of nuts right now."

Eluvia made a zip-it line across her mouth with her finger. "Sorry. Just nervous."

But they formed the line, and made ready to book as soon as they got the word. Jitters and taunts aside. Fear also aside. Other things, inside.

They spent the next half hour on high alert, perusing the still-bulging, still-churning hall of the damned. Each hoped to be the first to see a triumphant Moon-Ra coming back from wherever he went.

CHAPTER 18

Wednesday, August 31, *dawn*

He did show up, which everyone knew was a toss-up, but no one ever said. He was sweating and wild-eyed. Like some bad spirit had been inside him and was flaring out of raw flesh. The news was mixed. The door to the street that he tried was locked with a chain from the outside. He said no one knew why, but Cray-Cross was in the thick of it trying to figure it out.

He said people had huddled against the door overnight and were still either sleeping or leaning against it. He said they looked like they were dead. He said the expressions on their faces were like things from horror movies. He didn't realize the expressions had infected his own countenance. But as he explained what he had seen, he knew everyone around him was glued to something in his own face so terrible that no one, not even the kids, could look at him straight on.

But he said there might be another way, and they had to try it, because everything he saw was proof they had to get out of there. He'd seen another entry door about a block or so down the hall, in the upriver direction. There was no chain inside or out. He said he waited until no one was paying attention to him and pushed down the handle and it opened. He could tell somebody had already broken the lock to escape. The briefest smile flashed across his face, for even in this time of torment, Moon-Ra had a sense of the spiritual and the confused strivings of man. But he had details to spell out. That was the core of his story. So he got back to it.

They could get out that door, but to get there, they'd have to work through a shitload of people who were getting nastier with every minute. Daylight meant they could see and find new misery in every step. Outside was worse. Humans were clumped together like mounds of trash needing someone to load them up and dump them in a big landfill where the wild dogs roamed and crows and buzzards and flies zoomed.

With daylight, the sidewalk people, too, could see how bad it was and how much worse it could get, but they were also afraid that leaving the Center would mean they wouldn't get any food and water at all when it arrived. Which it still had not.

Moon-Ra said he understood better than before the confusion inside and outside the Center about what to do, and how, and when, and why. They really had been abandoned, like everyone was saying. In the heart of the city. He said that not one politician nor cop nor sheriff nor city official had offered guidance or help to the souls in the Center. He said outside he heard an older white woman call it a "concentration camp disguised as a shelter."

Po-po did drive by at intervals but accomplished little. They were afraid of what might happen, too. And the damn thing was they were right. So they were doing what cops always do under stress. Looking for people to arrest, so it would seem like they were in control.

Everywhere in the city, they were eager to catch looters and strays and desperadoes who until Sunday night before Katrina hit had been living in their own homes or apartments or maybe even on the streets but now were parts of the menace. Instead of being rescued, they were under suspicion. As far as the police were concerned.

Same with the busloads of quasi-police on generous per diem from all over the country who'd arrived and soon would be walking the streets and driving the boulevards and acting like tough hombres sent to quell an insurrection. A black one, of course.

And then there were the snipers. Everyone was on the lookout for snipers. Snipers! Because a few shots had been fired. Maybe. Later, in the outside world that awaited them, people would ask Duane if any of that back then was really true. Was it really that bad? Were there really snipers? It got to where he didn't even want to respond.

They had to get the fuck out.

Duane and Moon-Ra and Maybelle and Eluvia huddled for a moment to try to figure the most direct path through the chaos to the unlocked door. It wasn't rocket science. Just start walking. Everyone spent a few minutes double-checking that they had everything that was left of their supplies. They stuck to the formation plan: Moon-Ra leading the way, Duane as back-up. Then the moms and kids, then Maybelle and Paulus.

"We're good," Maybelle called out from back of the line. Moon-Ra raised his arm and pushed it forward. "Let's go. Stay tight."

Getting out meant plenty of bumps and minor detours. "I can't believe they haven't even opened up the damn exhibit rooms," Maybelle called out to Duane, not caring anymore if anyone was listening. "Good God, all these people could at least be able to spread out."

Nonetheless, they made it to the exit faster than expected, then stopped because a middle-aged man was stretched out prone in front of it. Duane raised his arm in a signal to hold up. Moon-Ra leaned down and asked the man to move. No response.

"Let's slide him," Duane said, and bent down to grab the man's ankles. Moon-Ra took the man's wrists and gave him another look. "I think he's passed out. Drunk, most likely." They slid him a few feet away, against the windows. A man and woman walking by watched them and stopped, maybe thinking they were muggers, but figured it out and moved along.

"Cops or anybody out there gonna try to stop us if we leave?" Duane said, looking at the man again to make sure he was still out cold.

"I don't see how they can," Moon-Ra said. "Ain't nothing out there to stop nobody."

"I overheard some gossip about that."

"Nobody knows anything," Moon-Ra shrugged.

"Let's go, then."

Duane opened and held the door and Moon-Ra raised his arm to the family in a follow-me sign. They squeezed out. Duane called out to Moon-Ra when they were clear, and pushed the door shut. A few people on the sidewalk noticed them but didn't care. Maybelle thought it strange. On the other hand, what were they supposed to say, "Hey, nice meeting you, have a nice day?"

Duane guided the file along the sidewalk as Moon-Ra fell in with Eluvia and the boys. People were bunched up, some still asleep, some on the concrete, some in folding chairs or sleeping bags. Thousands in every direction, as far as he could see. Maybelle's estimate of the numbers was looking accurate. Maybe even low. There was no way to take a straight path to the boulevard and cross it. Duane looked back over his shoulder constantly to make sure everyone was still with him.

Once they'd made it to the curb, Duane had everyone pull up into a huddle to catch their breaths. While they all confirmed they were okay, they were able to get a good look, too, at where they had been. "My God," Nadia said. Her kids clung to her arms. And who could not be mesmerized by the sheer monstrosity of it? It was like watching giant schools of fish in the ocean, moving and changing shape constantly. Unpredictably. Evading the predators for as long as possible.

Eluvia drew Samuel and Edwin close as an older couple who smelled worse than they looked stumbled past, mumbling about rumors of free food. "Let's go," Duane said, when he saw a good opening and signaled Moon-Ra to get everyone to follow across the boulevard's grass median. They did, but slowly.

"My Lord, they's a dead man in that strip in the middle of the street," Eluvia suddenly said, grabbing Moon-Ra's arm. Moon-Ra could see it, twenty or thirty yards away, toward the bridge. It was a black man, maybe middle-aged, stretched on his back. Bloated and distended. Moon-Ra couldn't tell if it was the same body he'd seen before, but it looked different.

"Where?" "Can I see?" the children asked. First one, then all. Paulus and Nadia glanced at Eluvia and exchanged quick looks. Moon-Ra called out to Duane, who stopped the column on the median. Moon-Ra and Paulus lifted the kids up to satisfy their curiosity. Paulus said they ought to see it so they wouldn't just keep wondering. But very quickly. "They need to remember this, but that's enough."

"It's not the only body," Maybelle said, walking up to Duane while the children were still trying to see the dead. She waved in the direction of the casino. A corpse of some kind was slouched in a wheelchair, covered head to foot in black trash bags, as if they would provide privacy or respect. A few scared-looking dogs moved around the body as if it were a pile of debris.

"Keep going," Duane said, and started for the lot on the other side of the boulevard, passing behind an abandoned pickup truck with a cable repair service sign pasted on its doors. The lot had once been for public parking but was now just an urban eyesore covered with puddles, mounds of wind-strewn junk, a half-dozen cars that no one had been able to rescue in time, and piles of human and animal shit. Also two dead cats and what might have been half-eaten rats.

A few people wandered past, seemingly trying to figure out if there was anything they could use amid the debris and ready to head off toward downtown if not. A few others were camped out at the far end of the block, across a narrow line leading to the hotels and business buildings. This was called the warehouse district, or maybe the arts district, depending on how you wanted to look at it. Duane looked at it as a place to regroup.

One good thing: they could see the sky again. It was enough to bring them to a stop to look up at puffy white clouds and patches of blue. "Thank you, Jesus," Paulus said.

Duane said they had to keep going. "Still think you can you make it to the Portia?" he asked Moon-Ra. "I mean, can they?" Duane waved one arm in the general direction of Uptown, and another at their exhausted group. They had all heard him.

"I know what you're saying, man, but look, we made it here. We can get back the same way." He looked at his sister. "Eluvia here, and Nadia, they already told me the kids could make it."

"We did," said Nadia.

"And I mean, where else would we go?" said Eluvia.

"What she said," echoed Paulus. "It sounds lot more likely than trying to get back to our place."

"For sure we can't even go back to ours," Eluvia said, instantly regretting it when she saw the looks on the faces of Sam and Edwin.

"So we agree? Keeping on to the Portia?" Duane said.

"Yeah, and we need to keep moving," said Maybelle. "I think some of those guys over there are looking us over." She started walking in the direction of Uptown. The adults glanced at each other, and at the people Maybelle had pointed out. Moon-Ra started off after her and then everyone else fell in step. This time Duane taking up rear guard.

For about a dozen paces.

Which is when they heard the booming holler of a south Louisiana drawl.

"Yo, Portia dude! Remember me?"

Duane stopped. The others did the same. Even Maybelle, though she was several yards ahead and determined to get out of that lot.

Duane's head was the first to turn, warily. He couldn't locate the voice at first. Then, almost 180 degrees later, target acquired. Son of a bitch, he thought. Son. Of. A. Bitch.

"Boy Jack? That you?" He had to yell, too, because of the distance.

"In the fucking flesh, movie man."

"Son of a bitch. You okay?"

"All good, brother. Where you headed?"

He began crossing a side street from the hotel he'd just abandoned, and on to the lot. Stepping around a puddle, he almost tripped on a busted-open suitcase that probably had been destined for one of the big cruise ships that tied up on the wharf behind the Center.

"Back to the Portia, turns out. You?" No more need to yell. Boy Jack was closing fast.

"I got nowhere to go, man. Mind if I walk with you a ways?"

Duane smiled, turned back to the others, including Maybelle, who'd come back from her lead-scout position, and shrugged his shoulders. Raised his hands like "who knew?"

Then, "He's okay. Met him just before the storm when he came to pick up his free tickets for the Billy Jack retrospective. Works for an antique store down around the Quarter. I forget which one. He helped me board up the Portia building. He's a good kid."

Maybelle and the others looked at each other. Then at Boy Jack, standing like a guy hoping to get hired on a job call. "Fine," she said. Her tone a slack-jawed, overtired, blind-sided kind of what-the-fuck-now sense of resignation.

"Okay by me," Moon-Ra said, a little more welcoming. "If he can keep up."

"Can you?" Duane asked.

"All the way. No problem."

Maybelle strode off again, waiting for no one. Eluvia and Nadia and the kids right behind her, then Paulus, and Moon-Ra, and then Duane and Boy Jack. Not exactly a column anymore, more like a bunch of people walking in the same direction. Within a couple of blocks, Duane and Moon-Ra closed the gap with Maybelle and took the lead as it was in the previous column formation.

Maybelle didn't care who was in front. Such a man thing. Actually, it was all good with her. If they ran into any trouble along the way, better that the big boys run into it first. Serve them right, too. The thought crossed her mind that she wished she had a gun.

She never had wished for anything like that. But now she did, and she didn't care.

Boy Jack stuck to the back, behind Paulus, aware he was the add-on and not wanting to press his luck. In his nervousness to fit in, he tripped over a chunk of tire tread and dropped his bag at one point. It took him a minute to get it all back together but he caught up by the next block. He apologized to Paulus and struck up a conversation, giving him a brief sketch of his last couple of days on the fourteenth floor. Paulus thought it was cool.

"Hey, your boy here was holed up in that hotel across the street. We shoulda thought of that," Paulus yelled up to Duane at the front.

"So what was it like in there?" Duane yelled back.

Boy Jack glanced at Paulus and stepped up his pace to be sure everyone could hear him. But he still had to shout. "I had to bust in and there wasn't any air or anything else and I was always afraid of the dicks finding me. So I got out. Y'all would never have made it in there, believe me. But I'm glad as hell I found you now. We need to catch up." He realized he was short of breath from talking and walking. And maybe a little tired after all.

"Well, we got time for that," Duane yelled back. "Don't need to tell the whole street anyway."

"10-4 on that," Boy Jack said.

"You missed all our stories," Maybelle called out over her shoulder.

"Stories?" Boy Jack said. He liked her, and not just because she was a babe.

"Yeah, we had a real storytelling thing. Couple of hours at least. Pretty big audience listening to us spin out our yarns there in the pit of fucking hell. Lovely night, really. I think I reached a new level of mystifying even myself. So your hotel doesn't sound that bad." She knew she sounded irritated and stayed silent after that.

"Anyway, thanks for letting me come," Boy Jack said.

"Wait and see about that," said Paulus, just to him, and then they concentrated on the route, because there was no long stretch of street nor sidewalk nor intersection nor storefront parking lot that wasn't festering in the heat with things that could cut or infect or bite or trip you or most definitely kill you and vanish you into the void. And Boy Jack definitely could see that.

They passed beyond sight or sound of smell of the Convention Center, past the high bridge that seemed to have had as many police cars parked across the lanes as they did people trying to cross over to the West Bank. They stuck with Tchoupitoulas as the most direct street. The Portia lay ahead. On the previous hike with Moon-Ra, taking the reverse route, it had taken nearly three hours. It might run a little more now with the children in tow, and more people on the streets. More chaos.

Everyone they passed had to be eyed carefully. True or false, the rumor mill was filled with stories of muggings and murder. Also with better stories—perhaps more suited to the city, of rescues and sharing. Still, it was like wading through alligators. About which there also were stories.

They had a half-dozen bottles of drinking water left, and finished them off quickly as the wet heat ratcheted up with each block. Boy Jack's backpack was crammed with purloined snacks and soft drinks and several bars of soap and a dozen coffee packets he had scrounged off a cleaning cart someone had left in the hall on the twelfth floor of the hotel. He had checked all but the lower three floors for supplies. He didn't go down there because he had heard noises and voices. He didn't want to risk running into anyone. Not just dicks. Anyone at all.

They devoured Boy Jack's stash as well as the remaining snack bars Moon-Ra and Duane had liberated from the Portia. Duane asked Moon-Ra if he could remember if there were any more supplies in the theater. Neither of them knew for sure, given the confusion of leaving, but figured there might be something in the upstairs closet, which generally provided space to everything from floor mops to peanut butter crackers.

Maybelle knew her eyes were rolling as the boys talked about plans to leave the city. Like they had any fucking idea at all of what to do when the Big Easy was blown out its own ass. But she said nothing. Who knew, anyway? Who knew anything? Except they were walking, and passing stragglers and miscreants and far too many people with wild eyes and taut expressions. And the stubborn types who "rode out" the hurricanes as a matter of principle instead of misfortune or lack of means. Maybelle considered the Portia family part of the latter, all things considered.

Either way, Katrina's lesson was that she couldn't be ridden out. She might be out-ridden, though. And that's where Maybelle's head was. She knew Duane was already there. That's why they were such lovebirds.

CHAPTER 19

Thursday, September 1, morning

With the windows open and the broken front door once again propped ajar by wind-ripped wood and branches, what breezes there were flowed with little impediment through the wreck that had been the Portia. It had helped everyone sleep through the night for a change, spread out from the lobby to the balcony to the stage around the building. That, and the extra boxes of concession stand snacks and water that Moon-Ra had found upstairs under the projection equipment, for whatever reason Gretchen had put them there. That, and exhaustion. Physical collapse finally outlasted fear. Fear required more than they had left. You could call it the sleep of the almost-but-not-quite-dead.

But worry could be a good alarm clock. Duane and Moon-Ra were up and moving around by 6:00 a.m. They went outside to look over Duane's Taurus one more time. Inadvertently, Duane caught a look at his face in the sideview mirror. The suture on his forehead had dropped off, no problem, and the sutures on his cheek finally had loosened up, but also reddened around the edges. Not good, considering all the ways they could be infected. He made a mental note to wash his face good with soap and pull the threads out first chance he got.

He flashed on the mugging that gave him the stitches. It seemed like another life, and he strengthened his resolve about what lay ahead in his new one. Then he and Moon-Ra gave up discovering any unexpected hope in the Taurus and walked around the neighborhood. To see what remained intact. To see what they could find.

An hour later, everyone else began to stir, all adjusting in their own ways to come out of their dreams and back to reality. In a movie theater. It was good the toilets in the downstairs restrooms worked.

Across the city, the late summer steam bath still ruled, and with it the smells and sights and bugs that Katrina had also added as a head-slap. Even more of the quasi-police were arriving, almost by the hour: black-clad DEA agents, cops from other cities and states, Homeland Security gestapo, all kinds of soldiers. More helicopters buzzing. What any of them were accomplishing was of debatable value.

But some arrivals brought actual help, and were welcome: civilian volunteers. They got called do-gooders, but they really did good. Their jeeps and trucks and skiffs and big motorboats were capable of navigating the flooded streets, picking up not only stranded humans but also pets and disoriented wildlife.

Sometimes, too, they found bodies.

Duane had zero intention of staying and dealing with any of that. During the night, when he had awoken from a nightmare he didn't care to remember, he made himself drowsy again by rehearsing exactly how to explain the urgency of leaving New Orleans—immediately—to his comrades. In a way that made sense. Even with Katrina, the city still had roots in everyone who lived there. The longer people had resided, the stronger the roots. In a way, that was why they all went to the Convention Center. Why they didn't head west as soon as they knew the hurricane would be bad.

Duane accepted that the roots were in him, too. But he was chopping them off. Of course that wasn't the way to convince anybody to split. He needed to have a forward action plan. A vision. A lure. A promise. Along those lines. In his mental preparation, he could barely get past explaining how he had this land in Texas—that he'd never seen—but could be just what they could all use to start over. He found it even harder to formulate an argument in his tired brain about the movie thing. He'd hoped to lay that out more back at the Convention Center. Which intent, now, seemed borderline nuts. He was still critiquing his wretched performance, and trying to fathom Maybelle's master class. Not to mention Moon-Ra's.

He wanted them, the Portia family, to understand that getting away, that the chance of producing a job-creating movie, could work. Would work. That he could wrangle enough money. That they could make a grand statement! Nonetheless, he felt it prudent to have a back-up plan.

Such as maybe once they got free of the city and on to Texas, they could go a whole other way. If they didn't want to do a movie, they could set up a new life. A commune of refugees and exiles, a free state, something like that, something away from the chaos and Katrina and everything that has been trying to kill them. Away from the city they loved but that would be impossibly slow rebuilding. That's when he had fallen back to sleep.

Now, walking around the wretched streets, he became resolute that he had to at least get the conversation about their evacuation destination started. Thus, when everyone had shaken off the shrouds of sleep, finished the breakfast of soft drinks and peanuts and potato chips, and done their shares of staring at the mangled wreckage outside the theater, he led them into the amphitheater, to the fortunately dry seats, which the children thought were especially cool. He ran through the plan.

Also, the back-up plan. It wasn't a perfect pitch, but it was more-or-less along the lines he'd rehearsed to himself last night, and it was good enough. Considering the context.

Elaborated, of course, with random Q and A, including a Q for which he had no A. To which he'd never given a thought: "Where will the kids go to school out there?" But essentially his theory— "vision" might be overdoing it—about what they could try during the next few days or few weeks seemed plausible enough to hold their attention. In context. The context being no other options. Nothing else. "Nothing else" being to stay and die.

It would not be until several days later, when Duane and Maybelle were sitting outside under the stars on a bench in the backyard of a house in Cut Off, along Bayou Lafourche, everyone else asleep or half asleep in their rooms, that she would tell him, almost offhand, that it didn't matter that much what he'd said to everyone that morning at the Portia about plans and visions.

She would tell him they had listened politely, and not without interest, but they were already ready. More ready than he was, insofar as that was possible. They were like people under water bursting to the surface to breathe and escape the sharks.

"So don't take all the credit, *cher*. Katrina's the one with the Big Ideas around here," she would say. "News flash: People who can't go home have to go somewhere else. All that big talk—thanks, dearest Duane, but all they expect from you is to find someplace they can just hunker down. For however long it takes until they can go home."

"Maybe."

"Maybe what?"

"Maybe they feel it's time to make a real change, too. You know? They got minds of their own, too."

She would lean over, kiss him on the cheek. He would be surprised by how cold her lips felt. "Of course it's time, my love. I'm just saying we all . . . they all . . . might not all have the same motives or incentives, right? I mean, we aren't even a week out of the shit. But we do want out of the shit. And don't feel let down. I like your ideas, me. I think everyone does. But you know, like I said, in their own ways."

In that backyard along the bayou, he would look at her. She

would be really something in the starlight. He would kiss her on the lips. And they would still be cold. He wouldn't know what to make of it.

"You know, maybe we can all have a fresh look at everything. Now we're out of the city. On the road kind of thing."

"Me and you, sure. But these are families with us. They have roots."

"Maybe."

"Maybe? Are you kidding?"

"Nobody forced them to leave."

"So they're glad to leave home?"

"I just mean things have changed."

"Maybe—that's the word you like, no?"

They would stare at each other. Hard. Deep.

He would say, "Don't tell me you didn't go through something back there in the Convention Center. I mean, seriously. That story. Holy shit, Maybelle! All those lives you said you went through. Including this one? I never heard anything like that before. Definitely not from you."

He would watch for her reaction and she would go silent for what seemed an eternity. Then say, "It just came to me. And I was telling stories. And I mean, dear Duane, it's not like you never veer off into your own world when you go on about movies or life or art. I mean, really."

To which he could only try to smile or nod and eek out, "If you see it that way."

To which she would gently touch his cheek and they would sit quietly. Then she would say, "I just mean, don't set your heart on everybody following your dream, or plan, or vision, or whatever you want to call it."

He would look at her, almost lost in the universe of her eyes, and say she was right. That she meant everything to him. The stars overhead would sparkle on the flooded landscape around them, cast faint illumination on the broken trees beneath the horizon.

She would squeeze his hand.

The mosquitoes would get really bad and force them back inside the house where refuge had been offered, and accepted. Because hurricanes could produce that response, too, among the surviving humans.

But for now, they were still in the city, still in the Portia, still rummaging for anything that could be eaten, worn, or used for the trip. Duane was sifting through the drawers in his office desk when he came across a yellowing Polaroid of him and Carlos, sitting on the tailgate of an old green pickup. He tried to remember where it was and finally decided it was probably in northern Mexico. They looked thinner and younger, and they were. It made him wonder, again, if Carlos was still alive.

Speaking of whom, Duane needed to pay more attention to the bequest of the ranch. It figured heavily into his plan, and yet it was exactly as Rhys had said, and likely what Carlos intended: a mystery. He made a mental note to get in touch with Memo Barrios, Carlos's lawyer up in Dallas, once they got on the road and could find cell service.

Memo and Carlos went back a long time, too. Duane also had worked with him at various times. Memo developed a habit of occasionally disappearing from his law practice into Central America, maybe Mexico. Much of that involved Carlos. The last time Duane had talked to Memo, which must have been at least six or seven years ago, the lawyer said he'd drawn up Carlos's will and a few other documents.

He said that Duane should make sure to keep him up-to-date with a mailing address. He said he would share the address, as well as any information from Carlos, with Sofia, the law firm partner with whom Duane had once failed miserably in a long-distance relationship. Miserably meant it lasted about three months. One, really. Three sounded better and was technically true.

Despite knowing little about the ranch, Duane had a good feeling. Moon-Ra called things like that "second sight." Who knew? And was not so-called actual sight overrated? Sight of land, people, events, massive destruction. The actual sights that Katrina had left behind. Those were nothing that anyone wanted to look upon. Even with eyes closed.

He put the photo back in the drawer, gave the office another look. Picked up what had been blown away and marveled again that it hadn't been worse inside. He and Maybelle had already packed up things before heading over to the Portia the night Katrina hit. But she had done some repacking of her backpack, and he did the same with his duffel bag. Also taking a second, smaller bag for his laptop, which he'd realized he would need, and the $2,500 from the safe. He thought about leaving it, but would probably need cash more than the computer. Two thousand into his bag and the other five hundred in his wallet. He just had to be careful with it and wouldn't tell anyone except Maybelle.

A flash of light seeped through and he looked outside, through a window that hadn't been broken. Out there, very bad. Everywhere that he'd been or heard about on the radio. The result of a hurricane. The word that had clogged up his throat and Maybelle's back in the Center, trying to tell stories. Just a word. But it stuck in his head again. Just thinking of it.

The Buddhists would say a word was just a word for something and not the something itself. A word and nothing more. And the city? Same reasoning—New Orleans was just a name for a place and not the place itself. Nothing more. Thus did Duane consider New Orleans a very Buddhist city.

As for the movie, who knew? Rhys was of course right that since it was supposed to be about the South and the city and Carlos's land was somewhere in the Chinati Mountains, there could be visual disconnects. But Duane believed, without any real evidence, that a good director could shoot the Arctic in Brazil if need be.

179

Of such was Duane's creative arrogance and his evacuative confidence. Of such would be the days future past for all who were with him. He put the photo in his pocket and would throw it away somewhere down the road at a gas station trash can because he was remembering that Carlos had never liked having his picture taken. In case it fell into the wrong hands.

CHAPTER 20

Thursday, September 1, late morning

Duane went back downstairs to help with whatever else needed packing or bolting down before they left, but there wasn't anything else to do and it was hot and the mosquitoes were hungry. It was a good thing the repellent hadn't run out. Eluvia told Moon-Ra she had heard on the radio about people getting stuck for hours at a time on the highway to Baton Rouge. She said that would make her crazy and everybody else joined in with variations of "hell, yes" and then she said it didn't really matter since they didn't have their cars anyway.

Duane went outside yet again to be absolutely sure one last time that not just one but three tires on the Taurus were flat and unfixable. He cranked it just to see and sure enough the battery was dead. So, who needed tires? Moon-Ra and Paulus and Boy Jack came over and made some car-talk commiseration, like they knew what they were doing. Then they split up for another neighborhood recon. Maybe they'd missed some vehicles that had been abandoned but might start up. They found nothing.

Regathered at the useless Taurus, they tried to think their way past the problem. Moon-Ra said if he could get hold of Feliciana, maybe her car was okay and she could meet them and they could check out his Civic, just in case it might run after all. Paulus assumed his Altima was under water and no point in even checking. Whatever might start wasn't enough. They'd need at least two cars for the road.

Then Boy Jack had an idea. A Boy Jack idea. A church van he'd come across on his part of the recon. He'd written it off, he said, since it belonged to a church, and maybe somebody was using it. But it was coming to him now that maybe he was wrong. Because after Katrina, nothing really made sense.

Such as, why exactly would the Church of Holy Sanctuary from Topeka, Kansas—for some damn reason the name stuck in his head—leave a muddy, twelve-seat, white passenger van on a street just off St. Charles? Unless maybe the water up to the bumpers and the downed tree in front of it might have been factors.

"I mean, it's worth a try for sure," he said. "I mean, it might be abandoned, and not broken, right? It's not but a few blocks over yonder way. I mean, don't you think?"

They did. Duane told Maybelle and Eluvia they were going to check something out and would be right back.

The van was close, sitting in a water-filled pothole behind a fallen tree, just as Boy Jack had described. They swarmed around it like it was a NASCAR legend and made mental calculations as to whether it could be started and was roadworthy. And if so, if it was okay to steal it.

If it could be called stealing, in context. The answer to the second question was yes. As for starting it, hard to say.

"Unless the engine is flooded I can hot-wire it," Boy Jack said.

Moon-Ra was busy pulling open the double-wide door on the passenger side. "Hey, we can get in. They might all be unlocked if they left in a hurry."

He was right. Boy Jack opened the driver's door and jumped in. The upholstery was still wet and he noticed the window was open just enough at the top to have let in the rain. He thought that was either stupid or desperate, but a wet seat was the least of their problems.

He found the release lever for the hood and popped it so Duane could look at the engine. But the hood latch stuck and took some fiddling to open. When Duane could lift it up, he saw hubcap-deep water below the frame, but not up to the sparkplugs or electrical wiring. Moon-Ra and Paulus came around to share the look. They had the same reaction.

"Well, let's just see if it cranks," Duane said.

Boy Jack touched the wires he'd pulled out under the steering wheel. After backfires and gray smoke coughing out the tailpipe, the motor shuddered and started like a champ. Like it had been in a garage all night.

Boy Jack left it running and joined them studying the engine. "That's why I drive a Ford myself. You just gotta work with them sometimes."

"Let's never turn it off," Moon-Ra said. "Or does it have enough gas?"

"Three-quarter."

"They must have been planning on going somewhere," Paulus said.

"Whaddya think," Duane asked Moon-Ra. "Good to go?"

"What I think is it's the only ride we got."

"So, yeah?"

"So, yeah."

"Anybody disagree?"

They laughed.

"Must be a big church, to have a ride like this," Paulus said. "Looks like they kept it in good shape."

"Battery looks okay." Duane said, before closing the hood. "But yeah, let's keep it running."

Boy Jack went back to the driver's seat. "I can hot-wire again," Boy Jack said, as if it were too obvious to have to discuss. "And nothing on the warning lights in the panel to give us worry."

"Well then," Duane said, "let's get back to the Portia and load it up. Get the fuck out of here. Getting close to noon."

"Hop in," Boy Jack said.

Duane and Moon-Ra got in back to look over the seats. Paulus took shotgun in front. Turned out only the driver's cushion had caught the rain.

"We're gonna have to put that back seat down for all our stuff," Moon-Ra said. "But that'll still leave enough seats."

"It'll be cozy," Paulus said.

Boy Jack eased into drive and was able to glide slowly back out of the water, and then around the fallen tree. It was so easy to do that whatever had caused the people to leave the bus became even more a mystery.

He proceeded slowly, avoiding the other potholes and downed limbs. Also a clump of a half-dozen tricycles that made no sense. Not that anything did. They were in the Portia parking lot in five minutes. The smiles on the faces of Maybelle and Eluvia and Nadia, though tentative, indicated they were happy as clams.

They loaded up quickly. Edwin, meanwhile, found a black box stuck under the back fender while he was bouncing on it. And got properly scolded by his mom, who turned her words to "Praise Jesus" when Edwin showed her his discovery and asked why it had a key and a magnet.

Boy Jack laughed and said he "didn't need no stinkin' keys," hoping Duane would catch the *Treasure of the Sierra Madre* reference. Which he did, and laughed more out of obligatory manners to his new friend than actual humor, but the times were very accommodating in terms of levity.

Then, just to be clear, Duane said they did need the key because no one else knew about hot-wiring. For the briefest of moments it was apparent that the car-jacking skill had been Boy Jack's insurance that he wouldn't be abandoned. And Duane taking the key was everyone else's insurance that Boy Jack wouldn't lord it over them.

From such whiffs of mistrust can arrive the beginnings of deeper suspicions and tentacles of paranoia. And in fact these soul-worms were at that very moment also spreading across the city and the state. As said worms burrowed deeper and expanded and multiplied, they would engender the most unwelcome of all the reactions to evacuations and shortages and lack of housing and permanence or self-sustainability of any kind. Katrina had shown her hand and now she was adding as a codicil that the displeasure of nature was not an isolated thing. It was an ongoing insatiable web of destruction for all living things who thought they could stand against her, ignore her, or survive her unscathed.

Additional scathing, therefore, remained.

Wading past I-10 sign.

Photo by Nicole Fruge/San Antonio Express-News/ZUMA Press.

WESTWARD

Mama exhorted her children at every opportunity to 'jump at the sun.'

We might not land on the sun, but at least we would get off the ground."

—Zora Neale Hurston, *Dust Tracks on a Road*

"You don't have to live like a refugee."

—Tom Petty and Mike Campbell, *Refugee*

CHAPTER 21

Thursday, September 1, afternoon

The usual way west from the Big Easy on I-10 was a barren, fast-moving stereotype of speed traps, tricked-out pickup trucks with Confederate flag decals and gun rights bumper stickers, barely roadworthy old sedans with duct tape sealing up broken windows and tail lights, right-wing evangelicals on the radio, and deep-fried everything. Pretty much a reflection of life as they knew it in Baton Rouge, Lafayette, Lake Charles, and on into East Texas. Which gave Louisiana a serious run for the money with pointless violence, pervasive intolerance, and Klaverns, albeit a little better financed with its oil and timber and fishing. Once in Texas, Orange and Beaumont, which basically might as well have been in Louisiana, would yield to the flat sodden plains of the extreme suburbs until the megapolis of Houston rose like another world.

But they would not be going the I-10 way. The destructive path of Katrina was so vast and complete that it disrupted not only the pre-storm evacuations, but also any kind of subsequent travel to or from the city. Interstate 10 being a case in point. It was all but impossible to use.

Completely impossible if you wanted to go east out of New Orleans. The causeway to Slidell was smashed into pieces and sunk into the water by the storm surge.

The westbound lanes leading to Texas and eventually LA were clear to drive, but the traffic was horrendous. If you tried bypassing the jam-ups by exiting onto the back roads through the small towns, it could get even worse. You might come to a dead end because a tree or phone pole had fallen over the right-of-way. Or you might run over nails or hunks of glass or metal scraps and lose your tires. Any kind of breakdown or accident left you stranded.

Sometimes squad cars or hasty red and white barriers were there to warn you, but just as often you found out for yourself that your brilliant shortcut meant you'd have to turn around and retrace your route and end up in the traffic knots you went to all that trouble to avoid in the first place. Unless you ran out of gas. Or just got lost.

Which is to say that while getting away from the city before the storm hit was the smart move, afterward it was just asking for trouble. Which hardly stopped anyone, of course. The entire state had become a slow-moving parking lot of evacuees.

When the Portia family had been inside the Convention Center, the gossip, such as they had heard, was full of notions of flight. But also of staying. If you had lived through the storm, and could hang on a little longer, even in a place like the Center, maybe you were better off in the long run by hunkering down. Thus, all over New Orleans, even where the water was up to the roofs and where more than a thousand had died, people hunkered down. Better said: They got hopelessly stuck.

Duane and everybody in the family had heard plenty. Rumors and facts and advice and sheer gossip spread throughout the neighborhoods and wards and reverberated in the Convention Center and no doubt in the Superdome. Real information, such as from Garland Robinette and WWL, became a literal lifeline. If you had a radio. Which Duane did.

And now they had a van. It had enough seats for everyone, and enough gas to get at least as far as New Iberia or Lafayette, stop for the night. All they really needed was a way other than I-10 to cross the river. And there was one: US 90. By all accounts and rumor it was open right through to Texas.

US 90 was considered a scenic, even tourist route, more or less paralleling I-10 to the south, but that also made it close to the Gulf and hurricane collateral damage. Moon-Ra objected, saying 90 was a crap shoot even if rumor said it was open all the way to Texas, because who really knew? Katrina went the other direction after New Orleans, but what if she had left behind flood water from the outer rain bands?

Moon-Ra said they should skip both and take back roads to Baton Rouge, and jump on I-10 there because the worst would probably have cleared up by that point. Paulus disagreed. He said anything was better than I-10, and it was far more likely that 90 was clear all the way out of the city. Maybelle sided with Paulus. She had used the old highway many times to visit law firm clients in Houma and Cut Off, a tiny fishing town on Bayou Lafourche. She said if 90 was blocked off or any kind of a problem, they'd have heard about it. Moon-Ra was outvoted.

So US 90 it was. Duane and Moon-Ra made a final check through the Portia. They closed the broken front doors as best they could, propped up plywood sheets against the window panes, and pushed a crowbar through the handles even though there was still a gap big enough to put an arm through. "This will stop anybody but thieves and looters," Moon-Ra said. They laughed, the way people do to blow off steam. Then they gave a last look at the ticket booth and the downed marquee sign. By the time they got back to the van, the others had finished the loading and were just waiting to head out. Everyone was sweating and hoping the a/c in the van would kick ass.

Duane had reserved the front passenger seat until they got out of town, so he could help with directions. Then anyone could swap off with him. Paulus and his family were in back, and then Eluvia and her kids in the middle row, and then Maybelle and Moon-Ra just behind the driver's seat.

Boy Jack was at the wheel. He could navigate the best through the clutter and congestion, everyone agreed. There was no need to worry about traffic tickets or anything that might interfere with his penchant for shortcuts, speed, and disregard of the usual rules of the road.

When all were settled, he cranked the engine, turned on the a/c full blast—it definitely was working—and they were off.

Getting over the river to the West Bank to take the "Westbound Expressway" section of US 90 was less a problem than they imagined. All the outbound lanes over the Crescent City Connection bridge, aka the CCC or its older nickname, the GNO, were open, although a few were speckled with parked cop cars, government pickups, and all manner of service trucks. None of them paid the van any attention. It might have helped that they had a church logo on the side. Bottom line was that traffic flow for leaving the city was busy, but moving along.

Just the opposite for traffic coming into the city. "Good thing we're not in those lines," Boy Jack said. No one had to affirm, because they were glued to the windows, watching the bottlenecks and jammed up lanes, the entire range of vehicular chaos. City and state cop cars in abundance, their checkpoints overwhelmed. People who evacuated before Katrina were now trying to get back in, to check on their homes and relatives, and now they were blocked from that. And it was hot, and idling cars and their air conditioners broke down, and if anger and frustration could be seen like storm clouds, the skies would have been pitch-black.

Boy Jack kept at a steady clip, a little over the speed limit, and said he could slow down if they were concerned about all the law. Maybelle told him to keep the heavy foot until they'd cleared the mess. So he did. The traffic thinned just past Westwego, Paradis, and Des Allemands. Boy Jack said he figured traffic before long would lighten all the way into Lafayette.

About a mile after that the engine shuddered.

"I thought we had plenty of gas," Duane said.

"We do. Look." Boy Jack pointed to the needle. "It says half full but it feels like the engine wants to quit."

Duane leaned over, pursed his lips, looked back at Moon-Ra. It wasn't necessary to say what both were thinking, that maybe they were finding out why the van had been abandoned. That it had nothing to do with the flooded street.

Another shudder and then the engine settled down.

"Next exit is for Houma," Duane said, looking at Maybelle. "You still know people there?"

"In Cut Off. It's closer. Unless they evacuated. I would have."

"If we need a place to stay if the van needs some repair? Could they help us?" He stared out the windshield again. "If. If. If."

"If they're there. I mean, like I said—"

"Should I take this one? Says Raceland and Highway 1," Boy Jack interrupted. "I think that goes all the way down to Grand Isle."

"Take it," Maybelle said.

Duane turned quickly to Moon-Ra again and got a thumbs-up.

"They's a sign for a gas station over there across the highway I can barely make out," Boy Jack said.

"Go. Go," Duane said.

He barely caught the exit, squealing the tires at the sharp curve off the highway. It put them on a crowded two-lane along Bayou Lafourche. It was the only land route down the thin peninsula of hard-core Cajun hamlets starting with Larose and on to the vacation and fishing haven of Grand Isle. Including Cut Off. Although, as they would soon find out, Cut Off was about as far as they could get, because of state police barricades at the lower end of the flooded highway.

Which was fine, because Cut Off was where Lenny Bacquet lived. He was a former oil patch tool pusher turned part-time deep-sea fishing boat pilot. Maybelle was pretty sure Lenny'd remember how last year the law firm had gotten him sixty thousand in damage claims on a delivery van whose driver was drunk and crashed into his garage dropping off a new mattress. The company refused to pay, basically because they were dicks and somehow it had pissed off Lincoln and he took the case for a small fee.

Lenny and Madge, his wife, would certainly remember Maybelle staying at their house a few nights doing legal research and depositions and playing drinking games and garbling the French words to Cajun country songs over at their friend Bertran's "Lordy he's 40" birthday party that turned into a *fais do-do*.

Getting there, and finding Lenny, if he hadn't evacuated, was still a crapshoot. Although partly open, Highway 1 was barely cleared of fallen trees and dead animals and farm and fishing equipment that had been pushed around by the wind and water like toys. Nor was there the slightest guarantee that the Ford van that Boy Jack had thought so reliable would have enough gas, or spark, or unclogged lines or whatever was scaring the hell out of them every few miles to even make it. They passed two gas stations and thought of stopping, but one was closed and the other had lines of cars twenty or thirty deep. Neither looked like they had any repair services.

The only other business they passed was a seedy motel with two pickups in the parking lot and a telephone pole adorned with the neon marquee sign which said, just to be clear, "Motel." Maybelle kept trying to reach Lenny on her cell, but it didn't have a steady signal. She told Boy Jack how to get to Lenny's place, which was fortunately on the same side of the bayou they were on, and maybe not that far now.

They made it. Cut Off looked badly storm-whipped. Most of the buildings were intact, but damaged, but there were still a few lights in houses and a café that appeared to be open. The bayou neatly divided the town. Boats were scrambled in the water and against broken piers and docks on either bank. Some were sunk at the bow or stern. All seemed busted up in some way, but the fleet was a long way from wiped out. Duane was pleased to see the resilience. The not giving up.

Boy Jack slowed as they got onto Main Street, using as little gas as possible, avoiding any sudden braking that might shut down the engine.

"A little farther," Maybe said. "Everything's really just all along the bayou."

They passed a few cars and pickups. It started to drizzle. Boy Jack turned on the wipers.

Duane leaned forward. "See that gas station right up there? Place next to it might be a mechanic." Then he shifted in his seat to see Paulus and Nadia in the back row. "We might have lots of problems along the way. It's just the way it is. Will be for a while. Half the damn city is trying to get out of the state. At least."

"We're good," Paulus said. "I read you a hundred percent. It ain't nothin' real bad in this truck, I expect. And I bet any mechanic's gonna be happy to have work, given nobody's driving around much."

"Better than being back in that Convention Center or even in the city, period," said Eluvia, her arms around her boys.

"That's how I look at it," Duane said.

"Grab a right, just after that little store up there on the corner. We'll be fine," Maybelle said, leaning forward to be sure Boy Jack could hear her over the sound of the wiper blades.

Boy Jack turned where she had indicated, and then, with Maybelle's additional directions, two more turns along small pot-holed asphalt or gravel streets. They were in what could be called a subdivision—modest blocks of modest ranch-style brick or aluminum siding houses and converted doublewides on concrete pads. A few roofs partly blown off. Lots of broken tree limbs and dangling wires and scattered trash and belongings, but not rows of smash and tatter. It was a hard hit—not as hard as she had expected, but bad enough.

"That blue one," Maybelle said. Boy Jack slowed to a crawl, and eased to a stop on the gravel apron in front of a half-flooded stretch of yard. A dark blue Chevy pickup with muddy wheels was in the driveway. A light or candle in a kitchen window. "They're here," Maybelle said, unable to disguise the note of surprise in her voice.

CHAPTER 22

Thursday, September 1, late afternoon

No one answered the doorbell or Maybelle's knock. The rain had slackened but was still enough to soak the top of her shirt as she waited on the front porch. She tried twice more, then looked back at Duane. Boy Jack kept the engine idling.

"I don't know," she called out. "Seems like somebody's here."

"Should we wait?" Duane called back.

Maybelle looked at the houses on each side. Both were brick, like Lenny's, and definitely vacant. The one to the left had lost about a third of its gray shingle roof. "Hold on." She hopped off the porch to walk around to the garage side of the house and then hooked a left toward the backyard. She'd barely cleared an overturned riding mower when a voice yelled from somewhere she couldn't see.

"Stop right there and don't take another step, motherfucker. It's a 12-gauge and it's aimed right for you."

She stopped. She'd had this kind of experience before and was lucky to have lived through it.

"My name's Maybelle Delaforte and I'm here looking for Lenny Bacquet or Madge," she said as loud and forceful-sounding as she could manage. "Is that you, Lenny?"

She didn't get an answer, other than the squish of heavy steps through mud and soggy grass. Then a big guy, heavier than she remembered and with a new beard, appeared around the corner. The shotgun he carried was leveled directly at her gut. As soon as he saw her face, his own lit up. He stopped mid-stride and lowered the weap-

197

on immediately.

"Goddam, Maybelle, it really is you."

"It is."

"C'mere, girl."

He closed the gap and bear-hugged her, clenching the shotgun in one big fist. Then he backed off, looked her up and down.

"So why in God's name are you down here in the bayou, girl?"

Maybelle looked him hard in the eyes.

"I got flooded out. Me and some of my friends back in the city. We're on our way to Texas."

He nodded, studying her intently.

"But something happened with our van up on 90 just before the exit down to here and I just took a hunch maybe we could find you or somebody in Cut Off could help us with it. I just didn't know if you'd be home. I never could get through on the damn phone."

Lenny touched her arm gently. He knew she was tough as nails but he could see she was nervous and rattled, even if she tried to hide it.

"Well, I'm here." He stepped back, spread both arms like bird wings, including the one holding the shotgun. Then he laughed and reached out to pat her arm again. "Madge is, too, but we sent the kids to Dallas with Madge's mom and her dad and them that left in time. Me and Madge just thought we should stay. Looters, for one thing." He looked away for a second or two. "Sorry about that."

"No worries."

"We been through this before. We just didn't know it would be this bad. I guess we wish we'd a gone, too."

"I know the feeling."

They laughed humorlessly.

"Anyway, she's gone up to Raceland to try to get some groceries, but she'll be back."

He walked toward the front of the house, Maybelle beside him. She knew something wasn't right but this wasn't the time to push it. Actually, nothing was right.

"That's them."

"That looks full of people."

"There's ten of us. Four of 'em are kids. It's a twelve-seater. But ten is plenty."

"Huhhn. Church van? Kansas, it says?"

"It's a long story. Anyway, we just need a mechanic to look at the engine and see what it is. We don't mean to burden you. Although, if your bathroom works, that would be great."

He studied the van a little longer. "So I guess them Holy Sanctuary church folks is gone back home. Is why they left their rig."

"Best we could tell."

"Huhhn."

"It's the way it is in the city, Lenny. We had to get out."

He coughed out a kind of chuckle. "Well, it is strange times, for sure. Still, you boosted a church van?"

"I like to think of it as rescuing an abandoned vehicle."

He grinned. "No problem, *cher*."

"For real?"

"Absolutely. Now you just tell 'em to get out and stretch. This here property belongs to me and you're always welcome, whatever the case might be. And all your friends, too. Damn, Maybelle. Me and Madge love the shit out of you."

This time she did the patting—on his back hard as she could, but it barely made a dent and actually kind of hurt her palm. Lenny was what they call good people. Even in a hurricane, good people made you feel good.

"They can use the toilets or pee out back if they want. It's the fucking swamp back there so it don't matter," he said. "I was just started trying to clear it up, but it'll take a week at least."

"Thank you. That's all I can say."

"No need. We're all in this shit, ain't we?"

"You got that right."

Maybelle waved at Duane, who had opened his door and was standing on the passenger side step-up, looking across the van roof. "Y'all go ahead and get out," she called as she walked up, pointing back with one arm. "This is Lenny here. He'll help us find what we need."

Duane jumped down from his perch and walked over to meet Lenny while the others were extricating themselves from the van's cramped seats. Duane and Lenny shook hands, and then, not quite sure what else to say, watched as the Portia family slowly gathered outside at the edge of the lawn. Except Boy Jack, who stayed in this seat. Like he was guarding it. Or, maybe, like he could take off if he wanted to. If the damn thing actually ran.

"It's raining, Mama," Elena said.

"Just a little. It'll be okay."

Lenny shook hands with everyone. He still had the shotgun, but it wasn't threatening and nobody really cared. Then he led them to the house. He pointed out the two bathrooms, which the kids and moms headed for right away, and then put his shotgun in a corner by the door and went back outside to talk to Maybelle and Duane. Paulus and Moon-Ra followed.

"I've done a fair amount of work on cars and pickups," Lenny said, as they gathered. "Any idea what's wrong?"

Duane summarized. "The guy driving, Boy Jack, can tell you more. You want me to call him over?"

"Nah, I need to look under the hood anyway. He can turn it off, though, if you want." Duane looked at Boy Jack and did a throat-slit gesture. Boy Jack flashed back a thumbs-up and then shut off the motor. It shuddered to a stop. So did the drizzle.

"It kind of sounds electrical, the way it jumps on you," Lenny said.

"I guess none of us have too much knowledge about this kind of thing," Duane said. "I guess it took a hurricane to show why that's not smart."

Lenny laughed, the way country folk do when city slickers show they don't know shit about practical stuff. But not much of a laugh, because everybody knew that neither country nor city could ever know what would happen in a hurricane.

Lenny and Boy Jack had a long look at the engine, and Duane

could tell they hit it off. Moon-Ra and Paulus smiled at the bond between white dudes of the same cloth. Leaning across the front of the van to get a better look at something under the cylinders, Boy Jack laughed, said something to Lenny. Lenny looked down and just said, "Yeah," then turned to Duane and said he could probably fix it himself. Unless it needed a part, which he might could find at a buddy's shop. Duane said that would be great and they'd be out of his hair as soon as they could drive.

Lenny said they were welcome as long as it took. He said, as a matter of fact, it was good to have company. He said he and Madge were the only ones on the whole street who had stayed, who'd ridden it out, although they didn't think about it that way.

It was especially bad at night, though, Lenny said. He said that's why he always kept his shotgun with him, even in bed. Not that he could sleep.

Then he went to his garage, brought out a toolbox and a flashlight, and went on with his examination of his new friends' only means of transportation. Boy Jack stayed at his side, and Duane went into the house to check on Maybelle and Eluvia and then came back out and did what Southern males have done all their lives. He squatted and watched the experts clank around tools and finagle with an engine and throw out a continual string of possible defects until they hit on the problem.

Fuel pump.

CHAPTER 23

Thursday, September 1, *late afternoon,* continued

Problem was finding one. For a van. Lenny said probably his friend Louis who had a shade-tree-mechanic kind of business might have one or know how to get it. So he tried calling, but Louis's cell still didn't work, and for that matter neither did Duane's. So Lenny and Duane and Boy Jack got in Lenny's pickup and drove over to Louis's house just across the bayou, which they were able to get to because the draw bridge was down and intact.

Turned out Louis didn't have a fuel pump either but said Big Tiny might. His auto parts store was on the other side of the bridge but still only a couple minutes away, if the streets were clear, at the lower end of the town near the church school. They got there without much trouble. They could see lights through the plate glass and the "OPEN" sign hung from the door.

Big Tiny was back in the parts stacks and hollered out that he'd be with them in a minute. Then he saw who it was and they all shook hands and talked a couple of minutes about Katrina. When that topic was spent, Lenny asked about the fuel pump.

Tiny looked through his inventory book, then went into the storage stacks. He came out with a look of disappointment and an open palms gesture that he had nothing.

"But hang on," he said, and pulled his cell phone from his jeans. He punched in some digits and to everyone's surprised he got a ring tone. Then an answer. They could hear him say things like "Yeah, I'm sure that'll be okay," and, "As soon as you can. They're stranded and want to get going." Then he held the phone down against his leg and looked at Lenny.

"So, it's Fred's Parts over by Des Allemands. He's open a few hours a day because of all the people there need stuff. He said they stock it and can send it down but it'll be tomorrow morning."

Lenny looked at Duane.

"Thing is," Big Tiny said, "they want an extra hundred to drive it over, because of all the trouble and all. So with the part it'll be about two-fifty, estimate. It'd be less but they're charging about double."

Duane looked at Big Tiny, who clearly felt it was still a fair deal, considering.

"Tell him to bring it. Soon as he can."

"He'll want cash."

"I got that."

"So I tell him you want it?"

"I want it."

Big Tiny told Fred's guy and put the phone to his leg again. "They want me to take the money now and hold it and confirm I got it." He rolled his eyes. "Sorry, man," he said to Lenny, and then to Duane. "That still work for you?"

"I'll give it to you now if he can figure the final bill."

"$260."

Duane took out his wallet. He had the cash but didn't think he'd be needing it so soon. He gave Tiny $300, just to be sure everything was covered. He also caught Boy Jack looking at his open wallet as he pulled out the bills, then immediately turning his head away.

"Just for this kind of thing," Duane said. "You know."

"Sorry, man. Didn't mean to be nosy."

"I'm just making this up as we go," Duane said.

"Ain't we all."

Lenny started for the door. "Call soon as it's here," he said to Big Tiny.

"I will." Big Tiny put the money under a notepad by the register.

"Glad you could help us," Duane said. "I understand about the cost. I'm just grateful as hell." He followed Lenny out, Boy Jack right behind.

"See y'all tomorrow morning, most probly," Big Tiny said. "If it ain't that whole amount, I'll have your change."

Back at the house, Lenny went to his garage and found the meter and wrenches he needed to check the alternator, just to be sure it was okay, which it was. That loose end was settled in his head.

What wasn't was where to put ten people for the night, and what to feed them. And how Madge would feel about it when she got home.

By when, he meant if.

Lenny hadn't mentioned to Maybelle that Madge had gone off the wagon a couple months ago. Not so much the booze as the meth. It had actually been a good year of sober for her, and as usual she couldn't pinpoint exactly what led her to the bar over in Houma that night. It just had a way of swarming over her is the way she put it, and even when she knew it was happening she couldn't stop it. She said she wasn't giving excuses. Just explaining. Lenny loved Madge and would never give up on her, but it could be bad. But he knew they could beat it again, like they always had. And they were real close. And then Katrina started moving in.

Madge was watching it on TV, and just after it slammed Florida, she saw something, maybe a family losing their home, that got under her skin. She was unusually quiet for the rest of the day, but Lenny never saw anything beyond that, and she didn't drink anything stronger than Dr. Pepper.

The next morning, as Katrina took in the Gulf, Lenny could tell Madge was scared. She went around the house like a cat trapped in a cage until they agreed to call her mom in Dallas to come down for the kids. Lenny thought she'd hold.

She didn't. She drove off Friday night before Katrina came in, probably to that same bar in Houma, the Frog Hair, and didn't get back until Saturday noon just after the grandparents, tired and stressed from the drive, had taken Bart and Lilly and left before the traffic home got worse. Which was one more blow. Marge leaned into her stashed vodka and pills and had been in them ever since. Just him and her in the house. Her taking off at any time, except the night Katrina hit, and coming back saying she was sorry.

Lenny knew the real business of her trip up to Raceland just now—getting refills from Connie or whoever was her connection. But he couldn't stop her. Even if he did, she'd just sneak away later when he wasn't watching. So he wasn't really counting on resupply of milk and coffee and anything else.

Mostly, he hoped she wasn't driving around too much, or too high, because she'd never see the washouts or junk on the roads. On the plus side, she wouldn't have to go too far. Drugs weren't particularly hard to find on the bayou or anywhere in the fucking parish for that matter.

It was still an open question whether she would ever come back. This bender was shaping up like a bad one. He was familiar with the territory. Sometimes as long as two weeks with her gone.

Lenny had tried to lie and tell Madge's mom and dad as they picked up the kids that she'd had to run up to Houma for some women's things, and then decided she would get all the way to Lafayette for that part they needed for the refrigerator. They weren't buying. Neither were the kids. Lenny couldn't shake the memory of the anxiety on their faces as they drove away. Or the blank mask of defeat on the face of Madge's mom.

Lenny was glad Bart and Lilly were safe, though, even without the storm. It would be awhile before the schools opened again, so they might have to stay in Dallas longer. He would miss them, but watching them around her like that was like having his soul raked over hot coals.

He was glad for the company now because he grew up knowing you helped people in the time of hurricanes, and also because they helped him. Helped him not think about things. But he wasn't going to tell Maybelle or any of them anything about Madge. He could barely tell himself.

CHAPTER 24

Friday, September 2, morning

Except for the heat, the night had passed so easily that Lenny wished they could stay a week. Everyone had a place to sleep, except for Boy Jack and Moon-Ra, who joined Lenny on the screen porch in back. It was cooler out there anyway because the air conditioning still wasn't coming on. Plus they had the fans Lenny had hooked into one of the big generators he'd bought from the lumber supply store years ago just for this kind of thing. They also kept the refrigerator going and a couple of the floor lights on. Word was the power would be back tomorrow or maybe the next day. But you never knew.

Dawn got everyone up because once they had slept out their exhaustion for a few hours, it really was too uncomfortable. Then came the bathroom rounds. The men made it easier by going into the backyard to pee. All of them were taken aback at the sheer amount of broken trees and assorted weeds and branches and trash that had washed into the yard. And what was left of the toolshed. As their pee streams splashed into the pools of standing water, the guys could hear dogs and roosters off in the distance. But no birds. Which Paulus thought was weird. And it was.

Breakfast was simple. Cereal for the kids, bread and butter and jelly and peanut butter for the grownups. Whatever was available in the cupboards and in the fridge. Just enough milk. The stove was natural gas, and it worked, and Lenny was able to brew up some coffee. Rael said it was fun, "like camping out."

Last night they'd been able to grab some burgers and shrimp po-boy sandwiches from Irma's, the only café nearby that somehow was open, and also as much bottled water and soft drinks as Irma was able to ration to them. Lenny had offered to cook up two big bags of rapidly thawing Gulf shrimp from his fridge just to use them up, but they decided to eat out instead, just to see how the town was doing. They encountered one family Lenny knew at Irma's, but all the other diners were contractors working to clean up the roads and bayou.

Cold food for breakfast reminded Duane that they were not just in transit but in dire straits. The journey likely wouldn't get any better lingering in Cut Off, no matter how hospitable Lenny was.

It was sad, even odd, to see the big guy's loneliness, how much he wanted them to stay. When Duane said so to Maybelle, she snapped, "Don't be such a jerk. Can't you see what's missing?" Duane said he could. But he couldn't.

He did understand why Maybelle might think that was being a jerk—a limitless quality in a man—or something along those lines. And he would give her that. But he had to stay focused on their own problems, not Lenny's. His role in where they were now was clear and cold: the completion of the plan and the successful relocation of the Portia family to Carlos's ranch. By successful, he realized he was thinking of survival.

For the next few hours, they waited for the call about the fuel pump. Lenny made more coffee, which went down in gulps, and so he made more. Then Elena happened to tell her mom that she smelled bad. Which led to a chain reaction of quick showers. Because the water heater also was gas, there was enough for the kids and their moms and then for Maybelle. Lenny asked the guys if they could take field showers, and that he could rig up a hose in back on the other side of the storage shed for a little privacy. And so they did that. And changed clothes, putting the dirty ones in trash bags Lenny gave them so they could wash them on the road whenever they found a laundromat that was open.

Duane took the last shower, and while he was finishing up, Lenny got the call from Big Tiny, who said they were "damn lucky." Turns out the pump would be coming from Oubre's Auto in Houma, because Fred's in Des Allemands had written down the wrong year for the pump and so the one they had in stock was actually wrong. So they'd called Oubre's, which was bigger and did have the right year and model. Oubre's would be sending over a driver with it. The Oubre's driver would stop by Big Tiny's to get the money that would have gone to Fred's in Des Allemands. And leave the pump. Big Tiny told Lenny it should be there by 9:30.

Lenny said all those phone calls and changes of plans made him wonder for the first time since the storm when he might be going back to regular work hours himself. Probably soon. Fishing might be zero, but he could pilot boats for the government inspectors and oil company researchers who'd be coming in to check out whatever the hell had happened out in the deep waters.

At 9:40, Lenny and Boy Jack drove the pickup over for the part and were back in a half hour. There was twenty dollars in change for Duane from the three hundred he'd left. There actually had been forty, but they had left twenty with Big Tiny for his trouble.

Lenny parked his Chevy in front of the house to free up the driveway and then went into the garage to get his tools and lifts and tarps and whatever else they needed. They got the van moved up near the garage, then opened the hood and got to work. So as not to bother the repair job, Duane and Maybelle and the others took off on separate walks around the neighborhood.

By eleven-thirty, the work was done and the rest of the van given a quick once-over. Lenny said they were lucky it was actually in pretty good shape. He said the church might miss it before long, even if it was being put to good Christian use.

Boy Jack laughed and said yeah, they might be looking for it. Then he backed the van out the driveway and drove off. He passed Duane and Maybelle and honked and rolled down his window to yell "test drive" and flash a thumbs-up.

They turned in their tracks. "Shit," Duane said. "What do you think?"

"I think he's about to make an existential choice."

They got back to the house and waited. Lenny asked what was going on with Boy Jack taking off. Duane said not to worry, he was just making sure it was running okay. That he did stuff like that. Maybelle gave Lenny a look that he remembered from some of her research findings on that lawsuit. It went with the phrase "measured skepticism" that she had used frequently.

Ten minutes later, Boy Jack pulled back into the driveway.

"Worried?" he laughed as he got out and tossed the keys to Duane.

"I know where you live."

Boy Jack thought that was even funnier than Duane did.

Shortly, the others returned from their strolls and went inside to pack up their gear and load it into the van. And then inside for a final pee. Once again, the men took to the backyard.

That was where Paulus told Duane they needed to talk.

"When we were walking, we couldn't get anything on our phones and then after I'd given up, mine rang," Paulus said as he zipped up and walked with Duane toward a dry patch in the yard. "It was mom."

Duane's face lit up with a smile bigger than he thought was in him. "Damn, man, that's great news. I mean, I assume it is, right?"

"It is. She's up in Shreveport, or has been, with some people from the church who all went and stayed in one of the churches up there."

"Wow." Duane worked to keep the smile on his face. They both knew where the talk had to go.

"She said it all happened fast and her phone stopped working and they had to leave so she just left, and she's been trying to reach me. She already got hold of Jean-Pierre and my sisters, who are back in Gentilly or also in Baton Rouge. I was a little mixed up about all that part."

"But she's okay."

"She's okay. She thinks her church back in the city might have got flooded. I told her she was probably right. So now she wants to come back and see what it is, and is hoping Jean-Pierre or Tina can get over there maybe. I didn't go into why they probably can't. I bet you need a boat to get anywhere around there."

"I wouldn't be surprised."

"I mean, she's a strong lady, my mom, but hell."

"The Reverend Corina Youngblood is definitely known for that."

They both looked out at the backyard, and its shattered storage shed, and beyond. Some blue sky, finally, above the fields of brown and green and muddy black.

"Anyway, while the line was still good she said she wanted me to come back. I told her where we were, here in Cut Off. She said too damn many Cajuns for black folk and I ought to get out of there. I mean, that's the way she is."

"Fair enough."

"She said they were driving back to the city tomorrow, when the roads were better, and said they could pick us up on the way. They were in a big SUV from one of the people at her church who had some money. So we could all fit, me and Nadia and the kids, at least for the rest of the way across the river. Then we'd go on and find somewhere to stay. She knows people who'd put us up."

He glanced at Duane then back at the sky. "I told her that might be harder than she thought, but she said they had it worked out. She said she needed me, and also Nadia." Another, longer look at Duane. "She said even if the church was flooded out, her house in the Seventh was on stilts and might be dry. But it was street by street from what she heard, and she had to look for herself. She said Cray and the Sanctified Knights would help and she'd get ahold of them as soon as she got back. Assuming the phones and streets let her."

"You guys ready? I think they're probably waiting for us." It was Moon-Ra, coming out the back porch door.

"Be there in another second," Paulus said, signaling a thumbs-up. "See you out front."

Moon-Ra returned the gesture and went back into the house, glancing back at them as the screen slapped shut behind him.

Duane looked at Paulus. "She wants you back. Sure."

"So I just found that out, though. But I guess it's better than if we were on down the road."

"It's fine, man. It makes a lot of sense. You found your mom."

"Yeah. You know, though, Moon, he still hasn't found his."

"I know."

"I kind of hate to tell him about this."

"It's okay. He'll get it. I mean, he'll be happy for you. He will."

"I just thought . . . "

"No, I appreciate it. And damn, we need some good news."

"I guess so. I mean, I know so."

"So you want to wait here for her? I'm sure Lenny would be okay with it."

Paulus shook his head. "He sure seems the loneliest man I ever seen. But I was wondering if you could drop us in Houma. She said she could pick us up there. There's a church where she knows the preacher and we could just relax awhile. I mean, if he's there."

"If not?"

"Well, we can find something to do. I mean, if we need to. Just for a few hours."

"Sure. I mean, if the road to Houma is open. But if the parts guy got through, I guess it must be."

"Yeah, that's right. I mean, if not, you can leave us back here or somewhere easy for you."

"I think we can make it."

Paulus looked at Duane and then away quickly, in case something might have gotten in his eye to make it moist. They both stared out into the yard and sky a little longer. "I guess we better go out and tell everyone. Probably get moving," he said.

"Yeah. We better."

The family was standing around the van. Duane announced what was going to happen, and then turned it over to Paulus for the details. Elena and Rael didn't like it but didn't make a fuss or cry, and neither did Edwin or Samuel. Moon-Ra shook Paulus's hand and told him how happy he was, just like Duane had said.

Moon-Ra gave his cousin a key to the Portia front door, which they had locked but might not actually even be a barrier, and asked him to check in on the place when he could. Maybe everyone's houses later on if it could be done. Duane told Moon-Ra thanks for thinking of that and also thanks in advance to Paulus. They exchanged a couple of sentences about maybe the Portia reopening at some point although none of them put much stock in it. But it felt good to say it aloud.

Meanwhile, in Moon-Ra world, something inside was stirring. He had kept it deep and tried to bend it in his mind into a sign of hope. But it wasn't hope. It was a widening abyss of dread and fading chances. But no point in bringing that up. He and Eluvia wished Paulus and Nadia the best, exchanged hugs, and went on about how they'd be seeing each other before long when the city got back on its feet. The way people do when they know something probably won't happen.

"We should get going so we can get to Lafayette or around there before too late and be sure we can get a place to stay for the night," Duane said when the hugging was done.

"If we can't?" Maybelle asked.

"We might have to drive into Lake Charles and stay at a casino," Duane laughed. Although he realized it was a possibility.

Lenny had been in the garage and came out with a small ice chest. "Maybe you might need this out on the road, if it'll fit. Ice already in it."

"Sorry about all that shrimp you got to cook," Eluvia said.

It seemed to touch him, the comment, coming unexpectedly. "Thanks, but you know, I'm just going to take it into Irma's. They can cook it up and feed some other people with it."

"You're a good man, Lenny," Eluvia said.

"Definitely," Maybelle added.

"You need any help there?" Lenny said, turning away from the women quickly.

"I got it," Boy Jack said, wedging the ice chest into the last bit of space in the back of the van. "Man, I had to learn how to find a spot for anything in my delivery job. You wouldn't believe."

They both laughed awkwardly and then it was Lenny's turn to hug or shake hands with everyone as they started loading into the van. Boy Jack got in his seat to start the engine and get the air conditioner blasting.

"I don't know how to thank you," Duane said across the roof as he opened the front passenger door. "I'll let you know when we get back. I'm good for anything you might need."

"No charge," Lenny said. "I'll be seeing you for sure."

Maybelle waited to be the last to board. She gave Lenny a hug, and he squeezed her so hard she almost couldn't breathe.

"Madge'll be back," she said. "I'm sure she would've called if she had a phone connection. She knows this place. I might've done the same if I'd run into trouble, or my car broke, or even if I had one too many."

She said that last before thinking it through and as soon as she did she hated herself for ruining the good-bye. "I'm sorry. I mean, I just think she's fine. Had to spend the night somewhere in this horrible mess and you'll be seeing her before we even get to Houma, most likely."

Lenny looked down at her face and wanted to say something but it wouldn't come out. So he hugged her again, not as tightly as before, and whispered, "It was so good to see you, *cher*," into the top of her hair before letting her go.

"You, too."

She took the same seat, behind Boy Jack. Moon-Ra and Paulus next to her. Eluvia and Nadia and the kids in the back rows. She watched Boy Jack lower his window to give a salute of thanks and adios to Lenny. And put it in drive.

CHAPTER 25

Friday, September 2, late morning

Highway 24 to Houma was clear enough. The standing water spots weren't deep, and parish crews or local drivers had pushed aside fallen branches and assorted trash. Houma itself was easy for Boy Jack to navigate. Some wind damage but houses were intact, streets mostly open, plenty of local traffic. Good thing Her Satanic Majesty and Her Outer Bands had not lingered longer.

Duane realized that in seeing promise in a town that hadn't been totally destroyed, he was leaping at the chance to be an optimist. Which tendency he recognized because it was part of trying to keep a movie theater in business. Trying to see the upside. And usually paying the price. Figuring he'd have a good crowd for some retro festival week-end, only to settle for a handful of movie freaks. Or drawing a crowd for an expensive reel and then the projector breaks, or the a/c goes on the fritz, or Gretchen calls in sick and he has to handle the ticket booth himself, which he hates.

Which reminded him of Gretchen. He turned in his seat to ask Moon-Ra if he'd heard anything. "No, man. Nothing." They both knew what that might mean. They agreed to call her at least twice a day until they got an answer. Duane said he still felt like a shit for forgetting to call her earlier. Moon-Ra said he damn well should, but admitted he did, too. Then Moon-Ra started to talk about his mom again but stopped. Maybelle didn't say anything to either of them. She only knew Gretchen a little. And there were so many she did know. She began thinking of them.

"Are we anywhere close?" Boy Jack asked, impatient with the conversation because he needed their full attention. While they were talking, he'd been crossing the town back and forth, first on the main street then on side streets, with only Paulus to guide him from his seat in the back. And he was struggling. His mom had given him directions, but he hadn't written them down and was going by memory. He hadn't been to the Houma church but once, and that was years ago. "Maybe you better stop so I could ask someone," he finally said.

Which is when Boy Jack interrupted whatever Duane and Moon-Ra were talking about to help decide what to do about being lost. Which is when they came up on a big discount store not far from the relatively small convention center, compared to the one in New Orleans, and at the edge of downtown. The store was open, with a full parking lot. Paulus said to pull in so he could ask someone where the church was. Duane said they could also get some water and whatever they could find to eat. For the road, and in case they had to wait a while for Paulus's mom to show up.

Boy Jack made a quick right turn into the lot and parked as close as he could to the store entrance. Nobody wanted to go in with Paulus, because of the probable crowd and the vibes, so Duane said he would. After he and Paulus jumped out, Boy Jack turned off the engine to save gas. It wasn't long until everyone else got out to stretch and loosen up. Cautiously.

Around them were all forms of human evacuation, including more than a few redneck types who clearly didn't think whites and blacks ought to be riding in the same church van, no matter where it was from. Confrontations and beatings and shootings were their preferred responses, but for now they settled for firing off dirty looks.

Maybelle returned the looks with her own patented glare of contempt. She thought about how a hurricane could be effective in deterring spontaneous acts of violence. Her conclusion was that it provided no more than a false, temporary bond among diverse segments of the demographic. She briefly flirted with the idea of a research paper on the subject that might get published in some kind of radical law journal. And then she realized she was thinking like Duane, and it had a mixed impact on her self-perception.

She went back to knife-eyes at a bubba in baggy jeans and matching camo T-shirt and cap, and just in case that wasn't clear, a tattoo of the Confederate flag on his left bicep. He was walking away from a red pickup where a bleached blond woman in her thirties, about the guy's age, also in jeans and T-shirt, sat on an upturned plastic box in the cargo bed. She was watching two toddlers trying to get over the sides or out the back gate. Maybelle felt no warmth or empathy for any of them.

Duane and Paulus were back in less than twenty minutes, carrying a flat of bottled water and a few plastic bags that held a variety of whatever they could easily grab—peanut butter crackers, chips, questionably fresh lunchmeat and cheese, two loaves of squashed bread, some juices for the kids, assorted candies.

"It's like an Atlanta traffic jam in there. And then the credit card machines didn't work and people were getting mad as hell. But I had some cash and that got us through the line faster. Shit, there's a hundred people in lines back in there. All of them pissed off."

"But at least we got some stuff," Paulus said. "And one of the old guys who worked for the store at the front door told me where the church is. We're actually not too far." Duane passed the bags of food and snacks to Nadia while Paulus managed to cram the water into the back of the van next to the ice chest Lenny had given them.

Once everyone was resettled, Boy Jack asked Paulus if he really knew where they were going this time. Paulus was rightfully irked, but was learning how Boy Jack often lacked any regulatory mechanism between his brain and his mouth. So he simply said he did, and he guided them with no detours.

The True Blessing of Jesus was in a frayed neighborhood, now even more so, on the side of town more or less on the way back to Cut

Off. A vivid green, red, and black paint pattern brightened the brick and siding and signaled what must have been a brave declaration of African lineage in Cajun country. Maybe also a welcome invitation to more and more black searchers of the soul. The windows on the east side were broken out and the front doors looked like they might have some damage. An older dark gray Chevy Suburban was parked in the small gravel lot in front. Boy Jack pulled in.

Paulus hopped out, went up to the door just as a black man with a gray beard, dark T-shirt, jeans, and rubber boots came out.

"Reverend Becker?"

The man raised a hand. Paulus met him halfway and they talked. No one in the van could hear because the windows were up because Boy Jack kept the a/c and the engine running. After a couple of minutes, Paulus turned, signaled a thumbs-up, and started walking back to the van.

"Praise Jesus," said Nadia. "We going home now."

"How, Mama?" asked Elena.

"We gonna wait here and grandma will be here to get us maybe around lunchtime. Then we going back to our house, or at least back to New Orleans and our hometown."

"Yay," said Elena.

"Yay me too," said Rael.

Paulus opened the side door and his family poured out, pulling their packs and the plastic bags of food with them. Then they went to the back of the van while Paulus and Duane opened the hatch and carefully picked out a few other of their things without letting everything tumble down in the process.

Reverend Becker introduced himself to Paulus's family and waved to everyone still in the van. They waved back.

"Bless you for bringing this family to us. We ain't got much, but at least it's safe and it's dry and it's still standing like the rock of the Lord."

"You just never know who's going to be still standing anywhere right now, Reverend," Duane said. 'This is a big help."

"You can stay, too, if you want. Church of Holy Sanctuary with

Kansas plates and all."

Duane looked at the preacher and then off into the distance, and then back at him. "You know, that's kind. But we have to move on. We have a ways to go yet today, maybe get to Lafayette, even farther, if the roads are good."

"Everybody's on the move now. I don't think I've ever seen people getting away like they are after this Katrina. And I mean I seen a lot of these hurricane times."

"Yeah, it's pretty bad."

Reverend Becker looked at the name on the van again. "Still, you never know what will come of it. God's ways are mysterious. You know that, I can tell."

"I didn't think it was that obvious."

The reverend laughed. "Well, you should maybe think again." He clapped Duane on the back and turned to Paulus. "So you know when Miz Corina's gonna make it here?"

"Just sometime around middle of the day. It all depends," Paulus said.

"It does that. But come on inside. You can unload your stuff, use the bathroom, whatever you need. I got the windows open until the electric kicks back on but it's not all that bad."

"Sounds perfect," said Paulus. He took Nadia's hand and walked with the preacher to the church, the kids running and horsing around behind them as they went.

Paulus paused at the church door to look back at Duane. They'd already said good-byes riding over, and so he just waved. Duane did the same, and so did the others. Boy Jack used the horn to toot his own burst of farewell.

Then they were gone. More room in the van now, so Moon-Ra and Eluvia and her kids spread out a little. Maybelle stayed in her seat behind Duane and watched the church recede from view. Boy Jack cut back through the town to get to the highway. Duane stared out his side window, not really sure what he was seeing.

In no time they were up on US 90, pointed toward western

Louisiana and eastern Texas. And beyond. Way beyond.

The kids fell asleep in an instant and no one said anything for almost an hour.

CHAPTER 26

Friday, September 2, afternoon

It was hard to know if the traffic was heavier on US 90 than usual, but at least it was moving. It usually took a couple of hours to get to Lafayette, maybe three with traffic. Still, so far there were no detours or major back-ups. If they'd taken I-10, they might be in a traffic parking lot and would be lucky to get as far as Baton Rouge for the night, which probably wouldn't have any rooms anyway, and would be triple the usual price if so.

Duane was glad to be on the road. They all were. But he had a secret gladness that wouldn't sound right to say under the circumstances. The howl was still loud and clear and incessant inside his mind, or more accurately what could be called his soul. He felt he had a soul. Because he didn't know what else to call it. He might speak to Maybelle of this later. Maybe Moon-Ra.

Morgan City was definitely slow, and the bridge was more clogged than the streets. Once they got across, Boy Jack said they ought to top off the tank even though the gauge still said half-full. Because who knew if it was accurate.

Duane agreed right away and they found an off-brand gas station with only a dozen cars in line. It gave everyone a chance to pee, in facilities so filthy that Maybelle said she ended up straddling the toilet bowl and peeing like a guy. Eluvia said she was lucky she had boys instead of girls but for herself ended up standing on the toilet seat and squatting over the dark yellow and brown in the bowl. They were all glad it took a while for the van to get to the pumps, because they needed the time to breathe once they escaped the disease pit.

"It's the thousand little dagger wounds that'll drive people to insanity and homicide. Trust me on this," Maybelle said to Duane as he held the gas hose.

"Sorry. We'll be past it soon."

"You don't have be sorry. I wasn't asking. I was just saying." He could tell Maybelle was on that edge that often took some talking down, but he knew she could handle it.

The pump clicked off and he paid right there, using his credit card, which he was glad was possible. He decided he could hold his bladder until the next stop. Boy Jack couldn't, having waited for everyone else. He hurried off to the men's room and came back with the grimace of having waded through an acre of raw sewage. The gas fumes floating over from the pumps were like restorative perfume.

Someone in a Suburban waiting in line honked for not moving on fast enough and got a Boy Jack double-finger return and fuck you glare. The honking stopped.

Boy Jack dropped his shades back over his eyes, hopped in, and they were on the road.

Duane turned his attention to the radio buttons. They'd gotten past WWOZ range and WWL was spotty, so the only choices seemed to be country-western or Bible stations. Then, finally, Cajun music and blues. An NPR program that turned out to be from Lafayette.

After about ten minutes there was a headline update that basically said New Orleans was flooded almost everywhere. That Mississippi had been hit even harder than everyone first thought, and the roads out of both places that were still open were jammed. And that the National Guard and the Army were in New Orleans and that people had drowned trying to get out of their homes. By the time the music came back, the entire Portia family was depressed.

Moon-Ra tapped the buttons on his cell again but reception was even worse on the open road. He bounced his phone on the carpeted van floor, stared out his window.

"We'll find your mama," Eluvia said, picking up the phone and giving it back. "I know we will. It's just all a mess."

"I know. Still."

"We'll find her. I got faith. You ought to, too. Mama probably out there worrying about us, so we're all just kind of together in that way."

The road delays that weren't supposed to be on US 90 began just past Franklin and continued for most of the next two hours until they hit New Iberia. It wasn't the highway that was bad—it was the drivers. First slow-down backed up the westbound lane for several miles and turned out to be a collision involving a horse and a Dodge Ram pickup. By the time Boy Jack was able to steer around it, the dead horse was pulled over to one side of the highway and the Ram, with a bashed-in grill and crushed wind-shield, was in a field lying on its side.

Flashing lights on the state trooper cars cordoned off part of the open lane, impeding traffic more than needed, in Boy Jack's opinion, as did a fire truck that seemed to have no apparent purpose. Nobody was standing around the Ram, so it was a good guess the driver and any passenger had long since gone to the hospital in Lafayette, if not the morgue. It looked pretty bad. The horse's guts and what looked like legs were still strewn on the roadway, to be driven over just to get past the wreckage.

The next two delays weren't as lethal but ate up another couple of hours. An 18-wheeler had blown a tire and part of its trailer was jack-knifed across the highway, so it was single lane again as a trooper waved his flashlight back and forth, even though it was broad daylight. This one was an oil or gas or maybe chemical tanker, so it wasn't long until fire trucks with lights and sirens came speeding in, probably out of Lafayette.

Around the Jeanrette exit, somebody in a late-model silver SUV hadn't been paying attention and banged into a flatbed carrying a bulldozer that had slowed to get off the highway. That caused a chain reaction of fender benders, with seven or eight vehicles scrunched and lined up behind each other. Their drivers were standing on the gravel shoulder talking to one another or on their cell phones, which Duane seriously doubted were pick-ing up any service. That was going to be a nightmare for all involved and so far no cops had arrived.

It was after three when they took the New Iberia exit. Duane said what he usually did when he was there, that this was the home of Dave

Robicheaux, the famous ex–New Orleans cop, who actually didn't exist but was made up by a writer named James Lee Burke, who didn't live there anymore. But anyway the town was cool and had even been in a couple of movies, and now all kinds of visitors knew where the Bayou Teche was, and even what a bayou was in the first place.

You could never assume people in other parts of the country would be familiar with Southern names any more than with Southern ways of life, Duane said, after telling Boy Jack which roads and streets to take through the town to stay on the path to Lafayette, adding that "telling them more about us" was one of the things he planned on covering in his movie. He noticed Maybelle and Moon-Ra share a glance when he used the word "movie," but he went ahead with his thought-train, sounding more each minute like a lecture in a community college English class, and said that aside from the literary fame, New Iberia was just another racist enclave of old rich families and rednecks, and black folks that had learned how to survive.

Boy Jack concentrated on driving. Moon-Ra had heard this, what Duane said, before and so had Maybelle. So Duane was really only talking to Eluvia and the two kids, but he felt good going on about something other than the hurricane.

They lucked into finding a local diner that was open, and everyone filled up on greasy burgers and chicken. Back in the van, Maybelle said she was glad they were taking this back road way instead of staying on 90 to get to Lafayette because they'd have to go through St. Martinville, and she knew of a little hotel if it was open. She said she was getting less and less sure about finding a place to stay, given all the traffic headed that way and on to Lake Charles.

She said her friends Will and Bonnie from the law office had both bragged about St. Martinville as a getaway, supposedly with good music, and then she fell silent for a while, looking out the window. "Well anyway, Bonnie would go there." She looked out the window again, chiding herself for making a terrible joke at Will's expense. Being dead and all.

"Mama, what's wrong with Maybelle?" Edwin asked softly.

"Shhh."

After a silence, Duane said, "Sure, let's check it out. Maybe I can get something on my laptop there, too, and we can check for hotels in Lafayette if we need to."

"Good plan," said Boy Jack. He had some idea where Maybelle's mind was right now.

It was only ten miles but took a half hour to negotiate the winding road through green, tree-filled countryside and farmland, past a few gas stations and rural groceries and laundromats. There were plenty of downed trees to dodge, and every car they came up on seemed to be content to drive thirty miles an hour.

In St. Martinville, it was easy to find the hotel that Bonnie and Will liked, right along Bayou Teche, next to the massive Evangeline Oak, dedicated to the Acadians expelled from Nova Scotia in 1755. They had one room left, at $200 a night, but thought there might be a cancellation later. If not, the lady at the front desk said, there might not be anything else in town she knew of.

Lafayette probably might have something. She said Duane could use his computer on her internet if he wanted.

Maybelle said it might take some time, and offered to take the others, especially the kids, on a quick tour around the square hosting a historic Catholic church. Maybe get some snacks at a little shop near the bayou bridge, if it was open.

The connection was still good, thank you, Jesus, and it took Duane only about ten minutes to link up a motel not far from the University of Louisiana campus with two rooms, $125 each, but one had only a king bed. Duane and Maybelle would have to share a room with Boy Jack, while Moon-Ra and his sister and her boys took the other. They had to check in by 6 p.m. He booked right away.

By the time Duane got back to the square, Maybelle was shooting him an eyebrow raise followed by a subtle turn of her head up the street. The others sat quietly at the bench where they had gathered, smiling as if by force and as if trying to appear utterly normal and happy and in fact quite delighted to be traveling through a strange town because where they lived was submerged by unmeasurable pound-feet of hydraulic force stretching over an entire city. Maybelle's mouth formed a silent "cop" as Duane glanced in the direction she had indicated.

It was. A fucking cop. City, not state, which probably was worse, but you never could be sure about that. The "probably" meant the cop would know everyone who lived in town and by elimination everyone who didn't. And even in the time of hurricanes, you didn't want a cop in a small Southern town to take an unusual interest in you if you weren't from around there. Mixing races prompted such interest.

While Duane was still thinking of all that, the cop car eased across the street and stopped along the curb. But it wasn't a city cop. It was a deputy from the parish. He lowered his window. He was a young guy, reddish-blond hair, aviator sunglasses, pressed uniform, the whole macho thing.

"Sir," he called out to Duane.

Duane turned, all innocent smile.

"Y'all in from New Orleans?" He shot a hard look-see toward the bench. Duane walked up to him slowly, stopped a respectful few feet away. "Yes, officer, we are. Just looking for some place to stay."

"Kinda all booked up around here, I'm afraid."

"That's what we're finding out."

"So you'll be taking off, I guess."

"Unless you know somewhere might have a vacancy."

The deputy's grin wasn't really. "Not that I've seen. But you know, I have to ask people now where they are. We're getting all kinds from the city. You know?"

Duane did. "Sure. It's pretty awful back there right now. I guess everyone is spreading out."

The car radio squawked and the deputy looked at the blinking red light, but it stopped. Then back to Duane.

"So then you're just taking a break I guess," the deputy continued. Duane could feel the tone turn straight-up aggressive.

"Yes, sir. I guess we'll be heading off, though."

"That your SUV over there?" he said, tilting his head toward a blue Chevy Tahoe down on the main street strip a block away in front of a bar.

"Oh, no, sir. We had to park on the other side and just been walking around. Been in the car all day, feels like."

"I thought you were looking for a place."

"Yes, that, too."

"Well, I guess you might want to get a head start. And you sure don't want to leave a vehicle too long, even in this little town, because of all the people coming through day and night. You know?"

"I guess I do."

"So where you headed, then?"

"We might try to get to Lake Charles if we can."

"That sounds like a plan. Those casinos can take a lot of people. Or then there's Beaumont and all that over the state line."

"I guess we'll see how it goes. I guess you know how it is out there."

"I sure do."

"Well thanks for your help, officer."

"No problem." He adjusted his sunglasses. "Well, I can make sure you get back to your car okay, if you like . . . with all your friends there, or maybe it's family."

"Thanks. I think we're fine. We just had a nice time resting up here in your town and now I'm sure everybody's ready to get going."

"Just doing my job—"

The squawking came again, louder and continuous, and this time Duane could hear some kind of static-filled voice spewing out a number, some kind of cop code.

"Hang on," the deputy said to Duane. He rolled up his window, pulled a hand mike from the radio mounted under the dash, and said something Duane couldn't hear. Then he rolled the window back down. "Anyway, be careful now. I'll be sure to check on you later."

He closed the window again, adjusted his seat belt, reached to turn on the siren flashing light, and basically burnt rubber peeling out. He veered across the street so fast that an oncoming flatbed utility truck carrying big piles of brush and tree limbs had to slam on its brakes just shy of a collision.

227

Duane watched until the deputy was well away. Then he turned to Moon-Ra and Maybelle, who were already off the benches in front of the church and walking back toward the van, making sure to stay on the sidewalks and not transgress the manicured lawn.

"Fuck," Duane said, catching up with them. "He's all over us. He got called off but he'll be back, you can bet on it."

"Fucking Cajuns," Moon-Ra said, striding hard. "Every fucking time. Paulus's mom was right."

"It's just fucking cops," Boy Jack said. "Don't matter whether they're Cajuns or Anglos or whatever."

"We were lucky," Maybelle said. "That boy was a killer. I could see it from where we were."

"You're right," Duane said.

"Mama, why are we walking so fast?" Samuel asked. "Are we in trouble?"

"No," Eluvia said, gaining on her brother. "It's just time to go. We wanna make sure we get to Lafayette."

"I can run," Edwin said, and did, across the back half of the square, Samuel catching up with him quickly. They got to the van before anyone. A few more cars were parked around it that hadn't been before, and a few more people walking around. They didn't look like they were local, either. But no cops. They left.

Someone else had paid the price for their getaway. Somewhere, some other person's misery, relayed by police radio, had attracted the unusual interest of the law in a way that would escalate into yet another live-action scene in a never-ending movie of arrests and possible beatings or even shootings. Over maybe nothing more than a speeding ticket.

If he were back at the Portia, Duane would have lit a votive candle to the Virgin, or maybe St. Jude, or maybe both. He wasn't Catholic, but he had learned that much about gratitude from living in the city. And he was sorry for whoever was bearing the burden. Whoever was in that movie instead of him.

CHAPTER 27

Saturday, September 3

The motel was good enough and they were too tired to care. They stayed awake long enough for another round of fast food and then pretty much collapsed for the sleep they had been without for days. By 9 a.m. they were loaded up, continental-breakfasted, bathroomed out, and back on the road.

The idea was to get to Houston by afternoon, joining up with I-10, even with traffic, and reconfigure how much farther they would drive. Maybe San Antonio. Then cut south for the Lower Rio Grande Valley and on to the Big Bend. Eventually picking up US 90 again along the Rio Grande and then some state highways.

He hoped to be wherever they were supposed to be within the week. To breathe. To take stock. All that. They could easily make it to the Valley that soon. Even if it wasn't their final destination, he wasn't opposed to resting there. It was a good place, the Valley. They would be surrounded by many people and many towns and not feel alone and abandoned by their storm-smashed city. They would not be threatened by hurricanes. They could relax, rethink. They could give thought to relocating that wasn't based on desperation and nothingness.

Duane liked having Boy Jack doing the driving and liked sitting shotgun in the front passenger seat. It was like having your own thought bubble. A cone of silence for your own brain. Which, according to Maybelle, Duane often needed.

Which made him think of Maxwell Smart in *Get Smart*. But he wasn't that guy. Nor was Maybelle Agent 99. And it was a good thing

Duane's thought bubble was in an imaginary cone of silence and that he didn't even have to look at anyone else as the van ate up the miles to a place along the Texas border that was yet to be certified as imaginary or real.

As they drove, Duane wanted to call Memo, the lawyer in Dallas. He would still have Carlos's deed, assuming it hadn't been mailed. Maybe Duane was channeling Rhys, but he was reluctant to go much further in this impromptu odyssey until he got the legal deed and any important details for taking possession. Also keys to gates or buildings, if any. And more to the point, an address.

Duane began to half-wonder if his assumption about the "ranch" location was correct. What if it were actually in the Valley, not the Big Bend, because he was starting to recall that Carlos had family down there. Around maybe Brownsville or McAllen.

But for the most part he did think it was in the Big Bend, and probably near Presidio, in the mountains in the general direction of Marfa. Bits of memory were popping back in now that there was time to think past immediate survival from one day to the next. One clear memory was through the foothills with Carlos near the river when coming up from the south of Mexico on a smuggling run to LA. They were picking up a dozen crates of rifles and boxes of ammo and then taking them back across the border.

Carlos said he chose the spot for the crossing because he was familiar with the area and because you could drive a truck across the Rio Grande near there and no one would care. So they did. At night. Duane had no idea where in Mexico they were going, other than southwest of Presidio on really bad roads, for hours. Carlos, the contact for the job, said it was better Duane didn't know anyway.

After they delivered the weapons, they had to get back into the US fast to stay safe. They crossed back over in what seemed like the same low-water bed of mud and gravel, then drove up into some foothills on a steep gravel truck path full of wash-out ruts, past what sounded like a prowling mountain lion, until reaching an old tin-roof line shack. It wasn't much but it had cots and kept out the mosquitoes.

They caught a few hours' sleep at what Duane now had to think was the "ranch." Almost had to be. But his memory was blurred. So he really needed the deed for the address, and he had to find the ranch. And he was pretty sure it had to be done as stealthily as possible.

Which put his cone of silence head into a covert panic about where exactly he was taking all these people. Various scenarios popped up, none of them what he really wanted, and he must have exhaled loudly because Boy Jack glanced over at him with a quizzical brow for a second as if he'd said something. Duane waved his hand to indicate it was nothing and Boy Jack went back to driving and watching for cops. And Duane.

For the next several miles, channeling Rhys, Duane's mental calibrations shifted yet again to how he could make a movie at the "ranch," if indeed that's what it was. A movie about the lush, fertile South. Using desert land west of the Pecos.

Oddly, and ironically, he still had confidence that he was doing the right thing. Which confidence gave him even more confidence. He understood that circular reasoning could produce flawed judgment.

But could it not also be a source of visionary transcendence? Or what good was "transcendence" as a word anyway? How could a word which claimed to transcend actually be held accountable by the very cognitive processes it no longer required? This could lead to much more exploration in his head, and perhaps push out the panic. He felt it important to keep that kind of mindset, not just for himself, but for those now almost totally dependent on his securing at least a landing place on solid ground. He also hoped to stow that somewhere in his brain for possible subtext in the screenplay he really needed to start writing.

A person looking at his situation from the outside would have to conclude that the entire odyssey, while having definitely taken Duane's flock out of harm's way in the face of forbidding odds, was in fact little more than a tapestry of dangling loose ends. Requiring transcendence. And mobility. And, ultimately, a destination.

Meanwhile, everyone was feeling cooped up. The boys fought with each other every so often and could require pit stops along inconvenient stretches. On one stretch, they'd had to pull onto the gravel apron of the highway so Sam could pee in the weeds. People in passing cars shot them looks, although most, especially those with Louisiana license plates, knew the situation. The situation was itself a situation.

Understanding the situation had even become kind of a code Duane had observed whenever they stopped. Some of the fellow travelers were on the edge and lost their tempers over lines at gas pumps or fast-food windows, but for the most part, the push of people recoiling from Katrina brought out more patience than tantrums. Knowing that it did gave Duane another sense of resilience. That maybe there was something worth exploring in humanity. Perhaps even saving.

Duane wanted to talk to his van mates about these loose ends.

They seemed down, cooped up with all the driving and confusion, but he wanted them to remember what was most important. They had escaped. The storm was gone. The flooding was worse. The Convention Center was behind them. The deputy in St. Martinville didn't arrest them. The ten thousand potential mishaps that could have killed them without pause had not done so. Their search for tomorrow was courtesy of a stolen church van. They were evacuees. They were really refugees. They were homeless. The most they could hope for was a place to survive. Maybe start over.

That was the appeal in Duane's idea, at least to him. Starting over. But where? Should such a life change be entrusted to a man with visions of movies in his head empowered by a mysterious friend with experience of revolution in his? If said friend still had a head? Those men would be Duane, and Carlos, respectively.

Yes. It made sense. They were revolutionizing their lives. In that sense, they were no longer refugees! Forget that word! They were *warriors*. In the New World, in the place where the New World made the most sense. They were citizens of the South. They were free. Even if not by choice. They were pilgrims. *Merci*, Katrina!

This was going to be a great fucking movie.

CHAPTER 28

Saturday, September 3, afternoon/evening

It had been a while since Duane had been to Texas, and he was surprised at the sense of coming home. It wasn't his home anymore at all. But it had been, and, now, he had no real basis for pretending he'd given up the connection. Even though he was long since a Big Easy convert. Like everyone else in the purloined and recently repaired Church of Holy Sanctuary van from Topeka, Kansas, he hadn't taken off for the endless Lone Star state because he wanted to. He had left for Texas because it was there.

After a few miles he saw the green mileage signs for Orange and Vidor and Beaumont. Whatever Texas was now wasn't whatever it had been in his indoctrinated mind as a kid, or for that matter his liberated mind as an adult. But it had the land he needed to make the movie he wanted. That movie, it was just beginning to occur, might not wind up exactly following the storyline he had in mind before Katrina provided her own notes. "Notes" is industry jargon for fucking with your ideas.

They hit the Houston slowdown just past noon, coming into the eastern edge. Boy Jack missed the exit for the I-610 loop around the city, so they stayed on I-10, straight past downtown, which didn't seem too bad at midday. Then it was.

It was a good stretch to San Antonio, but cell access was no longer a problem, and the phones helped to pass the time. Duane tried Memo again and this time left a message that the call was urgent. He also tried Rhys again, with no luck.

Maybelle tried Bonnie's number, twice. She also called her mom, with better luck. She was in Dallas with grandma and Aunt Ouisa and doing fine. "We're good down here, too, Mom," Maybelle said, as everyone in the car listened. "Headed to San Antonio now. Duane, yeah, and some of our friends. Let me call you when we stop and I can talk more. Yeah, okay. Love you too, Mom. Tell Dad and everyone." Then she clicked off, looked around like, so what, and tried a third time to call Bonnie.

Moon-Ra took Maybelle's cue and tried for Miz Claudia and Feliciana. Eluvia called her half sister, Jolia, in Alabama, and for a few minutes the car was as full of different voices, different conversations, as an airport lobby. Even Duane called his mom, who scolded him for not checking sooner but was also glad he was okay. She would pass on the news to his sister and brother. Boy Jack hadn't called anyone yet. He knew he needed a conversation with Mr. Croydon, but he didn't know where to start, and still didn't want an audience.

Following I-10 into San Antonio, they found a hotel with a decent price near downtown. Again, the primary goal was to stretch, relax, and hope for plenty of sleep before taking off in the morning. They'd meet later for dinner. Maybelle said she wanted to go for a walk, and Duane would have, but he fell asleep. Until a call woke him up. She didn't identify herself, thinking he should know, forcing her to finally say, "It's Sofia, for fuck's sake. Memo's out in LA and told me to call and also to give his, you know, his fucking regards. Okay?"

Duane worked to get a clear head and remind himself what this was about. It wasn't about old times. "Sorry. I just didn't expect." He hoped his tone sounded better than hers. He flashed on something Carlos had once said when they were drunk: "She dresses like a Republican but moves like Ché."

Sofia famously didn't care for small talk and got right to the point. Carlos, in fact, owned two ranches. Or farms. Or small tracts of land. Depending on how you looked at acreage. One was in the Big Bend, near Presidio, and that was the one Duane had expected. He breathed in relief, causing Sofia to pause as if he was going to say something. Which he didn't. Then she went on.

This other property was much closer. She said even Carlos might not have known about it, since they'd been unable to reach him, but Carlos's instructions to Memo had been to transfer "any other related properties" to Duane, also.

In this case, a smaller parcel of land just outside McAllen, somewhere in Hidalgo County. It had come to Carlos through an estate settlement just last month for an uncle who had lived in Seattle and made a lot of money in computer software. His name was Roberto, but he was mostly known as Beto. He had left the family decades earlier and was scarcely known to anyone.

He had deeded the new property, about twenty acres, to Carlos in part because he had heard of Carlos's exploits and in part because he had no children and didn't want to leave everything to charities or the courts. And especially not to his niece, Carlos's sister, Victoria.

Who, Sofia explained, in flat methodical lawyer-voice mode, had already filed papers to get the Hidalgo County land from Beto, just as she was trying to with the ranch at Presidio, which originally had come from Carlos's late father, Benito, after the Mexican hero, because that was just the way she was. And Victoria's husband, Phil Reagan, a gringo from Dallas, was even worse.

It was a lot to take in, so Duane had to ask Sofia to repeat a few things, which she did, not hiding annoyance. Sofia said that was pretty much it other than the deeds were coming to him tomorrow on FedEx and he had to give her the hotel address.

They shared small talk about themselves for a few minutes. She said she was glad to be in touch, even under the circumstances, which were enough for him to detect a slight note of disappointment when he explained his traveling companions, specifically Maybelle. It occurred to him he wouldn't mind seeing Sofia after all, but it was more a product of his ego and flawed memory than his feelings. Also, it was extremely stupid, and Duane's mind issued a very brief electronic pulse of congratulations at his maturity and reprimand for his disrespect for Maybelle. They said good-bye and hung up.

That evening at dinner on the patio of a Mexican place on the Riverwalk, he wanted to talk more about what lay ahead. He remembered Maybelle had told him that everyone was only going along with his plan because they had no other choice.

He waited until they were done reminiscing about New Orleans trivia and pet peeves and missing it, while proving how hungry they had really been for something other than road food.

At the flan desserts, Duane told them about Sofia's call, his lawyer, Memo, in Dallas, and the letter from Carlos that got all this started, that only Maybelle and Moon-Ra really knew about. He said the deeds to both properties would be at the hotel tomorrow morning, and they could go over as much detail then as anyone wanted.

Then he told them what he remembered about the ranch. He said he didn't know enough about the second property on the border at McAllen, but he'd find out as soon as he could.

"So this Big Bend ranch," Moon-Ra finally said, "it has a house or something like that, I think you had told us?" At almost that exact moment, mariachi music erupted when a door opened from the restaurant.

"I think. Maybe. But I have no idea, really."

"He doesn't," Maybelle said. "No idea."

Duane looked at her, then back at Moon-Ra.

"Okay, but you asked for questions, man. Sure looks like we got a long drive for a lot of 'maybe.'"

Duane glanced at Eluvia, whose expression had slid to stone, then at the others. He wanted to be careful with his words. "I get what you're saying. That's why I thought tonight we could clear the air or whatever before taking off tomorrow."

"You hope we'll still buy in," Maybelle said.

The mariachi horns hit a crescendo and they had to wait a minute to talk.

"It's not just about the land. Or even the movie. Like I said back at the Portia, we could build a new life, too."

"Doing a movie?"

"If I can make it work." He adjusted himself in his chair. "But you can do what you want. Of course."

"Maybe we all want to go home," Eluvia said, after being silent most of the evening.

"We can't. I mean, you know," Moon-Ra said.

"Not right this minute, I do know. I mean when the water's gone and we can go home. Go to our own houses." She looked toward the boys. "I mean, you know that."

Moon-Ra scratched his cheek, looked up through the oak trees.

"I'm in," Boy Jack said. "I always thought about moving to Texas. I mean, why not? It's not like I got anywhere to go back to. Except maybe to get my truck."

Maybelle said nothing.

Duane took a deep breath, and another draw of his beer. "Nearest town to the ranch, if I'm right, is called Presidio, general vicinity of Marfa. Maybe I already told you that. And it's near where they filmed *Giant*." Blank expressions. "It was a classic about Texas, with Rock Hudson and Elizabeth Taylor and James Dean."

"James Dean!" Boy Jack exclaimed. "Totally fucking awesome. It's out there? That's the ranch that guy just gave you?"

Duane smiled.

"But what about this brand new *other* ranch?" Maybelle said, just enough edge to be noticeable by all.

"That's what she called it, the lawyer in Dallas," he said. "She said it was a ranch. I'm not even sure Carlos knows it's his. This new thing just came out of nowhere."

Maybelle looked over at the tourists walking by. She wanted to say it reminded her of all the people in the hall at the Convention Center. She didn't.

Eluvia's face showed she was having trouble registering anything. Boy Jack nodded.

"That property is whatever it is, y'all, although it belongs to me and I'll make it work for all of us," Duane said.

"The boys are ready to go back to the hotel," Eluvia said.

Short silence.

"Okay, but just let me get this out real quick. I just wanted to kind of give us the big picture. At least the one in my head. I mean, we're just a few days out of a hurricane and we kind of need to remake our world, like half the city has to."

No one spoke but they all looked at him.

"I know I tried this back in the Convention Center, trying to explain what my idea is, and blew it. But maybe now I can make more sense. I haven't ever shared this with anyone"—awkward look at Maybelle and Moon-Ra—"so let me go back to something a regional rep for our film distributor had told me a few years back."

Awkward looks from Maybelle and Moon-Ra. Eluvia waved her hand in a go-ahead gesture, the kind she usually gave to her husband Timothy, and where the hell was he?

Duane nodded to her.

"So I didn't think much of it, what he said, at the time other than an interesting story because of *Giant*. But now, well, word is that somewhere around there in those mountains in the Big Bend— where the ranch is—is the remains of a movie set some rich guy and his cousin from one of the cartels were backing. Some kind of film project they were calling 'The Sons of Aguirre.' It was a kind of spin-off, or maybe just a reference, to a cult film called *Aguirre, the Wrath of God* by a famous German director. I know, nobody's heard of it. I couldn't even find it one time to book at the Portia because the distributor, same guy who told me this story, couldn't get it for me. In fact, I think that's what led to him telling me about the spin-off thing."

Maybelle was looking at him hard. It was the look that always told him to get back to the point.

He took a drink. He might as well be talking about aluminum siding.

"Anyway, 'The Sons of Aguirre' was supposed to be some high-concept kind of art film set in modern times, was the rumor. Some cult director nobody hardly had heard of brought in from Barcelona."

Duane paused. Maybe Maybelle was wrong. Maybe they were actually paying attention. Except maybe Eluvia. Anyway, he'd finish the pitch.

"So one of the cartel guys was into movies and couldn't get his money into any of the Hollywood studios without getting arrested, so just decided to do it on his own. But, you know, it stopped because the money ran out. About the time the cartel film wannabe guy fronting the money suddenly disappeared. Poof!" He made a poof sign with his hands. "Anyway, they say the set is still there."

Silence and beverage drinking. Some wriggling by the boys.

Then, from Moon-Ra. "So they were going to do that movie on Carlos's ranch?" He looked at his sister. "I mean, that's the basis idea for this whole trip?"

"Kind of a strange coincidence, yeah, including Katrina."

"You know all this from a film distributor?" Maybelle asked.

"Yeah, but it kind of made me curious, so I also did a little research of old movie industry magazines in the Tulane library and found some stuff about it, articles about an *Aguirre* spin-off, they called it, scheduled and nixed near the *Giant* location on the Texas border. So at least there was something to it. As for a movie set, I never found anything. The distributor guy said he doubted they ever built any sets and he never knew anybody who knew anything about it. But, you know, it just seems to me something is out there. Also, never got me the *Wrath of God* reel."

"Sounds cool," Boy Jack said. "You know, reminds me of Mr. Croydon. He hears shit all the time about where some kind of antique might be, or something valuable that got forgotten about in some old run-down house or plantation shed or whatever. You know, he always checks them out and more than half the time he makes pretty good money at it."

"That's all I meant," Duane said. "Who knows what we'll find?"

Maybelle looked at them both.

"No crazier than anything else we're doing right now," Moon-Ra said. Eluvia laughed at that one.

Duane sat forward again, grabbed his Dos Equis. "I mean, that ranch isn't 'Southern' or anything, but I was thinking of a dream sequence that maybe could include some of that scenery . . . "

"Duane," Maybelle said, touching his arm. He stopped.

Even the boys sitting next to their mama knew something not quite right was in the air. They paused in their fidgeting and gawking.

Which is when Eluvia pushed back her chair and stood.

"All that's good, Duane, but you know, and I appreciate all this, but I don't really need to hear anything else about movies and ranches and what-ifs and where-tos." She glanced at her brother. "You want to know what we want? Well here is what Eluvia wants. I just want to go home."

No one moved.

"That's *my* opinion. That's what I want. The boys got schools they know back home. Sooner or later, everybody be back. It's always that way. I don't know nothing about anything in Texas and don't really want to. I just want to be home. You know?"

Moon-Ra nodded, looking down at the table.

"How long do we have to wait?" she said.

"For the city to come back? Nobody knows," Moon-Ra said.

Maybelle nodded. "That's true."

"Well then you can just send us back on a bus or something up to Birmingham. We can live with my sister Jolia or go on to Georgia to stay a while with Timothy, supposedly working on the power lines. And we could get back in our house in New Orleans as soon as they let us."

"You'd stay with Jolia? With Timothy? I thought—"

"Yeah."

Moon-Ra looked at Eluvia, the boys, the crowd at the entry. Took a breath.

Then, to Duane: "Maybe we can get her a ticket tomorrow?"

Duane looked at Eluvia. "It's your call."

"Damn straight it's my call. You don't have to tell me that."

"He just wants to know what you want to do," Moon-Ra said.

She exhaled slowly. "I know." Her look at Duane softened. "We're just not cut out for this."

"You're being pretty damn sensible if you ask me," Duane said.

Eluvia's mouth shifted into a smile. "I guess so. And look, I know you got us out of there. We'll never forget. I just—"

"We needed you, too," Maybelle said, reaching across the table to put her hand atop Eluvia's. "I know I did."

Boy Jack raised his bottle. "To getting back to your own family, your own places. I totally get that."

They all joined the toast, mostly because, what else?

CHAPTER 29

Sunday, September 4

By nine in the morning, Eluvia and Moon-Ra and the boys had gotten dressed, finished breakfast, and loaded up the van. Church bells from the cathedral downtown were loud and sad.

Eluvia had things she needed to say. She told Moon-Ra all those big ideas of Duane's were just to help get through being lost. Except he should have been looking for a safe home back home, like she was. Doing that, thinking about home, instead of rambling all over the place, into strange places at that, talking up some movie idea to make us all rich or happy or whatever, and just driving us along in that beast of a church van.

She said she was the one who'd made the smart call. Then she went quiet as they closed up the van doors and got the boys inside. Then she told her brother she didn't mean what she said in an angry or judging way. Just something she wanted him to know about the way she felt. Before she left. Because she wished he'd come with her. But would pray for him to find what he wanted.

Duane came out the hotel door ready to drive to the Greyhound station. Boy Jack and Maybelle were staying so as not to crowd up the ride, but had said their good-byes.

At the station, already swarming with travelers, Duane parked across the street and helped Moon-Ra unload Eluvia's bags. Moon would stay with them at the station until the bus came. As soon as Duane closed the rear hatch, Eluvia came up to him with a strong embrace and her eyes teared up just enough to almost force the same from Duane. But he just couldn't go there.

243

He gave the kids quick hugs and Moon-Ra a strong pat on the back as support, and drove off. He didn't look back. He realized that was a kind of philosophy for what was coming. Moon-Ra said he would call for Duane to come get him when his sister had gone.

The morning crawled by, and for ten bucks the hotel desk clerk let them stay a few hours past check-out, so they could get the FedEx. When it arrived, he didn't want to talk over the contents in the lobby, so they drove to a small park near the river about ten minutes away. At one point it might have been intended for nearby King William swells, but now it anchored a mixed neighborhood of newish apartments and old Spanish-and French-style houses in need of rehab. Perhaps like the people who lived in them. It reminded them of parts of the city from which Katrina had pushed thousands away. Including them.

They sat at a moss-stained concrete picnic table barely in the shade of an oak and went through what Sofia had sent: various legal docs, six worn-looking keys taped to an index card, and a letter from her. Duane pushed it all to the center of the table so the others could look over. He said the letter was pretty much the same as what he'd explained at dinner last night, but they were welcome to read it for themselves.

Boy Jack gave it little more than a glance and called it "lawyer shit."

Maybelle jabbed him with her elbow.

"No offense. I mean just these lawyers. Not yours." They both laughed.

But the papers did serve a purpose. Despite the dry legalities, the arrival of facts in print—actual deeds—instead of Duane's grandiose visions was morphing the expressions around the table from week-long anxiety to pleasant surprise to relief. Maybelle in particular. Especially the letter from Sofia. The telepathic message beaming from her eyes was, "Well, buster, I guess you're only half full of it after all, and it sounds like that Sofia knows it." Actually, she also said that aloud, and then laughed.

When everyone was done, Duane gathered the papers back into a stack. He noticed they were damp along the sides from being handled. The steamy heat was already inducing sweat.

Maybelle wiped some from her eyes. "So that's it, then. Nothing else to wait for? To talk over."

"It's all here."

"And we have a destination. For reals."

He let it go. "So I'd say the plan from here is that we head down to the Valley, just like we were doing anyway. But now we check out Weslaco, even though she said McAllen, which is pretty much on the way. Then on to the wild west."

"Sounds impressive," Maybelle said, using her dramatic voice. "So we're off, *Los Conquistadors de Katrina.*"

"*Conquistadors?*"

"You know, search and destroy. Find gold. Make our mark. All that."

"You got it," Duane said. More like a snarl.

Moon-Ra thought of intervening, but whatever was going on between them wasn't about plans or properties.

"I'm ready to roll," Boy Jack said, hoping to change the subject.

Moon-Ra gave him a quick glance of hell yes.

Maybelle turned with deliberate body emphasis toward Duane. "You're the one fascinated by Aguirre and that movie. I mean, wasn't he some kind of *conquistador?*"

"Actually, like I said, that movie was *Aguirre, the Wrath of God.* From Werner Herzog, and yeah, it is fascinating. And yeah, like I also said, it somehow must have inspired 'The Sons of Aguirre,' which was just a working script, if that. And yeah, I am intrigued as to how it might affect what we find at the ranch." He tried to modulate his pique. "So that makes me a *conquistador?*"

"*Claro que sí, mi amor.* Because Aguirre was this European mercenary who had a vision and went looking for gold in the New World, which is the very definition of *conquistador*, ain't it?" she said. "Plus, he ended up killing his daughter. Down in Peru, somewhere. I mean in the movie."

"Yeah, quite a feat when you put it that way."

"Well you know, connections. I'm a big believer in connections, right?"

"I remember your stories back at the Convention Center."

"Well you get an extra kiss later for that, my dear *auteur*, née *conquistador* thou never wert."

They eased back from each other. Car horns in distance.

"So what I'm saying," she resumed, "is that all that insanity from five hundred years ago brings us to now. Which brings us to your movie idea. That you still need to write a script for. You know, the one about the South that we're doing all this exploring about. 'Southern Guide to Self-Improvement,' right? And by South you're thinking it could be . . . in the Big Bend of Texas."

Duane looked down at the package on the table. "Nobody has to go past here. Just like with Eluvia." Barely audible.

Maybelle looked him over, a long, tense moment. Then at Boy Jack and Moon-Ra. "Never mind the girl in the jeans and soiled T-shirt," she said. "She's just expressing inner anxiety about being homeless."

Duane put his hand on hers. To his surprise she didn't withdraw. Then she did, resting her arms and elbows on the table top, cupping her face with her hands, her stare now way beyond the park, way beyond a thousand yards. Or miles.

"What do you say, Moon? You still in?" Duane's voice barely broke a whisper.

"I don't feel there's any way to be 'out.' But sure. I kind of get it."

"Maybe we could just get going," Boy Jack said. "It's way too hot for all this."

More silence. More sweating.

"So let's do it already," Boy Jack said, voice rising. "I'm boiling."

Maybelle looked across the table, then at her Duane beside her. "I don't think your idea of getting us out of there, maybe starting a new path. I don't think it is in any way flawed. You know, as a concept." Then, almost to herself, "But I might be, darlin'. Flawed."

They looked at each other like they had the only eyes in the world. They kissed.

Boy Jack and Moon-Ra were already up and walking to the van.

Fifteen minutes later they were on I-37 headed south toward the Valley. Ten minutes after that they had to stop for gas. South Texas was no place to come up empty.

Big Bend ranch entry near Presidio.
Photo by Rod Davis

PART IV
THE HOWL

But through unreality, the Dominicana thought, they understood at least one important thing: that people could be other people, cities could be other cities, and worlds could be other worlds."

—Michael Zapata, *The Lost Book of Adana Moreau*

CHAPTER 30

Wednesday, September 14

Ten days later.

They followed highway 170 alongside the Rio Grande for about forty miles, keeping an eye out for an abandoned wooden shack next to a turnoff, possibly overgrown with weeds, leading north up into the mountains. If they got to Candelaria, where 170 stopped, they'd have gone too far. From the turnoff, it was supposedly seven miles of what Memo had described as "the nastiest-ass tire-track rut road you've ever driven" until they'd get to a "hidden valley" and a barbed wire fence leading to a metal swinging gate. No cattle guard because no cattle.

Past the gate it still would be a half mile to the line shack. Memo said that was all he knew about the place. It might or might not have electricity or water. "So don't plan on spending the night until you check it out. And call me when you get there, for sure. I mean if they have service."

The seven-mile road, to use the term loosely, was as nasty-ass as Memo had described, even in the Jeep Grand Cherokee they'd picked up back in Weslaco after giving up the van. Boy Jack, squeezed into the cargo space with the seats turned down for extra room, groaned at the worst jolts but mostly was still asleep or groggy from Duane's leftover pain med from his own mugging.

Finally, the trail dropped into a valley and Duane spotted the barbed wire fence leading to the ranch gate. Rock and concrete posts on each side. He waited at the gate for Maybelle to catch up in Boy Jack's F-150. She'd been hanging back enough so as not to eat dust the whole way. She pulled in beside him. So they could look through their windshields, as if in a dramatic shot in a movie, and see it together. The ranch. Or whatever it was.

What it was not, in all its dream-dashing splendor, a film location.

From what they could see, Memo had been mostly right. About the mountains, the valley, the line shack. What he had failed to mention was now in view from the gate: a hard-packed dirt airstrip, a military-style Quonset hut, and a tin-roofed outbuilding that might be a tool shed. All surrounded by brush, bare land, mesquite, and salt cedar. Duane was pretty sure this was where he and Carlos had spent that gun-smuggling night. The passing years had yielded considerable upgrades and add-ons.

Maybelle noticed that Duane seemed lost in thought. There was no time for that. She lowered the F-150's window to make sure he could see her making a what-the-fuck hand gesture. When he did, he responded in kind, then held up his phone so she could watch him punch in some digits. But she couldn't see who he was calling: Memo. Or what flashed on his screen: "No service in this area."

He threw the phone onto the passenger seat and got out of the Jeep, hoping the gate was locked, for security, because he had keys. It wasn't. He pushed it open. "Fuck if I know" was all he could utter as he walked back past Maybelle. They drove in to the line shack. She had to grit her teeth so hard her jaw hurt.

Duane tried to take it easy on the rut- and stone-filled lane, hoping not to wake, or cause pain to Boy Jack. He had to admit he was excited about finally getting there, even if it was a challenge—that was a good word—for his entire plan. Maybelle had a different POV and wasn't hiding it. But he understood. The thread of solid purpose, which had embedded in his soul back on the levee when Katrina was but a possibility, had become bare and tattered. Not for him—the movie, the ranch, the new jobs, the new start in the desert mountains. All still his north star.

Not for the others, the ones who were gone and the ones who were left—which now meant just Maybelle and Boy Jack. For them, Duane's Epiphany on the Levee (he was trying that out in his travel-fatigued head) tasted more like a reality sandwich somebody'd left on William Burrough's grave.

Which reality was that Katrina had smashed their lives. There was nowhere else to go and nothing else to do.

"Out here is about the same as anywhere," Boy Jack had said at the hotel bar in Marathon last night, a few hours before getting almost beaten to death in Alpine. "You're wrong," Duane had said. "This, out here, this is a helluva lot better."

They shared a laugh and a toast. Maybelle shrugged. She was watching the other people in the bar who had not fled a hurricane. Who did not know.

That what could have been a two-day drive from San Antonio to Presidio, or even a three-day at an easy pace, turned into ten, wasn't a hindrance, more a window of recovery. Following the border along the Rio Grande Valley and then the Trans-Pecos and Big Bend, is magical in just about whatever way you want. Hurricane odyssey included.

Three days were devoted to Duane, Boy Jack, and Moon-Ra (before he left) throwing up over bad tacos at Donny's Delite at Harlingen. Maybelle had refused to eat them, saying they smelled bad. Three more days at Carlos's Weslaco property, because Maybelle was enchanted with the fact that the land was actually being used as a model co-op *colonia*, the Red Blossom, managed by a brilliant and sensual force of nature named Rosario, who tried to talk Maybelle into staying because they could use a paralegal seven days a week. And then the two days at Progreso it took to buy and transfer title for the Jeep Grand Cherokee from Rosario's friend, who sold it for a bargain price because otherwise her divorced asshole ex-husband might try to claim it and she would have to shoot him. And then just the driving.

They also took time to visit a butterfly park, a bird sanctuary, and the historic, semi-mystical old cathedral at San Juan, the last of which left them with a half-dozen bottles of holy water and varieties of introspection.

Which may have been what inspired Moon-Ra and Boy Jack to decide to drive back to New Orleans and return the van of the Church of the Holy Sanctuary from Topeka, Kansas. In turn necessitating Duane's need for the Jeep Grand Cherokee. Moon-Ra wanted to be near his family and his Feliciana, and Boy Jack wanted to retrieve the F-150 he had put in Mr. Croydon's garage the eve before Katrina showed up. Moon-Ra would stay in the city, but Boy Jack wanted to go back to meet Duane and Maybelle because he'd decided he was a young man with a sturdy pickup who definitely needed to Go West. So he did.

But the biggest distraction along the border was crossing into Mexico at Falcon Lake on the way to Laredo to see what Rosario had told them about the reincarnated village of Guerrero Viejo. It had been drowned by the dam that created the lake, but had risen again because of an extended drought. As long as it wasn't submerged, the village, filled with still-preserved buildings amid a dark, dank forest, was open to any visitors who could find it. Duane said it could pass for a true-life version of *Green Mansions*, with Audrey Hepburn. Except in this version, Audrey was a very old woman living alone with the birds and animals, selling fruit drinks and trinkets to occasional tourists.

Duane spoke enough Spanish to communicate with her, but there was only one word that counted: Xóchitl. What the old woman called out to Maybelle as she was walking with Duane among the mold-covered ruins. The same name that Maybelle had assumed in her monologue at the Convention Center. Maybelle had stopped, turned, and locked eyes with the woman. Maybe more. It would be fair to call it surreal. It would be fair to say Maybelle had not been the same since.

CHAPTER 31

Wednesday, September 14, *later*

At the line shack, Duane left the Jeep idling so the a/c would keep Boy Jack cool. Maybelle jumped out of the Ford to open the Jeep's hatch and give their Cajun bar fight casualty a look. His forehead was warmer than she'd hoped but he was asleep and breathing quietly.

She pulled out the plastic sacks of things they'd bought at the pharmacy in Alpine, hoping not to have to go to a hospital. Because they'd have to explain why Boy Jack was messed up. Duane had been thankful the pharmacist hadn't asked questions because they'd picked out quite a mix: Advil, bandages, hydrogen peroxide, gauze, Neosporin, water, Gatorade, vitamins, and a few things for themselves, including two cans of Red Bull. Forgot a thermometer.

"I mean, damn, how does anybody live in this godforsaken place?" she asked, stepping back and closing the hatch.

"I think that's the point."

They gave the line shack a closer look. The keys Sofia had sent in her FedEx package worked. It was actually more than a line shack, despite its description, although not much more. Still, it was in decent enough shape: rectangular, wood frame, aluminum siding, tin roof. No broken windows.

The inside was dusty. Obviously not recently used. A front room with small kitchen area, an eight-place metal and Formica table, and folding chairs. A narrow hallway led to three rooms, starting with a closet-sized bathroom with a shower and then two bedrooms, one with a bed and clothes rack. The other room was apparently for storage.

Full of cleaning supplies, stacks of taped-up boxes, wicker baskets of sheets and blankets, and a fold-up military cot. Also a couple dozen water bottles, all full, one in the dispenser.

Maybelle tried the switch on an air conditioner unit cut into a wall in the front room. Nothing. She tried pulling the cord on an overhead fan in the bedroom. It didn't work, either. Neither did the one in the kitchen. Nor did any of the various lamps. A transistor radio on the window ledge above the kitchen sink was likewise useless.

"Probably a generator around here somewhere," Duane said. "Has to be some kind of electricity, or they wouldn't have all this stuff."

She looked into the old refrigerator that was neither running nor had anything in it. "Ghost fridge."

"Pretty much sums it up. Weird, a little."

"A lot. Wanna try that Quonset hut?"

Duane looked at the key ring. "Not sure if there is one. Probably in here—"

"Like here." Maybelle had slid open a counter drawer next to the sink. Empty except for keys. Each had a tag saying what it was for. Duane compared them to the ones Sofia had sent. All the same. They laughed for a second. "I guess they're not worried about thieves. Whoever 'they' are."

"Either that or they don't have to. I'd say this is for frequent fliers. In and out. Nobody's ever gonna just drop in."

"I don't like it," she said, heading out the door.

"Only two kinds of crowd would," Duane said, following her. "Maybe three. But I don't think hunters would go to this much trouble."

"So, two."

"It's crawling with all kinds of cops and military around here, just like the Valley. So, I mean, it could be something they set up. Maybe don't use very much. People don't call this part of the border a DMZ for nothing."

"Feels more druggie to me," Maybelle said, stopping at the Jeep, opening the hatch to have another look.

"Yeah. Other than being too clean."

"Well, yeah."

Boy Jack was still zonked. She closed the hatch and followed Duane to the Quonset hut.

"Either of those possibilities, wouldn't they need permission of the owner to use the place?" she said, shielding her eyes from the sun. "You know, Carlos? Your mysterious pal?"

"Hard to figure out." Duane stopped to look at the air strip, filled with weeds and scattered rocks. "Nobody would want to land a plane out there."

"Black helicopters could. You know, the ones that don't exist."

Duane went on to the Quonset hut, tried keys tagged Q-1 and Q-2 . The first fit the black steel padlock and the second opened the throw-bolt lock.

"Like a charm," Maybelle said, pushing past him onto the unpainted concrete floor inside. "What the hell?"

The room was full of nothing. Or almost. Three long plywood tables, banged up and possibly military issue, a few metal folding chairs like the ones in the line shack, and an open cardboard box filled with wires and cables. No windows. Two a/c units, with plugs and extension cords leading nowhere, mounted into spaces cut into the curved metal walls.

"Smells like an armpit," Maybelle said. "Not that I'd know."

They walked the length of it. "Plenty of room for parties. Or, you know, screenings," he said. "The Portia at Presidio."

She went back outside. Then he did, but left the door unlocked.

"So," she said.

"So," when he caught up with her. "So might as well check out that big shed."

It was for tools. All shelves and wall hooks. The usual array of hammers and shovels and wire cutters and nails and wrenches and pliers and even some battery-powered hand tools. Drills. Saws. Air-compressor and industrial-strength tire pump.

Also a dozen red fuel containers that were filled with gasoline or maybe kerosene. Also, various 50-gallon barrels of oil, or something.

Also, two other barrels, apart from the rest, with pumps and stenciled lettering saying "Aviation Only." All thick with dust. It was the hottest of all the buildings. They left.

"I wonder where they keep the artillery."

"Really."

"And the bodies."

He didn't reply.

On the way back to the line shack they noticed another shed, much smaller. It was attached to the back of the shack, but hidden from front view. It looked like something just big enough to hold a generator. And it did. Two of them. Big, maybe twenty-thousand watts, fuel-powered, new-looking. Each connected to an electrical box on the wall, where several other cords of unknown use dangled loosely to the floor.

Both generators had pull cords as well as starter buttons and were also hooked to car batteries mounted on a shelf. Duane looked at Maybelle, who snarked, "Do or die." He rocked each of the generators and they both felt full of gas. He pulled the cord on one. It fired up smart and loud with only one tug.

Maybelle applauded and hurried into the line shack to test the light switches while Duane peered around for anything else that could help.

"We got power," she yelled, loud enough for him and anyone in three counties to hear. Finding nothing else, he closed up the shed. There was no telling how long the gas and the power would last, but Duane figured they'd find out. And probably there was a rule that all the cans and barrels had to be topped off and ready at all times. Which meant they were very unlikely to be alone for long.

"My man!" Maybelle said, affecting a swoon as he walked into the shack. "You fixed that faster than a broken reel in the projection booth." She paused. "Except for that fucking air conditioner."

Duane tried the a/c buttons and wall plug for himself. Nothing.

Maybelle rolled her eyes and pulled the brass chain hanging from an overhead fan. It began to whirl.

Duane held up his arms to feel the circulating breeze. She was already checking the fans in the bedrooms, which also turned.

"I'll go try the a/c in the Quonset hut," Duane said, heading for the door.

Maybelle shrugged, as if amused. "Why?" Then stood up steel-rail straight, which matched her expression. "I'm not staying here, Duane. It's creepy."

He stopped.

"I'm not staying here." There was something in the way she said it the second time. "And neither is Boy Jack."

"It'll be cooler at night. It's the mountains."

"It's not the fucking heat. We're not staying here."

"I heard you."

"We've been here half an hour at least. He needs to wake up and sit up or stand up. And a doctor. And turn the Jeep engine off. It's been on a long time and it'll overheat and we'll be stuck."

They looked at each other. It was too hot to argue. Not that she was wrong about anything.

Duane went out the door. She followed. They opened the Jeep hatch to help Boy Jack sit up and drink some water, but the best he could do was raise his arms slightly so Maybelle could look at his hands, wrapped in blood-soaked gauze from the pharmacy. There didn't seem to be any fresh bleeding, but the old stuff was ugly and smelly. He dropped them to his side. He tried to make words but couldn't.

"I think it hurts his mouth or maybe his jaw to talk," Maybelle said.

"We're here," Duane said.

"Sa's goo," Boy Jack mumbled before slumping back. Duane elevated his feet. Maybelle touched his forehead. Still warm. She said she didn't see any unusual dilation in his eyes. But they were still blood-shot, and he'd be looking like a raccoon soon enough.

"He's got an infection. I don't know where, but we need to go now to that hospital in Alpine. Can you put it on your card?"

"I can."

"I mean, I know he probably doesn't have insurance."

"I found a card in his wallet when I picked him up outside that club, so he might. But that's not what I was thinking about."

Duane took a step back, still looking at Boy Jack. "Like we talked about. They'll want to know what happened."

She didn't move. "So tell them."

"He was in a bar fight over drugs?"

"You'll think of something. I mean that's your thing, right?"

He let it pass.

"So let's go. Now. Just work it out."

He stepped back, calculating. "It'll be four hours again, at best, with all the bad roads. You think he can handle that?"

"Better than he can handle spending the afternoon, let alone the night, here without seeing a doctor."

"Yeah."

"What about the Ford?" she said.

"We'll come back for it." He looked at her. "Right?"

"Yeah, sure."

Whether either of them believed that hung in the air.

Duane locked up and turned off the generator. They were getting into the Jeep, which had been left running, when Maybelle said they shouldn't really leave Boy Jack's pickup at the ranch.

Duane tried to read her face. He asked if she was really up for the rugged drive in the Ford. She said it was better than wondering if it would be there when they got back. Or who else might be.

They rolled out, separately.

The hospital was on the other side of downtown Alpine, on the way to Fort Davis, but supposedly easy to spot, according to the receptionist he had called when the reception came back. They made it around 6 p.m. The parking lot looked empty, but once inside, they could see that the ER actually was busy. But that was good.

Nobody would pay unusual attention to a kid who looked like he might be a hanger-on from Sul Ross who got busted up in one of the usual late-night brawls around town. Which is what Duane ended up saying when they checked in, because Boy Jack didn't look remotely like a ranch hand who'd gotten injured mending a fence line. The kid had been in a fight. But nobody knew why.

The young doc didn't care. Maybelle followed him, a nurse, and Boy Jack in a wheelchair into the exam room. Duane stayed at the admissions counter for the paperwork. The doc looked over the multiple bruises on Boy Jack's face, body, arms, and thighs. The nose wasn't broken. Not as lucky with the ribs. He asked if they wanted an X-ray. No breaks, but three ribs had deep bruises and would take a few weeks to completely heal. As for the cuts on the hands, something yellow was oozing out. A nurse cleaned and treated them with antiseptic and put on clean bandages.

Duane stayed out front still filling out forms. Boy Jack's insurance, through Mr. Croydon, covered everything but the co-pay of $400. Duane used his own credit card.

All told, they were done, Boy Jack packed back in the Jeep, and out in less than two hours. Better than Duane had remotely imagined. First stop was the drugstore they'd visited earlier. Duane got the painkillers and antibiotics while Maybelle stayed in the Jeep.

"This is a great country," Duane said, carrying back the sack full of drugs. "I mean, if you got Blue Cross to pay for everything." Maybelle shot him a look because much of her paralegal work involved people who had no money, no insurance, and no chance.

Then she got out of the Jeep, started toward the Ford. But stopped, turned back. Duane could see it coming but he made himself think otherwise. But the Doobies had it: "*What a fool believes . . .*"

She came to his window, said Boy Jack couldn't make the trip up to the ranch again. And she wouldn't drive the Ford there in the dark. She said Boy Jack "obviously" should be in a room with working a/c and near a hospital for another day, at least. You never knew with ribs, and he'd coughed up blood, too.

Duane ran his hand over his own recently mugged rib cage, reflexively. He no longer felt even a twinge. Just laser beams from her eyes.

She reminded him she was never going back to the ranch. Starting now. It wasn't a debate.

They booked a floor-level room at a jacked-up price at a sufficiently anonymous chain motel nearby on the highway. Just for two. Maybelle and Boy Jack. And one vehicle. The Ford. Almost no conversation. They helped Boy Jack into a bed, then kissed good-bye. More or less politely, more or less sadly.

It was getting darker, but he and the Jeep headed back to his new spread. Something suffocating had settled in his soul, his heart, maybe his head. Could he really leave her at a motel in the Big Bend with a busted-up buddy that cops might actually be looking for? He could not. Could she want him to? Turns out she could.

He had barely made it to the Alpine city limits when he remembered the cell reception problem he'd soon be encountering. He made a U-turn back to the motel parking lot. Strong signal there. He could've called Maybelle, knocked on her door, just to patch up what just happened. To say he understood but still loved her. That both would be going their own way.

But he didn't.

What he did do was call Memo. There were questions. All he got was voicemail.

Driving on in the dark, he thought again about calling Maybelle. And again did not, probably could not. He stopped at a burger joint in Marfa because he hadn't eaten, and gobbled the grease on the way. Almost no traffic back to the border except for a speeding *migra* pickup headed the other direction. It zoomed past him like it was hellbent on ruining somebody else's life. Not that there were many lives around.

"*Despoblado*," some called the Trans-Pecos. Deserted, abandoned, unpopulated. All of that. For a certain temperament, that was an attraction. Maybe that was what was wrong with him. Maybe Maybelle had just been waiting for him to figure it out.

He pulled up at the line shack just past midnight. Still warm, but not hot. He turned on the generator in the shed and fans in the shack and opened a window in the front room and the bedroom, which helped a little. He stretched out on the bed, dust and all, just to relax from the drive and the tension.

Sometime in the night he woke up shivering. It was definitely cool with the elevation. He got up for some water. A small wicker chest at the foot of the bed was stocked with sheets, pillows and a few blankets, which he hoped didn't have any fleas. He left the bed as it was. He went to the bathroom, pleased to find that it had toilet paper.

Before going back to sleep he looked out the window at what stars he could see. He thought of Maybelle, at how she was right about having air conditioning for Boy Jack at the motel. And wondering what was so important about the damn ranch and the maybe-movie that he had to come back to spend the night in nowhere instead of next to her.

CHAPTER 32

Thursday, September 15

When the phone buzzed just after 7 a.m., surprising Duane that any kind of reception was possible, he was already up and making a cup of Nescafé in the microwave. Although he still had electricity from the generator, he hadn't quite figured out how to hook up the gas stove, or even if it would work.

He knew it would be her because who else. And he knew what she would say, and she did, and he had to admit it was reasonable. But he didn't like it, and once again it produced the inappropriate feeling of anger at Boy Jack. Good Lord, what kind of person would be mad at someone beaten so badly?

"But you could stay up here a few days until he gets better."

"He won't, up there. And I won't, either. Do we have to go over this?"

"It's nice here in the morning."

"Can you leave now? Bring all his stuff? And mine? I think it's all in the Jeep."

"What?"

"He can barely talk and sit up, Duane. But he said he can't go on to New Orleans or to LA all busted up. Or whatever he had planned. It was hard to understand him."

"So this is up to him?"

"That's not what I mean. But like I just said, there's really no choice. Shit happened, Duane. I at least need to take him to Weslaco. Rosario can help us. I called her just as a long shot, but she said yes right away. So we're going. I mean, unless you want to come with us."

Long pause.

"I'll leave now and bring down your stuff."

"We'll—" The line dropped. "No service" popped up.

He added a packet of hardened sugar that had been in the cupboard to the coffee. He drank it fast. He locked the door, as if it made any difference, went around back to turn off the generator. He retraced his path to the motel. It was almost noon when he got there.

Maybelle opened the door to Room 114 before he could knock. Their stuff was ready and on one of the beds. Boy Jack was sitting up on the other, propped against the pillows. He'd managed a change of clothes into a loose-fitting blue T-shirt, gray sweatpants that he probably slept in, and sandals. He looked like his parents were coming to take him home from summer camp after a bad fall from a cliff.

He attempted a smile but ended up waving one of his bandaged hands and saying something that sounded like, "Hey, man," from a mouth clogged with socks. He looked worse than he sounded. Duane immediately regretted giving Maybelle a hard time on the phone. But that call hadn't really been about Boy Jack.

They guided their patient to the Ford more easily than they'd gotten him into the motel room. Maybelle did what she could with travel bags and blankets to build a nook against the back seat window so he could at least elevate his legs. The pain pills would help him sleep.

Everything else fit into the toolbox in the pickup bed. Duane added the ice chest from the Jeep, filled from the motel machine. Maybelle said they would pick up more ice and supplies on the way. They'd probably have to stop fairly often.

She said it would be best to get going, not that there was much traffic in Alpine. They could stay at Rosario's "for however long." If they needed a doctor again, Rosario knew some. It occurred to Duane that had they not left their belongings in the Jeep or back at the line shack, Maybelle and Boy Jack would have already been gone and she'd have called him from somewhere on the road.

She told him that despite all the LA talk, she was pretty sure Boy Jack intended to head back to New Orleans once he had healed up. He had asked her to call Croydon for him, since his words all sounded like mush. She did, and Croydon was shocked. He wanted to know if Boy Jack was okay. Maybelle had said "pretty much for a mugging," but could really use a place to recover. Might not be able to work right away. Croydon said if the guest house wasn't ready, Boy Jack could use the upstairs room that was less damaged. Go back to work whenever he felt like it.

Duane gave the tailgate an extra check to be sure it was closed and walked around with Maybelle to the driver's side door. The engine was loud and throwing off heat. But that's not what made it uncomfortable to stand there, avoiding eye contact.

"I'll call from the road and Rosario's."

"I wish you could stay."

"I know."

They embraced.

"I can't talk about it," she said. "I do love you."

He kissed her. Her lips were soft. Her eyes were wet.

His countenance was like a cow's waiting for the pneumatic hammer strike.

"So, you're really going back up there, the ranch?"

"I am."

"I mean, you don't have to stay there, either."

"I know."

Exchange of looks that didn't need a second take. "So I'd better get going."

She climbed into the cab. "*Hasta*, eh, cowboy?"

"*Adios*."

She closed the door, then opened the window.

"Don't forget me. Don't forget Maybelle."

The pickup rolled out with him just standing there.

He watched as long as he could. In his head, the part that still worked, came the refrain from an old Tom Rush song: ". . . *she's gone, solid gone.*"

He drove up and down Alpine's main strip, through the downtown business stretch, then a U-turn and back the other way. On the occasions in which he was aware of where he was and what he was, like almost running a stop sign, he told himself he just needed to cruise a little longer, that he was looking for groceries or some coffee and a taco, that it was Saturday night, and he was a kid in small-town Texas.

But he wasn't fooling anybody. He was just driving. He did not want to be aware. Did not want to think. Just robot reactions to traffic, robot scanning for cop cars. Eventually, his mind rebooted and he took the turn leading back to Marfa.

But he didn't stop. He drove straight through and didn't really tune back into Earth until he was almost at Presidio. It was a bigger town anyway and it was easier to find a *supermercado* for supplies, and also a liquor store for a case of beer and a quart or two of Jack.

He affected the air of a gringo tourist getting things for a party. It made him forgettable to the townies used to such nuisances. He gave the slightest thought to crossing into Ojinaga, but that would mean customs and he had no business going through their bullshit.

He did need to use the phone, though. So on the way out of town he went back to the *supermercado* parking lot where he knew the cell signal was good and he wouldn't be noticed.

"You need to tell me, no bullshit," Duane said the instant Memo answered.

"What the hell?"

"The hell is there's a lot going on out here."

"So fill me in. I haven't heard from you for days."

"You have any idea what I've gotten myself into?"

"Like I said, tell me."

"Fuck, you tell me."

"This isn't making me comfortable, your attitude."

"My attitude is I drove all the way out here to see Carlos's twenty acres and it's built up like some kind of military black ops LZ that got abandoned. Which you already fucking knew."

The line went quiet.

"It was an opportunity."

"No fucking doubt."

"I'll tell you, but get it together, will you?"

"Waiting."

"Okay, so it's this way. About five or six years ago, not long after you and Carlos did a little work together, Carlos needed money. Not for him, really, but for the villages down in Mexico, or maybe Guatemala, he'd been working with. You know them, right?"

Duane had to take a moment. "I do."

"So cut to the chase. Carlos knew a guy who knew a guy who was willing to pay big bucks for a landing strip across the US border. To fly in stuff."

"*Drogas?*"

"Just stuff, okay? I'm only telling you as a lawyer, and not even your lawyer, really."

Duane tapped his palm against the steering wheel.

Memo broke the silence. "Anyway, Carlos had some land—the one where you are. He wasn't using it. So he made a deal. They could build something on it right away. But he kept the deed. The details and the money came through me. Actually, through a guy I knew in El Paso. For a cut, you know. Quite a profit."

"Jesus."

"That's the way Carlos wanted it."

"People stayed there?"

"Sometimes. Then they stopped."

"Hnnh."

"Yeah, like that."

"So, Carlos knew all this when he sent the letter."

"The thing is, he was worried his sister would figure this out and put a bullshit claim on the property if she found out. Like she tried down in the Valley."

Duane thought a moment. "So I keep her from getting it."

"Correct."

"And he didn't want me to know the details just in case there'd be a leak."

"Correct."

"Well, shit."

"Now, it's your play. Carlos still stays completely out of it."

"So I could live on it. Make a business out of it."

"Why would you do that, Duane?"

"Just thinking out loud."

"My thinking would be to sell it," Memo said. "Yesterday."

"This is totally fucked up."

"Way more than fucked up, but never mind the details. I've already researched the market value. You could make several hundred thou, easy. Maybe a lot more, with the water and all."

Duane hadn't been paying attention to his surroundings and noticed that a Border Patrol sedan had pulled into the lot, and two officers were headed inside the store. Maybe to arrest somebody. Maybe to get some Gatorade. You never knew with those fucks. One cast a quick look at Duane's Jeep. Probably nothing, but it was spooky.

"I need to go. I'll call you."

"You really should."

Duane made his way out of town and back to the ranch. The miserable trail up the foothills played another round of hell with the Jeep's shocks and tires. He finally made it to the gate and was relieved to see that it still was closed. I.e., nobody was hanging around with AK-47s or rocket launchers or skulking with bodyguards inside their black armor-reinforced Expeditions or Land Cruisers. Nobody, especially Duane, would get killed on this visit. Except time. The remainder of the afternoon with no one to talk to but plenty to consider.

The book and then the movie of the same name, *The Remains of the*

Day, popped into his head. He had given up on trying to understand what the continuous random zaps of film references might even mean. Perhaps something he might be able to work into a script, some kind of character indicator. Probably a flawed character.

By the time she got to Marathon, stopping at a gas station and helping him pee, to the consternation or amusement of other customers, Maybelle knew Boy Jack couldn't make the drive to Rosario's in one stretch. So she started thinking about where to stay the night. Nothing looked safe or clean until Del Rio.

She was able to get him into the motel room without either or both of them falling down getting out of the pickup, and had him in one of the double beds without further ado. It felt weird to get him undressed and under the covers, but mostly she was worried about banging into one of his many bruises or cuts. He had a slight fever, and she made sure to wake him enough to take his meds and a little water with a straw.

After he was settled, she made a quick run for a salad and iced tea at a fast-food place, and then back to give Rosario a call. She left a message that they'd be in tomorrow. That evening, with Boy Jack zonked out on meds, she fell asleep watching a cable TV movie.

Before dawn she dreamed about the old woman in the village that had risen from the depths and called her Xóchitl and that a bad storm had come out of nowhere and darkened the skies black as night and that she was right there with the woman, pushing back the devil.

CHAPTER 33

Friday, September 16

It was as bad a way for Moon-Ra to find his mom as it comes. Her friends had brought her down from Meridian, and they'd gone to see her house in the Lower Ninth. But couldn't because it was under water almost to the roof. And they couldn't even have seen that if her neighbor, Mr. Gulaut, hadn't been able to borrow a metal john boat with a trolling motor from one of his friends.

On the way to where her street would have been, Mr. Gulaut had gotten into an argument with an out-of-state rescue crew, from Colorado or somewhere, about using the john boat over their submerged neighborhood. The white men in yellow vests in their big power rigs said it was dangerous, that the water was full of downed power lines and sharp debris under the surface. They said they had to leave. "Hope your home and families get flooded out some day so you'll know how it feels," Mr. Gulaut had yelled as he trolled away.

Miz Claudia wanted to cry but she couldn't. What she could do was see that she'd never live in that house again. What she also could do was breathe the heat-steam wafting off the dark toxic canal water. Spores and fumes found purchase in her nostrils, and mouth, and throat. They ignited and fed a fever that pushed into her bronchitis-weakened lungs and her heart and arteries and vital organs. That killed her in her sleep three days later.

Moon-Ra got the call from Eluvia early in the morning while he was at Feliciana's, having coffee and inspecting his bass and amplifiers and speakers for a third time. Working out his "post-Katrina" options. That's what everything was now. Post-Katrina. Pre-Katrina didn't exist, except in memory. In present time, it had no use. It was not relevant. It did not give you a place to live or a job or a doctor or food or help you find the people you loved or keep them alive.

Moon-Ra and Eluvia and the family weren't sure what they would do about funeral plans. The consensus was to lay Miz Claudia to rest in or around Baton Rouge, where her family originated, after the war let them out of the plantations, and before most of them moved to New Orleans. But there was no place in New Orleans for a proper burial and ceremony, and she wouldn't have wanted to be cremated. She might not even be listed as a Katrina casualty, as if that would have helped with arrangements. They would have to make do. In any event, Miz Claudia would be buried and her family would make it for the service. Those who could.

Reverend Youngblood, her sister, sent word through Paulus that she would lead the graveside service, assuming that's what Moon-Ra and Eluvia wanted. Which it was. In the coming days he and his sister managed the unthinkable.

Moon-Ra could not help but reflect that the time of hurricanes was not only about life, but also death. Even the final wishes of the departed for their eternal resting place were not beyond the interference and power and control of the great winds and the sea, province of the great spirits Oya and Yemonja, as Miz Claudia's sister would likely put it. Moon-Ra's cosmic side understood this, but his personal side was "*all tore down*," as Johnny Winter might have put it. Duane liked Johnny's bluesy rock because he'd seen him at a Jazzfest. That phrase had gotten into Moon-Ra's own head after some thoughtless DJ played it on the post-Katrina radio.

Maybelle half-considered changing her route, skipping Rosario's, and shooting straight for New Orleans. She'd get Boy Jack home and she could see about her apartment and car and then head back to the

Valley for however long, when she was ready. No encumbrances. But one more look at him, slumped half-comatose against his blanket and cushions, set her straight. For a start, she wasn't completely convinced at least one of those bad ribs wouldn't pop and puncture a lung. And didn't know why he was peeing blood. Just as importantly—and becoming more important with each day—neither was she completely sure she wanted to go back to the city.

Sheltering at the Red Blossom was the right call. It turned out Rosario's daughter, Estrella, had a summer cold and slight fever, which might be contagious. Maybelle hadn't planned on that. But they worked out a quick fix that they could stay in a hotel at least for the night. Then over to the trailer if Estrella was okay. Maybelle said the hotel they'd stayed at when they came through would be perfect. Rosario said she'd take care of the reservations.

Wherever they stayed, Boy Jack might need at least a week before his hands could grip a steering wheel or he could sit up for more than a few minutes without coughing. Without her.

Turned out they didn't need a hotel. Rosario arranged for Estrella to stay with their neighbor, Miriam, and canceled the reservations. They were exhausted when they arrived, but Rosario had everything set up. Boy Jack in Estrella's room, and Maybelle on the couch. Boy Jack tried talking while they settled in, and before taking his pain pills, but his lips were swollen and so was his tongue. He asked for a piece of paper and wrote out, "Thanks for everything. Just really tired and it hurts to move my mouth." He drew a smiley face at the end.

It was good to be in the line shack, alone. If that's the way it would be, that's the way he would like it. Straight. Like the Jack he'd poured into the glass on the kitchen table. In fact, it was better that way. Now he could really bear down on what he was going to do. Movies, life, people, places to live. All those images and strands of thought and memory he'd been carrying inside like secret explosives, or cosmic tunnels.

He took a long drink. Friday Happy Hour! Early Bird version! Damn, that was Jack number three. He'd better get to whatever it was before he was shit-faced. In the middle of the afternoon. That would not be aloneness, in the good way. That would just be pathetic.

He looked at the notepad in front of him. He'd grabbed it back at one of those Walmarts for just this kind of situation. The top page was just a title: MAJOR POINTS TO ADDRESS. Fourteen of those points were on the following pages, with two-sentence summary explanations. And they were pretty good. But he knew he wasn't finished.

He picked up the ballpoint and started to add to the list but at that exact moment his stomach growled. Time to hit the fridge and cupboards, stocked with the replenished chow from Presidio. Along with the Jack and beer. He wanted to quell his appetite just enough to keep the thoughts moving and the stomach silent. So he settled for quick bites of the granola bars and various so-called protein snacks he'd bought but never really heard of. Definitely enough for two or three days. Not that he'd be that long.

But who knew? A couple more days on his own in the middle of absolutely fucking nowhere other than the intersection of cartels and SWAT teams actually might be good. Maybe it was just what Interior Duane needed. Brainstorming Duane.

Life after Katrina had been pretty savage, come down to it. In such circumstances, who could give proper thought to planning for a movie that, at best, did not yet exist? Let alone a basic recalculation of one's entire life vector. The shape of which now resembled a black diamond downhill run.

Indeed, solitude—the essence of creativity, or possibly a co-essence on a twin bill with unendurable stress—was one of the most major of Major Points. On the next clean notebook page, he wrote "How Long Will I Stay?" That made fifteen Major Points. Filling five pages. Probably would have been more like three, but the more he drank, the larger the handwriting, and the more elaborate the explanations, often beyond two sentences, as he now noticed.

He remembered that he stopped writing because his fingers had started to cramp and he had gotten tired of the whole stupid thing. Which is when his thoughts drifted off the being alone stuff. To Maybelle. Whom he had set free. Right after she left him.

He took a another quick snap of Jack and back to the table. He read the Major Points for maybe the eighth time. Some really were pretty stupid. Some were not exactly new thoughts. A few were insightful enough to bear pondering. Then he got an idea for Point Sixteen and wrote it down.

"Why Am I Here?" Ideally, it should have preceded the more practical Point Fifteen, "How Long Will I Stay?" But they were closely related, and probably the only two points really worth the trouble.

For what could have been a longish time Duane stared out the small front room window of the shack, caught up in which question took priority, which reminded him of the old philosophical riddle of essence versus existence and then he was standing on the Quarter levee again, in his mind. The really weird thing was that as he stared, the Mississippi River appeared just past the foothills at the far end of the airstrip. It might not have been real, but it was a sign.

The simple answer to "Why Am I Here?" was, of course, Katrina. Whose imperious assault also covered and complicated the issue of "How Long Will I Stay?" She had predicated or altered everything. Any other conclusion was hubris and folly.

Katrina reigned. Then and now. Himself and the other humans, and also the animals and probably the fish, were at best surfers, if animals and fish could surf, smashed onto the shore by her Shiva wave.

Which, plus a little more Jack, triggered another revelation, that "Shiva" would have been an altogether better name than "Katrina," but "S" was too far down the hurricane-naming alphabet for the season. Also, the Baptists would have objected vehemently.

As Duane recalled often, the Buddha said in *The Diamond Sutra* that a name for a thing is not the thing, but only the name that we give it and nothing more. The thing is unique in itself, and also a part of everything else. It takes some time to understand this.

Katrina was indifferent to any words or concepts. She did not come out of the void, and did not disappear into one just because we could no longer see her. Duane struggled with this point. All he knew for sure was that while Katrina had strutted and demolished in her hour upon the stage, she alone had made all the decisions of how, when, where, why, who.

She scoured pitiful human aspirations, at least those of Duane McGuane. To include: Carlos, the Portia, the Big Easy, the movie (The Movie!), the Maybelle.

Replaced them with: The Convention Center, the flooding, the death, the horror (The Horror!), the despair. Then the road, the Valley, the good-byes, the hellos and *holas*, the *colonia*, the ranch, and a completely new movie (New Movie!), maybe. Really, out of theoretical certainties, Katrina had revised Duane's life into practical maybes. He stopped his musings to think how much Maybelle would have appreciated this line of inquiry.

He turned over the next fresh sheet of paper and at the top wrote, in the largest print size yet:

LIFE IN THE TIME OF HURRICANES

Nothing more.

He wanted to think on it, on the words, on the thing to which they gave a name. Perhaps a new movie had been hatched. He didn't want to crowd it. He didn't want to burden it at its creation with other fears and visions. Or maybe just stupid thoughts. False leads.

Duane was aware by then that all his other thoughts had become monumentally stupid. Like his plans. Moot. Had been drifting that way for too long.

He started to write "Scoot the Moot" on the new page but didn't. He did scribble three words: "Clear as Mud."

He badly wanted to call Rhys and go over his "New Options," which he had written somewhere as a Major Point, but was quickly reminded he was in a "no service" area. Even if a few calls somehow got through. Like the one from Maybelle. No way was he sober enough to drive down that hellish trail to get reception in Presidio, then drive back up after dark, probably.

And he definitely was not going to spend the night in Presidio. Sure, there were cheap motels fit to sleep off the booze, and not a few bars and sexual possibilities for a suddenly solitary man. *"Because I used to love her, but it's all over now"* was a really inappropriate line of male denial of feelings from a Rolling Stones classic to pop into his head just then and he did his best to banish it.

Because he was more than a solitary man now. He was a landowner. He paused to think how close that word was to lawn mower. He was a landowner in the Chinati Mountains of the Trans-Pecos of the mighty state of Texas. He didn't wear his cowboy boots very often or own a Stetson or any of that sort of shit, but who cared? He had property. That's what it was all about. Always had been. Always would be.

Also, he had two badass generators and plenty of gasoline to keep them running and there was sufficient chemically preserved store-bought food. He would not be moved. And by God, he was close enough to Marfa to understand that a man, a Texas man for godsake, stood his ground.

Which he owned. The land. Duane did. He had the deed. And it was a good deed. From Carlos, off somewhere unknown tending to deeds of his own.

If Duane McGuane was desperate to find or retrieve a true vision, and had been all but deaf to the meaning of the howl that had hurled him hundreds of miles from the wet mess of New Orleans to the dry emptiness of the Big Bend, he *también* had great confidence that he, selfsame Duane McGuane, was absolutely and beyond any doubt a man of good deeds. Nor would he be a man of constant sorrow.

He spent the next five minutes devouring the turkey and cheese white-bread deli sandwich in the fridge, which was running like a champ, and trying to decide if he thought Carlos was dead or alive.

For some reason the eating made him think: fuse box. Actually, the reason probably was the insane heat. He looked through the shack for any kind of breaker box but whoever wired it must have omitted that feature or hidden it. But an a/c almost certainly needed one.

He grabbed a Negra Modelo and went to the shed in back and looked around among the generators and cords and there it was, mounted in a corner under one of the shelves. If it wasn't obvious enough, the box had "A/C BREAKER" written across the top with a black marker. He stared at it a moment, in the way you have to do when something stupefyingly simple presents itself to you after you've been wracking your brain trying to solve a problem that was never really there. Like looking for your lost sunglasses that are on your head.

He pulled the switch down to "ON" and even from the shed he could hear an a/c motor growl. He took a goodly gulp of beer and gave a small amount of thought to whether knowing the shack actually had a/c would have made a difference to Maybelle. Which, he prided himself on knowing with absolute confidence, it would have not.

He was walking back to the side of the shack to sit in a patch of shade just as a decent and unexpected breeze pushed through. This is the Big Bend, something said in his head. The Big Bend is not the inside of a cartel shack. It is the great motherfucking outdoors. He badly wanted to go over to the Quonset hut and drag out one of the folding chairs to sit in the shade and feel the breeze and finish his beer in goddam peace and quiet. And so he did. And it was serene as hell. And still almost as hot.

In his chair, he looked at the skies not for cloud shapes, because he was sick to death of cloudy skies, but to see if it really were true you could see, from Duane's specific vantage along the border, stealth bombers and black helicopters. Which, as everyone knew, were doing their bit to protect this great country, from its mountain deserts to its storm-besieged coasts. Said coasts currently as flooded as anything Noah might have encountered.

Speaking of whom, hadn't Duane loaded up a God-fearing ark of his own, the bountiful van from the Church the Holy Sanctuary from Topeka, Kansas? The aforementioned of which, had he been able to pinpoint its current location, which he could not, being in the Big Bend and all, was still sitting in a slow-draining puddle on a potholed street a few blocks off St. Charles in New

Orleans, Louisiana, where Moon-Ra and Boy Jack had left it. With the keys under the mat.

If Duane were a God-fearing man like, say, Paulus, he would conclude that the Almighty had no real interest in the Church of the Holy Sanctuary from Topeka, Kansas, ever finding that particular blessed piece of its missing transportation. A cynic might conclude that perhaps an inflated insurance claim had already been filed, and discovering the alleged loss might therefore bring less, rather than more, to the holy budget. It was well known on Earth that God was notoriously strict about keeping her books balanced.

CHAPTER 34

Saturday, September 17

Which is not to say that Paulus hadn't given a thought to retrieving the van where his cousin had left it and using it a little longer, in service of helping the congregation from his mother's church move their things around from flooded houses to unflooded apartments and in some cases the famous FEMA trailers. Such sharing of a vehicle would constitute church-to-church solidarity, and who would object to that? Certainly not God or the spirits.

On the downside, all it would take was one bored, sullen, or exhausted NOPD cop cruising the streets and pissed off about the other NOPD cops who had gone AWOL like little chickenshits after the storm to pull Paulus over for any number of reasons, including Driving While Black. He would be busted faster than said cop could slam down a free lunch at one of the surviving cafés on his beat.

So Paulus stuck with his Altima, which still ran. Also, it turned out some of the church-goers had pickups or relatives with pickups and it was actually pretty inspiring to see how everyone was helping each other. At the same time uninspiring because the reason they had to band together so much for the most menial of tasks was because no one in the governments at any level seemed to be able to do anything beyond condemning houses, pulling bodies from the water, and quarreling with each other over who was more incompetent.

The city, at least the black part, had become, or perhaps reverted to, a commune of the surviving. People said it went back to slave and Reconstruction times. That feeling would last, Paulus had told his mother the reverend and anyone who would listen. He said it was at least one uplifting thing, in its own way, that came from Katrina. Black people banding together as no other people could imagine. He said it was important not to lose the scent of anything good amid so much bad, such as anger that couldn't be measured.

Everybody already knew that when the rebuilding of New Orleans started, it would not be aimed at poor and lower-income black folks, but at the white bourgeoisie who would have the money to buy up the flooded properties and gentrify parts of the city that had been resistant to exactly that for too long to count. They'd even get into the Nine Ward, bless their condescending little property-wise hearts, if they could.

But Paulus was glad he had come back to the city that day in Houma, with his family, even if they were temporarily living out near the airport in the month-to-month that Nadia had taken over from a friend who gave up and went to Memphis. Nor any regrets at the family having gone on the road with Duane. It was the best option at the time.

But Nadia had been right that what they really needed was their home. No matter what. Home was home. As for the kids, there might not even be school in the fall, but what would they have done in Texas? She'd heard a lot about how it was to live there and told Paulus she wasn't at all sure black people, especially from New Orleans, would be welcomed except in some of the big cities that already had black people.

Paulus had told much of this to Duane when he called in from the Valley that day to explain why he and Maybelle might stay in Texas for a while but probably would press on toward that ranch he'd been talking about so much. Paulus couldn't remember the exact location. And maybe all that would work out fine, but if he and his family had stayed with that strange, maybe even weird course, what kind of life would that have been for Rael and Elena? Or for Nadia? Or himself? What work would he get? How long would it take to get it? Duane in Texas was not going to be the same as Paulus in Texas. Nadia had said that.

At least in his hometown, flooded as it was, Paulus knew the land-scape. The music store would no doubt reopen, just as Louis, the man-ager, had said. Nadia had a couple of leads on jobs herself. And he had plenty of friends, plus everyone at his mom's church, so they'd figure it out. That was the thing, maybe the whole thing, about New Orleans. You figured it out.

After dinner, Paulus went to meet Moon at the Portia to give the theater another routine check, as they'd promised. He'd also checked on Duane's house, and nailed back up some plywood over a broken window or two, but it had survived pretty well. A lot better than the Portia. About all they could do was make sure the locks were still on Duane's office and the projection booth where the expensive stuff was. Everything else was easy to get into because the lobby was busted up.

But he enjoyed going to the Portia because it gave him a chance to talk about things with his cousin. Like remembering that trip. Like dealing with the impossible details of life after Katrina. Like how frus-trating it had been making arrangements for Paulus's mom to get to Baton Rouge to lead the services for Miz Claudia. Like how the sisters hadn't seen each other recently. And now, never would.

Maybelle was sitting on Rosario's couch as Boy Jack made his way out of the bedroom. He was definitely looking better, but only in comparison to the previous. Still, decided improvement. Mostly the antibiotics, but also because Maybelle and Rosario had started a daily regimen. Temperature, pulse, pee check, gargling with peroxide, checking or changing the ban-dages on his hands, which no longer were red and splotchy.

They helped him as he started to walk a little inside the trailer, but usually it was too hot to go outside. His appetite hadn't returned, but he was starting to nibble soft bread and sip at chicken broth. He was always thirsty, though, and went through a steady diet of Gatorade. He was able to watch a little TV to cut the boredom and difficulty talking, but so far, mostly, he slept.

That evening, Maybelle and Rosario sat up for a couple of hours over beers and sandwiches and worked out what Maybelle might do if she stayed in the Valley. Theoretically, Maybelle said. There was still the matter of New Orleans. Her old job. Sure, Rosario said. She also said that she knew lawyers in McAllen and Brownsville and Harlingen who handled immigration cases and various things for poor clients and could use someone with Maybelle's experience.

Rosario said if she did stay, there was a vacant trailer in Red Blossom down the lane. They'd figure out the rent later. It wouldn't be much, because the trailer wasn't much. They could find her a car if the one back in New Orleans was drowned. Maybelle said that staying was sounding better all the time.

Rosario kissed her goodnight before they went to their own beds and damned if Maybelle could figure out exactly what kind of kiss it was. If nothing else, it was evidence that she was welcome.

CHAPTER 35

Saturday, September 17, late morning

Duane went through a pack of saltines from the cupboard along with a mug of microwave coffee and two bottles of water, but he knew the Saturday hangover wasn't going to get any better without actual food, and anyway he needed to call Rhys. So he cleaned up a little, threw fresh sheets, a pillow, and a blanket from the storage basket onto the bed so he wouldn't keep forgetting them, and locked up the shack and the Quonset. He headed out the gate and down the "lane of the insane," as he had dubbed it, for some hot food in Presidio. And gas. He hoped to hell he could make it to a station.

He did, duly thankful for small blessings. Then he stopped at a cinder block diner offering "The Border's Best Brekfast Tacos," the sign possibly printed too late to correct the spelling, or maybe just a gimmick. He had three of the best, not convinced the fare lived up to the brag, but good enough to wolf down.

The waitress gave him one of those knowing looks. She knew a late-morning hangover when she saw one. He also slammed down more water, an orange juice, and two coffees. He ordered three more of the Border's Best in a Styrofoam take-out box, plus another coffee in a to-go cup to help keep him alert on the way back to the ranch. He was calling it the ranch now without thinking it should be in air quotes.

He drove through the quiet streets to that same grocery store lot he'd used for cell reception before. It was still crowded, mostly with pickups and SUVs. He turned off the engine but stayed in the cab with windows down to get some fresh air. But the air was already toasty, so he closed the window and started the engine again for the a/c.

As he punched in the numbers for Rhys and waited for an answer, Duane gave a micro-thought to how many million gallons of gasoline Americans, especially those in the lower, hotter half of the country, wasted doing just this sort of essentially lazy-ass engine-idling that was probably at least as polluting as sitting in line at drive-thru fast-food joints. Perhaps it could be background setup for a contextual exposition scene in the new movie.

He was fumbling through the glovebox for a scrap of paper to write down the idea but Rhys answered on the sixth ring tone.

He said he recognized Duane's number or he would have let it go to voicemail. Also, he was curious to see if the voice that answered would be that of his friend and client, or of some sheriff's deputy who'd found a body propped up against a cactus or snagged on a brush pile along the banks of the Rio Grande.

"So maybe, seeing as how you're still among us, boyo, you could tell me exactly where in God's holy fuck you are."

"You ever hear of Presidio?"

"The movie?"

"The movie was *The Presidio*, and it was in San Francisco."

"So you're in San Francisco?"

"I'm hungover as shit, Rhys. Also, I was just getting ready to write down something important when you called."

"You called *me*, my man."

"Fuck, right. Never mind."

"But back to my question."

Duane paused. "Well I'm not in fucking San Francisco. Presidio, *Texas*, is somewhere on the border. Just west of the Big Bend State Ranch and pretty far southeast of El Paso and right across the river from Ojinaga, in Mexico."

"Well, then. You've been a traveling man."

"Including about an hour or two of shit road down a

mountainside from the little ranch I now own thanks to Carlos. You remember that, right?"

Rhys exhaled for what seemed a long time. "So you really went there."

"Went there and am here."

"Not in the Valley. Which is where you were last time you called."

"No, nor in New Orleans, which is where I was before that. Do I need to run the timeline further back?"

"Can we start again?"

The breath was from Duane this time. "Yeah. Fine. I don't mean to be crabby."

"Yeah."

"So I'm calling from down here in Presidio because I can't get service up on the ranch."

"Maybelle? How's she like it?"

"Not all that much."

Duane explained about her leaving with Boy Jack, whose beating he also had to explain because Rhys didn't know who Boy Jack was or why he was with them or why Maybelle had taken him back to New Orleans or was in the process of taking him there. Explaining it, even in abridged form, contributed mightily to what was becoming a merciless return of the headache. And the bottle of Advil was back at the line shack.

Rhys finally broke in. "Damn, boyo, I don't know what to tell you. I mean, I'm glad you're okay and all."

"Do you know anything about the Portia? Any of those damn lawsuits?"

"I drove past it a couple days ago and there's some guys, look like Latinos, doing some cleanup around the area but nothing at the Portia itself, that I can tell. Somebody's taped up plywood across the broken windows and doors, though."

Duane thought for a minute. "Moon-Ra, I think. Maybe Paulus."

"Anyway, not much else," Rhys said. "Also, your car's still in the lot out in front. I'd say the city would tow it off but nothing like that is getting done. Towing cars from the storm is a cleanup luxury. For rich people."

"So I'm trying to decide if I can open it again, the Portia."

Another pause.

Then Rhys. "Your movie? How's that going?"

"The movie? Hell. The moving. The Maybelle. The whole damn plan. I mean, whssst! It's all gone." He realized he was in his Jeep waving one arm to indicate something had gone awry and that Rhys not only probably realized that but couldn't see any arms waving anyway.

"You sound down, my man."

"You should see it from the inside."

"I guess you haven't heard from Carlos, though."

"Well, no," Duane said. "But definitely his lawyer."

"Memo."

"Yeah."

"He's not *your* lawyer. Like I said before. What's he telling you?"

"We settled up that extra land back in Weslaco I told you about, left it with the *colonia* and a lady there to manage it. I told Memo if there were any more legalities needed taking care of on the deed, that you'd do it."

"Yeah?"

"But look, the thing is this other property. The ranch. I'm thinking I need to get off this mountain. Memo says he could sell it, easy. I'll tell you about that later. When I'm not sitting in a parking lot. On a prime smuggling route."

"Interesting. You had no idea what really was going on?"

"None."

"Hnnh."

"Actually, I was so clueless I gave some thought to reviving 'The Sons of Aguirre' up here, but I really have no idea who owns the rights to it or even if there are rights and if there are, would I want to have anything to do with them. But this is certainly a kind of landscape that could work for it. I mean, I'd have to rewrite the whole damn screenplay."

"*Duane.*"

Duane stopped talking, stopped staring at the people going in and out of the store. They all looked exactly alike except some were *gringos* and some were Mexicans. That is, they all dressed alike, more or less. And were different.

"I guess I got off track. I wanted to see if you could handle the sale."

"As well as the *colonia.*"

"Charge me whatever you think is right."

"Just give me the word."

"As soon as I get ahold of Memo again."

"Do it soon, my friend. You don't sound good."

Duane clicked off just in time to startle-jump like somebody'd taken a shot at him, but it was a backfire and two air horns blasting from tricked-out pickups on the street at the edge of the lot. Courtesy of two buddies passing each other and feeling the need to record the moment. One even found a way to stop for a second and rev up his engine, producing black smoke from a special exhaust pipe. They called it rolling coal. Duane had a strong feeling that kind of shit should be illegal. Nor did it do much for his hangover.

He thought of calling Maybelle, but his cell battery was almost dead. So he wouldn't be calling fucking Memo either.

Back at the ranch, he was embarrassed to realize he'd left the gate open. He made sure to close it behind him. Pulling up to the line shack, he slowed to a crawl to look around the property he could live in if he wanted to. He parked the Jeep and walked the length of the airstrip and back.

The sun was brutal, but the air was clear and clean and there were no storm clouds nor rain nor savage winds, and the brown and green palette of soil and rocks and scrub and mesquite on the mountain hills merged perfectly under the brilliant blue of the cloud-flecked sky. It was a place that made sense as a sustainer of spirit. But it had gotten all fucked up. He understood Carlos completely.

CHAPTER 36

Sunday, September 18

Boy Jack woke without the headache for a change, and turned his face on the pillow to feel the rays of dawn through the window blinds. Before long he managed to sit up. It was definitely a girl's room, with the boy band posters on the walls and family photos taped to the dresser mirror. Not a big room, but good enough. Certainly as big as anything he'd had growing up, and doubtless with fewer nightly fears of the screams and thuds of fists in the rest of the house.

He realized he didn't have his phone, and hoped he'd left it in his pocket instead of back in the Alpine bar. His brain frizzled in and out for at least a minute like a TV in a lightning storm. Blocks of time flashed and shifted. He was in a trailer, with Maybelle. Then in a hospital with Duane. Then somewhere in some house in the mountains. Then riding in the back seat of his own truck, cramped as hell. Then in a parking lot and a man and woman he thought were going to sell him a little pot and maybe some snort were yelling at him and making fun of his accent and New Orleans. Then something hit him and he was on the ground and the guy was hitting him again and again. And then he was back, sitting on the bed in a little girl's room with the start of a new day. He had no idea what day that was.

He breathed carefully, because sometimes it hurt, then remembered there was a bathroom. There was no blood in his pee, and he tried to remember why he thought there had been before. He flushed and then out of habit turned to the sink and started to splash his face with water until the first touch stung like rubbing alcohol. He dropped his hands to the sides of the basin and looked at the mirror. His face looked like a rotten turnip with bumps.

That made him start to laugh, which hurt, and also showed him the condition of his mouth. All the teeth were there, which was a plus, but the gums were plenty sore. He gargled with the peroxide, which he recalled Maybelle insisting he do at least once a day even though it stung. He opened and closed his mouth a few times to see if he could and it actually felt close to normal to do so. He thought maybe he could talk and said "hey there, buddy" in a low voice. It came out okay. He almost gave himself a congratulatory clap.

Until he remembered his hands, now wet, and still partly bandaged, were—of course—stinging. Everything stung. He pulled the strips off. Which also stung. Three cuts on the right hand, four on the left. Some kind of goo coated each of the wounds, which he vaguely remembered was for infections. Some of the cuts were forming scabs, the others were still inflamed. He didn't know if he should wash them with soap, so didn't. His brain was working just enough to realize he'd had some kind of first aid, but beyond that it was hard to pin down.

He stood back, pulled up his shirt. Pretty much a turnip there, too, with swatches of beets. His thigh hurt and he pulled down his pants and the colors there were more green and yellow, but nothing cut that he could see. Especially the important stuff.

He dabbed at his hands with toilet paper so as not to mess up the towels, pulled his jeans back up, and generally tried to arrange his appearance in some way. Then he coughed. Maybe a half-dozen times. He may have groaned. Whatever it was drew a knock on the door.

"You okay in there?"

"Yeah. Give me a minute." He coughed again.

"I'll be in the kitchen."

She was making coffee when he limped in. She paused to give him an air hug because she knew the real thing would hurt. He thought that was about the nicest thing that anyone had done for him lately, and returned the air gesture, then sat on one of the chairs around the linoleum table and just looked at her, whose name he had actually blanked on for a moment: Maybelle.

"You look a lot better. Really. And it's good to hear you speak," she said. "What did you do with those bandages?"

"They got wet. I just unwrapped them." Still talking slowly, but it was getting better. He held his palms up so she could see.

"You scared the hell out of us."

"Me, too."

"I want you to tell me what happened when it doesn't hurt."

He shrugged. "Boy meets new friends at a bar. They fuck him over. Pretty much the executive summary."

She smiled.

"I know those kinds of business jargons," he said, although enunciating "jargons" made him wince. "I'm not just a delivery boy."

She touched his lips. He flinched. "Sorry. Didn't mean to make you hurt."

"I love you, Maybelle."

He really was a pretty boy, she thought, even with a busted face and all kind of crimson around the blue eyes. And she knew how he meant those three words. It warmed what was left of her heart. "Same. But you gotta stop with the spontaneous and utterly unproductive roadhouse brawling, okay?"

They looked at each other closely. To say it was a little brother/big sister kind of thing would not be entirely without justification.

She went to the counter and poured two cups of coffee—his with two spoons of sugar, for the energy. He only managed a sip. She was breaking the eggs to scramble when Rosario came in, a long T-shirt jersey hanging down to her knees, probably nothing under it.

Because he'd asked several times, the two women went over the various details of how he wound up in the trailer, after the bar, and after the hospital, and after the god-awful trip to that house on that ranch. And how he would be resting for a while before going on to New Orleans because Maybelle didn't think he could sit in the truck for twelve hours at a stretch. Not even half that long.

It was the first real conversation he'd had since, what, Tuesday? It was good to hear how it had gone down. It was as he thought. In fact, he had been there. But something had literally been pounded out of his short-term memory. He was happy they helped him recall even the bad stuff.

"I should probably call Mr. Croydon. I mean, do I still have a phone?"

"You do. For some reason they left it, whoever did that to you, or maybe didn't see it with all that was going on. Your one-night bar buddy Phil, that called us to come for you, gave it to us when we picked you up. I'll get it." She looked at him with a soft smile. "Not that you could have much of a conversation at this point."

She scraped the eggs out of the skillet onto a plate. She put it in front of him along with a glass of water with a plastic kid's straw. He got it all down, then stared at the table like he was trying to work something out. He knew she could tell.

CHAPTER 37

Sunday, September 18, afternoon

Duane hadn't meant to sleep until late afternoon, and had no idea why he had done so. Or why he was fully clothed, except no socks or shoes, and hanging half off the bed. All he could really piece together was the sharp sensation of a needle-like jab on his ankle in the back shed, where he'd gone, barefoot, sometime in the dark just before dawn when the generator went out.

He remembered it was odd how the morning air outside had been so much cooler than inside. Maybe the a/c had been off for a while. So he could've just opened some windows and gone back to sleep. No trip to the shed. End of story. Funny how little things like forgetting the basics of weather at higher altitudes, possibly from previously consuming too many shots of Jack, can change the arc of karma.

But, as a Texan, he knew he'd felt obligated to get the a/c going. As easy as switching over to the second generator and refilling the first one for the next cycle if he wanted to stay cool. Which he did. Took less than five minutes. That he could remember. That was why he'd gone to the shed. Why his ankle hurt.

Also, his big toe. After closing the shed door to go back to the line shack, he'd stumbled a couple of steps and banged it against a rock. He remembered that he'd barely uttered a curse on behalf of said toe when every synapse of consciousness fired. A mega-watt bolt of pain, a sharp, pile-driving rush of eye-popping agony that couldn't even be translated into a scream. And then it could. Probably freaked out the coyotes up in the hills.

Now, lying on the bed he could barely remember finding, he was starting to recall flashes of moaning and writhing in the dirt and weeds around the shed.

Something wrong with his ankle. Which is when his memory slammed shut. Vanished. Gone where such things go when the brain so orders. When the brain thinks it is more important than pain. But what if it isn't? Duane tried to snap himself back into the moment.

Maybe the briefest recollection of extreme pain was the demarcation between that's-what-happened and what-the-fuck-happened? Hell, he couldn't even account for getting back into the shack. But he must have made it because here he was. He could rise on an elbow just enough to see down his sweat-soaked body to what he could scarcely believe. Just below the bunched-up jeans on his left leg was a swelling the size of a baseball, decorated by a dark red striation of skin from a puncture clogged with dried blood down towards his ankle.

Forget seeing it. Feeling it was all-consuming. Drool was coming out from the corners of his mouth. He may have pissed his pants. He let his head fall back onto the bed.

After lunch, Boy Jack had a rush of energy and wanted to stretch his legs. He said he could walk okay. Just being outside, breathing the air despite a few coughs, seeing all the activity around the *colonia*, the birds singing and flying, the dogs barking, the distant road noises from the busy highway, gave him a fresh idea.

Maybelle and Rosario were outside drinking iced tea at a little table in the shade of a beach umbrella. He told them he wanted to try a little driving. "Just on the back streets. Just to see if I can." The swelling in his lips had decreased and he could both talk and be understood.

Maybelle asked to see his hands. No swelling. No sign of new blood. She bent the fingers on his left hand and he didn't wince. Just sensitive to the touch. So were his ribs. "Come inside for a minute," she said. "Let's take care of these."

She sat him at the kitchen table and put fresh bandages and oint-ment on the various cuts and scabs, told him to keep them clean. She looked him over head to foot. She said if he really wanted to test drive himself, just a little, it should be okay.

She gave him his keys and a tall plastic cup with iced tea. He got into the F-150 with some awkwardness, determined not to wince as long as Maybelle and Rosario were in sight. As he drove off, he could see them watching, kind of like Mr. Croydon would do sometimes when sending him on a delivery in bad weather or to a rough part of town.

He changed his mind about just sticking to the back streets, which seemed boring, and went up to the main highway. It was okay. He could handle the gas and brake pedals and manage the steering wheel if he didn't grip too hard.

He headed west, thinking there would be less traffic, and on a whim he took the exit for the cathedral at San Juan, which wasn't that far. He thought it would be a good place to give him a feel for navigating city traffic and stoplights. He made it easily to the parking lot across from the gift store, same one they'd used on their long drive before. Now he wanted to see if he really could walk.

He found a space close to the long sidewalk leading up to the cathedral and made his way, with a decided limp, to the holy water fountain. He didn't feel up to waiting in line to go into the cathedral, but that wasn't what he wanted. He wanted the fountain. Most of the spigots weren't being used. When he turned one, on it didn't even sting his bandaged hands. He splashed water on his face and head and a fair amount of it wetted his T-shirt. Then with those same hands he formed a cup and drank. A lot of it. Like he'd wandered in from a desert. Some of the people around the fountain were looking at him—bruised and beat-up and dripping water everywhere.

"I guess I'm baptizing myself," he said.

The people looked away.

He limped back to the F-150, saying "hello" as best he could to anyone he passed. All of whom looked at him as if he were a crazy holy man.

He had to sit a few minutes in the truck with the a/c to catch his breath and get his strength back. He drank the iced tea and thought of pouring it out and then filling it with holy water, but he knew people would be looking at him again. And maybe he'd overdone it with the walking. So he was "good to go," if that was the way to put it.

Back at the *colonia*, he told Maybelle and Rosario where he'd been. He said it was kind of a test, and that he had passed. He was fine to drive. He was able to get himself to New Orleans. He'd take it easy, but he could do it. Without help. Unless Maybelle really wanted to go back to the city with him. He said he didn't want to wait until Tuesday, but would leave in the morning. He'd like to get on with it.

He said he was sorry to have messed everything up and he wanted to let her get on with her life in the Valley, and he didn't want to bother Duane anymore, either. And Rosario's daughter would want her room back.

Maybelle said Duane would be staying up at the ranch for a while, and not to worry about him, that he was just frustrated with his own shit. She said he'd have the time he needed all by his lonesome to sort out all his visions and plans. Boy Jack smiled without meaning to.

Rosario said he needn't be in a hurry, and if he was worried that he was a burden, he was not. He said he just needed to be moving. He said his only worry was how Maybelle would get back. She said there was no problem. He knew right away what she meant. They both knew it was right, and the logic was clean and so was the spirit.

Nonetheless, Maybelle and Rosario grilled him one more time, like doctors giving a second opinion. They made him show them the bruises. Maybelle reminded him to gargle with the mouthwash in his pack no matter how much it stung, and to take all the prescriptions on time. Rosario looked in each bottle to be sure he had what he needed.

They fussed over him. He liked it.

He said he could make it home in a day, like before with Moon-Ra. Maybelle encouraged him to break the trip up if he got tired. She said you could never tell when the adrenalin would use itself up and you'd want to just lie down and sleep. He said okay, but they both knew he'd try to blast straight through.

Then his face seemed to flush, even with the bruises, and his eyes brightened inside the broken capillaries. He stood up, spread his arms like wings and said the truth was he wanted to leave right away. He wanted to get as far as he could for the night. It was already 4 p.m.

Maybe he could make it to San Antonio or Houston, break up the trip like they wanted. Easy shot to New Orleans the next day. "Red beans and rice when I get there, no place better, and I'll be able to eat it," he said, so enthusiastically that Maybelle could just about smell it and taste it and see it. And then she couldn't, and she didn't want to be back there.

Rosario gave him a giant hug. "Go for it, *hombre*," she said, kissing his cheek. Then Maybelle hugged him. Then Rosario hugged him again, and then Maybelle did again, and when she broke loose she knew her eyes were glistening.

He picked up Highway 281 that headed north toward US 59 that would take him on to Houston and then east to New Orleans and the Casa de Croydon. That was the plan.

But in almost no time, near the tiny town of Falfurrias, he noticed highway signs for Laredo. They led in the opposite direction from New Orleans. Something clicked. Maybelle had given him a Texas map, but he didn't want to stop to look at it, and anyway, he remembered the routes that they'd previously followed to Duane's ranch.

Instead of continuing north, and then east, and thus on to the Big Easy, all he had to do was divert over to Crystal City and then Laredo and after that an easy shot to Del Rio. From there, he could go a little north to catch I-10 West. Which led to El Paso. Which led to Phoenix. Which led to LA.

His friend Switch would be glad to see him. They'd already talked a little when he was holed up at Casa de Croydon as the storm approached and before all the phones went dead. Switch had said

301

what he really needed to do was to come on out west, brother.

Boy Jack had helped Switch calm down after he came back with a medical discharge from Iraq, which he volunteered for after 9/11 and all that, and they were both from Louisiana. They had things in common. As for telling Mr. Croydon, Boy Jack could call him from the road. It wouldn't matter when. It would be no fun.

He pulled to the highway shoulder and thought for a moment if he really wanted to do something so impulsive. So opposite what he'd just told Maybelle. But she'd made some pretty fucking major changes of directions, too. Right?

Later, he would reflect on just how little time—almost none—the decision took. It was like his brain was the fastest computer in existence.

How could he ever thank them anyway? Hell, they all knew. Nobody had to say it. That was the way life was now.

He figured he'd make Del Rio before midnight, stay at that same motel. Or maybe Eagle Pass. He liked that town, too. Maybe he'd stop around Laredo to stretch and for something soft to eat. Bean and cheese burritos sounded pretty good. A Mountain Dew for the extra caffeine.

Speaking of jolt, that San Juan holy water sure had woken him up. If that was the right way to put it. He tuned the radio to a random station playing Mexican polka music, which he couldn't understand but got him bouncing to the beat in his seat. It made his ribs twinge but it was a small price to pay.

CHAPTER 38

Monday, September 19

Duane got it together a little more when daybreak woke him, which is to say brought him back to consciousness, on Monday. Which it took him a minute to realize wasn't still Sunday. His entire left leg felt like it would fall off and the red puncture mark on his ankle already had some pus along the edges. But his head was clear. Except for the smothering layers of pain. His mouth was so dry he could barely part his lips.

He hadn't moved from the bed, which was wet from pee and sweat, but he was able to sit, then get up. His body tingled and his skin was on fire. He wobbled into the kitchen and leaned against the counter while he drank three bottles of the Gatorade he'd picked up in Presidio. When? Saturday? Had to be. But he was sure it was Monday now. So where was Sunday? Also, it was hot. The a/c wasn't on, but the kitchen light and fridge were.

This really would be the last straw, he thought, until he noticed the plug to the a/c was on the floor, out of the wall socket. He had no idea why or how but he limped over and plugged it back in and the unit revved up with an electrical pop and whrrr. Good old refrigerated air. Wasn't that the missing comfort that he had to have so much that he'd gone out to the shed to fire back up in the dark? Was the whrrr worth it, there, buddy? Which made him wonder what else he might have done since Saturday and would any of it come back to kill him?

Next stop was the bathroom for the new bottle of Advil. He popped eight capsules, choking them down with another half-bottle

303

of water. He had plenty of water. What he didn't have was a sense of balance and he barely made it back to the bed to sit. After some time, while he stared at the floor and walls, his head began to unbuzz. He almost lay back on the mattress but stopped himself. Stay awake, goddamit, he repeated like a drunk talking to himself on a park bench.

When things got clear enough, he gave his body another inspection. Definitely only one puncture mark, so probably not a snake. Maybe a spider. Or a tarantula. A scorpion. Any would do the trick if they had enough venom and felt the need to hit big animals. He decided it was a scorpion because it hurt so damn bad.

He was filthy and felt just enough energy to try to clean up. The shower was one of those hand-pull gravity types designed and stocked for occasional use. The overhead plastic tank had enough water if you didn't waste any. For soap he had the hotel-style packages from his shaving kit. He did the best he could. The water was cold, but it helped him to keep from passing out. It occurred to him there was probably a protocol to refill the tank, as with the generators, but he'd tend to that later. "Later" being an optimistic concept.

He dried off with a rough white towel hanging on a nail in the wall and made a pass at brushing his teeth, mostly because his breath smelled vile even to him. He limped back into the bedroom and dug a fresh pair of jeans and a shirt and undies from his duffel. Everything hurt to put on, especially the jeans. That was damn near a sartorial deal-breaker. Along the bottom of the duffel was the remaining cash he had continually neglected to make any more secure, as if it mattered. But he did cover it again with the mix of clean and dirty clothes. Nobody'd want to look in there unless they really had to.

All that was exhausting. He mustered enough energy to pull off the newly soiled sheets and blanket and sweat-laden pillow he had just put on the bed. The mattress wasn't really wet, except in one spot, so he lay down again, knowing he shouldn't.

It was nearly noon when he woke. He went through the same tedious process of getting up, this time happy to pee in the toilet instead of the bed. He limped around the room a few times so the blood would circulate in his leg. Then, leaning against a wall for support, he unbuttoned and gingerly pulled down the jeans, which electrified every nerve in his leg again, to see if there were any red lines shooting up from the ankle. So far no. The red was mostly around the epicenter. But it had darkened considerably.

Not good. He'd never be able to drive down the foothills and into town. He probably wouldn't be able to climb into the Jeep. Hell, he'd be lucky to put on a pair of socks. But he did, the one on his left foot just halfway. He didn't want to go outside barefoot ever again, even if socks had to do for shoes.

But he knew he needed to take some steps, some kind of motion, or he might clot up. And he wanted to see some actual daylight. It might help get back on schedule. He got as far as the front porch step when he had to sit down, but in doing so put too much weight on his foot and ankle. Yelping with pain and cursing would be a good way to describe the next half minute. He never wanted to stand up again.

As if on bad karma cue, he heard a backfire sound from the shed and then no sound at all. Had to be the generator. Fuck me, he said aloud, emphasis on both words. He'd have to go back into that shed to see what it was. Probably out of gas, which made him wonder why the a/c had come back on at all. Why the fridge hadn't been off. Or maybe it had been. Too complicated to figure out.

He'd just have to go back there. Suck it up and do it. Or die. It was not an exaggeration. Without a generator working, all the power in the shack would be gone. Forget the sting, the fucking heat would do him in.

The sun out on the porch did feel good, though. He got up slowly, leaning against the door frame, until he felt balanced enough to take steps. Which he did, awkwardly. Mostly on his right leg, the unbitten one, dragging the left. The sun was almost directly overhead but a tallish mesquite at the edge of the air strip offered a little shade. He made it that far and then sat down again, this time more carefully.

And remembered that the reason he had gone outside was to check the generator. He had limped right past it. He shook his head. It had the memory of a fruit fly.

Things faded. Next thing he knew he was on his back, still on the airstrip, halfway out of what shade the mesquite offered. His face felt on fire. He had no idea how much time had passed. Why he was there. The sun had moved lower, so it had to be afternoon.

What he knew for damn sure was that Mother Nature was burning him alive in Texas, as opposed to drowning him back in New Orleans. The fire this time for damn sure, respect to Mr. Baldwin. And Mom knew her stuff. To ready him for the grill, she had prepped him with hot, spicy poison from her world-class toxic ensemble, and now that he was tenderized, had laid him out like the helpless slab of meat that maybe he really was.

Then the earth shook. A sonic boom louder than he could have imagined pinned him to the earth. He managed to shield his eyes with his hand and look up.

Way, way into the blue, he could see the outline of huge, dark airplane. His mind said it was one of those bombers people said plowed the skies along the border and the government said did not. The people were right.

He inched on his back like an inverted crab into what sparse shade the mesquite still offered. His face ached and even his hands were roasted. None of his muscles cooperated as they were designed by the creator of all things to do. But at least he was out of the sun.

He managed to sit up, using one arm as a resting crutch, and tried to spot the plane again, but couldn't. Then, from behind, came another extremely loud sound. Not a big boom like the plane, but much closer, more familiar, more mechanical.

He'd heard of black helicopters, but this one was dark blue. It was up there about three hundred feet, or a thousand, he had no idea. It hovered for what seemed a very long time, or maybe not even a minute. Then it zoomed away like a hummingbird, possibly a pterodactyl.

It occurred to Duane that he was attracting visitors. Not tourists. Who in their right mind would tourist up here? To see a dude sunbathing next to an abandoned landing strip. Not tourists. That left only a few options, none of which did not involve cartels and termination.

He realized he sounded paranoid, even to himself, but wasn't it Yossarian's contention in *Catch-22* that you're not paranoid if they're really out to get you? Was he actually hallucinating with literary characters now? He needed to get up and move. Not just to get away from fever-induced fantasy. If he passed out again, mesquite shade or not, he was going to die of heat stroke.

Thus motivated by a simple desire not to be incinerated, he made his way to the line shack. It took a while. Inside, he half-collapsed on the same chair by the kitchen table where he'd drafted his Major Points. Here was a new one: Don't die. He really was burning up and damn damn damn damn fucking damn if he hadn't forgotten to check on the generator! Again! Why was that so hard to remember?

What would a shrink say? Why would a shrink even be there? That would have to be for later discussion.

He waited until he was recovered enough to get more bottles of water and Gatorade in the kitchen, then downed them so fast he spit part of the liquid back up. He wanted to make sure he didn't go prone again, so he leaned against the counter, almost feeling the blood flow the way it was supposed to.

He could see through the window near the door all the way across the compound lot to the Quonset hut. He felt that he ought to go check that place out one more time. He would get to that later, right after the generator.

He wasn't hungry but felt he ought to at least try to eat something. One package of granola bars was left and it went down grudgingly. He made it into the bedroom and sat on the mattress to catch his breath.

He knew he had to get to a hospital, even a doc-in-the-box. But he had no illusion he could drive to one. He couldn't call, either. No service. He felt that if he could survive the rest of the day he might live. A truism but it was true.

He remembered from long ago someone saying scorpions or poisonous spiders usually wouldn't kill, just make you wish they had. Of course sometimes they did. He didn't want to die not knowing what had killed him. Or who. All that line of inquiry.

Before he lay back, taking care to prop his fucked-up leg on wadded blankets at the end of the mattress, he thought that he would definitely want to go into all this in some detail—he liked that phrase, "in *some* detail"—with Carlos.

Then part of his brain immune to all other kinds of toxins began flashing out contemplations of how this experience, if survived, might make a pretty great scene, first or maybe second act, if he ever did find a way to shoot "The Sons of Aguirre." Which would never happen. So then he realized it would be a much better fit in a bayou scene for "Life in the Time of Hurricanes."

He woke once, burning up, and remembering, again, he hadn't remembered to check the generators, but then fell back asleep and writhed in sweat and dreams he would never remember. Of course she was in them. The other she, too. Shiva's handmaiden. Katrina.

Moon-Ra finally got in touch with Gretchen and went to see her. She was laid up at her apartment in Carrollton, on the second floor of a complex that wasn't too damaged. She was, though. She'd tripped over a broken bookshelf that had washed onto the sidewalk while walking around the neighborhood a couple nights after the storm. An ambulance actually showed up and took her to the hospital, where they said she had a broken ankle and also noticed that she had what looked like a rat bite on her back just above her hip. A nurse said she thought both injuries must have hurt but then it became obvious Gretchen was in a kind of ongoing state of shock and wasn't feeling much. They put her ankle in a cast and gave her a shot and meds for the rat bite, just in case. They'd seen a lot of that sort of thing.

Now her leg was mending and she could get around. But not drive. Since her car engine was flooded, that didn't really matter. They talked about the Portia and the odds against it ever opening again. Gretchen said she'd already made up her mind to enroll in classes as soon as UNO reopened, because she'd already put in two years there. Or maybe she'd have to transfer somewhere else if the campus stayed closed too long.

Or maybe she'd move. She said she didn't really know and was "just trying to deal, man," and Moon-Ra said he could definitely relate to that. He told her he'd let everyone know where she was and that she could call Duane when she got a chance. He got the impression she was not going to. At least for a while.

Later, he called Maybelle and left a message that he'd found Gretchen and what had happened to her but missed her call-back and didn't want to play phone tag. It had become a way of life with all the poor service and sometimes he just didn't want to do it. He'd get back to her later. Ditto with Duane, but they stayed in touch fairly often anyway.

He was still trying to figure out how he could find more paying gigs, in or out of town. And get through mourning for his mother, who would be buried just north of Baton Rouge on Wednesday morning, although there might be rain. But they'd hold the services no matter what.

The family would try to sell her house, if it was worth anything. At least the lot might be. But it would be a while before the waters lowered enough to have any real idea about the Nine, the people were saying.

Feliciana had a job lined up and they were fine living at her place for the time being. In a way, they had gotten closer. But she was despondent, like the frame of mind in the city. Moon-Ra had to admit being prone to despondency himself. Katrina was long gone and much of the water receded, but not enough. The wounds were obvious and unhealed. It would take weeks, months, years, depending on where you lived and what you did.

Word was a lot of folks would never come back, especially the black ones. That house prices would go up. People like Miz Claudia, had she lived, would never be able to go back to their destroyed homes, and never be able to afford to buy any other ones. They'd have to move out of the city. Maybe out of the state.

Moon-Ra had thought of being a Big Easy ex-pat himself, and he and Feliciana had talked about it almost daily, until they just stopped. They didn't want to move to Houston or Dallas or anywhere like that and feel like dolphins stranded on a foreign beach. But they didn't know how they could make it.

They watched their money and tried to keep an eye on the future, but it was hard. How were you supposed to feel with your past washed away and with a future that seemed to make no sense, or even exist. In the worst moments, Moon-Ra felt like he was back in the Convention Center, and that being there was somehow better because you knew where you were and what you had to do.

By the time Boy Jack got to Laredo, the high he'd been riding since jetting off so impulsively had dropped down a notch or two. Most of his body hurt, his hands were feeling tender, and he realized he'd had enough driving for the day. With the pain pills he wasn't supposed to take while driving and maybe a giant coffee he still could make it as far as Del Rio. But he gave up at Eagle Pass.

He had to try three motels because the first two were full with gamblers who'd come in for the reservation casino. The room was fine, if a little expensive. But no big thing. The clerk did give him a wary look because of the bruises and bandages.

He wasn't going to call anybody. Except Switch. Voicemail. He left a message that he'd be in LA in two days, and would keep calling to get the actual address. He almost called back to leave another message that it could turn out to be three or four days, but didn't. He knew it would be a slower go than he planned, but so what? He was on the road.

CHAPTER 39

Tuesday, September 20

Duane was sprawled on the line shack bed in almost the same position as when he'd passed out. And shivering in his own sweat. It took nearly fifteen minutes to get fully awake and muster the motive and energy to stand. First stop the bathroom. He flipped the light switch, but it didn't work. He realized why he had been sweating. Maybe from fever. Maybe from sunburn. But definitely from having no power or a/c all night.

He leaned over the toilet and peed in the semidark, his thoughts unable to get much past "fucking generator." He also realized his ankle wasn't hurting as much. He was able to bend enough to feel it, and the swelling had definitely gone down. He pressed the back of his hand to his forehead, and it felt hot, but at least not like molten lava anymore. He noticed a small shaving mirror on a nail next to the shower cabinet and had a look. Forehead to chin was plenty scarlet, but he couldn't see any blisters. His eyes were marbled with broken capillaries. He looked like shit.

He made it to the kitchen, fumbled in the first rays of light to fix a stale Nescafé. With cold dispenser water, since the damn microwave had no power. Not that he needed to be coming on like some French Quarter coffee snob, but damn. Then he drained another bottle of grocery-store water and lined the empty on the counter with the others. As if they were bound for recycling bins.

He grabbed a packet of peanut butter crackers, took the coffee outside, and settled, carefully, on the edge of the porch. Definitely still cool just before sunrise. Then he got up because he knew sitting down would lead to lying down and then to falling and then to sleeping and he'd already done that out by the airstrip.

Which reminded him about his face. He knew the sunburn should hurt more than it did, but maybe all the pain sentinels in his body were otherwise occupied. He made a mental note that his sensory perceptions might not be all that they should be. Point proven when he leaned too hard on his left ankle and lightning shot to and through his cerebellum.

Took him a few minutes to get over that one. He really had to stop doing that. When he could think again, he looked up to the emerging blue sky, highlighted in crimson, and saw no more black bombers or blue helicopters. And it came to him that he had actually seen both. He marveled at the way the poison was reorganizing his cognition and memory.

"So I'm not alone," he said, not much caring that he was talking to himself.

He wanted to call Memo and again remembered that he couldn't.

What he would have to do, somehow, was get down the damn mountain into Presidio. The live-or-die thing again. Go to a drugstore for some kind of over-the-counter meds. Or go to an ER. But that seemed pointless in the arc of his recovery.

Accordingly, he went back inside for his Advils. Popping eight more, he thought on how he must be one tough son of a bitch to have gone through all this with almost no professional treatment. Then he thought how that would be a nice epitaph on a tombstone. "Didn't Need Any Help." And then he thought how stupid all this was and that he needed to get the fuck out of there.

"I mean, do I need any more signs?" he said, going back outside.

"Hey, I'm asking a question." Not caring that he was talking to himself.

People in these circumstances needed to have some kind of audience. Movies, to name one example. Some kind of companionship. And witnesses. People in these circumstances also were known for having no idea what was going on in the real fucking world. Though they eventually would. Often dramatically.

He made his way to the shed, and sure enough the second generator was out of gas so he switched back to the first, which he had been prescient enough to refill. He flipped the breaker, and lo and behold. He was a Handyman.

Maybelle got through to Eugenia, finally, and had a good catch-up. The law office opening could still be a couple months away, if at all. She said most likely they'd move to a different building, or an abandoned house. Somewhere with less damage but not too far from Gentilly. It was hard to know, Eugenia said. Meanwhile, she and Lincoln were working out of their apartments, and having to meet clients in cafés and shopping malls. They still could never count on cell reception. It was generally dreadful. And there was talk of maybe another damn hurricane coming out of Florida.

Maybelle said Eugenia was welcome to stay at her apartment if that was easier, or safer, and also if she could check to see if her Toyota was still running.

Eugenia had everyone's car and house keys with the things they'd been able to box up at the office before Katrina hit. Eugenia said she might take her up on that and would check the Toyota regardless.

She said Maybelle's plan to stay in the Valley actually sounded pretty good to her, and so did the new friend, Rosario. She asked how Duane felt about it and Maybelle just said he was okay with it but was still out in the Big Bend. Eugenia didn't pursue it. They agreed to check in by Thursday, if not earlier.

Then Maybelle tried Bonnie's number again. She listened to the static-laden silence after the robot words "this number is no longer in service" were spoken and didn't want to hang up because she knew what it meant.

She'd been standing in the kitchen too long and went outside to find Rosario and borrow her truck keys. She needed to drive around. She decided to go back to that butterfly center. It was crowded, but she found one of the paths less traveled. She had to stop under a tree and hope no one saw the tears that had come out of nowhere. When her cheeks dried, she moved on. There were more tears inside, but they would always be there. And Bonnie would not.

On the way back to the *colonia* she picked up the groceries and a few other things, including more beer. She was glad she had let something out, among the butterflies.

Later, back in the trailer, she remembered William, and that she might never again visit his grave. She might never return to her home.

Boy Jack woke up sore as hell but better than expected. He went out for breakfast tacos, then came back to freshen his bandages and take care of business. He was checked out of the motel by eight and headed to Del Rio, where he'd turn north to pick up I-10 West. The big interstate would take him all the way to California. He knew he'd have to pass through at least one customs checkpoint along the way, but he had his driver's license handy and no weed for the dogs to smell so it would just be an annoyance.

If his mood and concentration and low level of pain held, he could be in El Paso by late afternoon, maybe Las Cruces if the traffic was light, and be the hell out of Texas. He'd just pull into any place that looked decent when he wanted to stop for the night. He might even pop a couple of those pain meds if he wanted to keep moving, but his body didn't. He was Boy Fucking Jack, aka John Caleb Pateau from Lafayette, Louisiana, originally, and he could handle it.

CHAPTER 40

Tuesday, September 20, later

Duane's idea had been to use a long piece of rebar from the generator shed as a staff and, with his faded Saints cap and bottle of water, to walk at least a little around the clearing and the airstrip to get his body loosened up for travel. Also to think a few things over and maybe say good-bye to the present from Carlos that seemed determined to kill him.

He didn't get far—maybe a quarter the length of the strip. The ground and the rocks in it felt hot against his left foot despite the double-socks he'd rigged up, since he still couldn't put on a shoe. Not even flip-flops, which he didn't have anyway. He expected to be strictly a right-shoe man for the foreseeable future.

He found a place to sit on a slab of rock under a big fluffy salt cedar, a notorious water-sucker, and he was surprised that he realized it might be proof of the underground spring Memo had once mentioned. Maybe.

If he shifted his body a certain way, one leg half-bent, the hurt one extended, it didn't put too much pressure on his ankle and foot. He laughed, possibly aloud, at the thought that it was at least an homage to a Buddhist meditation posture, if there were a one-legged version. In some Zen centers they allowed people to sit in chairs if they couldn't handle doing a lotus on a mat. So there was certainly precedent for improvisation. Duane felt he had to make that clear to himself, Zen-wise.

He adjusted himself several times more until he could sit without twitching. Over the next hour—if that long, he had no sense of time—came what might be called the Dreams. Not the nighttime versions. More the long-range, far-sighted variety. What might be called the Duane McGuane stuck-in-the-high-desert poisonous hallucinatory confrontation with his current predicament offshoot. Like magic mushrooms with fangs or stingers.

It started with his notice of birds, possibly buzzards, high in the sky. He followed their flight until he was on wings of his own, and then via slow dissolve to another bleak landscape and he was with David Lean, figuring how to do the whole Russian Revolution in *Dr. Zhivago* in a way an audience in a violent anti-Communist country could re-interpret as a love story because who in their right mind wouldn't want to love Julie Christie and Omar Sharif? Together! In fur hats!

And then turn right around and do pretty much the same thing with the deserts of Arabia and the high intrigue of World War II? With Peter O'Toole! *THAT* Peter O'Toole! Scope. Depth. Passion. Longing. Statement. Perfection. That was our boy Lean, *de veras*.

And why else would this come to mind at this particular moment in the life of Duane McGuane, arachnid-hexed on a cartel airfield in the Chinatis, if Lean were not a kindred spirit of the deepest sort?

Duane accepted the creative kinship, this shared galactic grandeur of imagination, without hesitation. Although there was a significant difference. Duane had to improve on his Spanish if he was going to make any movies in this part of Texas. Lean had plenty of money to hire interpreters when he shot on location around the world. Duane's budget was more limited. If he wanted to film anything out here, basically northern Mexico, and if he wanted to hire the crew locally, which he did for many practical as well as noble reasons, if it was okay with the unions, he would have to be able to handle at least business-quality *español*.

But back to the main point. If anybody could have turned "Sons of Aguirre" into a cinematic masterpiece of global scope, it would have been Lean. Or somebody who understood Lean. Such a man was not Fellini, whose head was clearly in another dimension. But it absolutely was Duane McGuane, theater owner (barely), Texas land baron (sort of), *wunderkind* of two great rivers (Mississippi and Rio Grande, kind of), and seer of both bayou and desert.

He had to readjust himself on the rock because even in his trance his leg was starting to hurt. And it was possible that a giant ant had bitten his thumb. Also, he needed to scoot more into the shade. The rock had gotten hot and likewise his butt.

Once that was settled, his slow-braising brain was able to return to the fantasy of cinematic creativity and ruthless dominance by directors. And what more relevant than a rewind of *The Man Who Would be King*? In which John Huston not only perfectly captured but gloriously expanded on Kipling's yarn, filling it not so much with Lean's passion for love and war, although both were present, but with grand views of philosophy and power, unflinching examinations of friendships and risks, and utter lack of fear.

And, as often follows, with bad outcomes. Certainly, Danny was an example of losing one's head to hubris, but could not the same be said of Huston himself? It could *not*. Huston did not have to experience the depths of depravity in order to film it. He only had to envision it to make it so. Duane got stuck on that part.

He had to wait a minute for his thoughts to re-collect.

Still, Duane was miffed but not unaware as to why Maybelle had seen Duane's Great Quest for the perfect movie as hubris. Would she have called hubris on Lean and Huston? She would not. Well, she might.

Then his trance permitted just enough actual consciousness that he understood he was now labeling the exodus from New Orleans and the search for a new life a "Great Quest." Much like calling a few scrawny acres left by Carlos a "ranch." Fuck Carlos.

He noticed he was not sweating because the air was so lacking in humidity that it soaked up every morsel of moisture that physics allowed. In fact, the air would suck every ounce of moisture from a body if the body didn't have enough sense to come in from the sun. Which, supposedly, was the problem with Englishmen not unlike Danny and loyal *cabeza*-carrying Peachy.

317

With that, Duane's mind shifted to trying to figure out exactly where he was. He heard what sounded like the cry of a very large animal. He was pretty sure that this swath of Texas still had a few mountain lions, or bobcats, or pumas, or whatever the hell could eat sheep and goats and just about anything it came across to keep from starving. *Chupacabras*, were they a thing, too?

That line of mental rivulets led him to Peter Matthiessen, and not in a movie but in a book. Matthiessen never found the object of his desire, in the Buddhist Four Noble Truths sense, but titled his search in the Himalayas for it anyway. *The Snow Leopard* was about a snow leopard. Or at least seeking one. Matthiessen wasn't like Danny or Peachy or Lawrence of Arabia at all. He didn't have a vision requiring fulfillment. He had questions in search of answers. So did Duane's Ranch.

He felt a thud in his ass and on the back of his head and it forced him to reckon with the reality-fact that he had slid to the bottom of the rock. Had he passed out again? And for how long? He touched his face and pressed his arms with his fingertips to check the redness and definitely new sunburn had been added to what he had amassed from yesterday. He had been a Handyman. Now he was a twice-baked potato.

He got back to the shack in what certainly seemed like the Bataan Death March without getting lost. He took off his clothes, slowly, and took another shower with cold water until the water ran out. He had no intention of refilling the tank.

Then a towel and back to the bed. He felt like he heard himself talking. Probably not good. He felt like he heard others talking. Definitely not good.

It was dusk when he woke. Half-naked again. On a damp mattress again. Another wasted day again. Fuck. Again. Too many agains, again. He put on clothes, gobbled more Advils, drank more water, and hobbled out to check the generators.

He closed up the shed for what he hoped was the last time. He could have sworn he heard rotors slashing overhead, but when he looked up he couldn't see anything. He looked for a long time.

After an hour or so he took one of the two slightly soiled Tylenol-3s he'd found in the bottom of his shaving kit so he could sleep without just passing out. He wanted to be in his Jeep at first light.

He had things to do. Starting tomorrow. Famously, another day, eh, Scarlett, if you're still counting. Starting with staying alive. He listened to the sounds of night falling outside. To the birds and insects. If there were any choppers, he'd be able to hear them. Once he was satisfied there were none, he gave in to the sleep of the exhausted and medicated. He dreamed of blue mastiffs and snow leopards in the Himalayas. Of deserts and Bedouin warriors. Of Maybelle's eyes.

The funeral for Miz Claudia was less draining than Moon-Ra had expected, despite word of the new hurricane named Rita. It was still in the Gulf, but heading maybe to Louisiana and maybe to Texas. Right now it was just something on TV, but Houston was evacuating. Also south Louisiana. All the surrounding highways were full and getting worse. Even in Baton Rouge it took them about an hour longer than normal to get to the cemetery, but everyone was patient. Reverend Youngblood was late anyway, so the delay worked out. When the ceremony was over, and Miz Claudia gone forever except for her soul and memory, family and friends headed home right away. No group lunch. No hanging around. They knew the pre-hurricane drill.

Still, Moon-Ra was glad to see the kin, to see Nadia and the kids, to hear even a few of the stories of his mother from a baby to a grandma. The gospel songs around the gravesite were so pure and transcendent that Moon-Ra understood once again why he, Curtis Lincoln Boyard, was who he had been. Became who he was now. Why he always would be. Feliciana held his hand most of the way back to New Orleans, except when he needed it for the steering wheel, and they spent the rest of the afternoon going through his things at his apartment.

They talked about whether they should both move back in there. She could give up her own place. They talked about that because they felt the need for some kind of permanence, some kind of plan, some kind of adherence to other human beings over the long haul. Because they had said good-bye to Miz Claudia because of one hurricane and had left her gravesite in a rush because of word of another. And back in New Orleans anyway.

In the end, not that far in the future, they would not move in together in the Tremé. It was Feliciana's final, if unwelcome, position. And his, come down to it. In Moon-Ra's view, the cosmic view he had sworn to himself to retain, too much had been torn asunder, even to those dulled to the terror and panic of nature. It would take much to pull it back together. If back together was the way it was supposed to be. Would ever be.

Street celebration in the Quarter.
Nicole Fruge/San Antonio Express-News/ZUMA Press.

PART V

SNOW LEOPARDS

I would like to see a snow leopard, but if I do not, that is all right, too."

—Peter Matthiessen, *The Snow Leopard*

CHAPTER 41

Wednesday, September 21

Duane woke to the crackle of glass hitting the floor as it blew in from the front room window facing the Quonset hut. Then a gunshot, then a zing followed. He was too hazy to put it together but clear enough to roll to the floor. He didn't move. No more sounds. Then, an engine of some kind in the distance. Then more silence.

He drew himself upright against the side of the bed, as alert as he had been in days. Still in the same clothes from yesterday. Dawn was just breaking. More like predawn. So probably, four or five. Hell of a wake-up call.

After a few minutes getting oriented, adjusting his pupils, he got up, moved along the walls in a half crouch to the small bedroom window. He didn't see any black cars or blue helicopters, at least from that view. He took another few minutes to think it through and found himself shivering from the a/c. A sense of irony did cross his mind, but there was no time for indulgence.

It hit him that it wasn't painful to stand. He pulled up the left leg of his jeans and checked his ankle. Even in the dim light it seemed less red. Definitely less swollen. He didn't feel feverish, either. All good signs. Except for getting shot at.

He made his way into the front room. Definitely not turning on any lights. The door was still locked, but not really much of an obstacle if anyone wanted to break in and kill him.

He went to the kitchen for water. He drank it slowly, as more sunlight filtered in. Now he could see broken glass all over the floor.

Maybe they were leaving a message. Whoever "they" were. Or maybe they were just poor marksmen. All bets on the former. And the message was to disappear. Or be disappeared.

He stuffed all the food he'd bought into the plastic grocery bags next to the trash can and went back into the bedroom for his duffel, double-checking everything. Careful not to step on glass. He also picked up the wad of bedding from the night he passed out after the bite. He crammed it into another big trash bag. Leave nothing behind—that was how he and Carlos learned to play it back in the day.

And suppose his predawn visitors weren't cartel thugs. Suppose they were cops or DEA, maybe looking for DNA left by traffickers. Who the fuck knew, but better safe than sorry. Then he remembered his fingerprints were all over everywhere and decided he might be a little paranoid and off-mission. What he really needed to do was to get gone.

He piled everything by the door and turned off everything electrical, including the damn a/c. He did one last recon. Now, with even more sunlight, he could see what he hadn't before: the bullet hole in the wall opposite the blasted-out window. It was not quite knee-high, so it had taken a downward trajectory.

So it had to have come from some kind of elevation. Maybe the hills. Or maybe just the bumper or roof of a Suburban or Expedition parked really close. Definitely a message. Whoever fired the round knew what he was doing. Tradecraft—what made America great. And Mexico.

He opened the door, gave it a twenty-count, and then pushed his bags outside onto the porch. He stayed inside for another minute, then went out, scouring the perimeter as best he could. He locked the front door, as if it mattered, and loaded the Jeep. Nobody was around, or if they were, they weren't going to shoot him. He realized the faint hum he was hearing was the generator. It'd have to run itself dry. He'd never go back into that shed.

He leaned against the Jeep's hatch a moment to take a few calm-down breaths. And now his ankle hurt again. Most of his calf. He wondered if there was an index somewhere of pain to energy and whether it was calculated and charted exactly how much extra energy was required to overcome each added unit of pain.

He wondered where he might fit on such a chart at that particular moment.

He realized he was about to detour off on another mental footnote, that this was kind of like being stoned in a really godawful way, and he pulled himself back into the game.

Now. Focus on now. Right now he was going to drive to the gate, shut it behind him, and bounce down that washboard patch of hell. Every rut and bump would have its price of impact pain jolting up through his leg. But he'd pay. He was getting the fuck out of there.

Adios, Carlos, and thanks for all the fish.

Duane's first stop in Presidio was for a large coffee and breakfast taco at Yo-Yo's Huevos, a bright green and white drive-thru, which he chose over "The Border's Best Brekfast Tacos" diner not for quality but because he didn't want to go inside anywhere. He had an attention lapse at the pick-up window and had to be prompted twice to move along in the line.

His second stop was for gas, and also a call to Rhys to bring him up to date. He stopped in yet again at the cell-friendly lot of the *supermercado*. Which also had two trash dumpsters off to one side. They were open, and Duane deposited the bags with the bloody clothes and bedsheets. Which made him feel like a criminal, although his only crime was to have taken a hot shot from a scorpion.

He got settled back in the driver's seat, took a bite of the taco and a sip of coffee and punched in Rhys's number.

"Coming back," Duane said, almost choking.

"What?"

"Coming back."

"You sound like you have a mouth full of oatmeal."

"I got bit by a scorpion."

"Jesus, Duane. You still at the ranch?"

"Of course not. Or I couldn't be calling. Remember?"

"So where?"

"Presidio. I'm never going back up there. I just wanted you to know while I could still get reception for my phone."

Duane relayed a brief tale of the sting, with unintended digression on the role of electricity in our lives and interruptions by Rhys to please talk more clearly.

"For sure it was a scorpion?" Rhys asked. "Not a snake?"

"Not for sure but for probably."

"Fuck, man."

Duane took two long sips of the coffee. "Swelling's gone down. Hardly any pus."

"So you can drive?"

"I'm testing that theory now," Duane said, trying not to cough.

"And you're headed back."

"It could take a couple of days."

Rhys was quiet for a moment. "So you don't know about Rita?"

"Who's that?"

"You don't get the news out there?"

"I don't get anything up on the ranch, remember? Who is she?"

"She's a fucking hurricane. Turn on your radio."

Duane swallowed so hard the coffee burned his throat.

"It's coming to New Orleans?"

"You know how they change paths all the time. But yeah, it might."

"Are you staying?"

"Me? Yeah."

"So you don't think it'll hit."

"Not here, no," Rhys said. "But it could be damn close."

"Shit."

"You think you should still come?"

"Do they know when it will hit?"

"Couple of days."

"I could maybe get there tonight if I push."

"You have to go through Houston," Rhys said. "It's really piling up, the traffic."

"Except I'll be heading in and they'll be heading out."

"Still."

Duane looked out into the parking lot for the usual suspects. Cops. Border Patrol. Reminding himself again he was not a criminal.

"I'll let you know when I get close."

Rhys sighed. "What can I do?"

"Did you call Memo?"

"I did."

"And?"

"He's kind of a dick but yeah. He's getting a good price."

"From a cartel."

"I ain't getting in involved in that part," Rhys said. "Neither are you."

"What the fuck did Carlos think was going to happen?"

"No idea."

Duane realized he'd forgotten to tell Rhys about the choppers and the gunfire. He kept it short, which was easy because there wasn't much to it.

"Shit. You keep burying the lede."

"Look, I gotta go."

"Listen to the news. Stay in touch."

Duane said he would.

CHAPTER 42

Wednesday, September 21, later

Marfa was an easy drive. Almost no cars on the highway. He coasted on through Alpine, barely looking at the country music club where Boy Jack had met his Waterloo.

He was just past Marathon when Memo called. He was worn out with calls and didn't want to answer but knew he had to. Nothing like being out of touch and hallucinating on poison and heat stroke for a few days to make everyone in the fucking world want to call you on one of the most fucked days or your life. In context.

Duane gave Memo the same update he'd just given Rhys, only shorter. Memo's main responses were "that sounded tough" and "oh, that makes more sense." Except for that part where Memo said the cartel guy had called him about finding a body lying in the middle of the airfield. Because they didn't know anybody would be up there. And because they were still watching it.

Memo said the history of the whole ranch was complex and muddled but it had definitely been used by the cartel, but also for a very short period by the US Army for some kind of special operation that no one ever knew about, and then they just left overnight. So it went back to the cartel.

Duane asked why they didn't just take him out and be done with it. Memo said that was the old way and the new cartel guys were more businesslike. But really, it might have just been a lucky break.

Duane asked if Carlos had known about any of it and Memo

said no, that he was unreachable down in Mexico or Guatemala or maybe Nicaragua or Costa Rica. Although the ranch deed was still in his name. Memo just let it all ride.

Duane said he wanted to see Carlos or at least talk to him. Memo said he had tried.

Duane said to try harder, then clicked off his phone and dropped it on the passenger seat. No more calls. He made a quick guesstimate how many hours it would take to get to San Antonio. By then he'd know if he could make it around the outbound Houston evacuation snarls. Maybe Rhys was right. Who in hell would be heading inbound ahead of a hurricane?

Paulus waited for word from the music store if it would be opening up again. Nadia stayed frustrated with the schools. Most weren't open, and now the city was saying there might be a new kind of school plan, maybe more private schools or charter schools. The teachers from the regular city school district were pissed off.

The bottom line was maybe no classes before Christmas. Nobody knew. Communication was a joke. Nadia spent hours a day with other mothers from all over the city trying to figure out the next moves.

She told Paulus they might have to leave, this time more permanently. Maybe all the way to Atlanta. She said maybe they could stay with his brother, Jean-Pierre. And where was his preacher mother going to wind up? At the funeral, she said this was the time for families to pull together. Paulus told her afterward that he agreed, but that it was also a time they had all been pulled apart. It had become an almost daily conversation.

Paulus had been glad to see Moon-Ra at the funeral, and so had Nadia and the kids. He had enjoyed their brief visits together to check out the Portia since they got back from Duane's escape, which is what they called it to themselves.

But he was surprised and confused when Moon told him Duane was on his way back from Texas. That he was coming despite Rita.

Duane, had he been there, would have understood Paulus's take. They had not spoken in some time, especially not in the last several surreal days, so Paulus couldn't have known that Duane was actually following one of the main points on the list of Major Points: "What to Do Next."

Nor could Paulus have known that "What to Do Next" meant getting away as fast as possible from the scorpions, the flyover bombers, the sharpshooters, and the entire range of Big Ideas of films about the South or about Aguirre's sons or anything else that he had floated out as visions of the future from the Moon Walk on the levee or the foul bowels of the Convention Center or face-to-face with his lost amour Maybelle, if that was really who she was. That "What to Do Next" for Duane led to its own kind of customized FEMA trailer. Which was a metaphor. Which Duane preferred not to use, but it was a long drive and he had to make allowances.

He hit Houston traffic as predicted, mostly going the other way. Mostly. Still, it took almost four hours to get to Lake Charles, including stops to stretch and keep his ankle from clotting up. He could make it to New Orleans, but his attention span was drifting.

For example, waking abruptly from the sound of the Jeep's tires crunching gravel on the highway apron. Three more seconds nodding off and he would have been in the ditch and that would have been that, plans and visions and screenplays and Maybelle and lifewise.

Problem was there were no motel rooms, not even at the casinos. He slapped his face a few times and made himself stay alert and finally some miles later at the Iowa exit he spotted a "Vacancy" sign. The motel was sketchy and the room price doubled, but it was late, and he was lucky to get it. Lucky they didn't call the cops on him. He looked like he'd just driven in from the End Times.

CHAPTER 43

Thursday, September 22

Maybelle tried Boy Jack three times, finally left a voicemail asking him to call because she had a favor to ask. And hoping he was at Croydon's and doing okay and feeling better and keeping his bandages clean. And repeating the request to call her even if just to let her know how he was.

So far she'd heard nothing. Couldn't they just fix the fucking cell towers? She even had trouble reaching her mother, to see how they were doing. But that call could wait, at least for a while. There would be questions. Many questions. None of the answers would be to her mom's liking, but Maybelle'd resigned herself to that long ago. She just wanted to know they were alive and well.

She was happy to be in the Valley, and it kept her busy. Hoping for a legal aid job Rosario had heard about in Rio Grande City, but it looked more likely that for the short run she'd have to settle for pro bono paralegal for the Red Blossom. And maybe waitressing. Pretty sure she'd get hired at the new French-Italian café in McAllen.

The clapboard one-bedroom Rosario had set up would be ready to move into within a few days. Main problem was getting the power turned on.

Maybelle would be settled. She would not drift. Would not jump. Would not be blown away or drown.

Maybelle also was pretty sure Eugenia would be coming to the Valley to join her. With similar motives and far better legal contacts. She might also live at Red Blossom. Between them they'd find plenty of legal work. Actually, Rita was more likely to hasten Eugenia's migration, even if, as Eugenia said, word was it might miss the city and hit Texas.

Maybelle knew she still might have to go back to New Orleans. For her car. Some of her things. But Maybelle would not go back to New Orleans for Duane, which is where she was sure he would eventually return.

Nothing back there would ever be the same. Nor the same with them. Even if she loved him, which she did. It wasn't that. It was things beyond that. He knew it, too. At least some of it. He couldn't know all of it. Only she could.

She was glad to be where she had washed up. In context. The context of Katrina, and the context of all the lives she had previously inhabited, and had revealed to no one before, ever, until that long night in the Convention Center. To total strangers panicked out of their minds by their own contexts.

She had never directly asked Duane if he believed it was true, what she said about who she was. About what was in the story that flowed out of her. But it was not really a story. The old woman in Guerrero Viejo had called it out. That Xóchitl was her name. That her name was her life. Her origin.

It took two more days for Boy Jack to reach the other coast, or at least the view of it. He didn't think he'd ever want to look at a mass of water again, but the Pacific is the Pacific. You had to succumb to its majesty, even if only where it pushed up to form a beach now all but erased by a city of endless expansion and lust.

Nothing could diminish the Pacific. Nor of the earth underneath. He could watch the waves and the never-ending blue and green for hours. Venice Beach, baby. He had finally arrived.

He should be calling Switch to go crash at his place, but he didn't want to yet. He'd had a lot of thoughts during the drive and the quiet nights in the motels. He had left the bosom of his being back in the swamps and bayous and rivers and canals and Gulf and had headed west. And even though Switch had been a bayou boy and might understand, no one but Boy Jack could truly feel the swell of his own soul.

He would be an LA boy from now on. He was one of those people who were reborn and baptized in it from the moment they arrived. He'd always liked Jim Morrison and now he really got it. And as soon as Morrison moved to Paris, he wound up dead. So, Paris and New Orleans. Not so far apart in some ways. Boy Jack took this as a revelation that he was in a place he must never leave. Ever.

Maybe he'd change his name. Or revert to John Caleb. Not sure about that. But for now he wanted a drink. There were plenty of bars at Venice Beach, although not so many parking places. He found a small lot and paid the ridiculous rate they wanted for a few hours. It didn't matter. He wanted to be close to the sand and water and all the people. What people! These were Boy Jack people for sure.

He locked up the F-150 and went to a place with a tropical theme where you could sit outside. He stayed a couple of hours and had a hell of a good time with newfound friends. One of them said he could hook him up with some prime weed and they went out back to do the business, as if Boy Jack had zero memory of how that kind of thing had turned out back in Texas.

But he was careful, kept his wits and awareness, and took off in his truck to find a place to stay for the night. Because he was a little stoned, he missed a turn or two and found himself among signs that said North Hollywood. Switch lived somewhere near there. But he could use another night to himself and pulled into a motel with a "Free HBO" sign and a U-shaped courtyard surrounded by two levels of rooms and wire-rimmed balcony walkways. He'd sleep his first night surrounded by classic LA attitude, he told himself when he checked in. Maybe he'd even go back to the beach to watch the waves.

It wasn't until the next day, when the maids came to the room after the guest had missed check-out time and found an open duffel bag and part of a six-pack and a plastic bag and no one there that they called the motel office and asked what to do. The office said they'd try to call the guest to see if he wanted another day, and to just get it cleaned up. The maids did, and put the stuff they'd found into a black trash bag and wheeled it on their cart down to the office, where the clerk, possibly an unemployed actor, taped it up and wrote the room number and date and put it in a storage closet behind the check-out counter.

Later, the police came and went. The young guest's credit card, JC Pateau, went through but wouldn't renew for additional nights. The police ran a check on the license plate number he'd left on the check-in form. It went back to a duplex apartment in New Orleans that had been abandoned. The police told the desk clerk to let them know if the guy showed up to get his things. They said missing persons were not rare and you never really knew.

CHAPTER 44

Thursday, September 22, *continued*

"The center will not hold" had become a cliché, and Duane would never say it aloud, not that anyone anymore had any idea who Yeats was, or even what poetry was. He'd put up good money that half the strangers he might ask on typical American streets couldn't find Ireland on a map. Hell, they probably couldn't find China.

But facts was facts. The center was not holding. At least from the Convention Center. Nobody who had gone into that vast building seeking a center of cohesion or meaning had found anything but chaos. More specifically, none of those who had then come out of the actual Center—such as seekers of the potential of the Portia—had wound up where they expected. Maybe the new foundation poem for the new century with its hurricanes and its centerlessness should just concede, "Center my ass. Everything is scattered."

That such thoughts were swimming in his brain on waking up in Iowa, Louisiana, was not unusual for Duane, especially of late, but he was impressed by the coherence. Beat the hell out of hallucinations. He looked at his phone, and it was just after 5 a.m. He'd slept hard.

He showered and brushed his teeth. He looked into the mirror over the sink. People did that in movies all the time because apparently some directors thought it conveyed deep self-reflection. Mostly he noticed the need for a shave. But perhaps there was some value in the ritual.

Accordingly, he tried to figure the best camera angle if he were directing a movie of whatever was happening inside the head of the Duane McGuane character who had fled New Orleans with a big idea and a stolen church van. And now was coming home so a Mexican cartel wouldn't kill him.

He was glad his mind was back where it needed to be. Conceiving things as part of a movie. He felt he had it in him to be a good director. Strictly independent, but that's where the brilliance was. Then he realized he still was doing the cliché shot with a mirror. Which was itself a mirror, no?

He got dressed, made some hotel room coffee, and flipped on the cable news. It showed enormous traffic jams moving out of Houston to the west and north. But nothing about New Orleans, until another report said the storm was changing course and the city was not evacuating.

The guilt he felt about giving up driving any farther last night turned into validation about his instinct for hurricane tracking. He turned off the news, dropped his key at the front office, and took off like he was Ulysses hellbent for home.

He stayed with I-10, stopping only for gas and food and better coffee, gambling that given Rita's changing direction, US 90 would now bear the most traffic. He didn't call anybody and nobody called him.

He got past Baton Rouge and the long swamp bridge and Louis Armstrong airport and into the city well before noon. He exited coming into downtown, taking the feeder streets to dodge the business district and the Quarter and then into the Marigny. Despite some rain.

He was surprised at what he saw, now almost a month since leaving. Like some streets being open, others closed block after block. Like hand-lettered X-markings from the National Guard and Army on boarded-up houses indicating if dead people were inside. Like trash and furniture and taped-up refrigerators all along the streets. Like endless pools of dark water covering the curbs and in the potholes. Like fewer people.

The streets to his house were mostly clear, which was a relief. He parked in the narrow driveway and went inside. It was in okay shape and no surprises, as Paulus had told him earlier. And as he inferred from Rhys not calling back with any bad news. Basically, that meant no looters.

Still a fair amount of downed tree limbs and assorted debris and overgrown yard and flower beds. Utility pole where it had fallen. Plywood repair still in place over the broken windows, thanks to Paulus. No mold or bad smells. Plenty of work to do. Real handymen to call. But it was livable.

He checked the switches and the power was on, the water worked. A welcome surprise. He'd unplugged the fridge and thrown away what little was in it before going to the Convention Center, and thus was spared the toxic garbage too many other residents of the city faced when they got back to their houses. The door was slightly propped open just as he'd left it. He'd plug it back in and give it another wipe-down later. He did turn on the a/c. When the motor clicked on he had a quick flashback to the ranch. He stood still for at least a minute until he could shake it.

He carried his things in from the Jeep and dropped them in the front room. He opened the blinds and sat on the couch that faced the big window to the porch and the street. The rain had increased a little, mostly on and off. He sat for an hour, watching, daydreaming, resting his leg and foot, but mostly thinking about the city. What had happened to it.

A few locals walked by on the sidewalks, carrying umbrellas and plastic bags of groceries. Cars and cabs occasionally passed, rattling over the broken pavement. His cell phone sat on the cushion next to him. He wanted to meet with Moon-Ra and maybe Paulus, at the Portia, if they could make it. He would fill them in on everything about coming back except the Incident with the cartel, which he decided would be a good title for a low-budget noir. Kind of like *Bad Day at Black Rock* with a border twist.

But meeting them, or doing anything, depended on whatever might still happen with Rita. And he didn't really feel like calling anyone. Being home was all he could handle.

He realized that just sitting there on the couch, he was fronting a thousand-mile stare. It was a little different from the traditional such stare. It offered greater maneuverability. Greater concealment.

He felt his stare become a smile, and, aware of itself, become a frown. Then just a blank face. Another level of awareness told Duane that an expressive facial transition like that should one day belong on the face of an actor in "Life in the Time of Hurricanes." Then he got bogged down on whether it would go in the opening scene or the finale.

Outside, in the city, day dissolved into night.

CHAPTER 45

Friday, September 23

What woke him in the morning were the sirens. Could have been any-thing, but sounded like fire trucks. It was near nine. He'd been out for twelve hours. His body was stiff from being still so long, but it didn't hurt. Until he stood. Then the pain in his ankle and leg reintroduced itself, but eased considerably as he hobbled into the living room.

He clicked on the TV. It worked, in spurts. The weathermen and women at three different channels repeated the forecast that Rita would continue shifting west, even though on the maps it looked like the storm covered the entire Gulf. They said it would "graze" the city, was the word being used. Before the day was over. So get ready for wind and rain at anytime now.

Then came local advisories for anyone watching or listening that the danger wasn't just from a direct hurricane hit. It was the power of the winds pushing up the Gulf tides into the waterways. The storm surges. Starting before landfall. Katrina being a case in point. They said although New Orleans officials didn't require evacuation, thou-sands were leaving anyway, and it wasn't a bad precaution for those who could.

Duane had the same thought everyone in the city probably had at one time another. Which was: *Can't somebody do something about the damn storm surges?* The answer being they could, but never would. He surfed the channels to make sure nobody was saying anything differ-ent. Nobody was. There would be no emergency refugee campout at the Convention Center. No tramping through flooded streets. No looking for the lost. No stepping around bloated bodies. But it would be hell for the parishes to the west.

He needed coffee, the real New Orleans stuff. The rain had let up, not for long, and his favored shop down near the docks probably would be open. He took off, his limp improving as walking loosened the muscles. As he rounded the block, he could see a line. It was worth the wait. When Duane's turn finally came, Eddie, the owner, smiled at him in that way one local did to another to acknowledge they had lived through it. Then he explained there were no muffins or anything that needed baking because the oven wiring got wet and nobody had any parts.

The regulars hung around with their coffee to gossip about Rita and make comparisons to Katrina, but Duane just carried his two large cups home, nodding to a few people he recognized as he left. The unopened pack of Oreos in the cupboard paired well with Ernie's house blend and all was good in the world. He'd worry about a real meal later, when he went to the Quarter. If going to the Quarter would be a possibility as the day wore on. And he should make those calls to Moon-Ra and Paulus.

He went out to sit on one of the wooden porch chairs, which, strangely, no one had stolen. Which prompted him to look over at his Jeep-from-the-border in the driveway. Which also had not been stolen. He looked at the Texas plates and tried to remember how long before he had to swap them for Louisiana. He was on the way back inside to write himself a note about that when Memo called again.

He said he was only checking the line because Sofia complained she couldn't get him to answer last night. So Duane said to wait a minute and he checked the recent call list, and sure enough there was Sofia's number but she hadn't left a message and so he had forgotten about it. Memo said it didn't matter.

"Really, I'm just waiting to hear from Carlos. But I'll get to that. The headline is the sale is final."

Duane had made it from the Jeep as far as the porch. He dropped into the chair, swatting away a mosquito. "We just talked about this."

"I'll get to that, but now I got a contract I need to overnight you and so the main thing Sofia wanted to know was your address. If it's the same. I mean since the storm. And, you know, assuming they can overnight to New Orleans."

"I'm sure they can, and it's the same."

Memo paused. "You haven't asked how much."

"You said it was a lot."

"A mil point two. One million, two-hundred thousand. US."

Duane had to take that in. "Isn't that twice as much as you thought?"

"Even more."

"But that much?"

"It's not the land," Memo said. "It's pretty worthless other than the scenery. And there's that spring, but it's not that. You must have an idea."

"All the other stuff."

"And maybe more to come."

Awkward pause.

"Like you didn't know," Memo said.

"Well, not at first, but then when they tried to kill me, that sort of gave it away."

"Damn, Duane, I just made you a damn fortune."

"Good thing I showed up at the ranch, huh. Sort of speed things along."

"You're welcome anyway," Memo said, gravel voice. "But look, we can chew the fat about this later. I really just wanted to send you the contract to sign so we can close. I mean, like in the next seventy-two hours."

Duane walked to the edge of the porch to look out at the street. Still quiet. Starting to sprinkle.

"You still there?" Memo asked.

"So what about Carlos?"

"I did finally get in touch. You know, we still have a code and some verifications. He's fine with the sale."

"Gosh." Now Duane's turn for sarcasm.

"But there's something he wants. I mean he has no legal right because the property officially belongs to you. But, you know."

A Harley putted down the street, maybe bound for the coffee shop. Or maybe headed home. White corporate-looking guy driving it. Arm candy behind, holding him by the waist. Duane wondered if she was thinking he was an idiot about to get her drenched just to show how macho he was.

"I know," Duane said, when the Harley noise was gone.

"He wants to split the proceeds. But only if you agree."

"But you were the one who contacted him, right?"

"Sort of," Memo said. "Sofia demanded that Carlos had a right to know, and I had to agree."

"I'm not disagreeing. Hell, it was a gift."

"So are you good with this?"

"Don't even ask me that," Duane snarled. "How will you even send it to him?"

"Transfers and banks. Only thing is he has to be in the US. But he's willing, and then he'll sneak it back down there."

"Fucking black ops again."

"This isn't going for weapons or anything like that," Memo said. "Something about villages. I mean, I think I know where, but I don't want to say."

"Me, neither."

"You know," Memo said, "now I'm thinking, Sofia could fly down Sunday and meet you at the airport. Sign everything and she'll come back on the next flight."

"What if the flights are delayed? And they will be."

"It's not going to hit New Orleans."

"It'll get close enough," Duane said. "Just send the FedEx. I'll sign everything and send it right back. Faster than trying to book flights for Sofia. Not to mention driving through these streets right now."

They quibbled over details another ten minutes, and then Memo agreed.

Duane stayed on the front porch a little longer, thinking about how he'd get to the airport if he had to. Then he decided hell with that. FedEx could handle it easier than he could. Part of him kind of wished he might have seen Sofia, just in passing, but most of him knew that would not play well.

He called Rhys to be sure he knew the latest on the sale but had to leave a voicemail. Then he finished unpacking his gear from the road and finally put what was left of the cash somewhere safe.

Rhys usually took hours to call back. It was his way. The cell rang in ten minutes. He was up in Shreveport and had to squeeze the call in because it was important, but he couldn't talk long because he was taking a break from deposing a witness in a wrongful arrest lawsuit. He'd be there until Tuesday, at the earliest. Unless Rita closed them down. He said the suit was against two construction workers who had committed the crime of being Mexican. Turns out they also happened to be cousins of a wealthy developer in Dallas. So there was a considerable defense and countersuit in the works. Rhys summed it up as "tawdry, vicious, bogus, and naturally about 150 percent racist to its fucking core."

Duane briefed him. Rhys said it sounded like Duane made the right choice, but also to have "that Dallas lawyer" call him. Not that he didn't trust Memo, but because he was "a fucking lawyer," and trust was not part of the business.

Duane milled about a little more, then got his REI rain jacket and an umbrella and set out for the Quarter. Since the storm really was veering off, he might just take a chance on a walk. Be good for his ankle and leg. Also he missed the Quarter, and it always made him feel better to be in it. Maybe especially now since he just became a *rico*. Putative. He might get as far as the Convention Center if his wound held up and the weather held back.

His basic take through the barely recovering streets was that nothing post-Katrina had changed all that much. There'd been some cleanup and fixes, for sure. Most of them still in progress. Some places open, some still closed. But that was the Quarter all the time. It was New Orleans all the time. *Plus ça change, plus c'est la même chose* never fit a city so well.

And then it was raining again. Harder. That was also New Orleans.

He ducked into a favorite restaurant that had reopened but said it was closing today at 3 p.m., and made short work of a shrimp po' boy with fries. Topped off with a Negra Modelo, with which he made a silent toast to his soon-to-be-former ranch in the Big Bend. And his already former friends in the Valley. And whatever might happen with Carlos.

He felt game enough to press on to the Convention Center, even on a full stomach and in the rain. He'd heard that some kind of temporary military hospital was set up or going to be set up inside. Or maybe offshore. Not sure which. Maybe he'd have a look. Maybe not. The sky was getting worse. The rain had slackened, but the wind gusts were picking up. His leg and ankle felt pretty good.

Just past Poydras, across from the Hard Rock casino, he stopped. On Convention Center Boulevard. The monster building was a block away. Where the thousands had waited for some kind of Godot. Who must have been busy elsewhere.

He didn't intend to stop, but he couldn't make his legs move. Not because of pain. More something in his brain. His mind kept going down the boulevard and into the place he had been. It jumped right onto the blood-stained carpets. The toilets. His mind let his nose smell everything. The vomit, the pee, the shit. He became lost again, visible only through the eyes of the old people in wheelchairs and the young children with no idea what was happening and the adults coping with self-medication or not coping at all, yelling or crying or lying in human puddles of fear and abandonment. The bodies. The stories.

He wasn't sure how long he had stood there, lost in time, space, matter of any kind. Until the hard kind of raindrops splattered and a well-soaked urban runner nicked him like he was taking up too much room in the sidewalk puddles. "Sorry," the woman yelled, jogging ahead, flipping water from her bob.

He mumbled something, then turned back and limped through the weather into the Lower Quarter and toward the Marigny. Not much choice but to keep plodding on.

He thought about calling Moon-Ra and Paulus whenever he got back, but no way they could get together until Rita had passed, or done whatever she was going to do. And it would be good just to have even more time at his house. No miles ahead on the road. No traffic to dodge. No helicopters. No scorpions. No lost visions.

Nothing to deal with but himself. And another hurricane. Which was sufficient unto the day.

At home he dried off, changed clothes, hunkered down. The cable came back on, and he happened upon the poor taste or bad timing or coked-out sense of humor of some programming geek in Atlanta or wherever who had scheduled *The Wake of the Red Witch*. He sort of watched, only slightly soggy, helped by a glass or two of red, while spending the evening rummaging around his house.

He was mostly intrigued with a wall shelf of old books and whatever other miscellany had wound up there over time. A stack of screenwriting guides were the first to catch his attention. He thumbed through them with the morbid fascination of someone passing a mangled car wreck. Also, he found a small stack of DVDs that were useless without a player, which he had left at the Portia or maybe at Maybelle's. Even came across some notes he'd scribbled, and forgotten, for "The Southern Guide to Self-Improvement."

He read only a few lines. They reminded him of her. And there she was. With him. Coupled in a motel bed in Eagle Pass. Walking under the birds in the trees through the dark, verdant trails of Guerrero Viejo. Something happening to them both. Being in the ruins had freaked him out, and she had seen that. And he had not. Not right away. Not seen it. Not listened. Not believed? Or had it all happened before?

Duane knew he was headed down one of those fever-induced time and space paths on which he'd trod after the scorpion and he didn't want to do that again. He tossed the notes into a wicker basket. Then he sat on the floor and stared up at the books on the shelves, per-haps not really seeing them, until his focus settled on a dog-eared, cof-fee-stained paperback of *The Snow Leopard*. He got up, pulled it down.

Thumbing through it held his attention for nearly an hour. Then a third, much larger glass of wine added to the feeling of no longer being in his bruised body, or being in his wind-whacked city, or imag-ining being in the Himalayas for that matter.

He made it to bed. Alone.

No snow leopard. No Maybelle.

CHAPTER 46

Saturday, September 24

Rita muscled ashore early Saturday morning near Sabine Pass at the Louisiana-Texas border, drowning and destroying everything in her path that hadn't already been drowned or destroyed by her outer bands. Only the people in Mississippi who had taken the full force of Katrina and were all but ignored could know what that entailed. In neither place, though, would the survivors imagine how long it would take to even start to become normal again.

Duane mostly slept through Rita's graze, as he sort of had with Katrina's body slam. Once again, the storm surges emerged as the villains. For New Orleans that meant fresh hell on the barely repaired Industrial Canal and reflooding of the Lower Ninth. Rita's swipes also busted up temporary walls on one of the canals from Pontchartrain and once again put parts of Gentilly, home to Maybelle's former law office, under water, though not as much as from Katrina.

He was up at dawn, but stayed inside, using the dregs of an old bag of Community Coffee to make himself a cup, until there was enough light to see what had been wrought. No new damage at his place. Maybe one dangling tree limb. The wires from the utility poles were still drooping, but hadn't fallen down. He'd make the routine useless calls about getting them fixed, and just get the same recording about "a heavy volume" and to leave a detailed message. TV remained iffy, but his cell phone worked. Who knew why.

The radio also worked. From all the latest reports, he was more convinced than ever that he'd come back at the right time, even if it was dumb luck the hurricane had veered. And now that he'd gotten the cartel-sale background from Memo, he felt validated that the risk of driving into the possible path of Rita had proven far less dangerous than would have been the deadly certitude of staying at Carlos's ranch even one more minute. If the scouts or *sicarios* had come back, and found him, they would have expedited his departure with extreme prejudice, as the military saying went. Instead of profiting from the sale, he would have been a minor adjustment in the fine print.

He became restless. Around ten, he actually did call Paulus and Moon-Ra. If they might meet tomorrow. If weather and streets were okay. Paulus answered but wasn't even in New Orleans. He said he and Nadia and the kids and his mom had been in Atlanta since Thursday, staying at his brother Jean-Pierre's, partly because of Rita and partly just to check Atlanta out. He said his mom had been thinking of finding a new church. She was convinced there was considerable saving of souls and imparting of the true ways of the African spirits to keep her busy anywhere in Georgia where the white people weren't too crazy to deal with. Paulus said he'd call with their plans whenever they got back to New Orleans.

Moon-Ra had stayed in town and said he could get to the Portia on Sunday, no problem. Would be glad to. They agreed on two o'clock and to call each other if for any reason flooding or wrecks or idiots driving through the streets held them up.

He knew he needed to call Maybelle. She was the one person who didn't know he was back. They hadn't talked since she left with Boy Jack for Rosario's. He was just waiting for a good time, he explained to himself. But Rita brought back related memories. He did want to talk. He wondered if her parents had moved back in at Lakeview yet? And if so, had they had evacuated for Rita? That could be an excuse to call. To launch an awkward conversation.

Didn't matter because she called him late afternoon. She had memories, too, she said, and she wondered how he was. She was completely surprised he was in New Orleans. Startled. He assured her he was fine, and they talked woodenly about Rita and how it had veered but then came the flooding and blah blah about hurricanes, but the larger question remained.

"Why?"

"Why did I come back?"

"I thought, you know, you were staying. Out there."

"It was like you called it. Creepy. Plus, like you also said, what was I actually going to do?"

"Work on your plans? The movie?"

"Oh, that."

"Duane."

"Okay. You want to know?"

"Of course I do."

"Well, a couple of things happened after you left." So he told her. About the scorpion sting. The pot shots. The sale. The conversations with Memo.

It took some time. When he was done, all she could manage was, "Jesus, Duane." Then, as if it took some effort to make her mouth work, "I had no idea."

"I was going to wait to tell you."

"You could be dead, lying out in the brush all this time."

"I'm not."

"Jesus, Duane."

"I'm okay. But look, keep this part to yourself. Really."

"Because?"

"Because you know why."

"Sorry. I know it's serious."

"It's okay. It's also beyond weird."

That settled in with each of them.

"All this time I thought you'd found your new home," she said. "You know, what you've been wanting to do for so long."

"I guess not. The part about finding a home."

She went silent. Then, in an entirely different tone, "So have you heard from Boy Jack? Or maybe you haven't had a chance to see much of anybody."

He was glad for the change of subject. "I'll see Moon tomorrow. Talked to Rhys by phone. He's out of town. Paulus and Nadia went to Atlanta but will be back. But no, nothing from Boy Jack. Nobody but you and Rhys knows about what happened."

"I see. I'm glad they're all okay. I'm asking about Boy Jack because I've left a lot of messages. Do you think you could go over to Croydon Imports and see if he's there?"

"You're worried."

"I am. He was getting better when he left here and he sounded excited to get back to New Orleans. But seems like he'd have called by now."

"I'll check."

"Maybe drive by Arturo's? If it's still open."

"Sure."

"I mean, I'm probably overthinking it but I'm not taking anything or anybody for granted these days."

Deliberate pause.

"Duane?"

"Yeah?"

"I wasn't going to tell, you know, but I really should."

"What?"

"It's Lenny, you know, from Cut Out."

"Something happened to him?"

"Not him. His wife. Madge. You remember she wasn't there?"

"I remember."

"She's gone. Lenny said they found her along the bayou. Her car was stuck in the mud and her body was snagged up against a clump of tires and trees. Lenny said it was a miracle she wasn't washed down to the Gulf. It was pretty bad."

"Damn. He always seemed so sad deep down."

"He just called me a couple days ago. He said he'd put off telling anyone but family. They came down to help with the services and all, and the kids. I should have called you then, but I guess I had to let it settle in my mind. And then Rita started coming."

"Rita's gone but Katrina just never leaves."

"I know."

Another pause.

"Me and Rosario, we're talking about organizing the Red Blossom more. Especially if I can get hired by a good law office. Which I'm working on."

"Sounds good."

"Eugenia is coming here, too. The Dillard office is just in too bad a shape."

"I think Gentilly flooded again."

Silence at both ends. "Duane, I do love you."

"I love you, too."

"So naturally we can't be together."

"I guess you called it."

"We won't be out of touch," she said.

He knew he had to ask. "When . . . you know . . . when did you know? I keep asking myself and getting different answers."

"Duane."

"It's okay. It was after Katrina, right? Not before. Somewhere on the trip. Maybe in that Mexican village at the lake."

"For me, it wasn't anywhere in particular. Mostly after Katrina, yeah. I guess. So much to take in. But, you know, we really are where we need to be."

"Just not in the same place."

"Like I said."

"I could feel it happening, maybe a little at the Convention Center. But a lot more on the road, in the village. You were so shocked by that old woman."

"Maybe she thought I was her daughter."

"Nice try."

Maybelle took a minute.

"You know, even with all our time together, we almost never talk about us. Analyze us. We just be us. You know?"

"Very Buddhist of you."

"Not really."

"Maybe not talking about our 'relationship' kept the spell. So to speak."

"I don't know. I don't know how it got that I wanted to stay here on the border and you wanted to stay out there in the Big Bend, and after all of that, you ended up going back to the city but I didn't. That we didn't make the same choices. To stay gone. Start over."

"Feels wrong, and right."

More silence. The call was filled with it.

"I will miss you," she said.

"And you."

When she spoke again, which wasn't right away, her voice was soft and calm and almost didn't sound like her. "When you're young, life is more interesting because it's more mysterious, right? Then later, you have different expectations. Different experiences."

"You're really gone, aren't you?"

"I think I'm going into a new life. Or another one. Yes. But you're in my heart. Still."

Duane started to make another reference to her story that night, or to "Aguirre," but he knew nothing he could say would sound right, or clever, or wise, or in any way understanding, but would only be words and nothing more. "*Yes, it's so hard, loving you, loving youuu . . .*" Beatles. Damn, where the hell did that come from? His stomach was knotting, and he was glad no one could see his face.

"Well, then," was the best he could do.

"I'm going to say good-bye now. But let me know about Boy Jack."

"I will."

"And call me. Especially if you move again. Or get stung again. Shot at."

"Stay safe."

He sat for a while on his couch, so lost in thought he didn't know he was lost in thought. Then he snapped back and started out for another walk, just around the Marigny, to loosen up. He didn't notice the return of the rain at first, but it didn't take more than a half-block to realize his folly and go back inside and dry off. But it was kind of refreshing. In context.

He put together something to eat, caught another very strange movie selection—no doubt from the same suspected coked-out cable programming geek in Atlanta—*The Last Wave*, an Australian art house film by Peter Weir with a very odd leading role for Richard Chamberlain. He tried to remember why he had never booked it. Then he thought of Marcello's last scene in *La Dolce Vita* with the young girl on the beach, how he had lost everything he loved, and looked like it. But had stayed alive. Damn, how did the Bee Gees get back in there?

After the Weir film, night had fallen, and he made himself stay put despite an urge to just get out of his house. Not to remain inside just because of the tail of the storm, but because it was his home—the house, the Marigny, the city, the people past and present, hell, the Jeep—and he needed to get used to it. A little vino, some music from the radio, then bed. Eventually falling asleep.

About 3 a.m. he woke with dull pain in his jaw from grinding his teeth and could do nothing about it but wait for the early birds to start singing perched on whatever power lines had endured.

Another song came into his head, and it wouldn't go away. Nor would her face. *"Baby please don't go, Baby please don't go, Baby please don't go, down to New Orleans, you know I love you so . . . "* Nor would the irony.

CHAPTER 47

Sunday, September 25

Duane waited until nine to call Moon-Ra. Sporadic rain and wind from Rita lingered, but the forecast was for clearing skies as the day wore on. They confirmed meeting at two.

It was a good thing, because just after ten, while Duane was looking around his house to see if he'd missed any damage, a FedEx truck pulled up. The driver saw Duane and gave him an overnight package that required a signature. The driver said they had to do that for some kinds of deliveries.

Duane gave it a quick look, asked if they still had a pick-up service, or if the driver could maybe wait ten minutes for Duane to send it back. The driver called his supervisor, and then told Duane that they could do that because since Katrina they had to improvise, to save time and fuel.

So Duane signed where Sofia had put yellow stickers and packed everything in a return package from the driver's supply, and gave the driver a twenty, because it was New Orleans. As the truck left, Duane stood for a few minutes in his yard, contemplating what he had just authorized with, literally, a few strokes of a pen.

At noon, the new millionaire, still putative, depending on Carlos's share, headed across town in the used Jeep from the Rio Grande Valley. Traffic was less gnarled than he had expected, and he took his time, switching over to St. Charles instead of Magazine just for a change of pace. Then back to Magazine because of too many roadblocks and traffic knots from tree limbs and stalled vehicles and trolley repair crews.

It was as bad as he remembered. He parked near the Taurus, still there and mostly covered in leaves and branches and mud, but also jacked up on concrete blocks and stripped of its tires. Then he walked up and down the block, looking at the other buildings and a couple of houses. Some had been cleared of debris. Some still waited. Some likely never to have a future.

He went back to the Portia and was trying from different spots around the building to get a good view of the roof when Moon-Ra pulled up in his Civic, which had been repaired in spite of the flood-water. They did the handshake/hug not so much because it was a male ritual as that they were really glad to see each other. Alive. Alive was a big part of greeting friends after Katrina.

They talked about the Valley, the Red Blossom, how things had gone, how they were coping now. Duane led him up the street a half block so he could see the setting in which the Portia now found itself. Then back to the parking lot, where Moon-Ra wanted to look at the Taurus a little closer.

They speculated on why anyone would just take the tires, even the flat ones, and leave the car instead breaking the windows to get inside, or towing it to a junkyard to sell for parts. No immediate reason beyond booze and drugs came to mind. Moon-Ra said Duane really needed to call the insurance company. Duane said he'd already made several tries.

Finally, they went inside. Which they did and didn't want to do. Accumulated mud and debris made it harder to pull open the doors, busted-up and half-open. And when they did get in it wasn't so much what they saw as what they inhaled. Rank, sweet-putrid spores of black and green mold, anchored in streaks along the lines where there'd been rising water, and in formless blotches on walls and doors and anything that had been flooded and slow to dry. Moon said it was dangerous to breathe, and they should work fast.

Each picked his way through different parts of the wreckage. Moon-Ra said the concession stand was in reasonable shape, except for the broken glass in the display window. Duane said the amphi-theater pit was still dry, the seats undamaged. The screen intact. So no vandals. At least none that wanted to go to that much trouble or harbored that much pent-up hurricane anger.

They also found that, unlike the lobby entry doors, the side exit doors had held. But the ticket booth windows were gone, and everything in the booth destroyed.

They went upstairs. From what they could see inside, the roof had withstood the winds except in a few spots, from both Katrina and Rita. The odor decreased considerably, and there was little or no water damage. Almost the same in Duane's office, but the broken windows from Katrina, not yet repaired, meant it must have taken rain from Rita.

There were a few wet spots near the windows, but none on the desk or cabinets on anything of importance. The safe was still there, bolted to the floor and locked. Moon-Ra told Duane he was lucky. Duane thought of looking around more, but they both wanted to see the projection room.

It was dry, as was the equipment. Moon-Ra had already confirmed that when he and Paulus checked the place two weeks ago, before Rita. And it was still good.

"Damn lucky," Moon-Ra said again.

Duane nodded but couldn't make words.

"We could run some movies in a couple of days as far as the projector and the seats go," Moon-Ra said, as Duane picked at a stack of reels and screening logs. "I mean, theoretically. We'd have to use this old inventory. Just a bunch of old foreign classics and a documentary about birds or something the distributors practically gave us for free. I hope to hell they don't plan on late fees getting them back."

Duane turned his attention to the projector. Ran his fingers along it. More good luck, but it was hard, seeing everything this way.

"Fuck 'em if they do," he said, leaving the projection room for the stairwell landing. "I wouldn't pay a goddam distributor for that shit anyway. But we can UPS them back next week. I wish Gretchen was still here."

"Yeah."

"You'd really work here again?" Duane said, starting down the stairs.

Moon-Ra followed. "If we had business. And you had money to pay me."

"I could probably work that out."

"Then, yeah."

When they were back in the lobby, Duane looked up at what he thought was a damp spot in the ceiling but was just an old stain. "If there are any city inspectors doing anything right now, they'd close us down in a second. I mean, not that we're open."

"They would."

"Shit. This'll cost a damn fortune."

"What about building insurance? They can't do something?"

"Rhys is having conversations about that."

"And you'd want to open it again?"

"That's the question, right?"

Moon-Ra started coughing again. "Damn. Let's hurry."

"I'm with you. Just give me a second." He was looking at a wall outlet that would have to be replaced.

"Gonna be a ton of electrical problems in the walls," Moon-Ra said, pointing at other places around the room.

"Hadn't even thought of all that," Duane said, bending down to pick up a shard of glass from the entry door. Then dropping it.

"Hey, man. I got to ask," Moon-Ra said, some hesitation in his voice. "All that way to Texas, you wanted to start over. Make a movie, all that. That was all you could talk about. Starting over."

Duane looked at his finger, which was bleeding. "True."

"And now?"

"I still do. Starting over. You?"

Moon-Ra cleared his throat.

"Paulus, you know, he's not coming back. "

"I talked to him. I know."

Duane licked the blood off, wiped his finger on his jeans.

"No point wounding yourself, man. Whole thing has to be replaced."

"I know," said Duane. "Everything's broken."

"Like that Dylan song."

"At least."

"It's not just Paulus. Eluvia says lots of people are never coming back."

"That's the word."

"Some say Katrina just brought it out," Moon-Ra said." The idea of leaving."

"And word is everything is still eighty percent flooded."

They started to walk out. Moon-Ra stopped, held up his arm so Duane would, too. "Holy crap, that's a dead rat."

"Fuck. Don't touch it."

"Not planning on it."

"What next?" Duane found a squashed popcorn box and scooped up the carcass.

Moon-Ra made a face and pushed the door open for Duane to get outside, where he went to the back edge of the building and threw rat and popcorn box against the real estate office next door, fuck those guys, which was closed.

They moved out into the parking lot. "But look," Moon-Ra said, "what I was saying, most of the people who leave, you know, they really do come back." He punched Duane lightly on his upper arm and started toward his car, the coughing getting worse. "Anything else? I told Feliciana I wouldn't be too long."

"Nah. She okay?"

"Other than depressed like everybody else?"

"And you?"

"You know. I call on my spirit side. Getting some gigs would be good, though. Might have something coming up in Baton Rouge. But now, with Rita—"

"With Rita. With everything," Duane said.

They looked back at the Portia. Like it was a ship pulling away from the pier. Or maybe a building waiting for the swing of the wrecking ball. Or maybe what it was. An Uptown art house theater beat to hell.

"Had some fun, huh?" Duane said.

"I expect we might again."

"You think I made a mistake?"

"Coming back?"

"And just in time for another hurricane. Even if it missed."

"Like I said. People leave. Come back. It's a thing."

"But my thing was starting over," Duane said. "Like you said."

"Maybelle did, I guess. Stay there. Start over."

Moon-Ra didn't mean for that to hit home, but it did. They stayed focused on the Portia like it was the only thing their eyes could see.

"You know what I meant," Moon Ra said.

"It was a tough call. For us all."

They looked at the Portia some more.

"So you're regretting it?"

"I'm not. How fucked up is that?"

Moon-Ra put his hand on Duane's shoulder. "She was looking for something else, our girl. I don't think it was about you."

"I guess."

"Anyway. I'm glad you came back, me. Feels right."

Duane watched his friend drive away. Then he looked up into the trees. Most had survived, though some were broken. Instead of going home, he walked back to the theater. He went upstairs and stayed in his office for the next hour or so. He looked through drawers and boxes and closets.

He thought about what Rhys had said, how a reopening could work and what it would cost. But he knew Rhys also would insist that any revival of the Portia would have to be powered by more than Duane's personal interest and funded by more than money. Even new-found cartel money. Good *koan* in there somewhere. What is the sound of one obsession crashing?

He slumped in the chair at his desk, which felt comfortable, considering, and studied the wall where he'd taken down the movie posters. One of those pointless precautions, as if anything could have staved off a hurricane intent on obliterating whatever she desired. He might have given that even more contemplation if his cell phone hadn't gone off. The voice at the other end was all too familiar. After all these years.

"*Hola*, man, it's me."

CHAPTER 48

Monday, September 26

They met in Audubon Park on Magazine Street across from the Audubon Zoo at 8 a.m. It was part of their ersatz tradecraft to use public places and routine times as much as possible. Carlos had said he would be coming in a cab from "near the airport" and Audubon was closer for him than trying to get across town to Duane's house, especially after a hurricane, which had been holding up flights. He didn't say where from. He didn't say much of anything.

Monday instead of Sunday worked for Duane. Not only had the remnants of the storm still been in play when Carlos called, a semi-shock in itself, but Duane had finally come to a delayed reckoning with exhaustion. Spending time at the Portia probably the trigger. Reality catching up, as Moon-Ra had put it. Whatever the cause, it had left him drained. Like the venom back at the ranch, minus the intense pain and intimations of imminent mortality.

So rather than an emergency scramble to quickly meet, a tactic Carlos was quite capable of forcing, Duane had done very little for the rest of Sunday. Then hard sleep Sunday night. Whatever was about to happen, best to confront it with "fresh eyes and clear head." Carlos used to say that when planning smuggling runs.

The portion of the park they selected was a parking and picnic area, where runners, especially the early risers, often started their laps. It was also the same park—though at the opposite end of its oval shape—where Duane had read Carlos's letter while sitting on a bench along St. Charles Avenue. Duane found the symmetry poetic. In context.

They recognized each other at once, despite the years, because both looked the same. Carlos still a Latin version of Tony Perkins, dressed in black even on hot days. Duane still with the Jeff Bridges approximation, but skinnier, thanks to the last few weeks. A loose Hawaiian shirt over his jeans. They exchanged "*holas*" and "god-damns" and went from a handshake to a brothers-in-struggle hug that felt to Duane as awkward as back in the day.

Carlos pointed to a green bench under one of the huge oak trees that covered the park, and they walked over as a pair of hard-breathing joggers slow-trotted past.

"So what the fuck?" Duane said, sitting down. "Also, how the fuck are you even here?"

"Good to see you, too." Carlos took the other end of the bench. "I would've called before, but I couldn't. I can't."

"Really?"

"Yesterday was an exception. You know the drill."

"It's been a while."

Carlos shook his head, like there was no time for this. "Look, I had to see you, and I didn't want to leave this to Memo, let alone Sofia."

"Yeah?"

"So once they told me where you were for sure, I just took a chance."

"So you're in and out."

"Red-eye from Atlanta, quick turnaround. Booked last minute and helluva price." He kept shifting around on the bench to recon the golf course, the jogging path, the street, the parking lot. "But look, I know you have questions. I'm the only one who can answer, and I owe it to you."

Duane almost said he was also the only one who could make everything up, including the flight.

"Jesus, man. You that far under?"

"I think so."

"So we can't even go get a beer?"

"I can't stay. Like you said. In and out. So what do you want to know?"

"What don't I?

"Really? Memo said he's been filling you in."

"He has."

"So I know you do know this, but like I said, I want it coming from me. First off, though, I understand you're keeping the tract where Red Blossom is. Which is good, by the way. Rosario is doing the right thing, and very well."

Duane shot a thumbs-up.

"But why I'm here is about the ranch. I hadn't gotten in touch before because I guess I thought it would take a little longer for you to get out there."

"Really?" Duane stared. "I mean, it's a little more complicated. Getting out there. Didn't take long because we were basically homeless and stuck in an honest-to-God hellhole after Katrina. Which you probably hadn't anticipated in your timeline."

Carlos raised a palm of peace. "I know all that was bad. And I want to hear about it." He stared up at the trees, then back at Duane. "But later. For now, here's the thing. We need to do this quick. So you're selling it, right? The ranch."

"I think I already did."

More runners walked by, more than Duane would have expected, prepping with stretching motions, drinking Gatorade, and talking about how humid it was and blaming it on Rita. Duane said he wanted to hit them with something. "People in those parishes out there are wiped out. These fucks are bitching about the weather."

Carlos managed a grin. "Good to see you still got the pissed-off in you."

"For some stuff."

"So anyway." Carlos eyed a man and a woman pushing a jogging cart with a baby strapped in.

"So anyway."

"So anyway. The sale. I mean, it's a fucking good deal, right?"

"From a cartel."

"Right, also."

"You're good with that?"

"I've been aware for some time. It actually seems like the best option."

Duane stared at his friend.

Carlos shrugged. "Not least because those gangs, really kind of minor league ones if you want to know, completely blocked out my sister and her fucked-up husband. They would have ruined everything. So I don't want them, or that, either, ever. I'm sure Memo filled you in on that nightmare." Carlos paused, nodded as if talking to himself. "So I knew you'd go out and see. What I didn't know was how you'd react. What you might want to do with it."

"How I'd react?" Duane stood, body tense.

Carlos rose, too. "You know."

Duane walked away a half-dozen steps, then came back almost in Carlos's face, walked away a few steps again, turned back. "I reacted to figuring out it was drug shit and to being swarmed by helicopters, maybe *sicarios*, on the ground. I reacted to getting hit by a fucking scorpion, which I hope was just nature and not cartel shit. Which now I'm almost starting to wonder. Could have been knock-out gas and a syringe." He tried to gauge that possibility in Carlos's eyes, but got nothing. "But maybe most of all, I reacted to losing my girlfriend, who hated the place from the get-go. But otherwise, you know, I reacted very well."

"*Cálmate*, man. I didn't know that part."

"But yeah, I thought about living there. For about two days. And then I put it together. Living there was not going to be living, actually. Know what I mean? Fuck, man."

Carlos looked around. Their voices had gotten loud. But no one was that close. Duane turned away. They stayed like that while something in each of them settled.

Then Carlos reached out to lightly touch Duane's shoulder. Duane didn't shrug it off. They returned to the bench but didn't sit.

"*Scorpions?*" Carlos said. He cocked his head like a dog trying to figure something out.

Duane put his left leg on the bench and rolled back the jeans cuff. The black and purple and green had faded, but it was still ugly.

"Damn. Haven't seen one of those in a while."

"Starts at the ankle."

"You sure it wasn't a snake?"

"No fangs."

Carlos shook his head. "How did you get to the doctor?"

"I didn't. I was stuck up there."

Carlos looked at the wound more closely. "*Hijo*! You could've died."

"It occurred to me."

"We used to lose people out in the jungle with that kind of thing. That's no syringe mark."

Duane rolled down his jeans.

Carlos looked away, shook his head slightly. "And the helicopters?"

"I didn't know what they were for sure, I was so fucked up. At the time. Now, I got a real solid idea."

"Memo said he told you it was a warning to get out."

"He did."

"Well, good. Good that you did. I mean, that you were able to. Shit."

"So, yeah, that was really good. That I was able to. You know. And more than that, it was interesting. Really interesting." Duane took a moment. "So, you know, it was totally worth it, as my young ticket booth cashier would say. Who, by the way, was busted up by Katrina and is damn near homeless. Hey, maybe I can front her some cartel profit money now. Good comes from bad. We're fucking saints! Like the team."

Carlos looked off into the trees again. "I'm sorry all that happened. And I admit I didn't know what really was going on, after the cartel first took an interest. I wasn't even in the country. But if I had gone up there like a landlord, it wouldn't have been for long. As you found out. I should have given that more thought."

Duane went to the bench, sat down.

"We can go into the details later."

Carlos sat, too. They took a minute. Some personal adjustments needed.

Carlos looked around again to be sure no one was eavesdropping, then leaned in. "I mean, I just figured you'd see right off it wasn't any place to live, and I knew Memo would have an offer. The cartel wanted it to look like a boring real estate transaction, not draw any attention. Instead of, you know, just taking it."

"'Just taking it'?"

"I mean, I never thought it would come to that."

"Nice to be a pawn."

"To be somebody I could trust. You know that's the truth."

"I guess it doesn't matter."

"It doesn't."

Carlos looked at his watch.

"You're still down there," Duane finally said.

"That's also why I'm *here*. I mean, to see you, but also get the money from Memo. It can get things moving, armed actions if we need, but mostly more village organizing. I'm starting to see that's where the long-range is. But, you know, you never know."

Duane nodded. The talk was familiar. But also different.

"I need your okay."

"Shit, Carlos, it's your money, not mine."

Carlos's eyes darted to one side. "Legally, no. It's yours. The property, and now the money. I'm just asking if we could split the sale. Memo and I will take care of the details as soon as the stuff you signed gets to the buyers. He'll fill you in later, or maybe through that lawyer he says you have. I'll get the cash across the border, like the old days. Your half, do whatever you want. Stay here. Do that movie Memo said you were 'obsessed' with. His word. Or just keep the *colonia* going."

"My girlfriend, the one who left me thanks to the ranch, is still there."

Carlos could hear a stumble in Duane's voice.

"Sorry. I really am."

Duane started to explain, but stopped when two utility vans and a big Dodge Ram with bad struts bounced into the parking lot, heading for a group of picnic tables and restrooms. They parked and the passengers poured out to unload cartons of water and ice and food. A banner in the back of the pickup was unfurled, with hasty-looking lettering announcing "5K Impromptu Screw Rita Fun Run and Belated Pet Rescue!"

Duane knew Carlos's only interest was if the gathering was any kind of threat. Which it wasn't. It was just New Orleans.

The people from the vans started setting up the tables and hanging the banner between tent poles. "I don't even see any dogs," Carlos said. Duane remembered that Carlos could be extremely literal. He also was the real thing. It was amazing he was still alive.

"I better get going. Lots to do."

"You want a ride?"

"No. Why take chances. You're important now, *hombre*. You got money. I can get a cab."

Duane grabbed his arm. "I'm glad you came."

"*Lo mismo.*"

Duane glanced at the growing crowd. "So, one question I forgot. Just to test my memory. The ranch—it's the same place, maybe a little spruced up, that we stayed that night on the way to LA?"

"Of all things to wonder about. You couldn't tell?"

"You know, continuity. I'm starting to appreciate that more than I used to."

Vehicles kept arriving. "All these people."

"They couldn't care less about us."

"Anyway, I need to go and you don't need to be around me."

"You really are being a spook."

Curt grin. "I gotta go."

"You can't even tell me where?"

"Memo, of course. But after that, just 'back.'"

"Okay, but you have to say it."

"Say what?"

"Think a minute."

It made Carlos irritated, until it hit him.

"I have urgent business in the south." He tried to sound gruff but couldn't fend off the laugh.

"Reference?"

"Peachy to Kipling. With Danny's head in a bag."

"Yeah. So watch out for yours."

Carlos looked at his watch again. Quick handshake. Brothers in the struggle. So long ago. Another time. Another Duane. Maybe it would come back.

"*Hasta.*"

"*Hasta.*"

"You know, you can always come down, be with us."

Before Duane could think of an answer, Carlos was off toward the street. Already on his cell phone, no doubt a burner. Speaking to who knew whom, who knew why, who knew where. Or maybe just a cab dispatcher.

Duane knew Carlos would want him to vanish, too, so he got in the Jeep, threaded through the 5K crowd, and headed home on a route he didn't usually take. He couldn't find anything he liked on the radio, felt restless and almost as disoriented as in the ruins of Guerrero Viejo.

He made a short detour to a sidewalk café he liked off Esplanade. It was still early for New Orleans, and parking was easy. He wanted to have a normal breakfast and a normal mug of chicory coffee and sit among normal people, if there were any.

CHAPTER 49

Monday, September 26, later

Duane took a large to-go cup of chicory back to his house. He didn't bother to lock up the Jeep. The morning was still quiet. Unusually so, even with storm-free skies. He began to wonder if it would be that way for a long time. It was disconcerting. He turned the radio to OZ and turned up the jazz just loud enough to hear on the front porch. No cars, no tourists, no delivery trucks, no school buses, hardly anybody walking down to Ernie's.

He was restless, and not from the caffeine.

He went back inside and channeled his unease into busywork, picking up where he had left off last night with storage closets and stacks of files. It was time to tackle the fridge. It had survived Katrina, and it deserved to get back to work. He wiped it down good, inside and out, and sprayed it with cleanser. He plugged it in and sure enough the light and the compressor came on. And it didn't smell. He closed the door so it could return to its normal state of cool. He was aware of the possible metaphor for his own life. But it was too obvious. It would never be used in any film he directed.

Enough housework. He went back out to the front porch for a half hour, sticky heat just kicking in. Now visible on the street: one cyclist, two pickups, a loose dog. Then back inside, where at least there was a/c. He happened upon the old clipboard with notebook paper pad he'd found in one of the boxes marked "Office." He grabbed a ballpoint pen and ambled over to the couch. He looked out the front window. The jazz from the radio was calming, but not enough. And his city was still too quiet. Like something was hiding something.

He stared at the blank top page of the pad. It reminded him of starting the "Major Points" from the ranch. A list that seemed ridiculous now, but at the time had served its purpose.

An art house cult offering like "The Southern Guide to Self-Improvement" now also seemed ridiculous. An embarrassment. Or at least a kind of humor that he could no longer engage. An indulgence. Justly indicted, tried, and convicted.

Nor did he feel that a "Sons of Aguirre" rebirth, if indeed it had ever been born, was viable. Talk about art house fodder. Not to mention impossibility. And now he didn't even have a ranch on which to build sets. Not to mention logistics. Not to mention every other possible problem that could go wrong on a shoot. Weather, overruns, actors, tempers, lawyers. Getting shot.

Not to mention actually writing a script, since he was sure whatever version of "Aguirre" that might ever have existed certainly did not continue to do so. Not to mention he had a whole new direction in the wings. "Life in the Time of Hurricanes" was nothing more than an idea. Not a single word yet written.

He needed to get back into the streets. Clipboard and pen in hand, he grabbed his Saints cap, locked the front door, and headed to the Quarter. It was a little like being his own ping-pong ball, these comings and goings, big and small, but he didn't care.

He was past the French Market in no time, barely a limp, and then up the levee steps to the Moonwalk. There was a strong breeze. Like a blast of a/c, except from a heater. Moon-Ra defended the city's steam bath climate, arguing the water-laden air was what had formed the cocktail of life when the earth was hatched. Which he said probably accounted for the reluctance of creatures back then to crawl out of the bounty of the ocean onto the naked misery of land. He said this was how the city always would be until it rejoined Atlantis.

Duane followed the levee downriver, past the lower end of the Quarter, pulling up along a stretch near the Governor Nichols wharf that hadn't been "improved," and hardcore locals liked it that way.

The slant of the wild, weed-covered embankment to the river's edge caught his attention as unusually artful, and he slowly picked his way down. It wasn't that much a descent, but because he was day-dreaming, he almost twisted his left ankle in a hole, which quickly redirected his thoughts to a sharp memory of pain back at the ranch.

He leaned on his right leg to take the weight off the left until the spasm passed, then found a slender patch of beat-down grasses and sat. Stretching his bones and muscles felt good, and when his legs felt loose again he crossed them in a half-assed half-lotus. He faced the river and Algiers Point.

He pulled down the bill on his cap and looked at the clipboard. Then at the waves. Then at the sky. Then at all that was out there, beyond what his eyes could see and brain process. Then at himself, standing bowed but not broken, more or less, in the lot in front of the Convention Center. Then at himself, sitting right where he was. Only two people he knew could understand his perspective, his coordinates in time and space. No wonder Moon-Ra and Maybelle had both shown up in his dream. Maybe one of them lived there now.

He began furiously jotting down plot points for "Life in the Time of Hurricanes." They might eventually yield a treatment, or a synopsis, or whatever the hell the industry wanted to call it, and then maybe a no-kidding actual three-act screenplay, which said industry ruled to be the proper format. He would be on the assembly line's fast lane.

His hamstrings began to cramp, really without any scorpion-related justification, and he had to stand and stretch. But he wanted to be even closer to the river, so when the cramping eased he made his way a few more yards down to the very edge.

The rush and spray were daunting. And loud. So were voices above him. He twisted his neck to look back up at the walking path on the levee. A half-dozen or so tourists, possibly delayed a day or two by Rita, were pointing at ships and boats on the murky waves, noting with snarls of disgust the opaque brownness and piles of floating debris jetted along by the Big Muddy. Where did they think it got the name?

Now they were watching him. He waved and they waved back. He thought he heard laughter. He looked upriver past them toward the CCC bridge, where cops and deputies had blocked thousands of people from crossing to the West Bank. He thought he saw the car ferry from the Quarter to Algiers starting to move, or at least fire up its engines. But he couldn't be sure. He was sure that he heard one of the male tourists call out, "Y'all, check out the dude down there. Might as well be on a toilet."

Maybe they assumed Duane couldn't hear them. He wished he'd never waved, like he was some kind of Big Easy greeter. But it wasn't the insult that bothered him—it was that they had trespassed him. So he ignored them.

He sat on a flat rock and drew his knees up so his heels could be anchors. When he felt stable, he rested the clipboard on his thighs and reviewed the four pages of his just-born script. The handwriting was godawful, but he was sure he had made good progress with the content. He twiddled the ballpoint between his fingers before fastening it to the pad and setting the clipboard at his side, topping it with a loose pebble so the wind wouldn't blow the pages.

He watched the river.

CHAPTER 50

Monday, September 26, almost high noon

The theater screen of his brain lit up again, but this time with a scene from only a month ago, when Katrina was getting her act together in the Atlantic and then the Gulf. When she could've gone anywhere, but chose this curve of the swampland on which the French had built a landing port despite all advice to the contrary.

Like most of the *cognoscenti* in New Orleans, not that he was one, Duane had mixed feelings about that long-ago choice, utterly based on greed and murderous violence against the people who already lived there. Bottom line was that it was the rationale for the city's very existence. Also a kind of original sin. Few who lived here pretended otherwise. Or was it that everyone pretended all the time?

Without warning, his brain-picture made a jump cut—still on the river that almost swallowed him, but transplanted into Texas. Then the brain-picture expanded to a massive screen. Then not a screen, but what it was, in the way of the Buddha. No screen, no words. A river, née a cosmic waterway in grander times. The aboriginal mythical majesty of the Mississippi Rio Grande, mystical immortal mother of all rivers, all life on this part of the earth. Florescent and starlit as it flowed down from the Rocky Mountain springs far in the northwest of the continent into the flat fertility of the continental expanse that was the Valley of Spanish France. Past the Red Blossom *colonia*, prosperous and beautiful and joyful, all the way unto the Tierra del Fuego and the End of the Known World of the Americas.

Before it was consumed by the Gulf of the Gods and the Oceans of Eternity, and split into even greater majesty, the Great River lingered on the land to host a party to its neighbor the heavens, with lights strung from trees and adobe houses and uncountable people laughing and dancing to *conjunto* music. And to one side were 35mm movie cameras on airborne tripods, Duane and Moon-Ra behind them, directing and filming at the same time.

Not even the panoramas of David Lean could capture the scope and depth, but Duane tried, until his floating camera found and lingered on a single face. Hers. Maybelle, dancing with Rosario, serene and ecstatic, a red flower beckoning amid waves of thick, dark hair.

A woman whirling nearby calling out, "*Que linda, Xóchitl.*" And the woman answering to that name, flashing a smile brighter than lightning. Thunder pounding the sky. Winds tearing through the party and ripping the lights from the trees. A man in a poncho who looked like Carlos.

Then the lens closed and the screen in Duane's brain cut to black. No fade away. No more time. It was like instant birth into another galaxy. Where he already lived.

His shoes were starting to get wet. He grabbed the pebble on his clipboard and threw it into the water. It wasn't the thin shape for a skip and it sank immediately. He stood and turned to look up at the levee. A gust of wind almost blew his cap away. The tourists were gone, but others had taken their place. They paid Duane no attention.

He just wanted to watch the river and be with the river and think only about the river. What the Buddhists advised. But he wasn't there yet. Not even close. In fact, he was about at the same place he was the first time he stood atop the levee and heard the howl. Just before Katrina.

And now he was speculating, once again, that if he were to wade out into the chop and swim upstream to reach Algiers Point on the other side, exactly how far downriver would he be vectored instead?

Bulldozed by unmeasurable hydrology into the sewers of the Quarter like so much Sunday morning street trash power-washed by cleanup crews? Beached somewhere along the Bywater? Or would he just be pulled under and funneled to the Gulf?

It was time to find out. Surely, such research would be a valid rationale for coming back, for having returned to sender. Damn. An Elvis reference? Really inexcusable.

He stepped into the water. Which was up to his waist almost immediately. His cap blew away and sank within seconds.

The latest round of levee tourists were screaming: "Don't do it," and "Look at that idiot," and "Must be drunk."

He had no interest in their interpretations nor fear of his immediate time and space coordinates. He moved deeper. Instantly, he lost his footing. He paddled energetically with his arms and hands. No luck with that. This was not fucking surfing. It was not lining up to catch a wave.

He'd always been a strong swimmer—he once saved a drowning comrade caught in the tides off the Mexican Pacific—but he was a joke in this churn. The revived pain in his ankle wasn't helping. Within seconds, all he could do was try to keep his head out of the water.

That might have been the last sighting of his mortal coil, his essence and existence of Duane, unless someone up on the levee happened to be using a camera to record and preserve his demise. But he lucked out as a tree branch shot along. He grabbed it like it was a raft to Jordan, and thusly did physics hurl it and him immediately back to the shoreline.

Within a desperate few seconds he found enough footing to push out of the water and onto the muddy bank. Within those seconds, it is true that a scene flashed in his brain of using the branch to propel himself again into the river and give it one more shot. The scene had no staying power.

He was on hands and knees, coughing, but stood up as soon as he could, moving up the slope a few more feet, but coughing even more. Then he dropped back to his knees. His ankle made him wince, but the pain seemed irrelevant. River water poured off his clothes and hair and face and trickled from his mouth. The taste was like nothing he'd ever imagined.

It helped remind him what was what. What he was. What he wasn't, including a fish. Nor was his mom, and he almost choked with the gasp of wet breath that came with realizing how definitively inappropriate a Faulkner wisecrack was at that particular moment.

After a few more lung heaves, he stood again, slowly, favoring the reignited burn in his ankle, not moving until he no longer felt dizzy. He wiped his face so he could look around but wasn't exactly sure where he was. Or why.

He could hear voices shouting from the levee but couldn't make them out because his ears were clogged. He was going to yell at them to "get a fucking life," but he lost his footing and all but fell back down the bank. The contortions to save his balance helped water drain from his right ear and he realized they were not talking about him, but laughing.

He didn't care. He really did feel incredible, like something had happened that had been a long time coming, like *Cleopatra*. Like all the deals to turn *A Confederacy of Dunces* into a movie. Like a trip to nowhere that finally arrived.

A strong breeze pushed against him and swirled up the hell of his smell into his nose. Add that to what he probably looked like, and it was time to go home. He lumbered part-way up the embankment only to remember that he'd left his clipboard behind when he went full immersion. He wiped his eyes and descended back to where he was pretty sure he'd been standing. Even if he couldn't find his notes, he knew he could remember them. Probably.

He looked up. A passing flock of birds speckled the sky, maybe bound for the Gulf, maybe just perches in a parish. Shiny flapping feather molecules, quantum-clacking particles in constant motion, continually rearranging themselves and changing their direction. He felt like yelling to the tourists on the levee, "Stop gaping at me. Look up at wings in flight. See the core of what the Buddha learned. That it is also science."

He decided against yelling, although what he would have said was true. Maybe almost drowning was worth getting the message. To wit: Taking a stand, going away, coming home are only conceits, or long- ings, for a stability that cannot exist. That is but the illusion of desire. Thus spake the birds, the river, the insignificant human soaked to the bone halfway down the levee bank. What was the saying—when you are ready, the teacher will come?

Anyway, the tourists had trickled away, having lost interest now that the madman along the water hadn't drowned and all they had to entertain their friends back home with was the story of a drunken bum instead of a bloated body. Maybe some funny videos.

A slosh of remaining river water got stuck in his throat and Duane coughed up a last bit of phlegm. As he spat out the residue, a glint of sunlight reflected off the metal on the abandoned clipboard he was trying to find. He sidestepped his way down to get it. His sneakers squished with each step.

Everything was safe, even the ballpoint, and he tried not to get the pages wet. Rather than slog back up again, he opted for a flat place among the weeds where the shallow wavelets were barely up to his shoes. He just wanted to stand there a minute, without jumping in. Without ridicule.

Almost immediately, another stray breeze chilled his wet clothes. He crossed his arms with the clipboard to stop the shivers—on a hot morning—an incongruity that made him chuckle, which led to a coughing fit. When that was over, he took a long breath, for which he was duly thankful, and another, and he was nothing, and he was part of everything.

He was not Marcello. Nor Peachy, nor Danny, nor Zhivago, nor Aguirre. He was Duane. McGuane. He was just a name. A name and nothing more. So was Katrina. So was Xóchitl. So was New Orleans. So was the Valley. So was Texas. So was the Mississippi. The Gulf. The Sun of Moon-Ra. It was blasphemous bad timing that Donovan's "*First there is a mountain, then there is no mountain, then there is*" would pop into his head at the moment of his Big Muddy enlightenment, yet it did.

He looked around, simultaneously toasty and trembling. Upriver, now bearing real Mississippi headwaters from the real and farthest northern plains of America, Duane could see the edge of the Quarter, the downtown skyline, the long sweep of the West Bank, and a barge pushing its load under the bridge. He could see Carlos, waiting. In the middle of it all, a ferry, bucking the waves.

ABOUT THE AUTHOR

A longtime journalist and magazine editor, Rod has done time at the Associated Press, the *Texas Observer*, Time Inc.'s *Cooking Light*, *D Magazine*, *Rocky Mountain News*, *San Antonio Express-News*, and the Southern Poverty Law Center's *Teaching Tolerance*. He is a member of the Texas Institute of Letters and PEN America and has served on the board of directors of the National Book Critics Circle. He taught in the English Department at the University of Texas and Southern Methodist University and was a cofounder of the first system-wide veteran service program at the Texas A&M University System. He is working on a new novel and a film project based in Juárez.

www.ingramcontent.com/pod-product-compliance
Lightning Source LLC
Chambersburg PA
CBHW041729081025
33746CB00041B/1008